psychopath

Keith Ablow, M.D., like his protagonist, is a forensic psychiatrist who has testified in some of the most highly publicized trials in the US. He has written three other Frank Clevenger novels, *Denial*, *Projection*, and *Compulsion*, and lives in Massachusetts.

His website is www.keithablow.com

PSYCHOPATH

Keith Ablow

This first hardcover edition published in Great Britain 2006 by
SEVERN HOUSE PUBLISHERS LTD of
9–15 High Street, Sutton, Surrey SM1 1DF,
by arrangement with Pan Macmillan Ltd.

British Library Cataloguing in Publication Data

Ablow,   Keith
    Psychopath
    1.   Clevenger, Frank (Fictitious character) - Fiction
    2.   Forensic psychiatrists - Unites States - Fiction
    3.   Serial murders - Fiction
    4.   Psychopaths - Fiction
    5.   Suspense fiction
    I.   Title
    813.5'4 [F]

    ISBN-13: 978-0-7278-6441-3
    ISBN-10: 0-7278-6441-6

All Severn House titles are printed on acid-free paper.

Printed and bound in Great Britain by
MPG Books Ltd., Bodmin, Cornwall.

For J. Christopher Burch,
whose creative gifts are an inspiration
and whose friendship is a treasure

acknowledgments

My agent, Beth Vesel, and editor, Charles Spicer, continue to make me a better writer than I would be without them. Many, many thanks.

The support of my publishers, Sally Richardson and Matthew Shear, is more wind at my back.

This book has had many friends who read early drafts and gave honest criticism. They are: Deborah Jean Small, Jeanette Ablow, Allan Ablow, Dr. Karen Ablow, Paul Abruzzi, Charles "Red" Donovan, Gary Goldstein, Debbie Sentner, Julian and Jeannie Geiger, Emilie Stewart, Marshall Persinger, Steve Matzkin, Mircea Monroe, Billy Rice, Janice Williams, Amy Lee Williams, Matt Siegel, and Joshua Rivkin.

For their encouragement, I thank: Michael Palmer, Robert Parker, Jonathan Kellerman, Dennis Lehane, James Hall, James Ellroy, Tess Gerritsen, Harlan Coben, Janet Evanovich, and Nelson DeMille.

Because I love them to the ends of the Earth and up to the moon and stars, I write, in part, for my kids, Devin Blake and Cole Abraham.

Finally, for many years I have benefited from the support of Dr. Rock Positano, who secretly runs the whole world and plainly is my brother at arms.

psychopath

part one

one

Mahler's *Tenth Symphony* played on the BMW X5's stereo, but even that serene music did nothing to calm Jonah. His skin was hot with anger. The palms of his hands burned against the steering wheel. His heart pounded, squeezing more and more blood with each beat, flooding his aorta, engorging his carotid arteries, making his head throb inside the skull, somewhere within the temporal lobes of his brain. At last count his breathing had risen to eighteen respirations per minute. He could feel a dizzying undertow of oxygen sucking him inside himself.

His hunger to kill always began this way, and he always believed he could control it, ride it into submission down a long highway, the way his grandfather had broken sinewy colts on the plains of the Arizona ranch where Jonah had spent his teenage years. So cunning was his psychopathology that it fooled him into thinking he was greater than it was, that the goodness in him could overpower the evil. He believed this even now, with seventeen bodies strewn along the highways behind him.

"Just keep driving," he said through gritted teeth.

His vision began to blur, partly from surging blood pressure, partly from hyperventilating, partly from the milligram of Haldol he had swallowed an hour earlier.

3

Sometimes the antipsychotic medication put the beast to sleep. Sometimes not.

Squinting into the night, he saw the distant glow of red taillights. He pressed down on the accelerator, desperate to close the distance between himself and a fellow traveler, as if the momentum of another—of a normal and decent man—might carry him through the darkness.

He glanced at the orange neon clock on the dash, saw that it was 3:02 A.M., and remembered a line from Fitzgerald:

> In a real dark night of the soul it is always three o'clock in the morning.

The line was from a short story called "The Crack-up," a title apropos what was happening to him—fine fissures in his psychological defenses giving way, splitting into bigger clefts, then into each other, becoming a gaping black hole that swallowed him, then rebirthed him as a monster.

Jonah had read everything F. Scott Fitzgerald had written, because the words were beautiful, and the places beautiful, and the people beautiful, even with their flaws. And he wanted to think of himself in exactly that way, to believe he was an imperfect creation of a perfect God, that he was worthy of redemption.

He was, at thirty-nine, physically flawless. His face suggested both trustworthiness and self-confidence—high cheekbones, a prominent brow, a strong chin with a subtle cleft. His eyes, clear and pale blue, perfectly complemented his wavy, silver-gray hair, worn just off the shoulders, pleasantly tousled. He stood six-foot-one and was broadly built, with long, muscled arms and a V-shaped torso tapering to a thirty-one-inch waist. He had the rock-hard thighs and calves of a mountain climber.

Yet, of all his features, women commented first on his hands. The skin was tan and soft, covering tendons that fanned perfectly from knuckles to wrist. The veins were visible enough to hint at physical strength, without being so visible as to suggest destructiveness. The fingers were long and graceful, tapering to smooth, translucent nails he buffed to a shine each morning. A pianist's fingers, some women said. A surgeon's, others told him.

"You have the hands of an angel," one lover had gasped, sliding his finger into her mouth.

The hands of an angel. Jonah looked at them, white-knuckled, clutching the steering wheel. He was within fifty yards of the car in front of him, but felt himself losing ground in his race against evil. His upper lip had begun to twitch. Sweat covered his neck and shoulders.

He opened his eyes wide and summoned the face of his last victim in that young man's last moments, hoping the image would sober him, in the way the memory of nausea and vomiting can sober an alcoholic, making repugnant the bottle that beckons so seductively, promising relief and release.

Nearly two months had passed, but Jonah could still see Scott Carmady's jaw drop open, utter disbelief filling his eyes. For how can a weary traveler, feeling lucky to get help with a broken-down Chevy at the side of a desolate stretch of Kentucky highway, believe the raw pain of his cut throat or the warm blood soaking his shirt? How can he make sense of the fact that his life, with all the momentum of a twenty-something's hopes and dreams, is screeching to a halt? How can he fathom the fact that the well-dressed man who has mortally wounded him is the same man who has spent the time not only to jump-start his car battery, but to wait fifteen minutes with him to be certain it will not die again?

And what minutes! Carmady had revealed things he had spoken of to no one—the helplessness sparked in him by his sadistic boss, the rage he felt clinging to his cheating wife. Opening up made him feel better than he had in a long, long time. Unburdened.

Jonah remembered how a plea had taken the place of the disbelief he had seen in the dying man's eyes. It was not a plea for the answer to some grand, existential *why?* Not some cliché last scene from a movie. No. The plea was purely for help. So that when Carmady reached for Jonah it was neither to attack him, nor to defend himself, but simply to keep from collapsing.

Jonah had not stepped away from his victim, but closer. He embraced him. And as Carmady's life drained out of him, Jonah felt the rage drain out of his own body, a magnificent calm taking its place, a feeling of oneness with himself and the universe. And he whispered his own plea in the man's ear: "Please forgive me."

Jonah's eyes filled with tears. The road undulated before him. If only Carmady had been willing to reveal more, to peel back the last layers of his emotional defenses, to give Jonah the reasons *why* he could be victimized by his boss and his wife, what trauma had weakened him, then he might still be alive. But Carmady had refused to talk about his childhood, refused utterly, like a man keeping a locker full of meats all to himself—keeping them from Jonah, who was starving.

Starving, like now.

His strategy was backfiring. He had truly believed that summoning memories of his last kill would keep the

6

monster inside him at bay, but the opposite was true. The monster had tricked him. The memory of the calm he had felt holding death in his arms and another man's life story in his heart made him crave that calm with every cell of his white-hot brain.

He glimpsed a sign for a rest area, half a mile away. He straightened up, telling himself he could go there, swallow another milligram or two of Haldol, and put himself to sleep. Like a vampire, he almost always fed by night; first light was just three hours away.

He veered off Route 90, into the rest area. One other car was parked there—an older-model, metallic blue Saab, with its interior light on. Jonah parked three spaces away. Why not ten? he chastised himself. Why tempt the beast? He gripped the wheel even more tightly, his fingernails digging into the heels of his hands, nearly breaking the skin. His fever spawned chills that ran up his neck and over his scalp. His ribcage strained painfully against his bulging lungs.

Half against his will, he turned his head and saw a woman in the driver's seat of the Saab, a large map unfolded against the steering wheel. She looked about forty-five years old. In silhouette, her face just missed beauty—her nose a bit large, her chin a bit weak. Crow's-feet suggested she was a worrier. Her brown hair was cut short and neat. She wore a black leather jacket. A cell phone lay on the dashboard in front of her.

Just looking at her made Jonah hungry. Ravenous. Here was a living, breathing woman, not twenty feet away, with a unique past and future. No other person had had precisely the same experiences or had thought precisely the same thoughts. Invisible bonds connected her to parents and grandparents, perhaps siblings, perhaps a husband or lovers, or both. Perhaps children. Friends. Her brain held data she had gathered, picking and choosing what to read and look at and listen to out of interests and abilities that were mystical and immeasurable parts of her. Of *her*, a being like no other. She harbored likes and dislikes, fears and dreams, and (this, more than anything) traumas that were hers and hers alone—unless she could be coaxed to share them.

Bolts of pain exploded into Jonah's eyes. He looked away, staring at the highway for most of a minute, hoping another car would slow to enter the rest area. None did.

Why did it always seem so easy? Almost prearranged. Even preordained. He never stalked his victims; he came upon them. Was the universe organizing to feed him the life force of others? Did the people who crossed his path come in search of him? Did they unconsciously need to die as much as he needed to kill? Did God want them in heaven? Was he some kind of angel? An angel of death? His saliva started to run thicker in his mouth. The throbbing in his head surged beyond anything like a headache, beyond any migraine. He felt as though a dozen drill bits inside his skull were powering their way out, through his forehead, his temples, his ears, down through the roof of his mouth, his lips.

He thought of killing himself, an impulse that had visited him before each murder. The straight razor in his pocket could end his suffering once and for all. But he had made only meager attempts on his own life. Shallow lacerations to his wrists. Five or ten pills, instead of fifty or a hundred. A drunken leap from a second-story window that fractured his right fibula. These were suicidal *gestures*, nothing more. Deep down Jonah wanted to live.

He still believed he could make amends in this life. Beneath all his self-loathing, at the core of his being, he still loved himself in the unconditional way he prayed the Lord did.

He flicked on the BMW's cabin light and sounded a short blast of his horn, nauseated at secreting the first sticky strand of his poisonous web. The woman started, then looked over at him. He leaned toward her and held up a finger, almost shyly, then lowered his passenger window not quite halfway, as if *he* wasn't sure whether to trust *her*.

The woman hesitated, then lowered her own window.

"Excuse me," Jonah said. His voice was velvety and deep, and he knew it had a nearly hypnotic effect. People never seemed to tire of listening to him. They rarely interrupted him.

The woman smiled, but tightly, and said nothing.

"I know this would be, uh . . . asking a lot . . . but, uh . . ." He stuttered intentionally, to sound unsure of himself. "My, uh . . . phone . . ." he said, with a shrug and a smile, "kind of died." He held up his cell phone. It was silver and looked pricey. He extended his arm and turned his wrist, checking the time on his shiny Cartier chronograph, a cabochon sapphire at the crown. He knew most people trusted others with money, either because they believed the rich didn't need to steal from them, or because they assumed the rich valued society's rules too much to break them. "I'm a doctor," Jonah went on. He shook his head. "Left the hospital about four minutes ago, and they're paging me already. Any chance I could, uh . . . borrow your phone?"

"My battery is getting . . ." the woman started, sounding uncomfortable.

"I'd be happy to pay you something," Jonah said. The offer was his way of leapfrogging the woman's better judgment by transforming his request for the phone into the question of whether she ought to charge him to use it. A generous person would offer it for free—which, of course, required offering it to begin with.

"Go ahead," she said. "Evenings and weekends are no charge."

"Thank you." He got out of his car and walked toward the woman's door, stopping a respectful distance away. Partly to trigger her instinct to nurture him, partly to discharge the electric energy coursing through his system, he stepped briskly foot-to-foot and shook his head and shoulders, as if freezing.

She reached out, handed him the phone.

He stood facing her, letting her take note of his chocolate-colored, quilted suede coat, his sky-blue turtleneck sweater, his pleated gray flannel slacks. Nothing black. Everything soft to the touch. He dialed random digits and held the phone to his ear.

"You can use it in your car, if you like," she said.

Jonah knew the woman's invitation to take her phone into his car reflected her unconscious wish that he would take *her* into his car. He also knew that the more proper he was, the freer she would feel to fantasize about him and the more penetrable her personal boundaries would become. "You've already been incredibly kind," he said. "I'll only be a moment."

She nodded, looked back at the map, and rolled up her window.

He spoke loudly to be certain she would overhear him. The words reverberated in his ears. "Dr. Wrens," he said, then paused. "A fever? How high?" He paused again. "Let's start her on some IV ampicillin and see how she does." He nodded. "Of course. Tell her husband I'll see her first thing in the morning." He pretended to click the phone off and knocked quietly on the car window.

She lowered it. "All set?"

He had obviously finished using the phone. Her question meant she wanted something else from him, even though he doubted she would be able to put into words what that something was. He felt a stiffening in his groin. "All set," he said. "Thank you so much." He held the phone out, waiting to speak until she was holding the other end of it, until they were connected that little bit. "Maybe I can return the favor," he said. He waited another moment before letting go of the phone. "You seem uncertain where you're headed."

She laughed. "I seem lost," she said.

He laughed with her—a boyish, infectious laugh that broke the ice once and for all. The beast was fully in control. The pain in Jonah's head seeped into his teeth and jaws. "Where are you trying to go, if you don't mind my asking?" He rubbed his hands together, blew out a plume of frosty breath.

"Eagle Bay," she said.

Eagle Bay was a small town on the Adirondack Railroad, close to the Moose River recreation area. Jonah had hiked nearby Panther Mountain. "That's easy," he said. "I'll scribble out directions." He had chosen the word *scribble* to conjure the image of innocence, of a harmless man-child barely able to write, let alone plot and plan.

"I'd appreciate that," she said.

Jonah felt as though he had sufficiently weakened her defenses to push past them. The average woman lacked the internal resolve to protect her boundaries, except in the face of obvious danger. And this woman could not see him as an imminent threat. He was handsome and well-spoken. He looked wealthy. He was a physician. He had been called by a local hospital to help someone in distress. A *woman* in distress. Now he wanted to help her.

He came around the front of the Saab, hugging himself. Walking around the back of the car, leaving the woman's field of vision, might make her wary. He waited beside the passenger door, making no movement toward it. The less overt his demand to be let inside, the better his chances.

She seemed to hesitate, again, her face registering what looked like a textbook struggle between the instinct for self-preservation and the quest for self-reliance. Self-reliance won. She reached across the passenger seat and pushed open the door.

Jonah climbed in. He held out his hand. It trembled. "Jonah Wrens," he said. "It must be ten below, with the wind chill."

"Anna," she said, shaking his hand. "Anna Beckwith." She looked confused as she let go, probably because Jonah's hand felt warm and clammy, not cold.

"Do you have a pen and paper, Anna Beckwith?" Jonah asked. Speaking her name would make them seem less like strangers.

Beckwith reached behind Jonah's seat and rummaged through her handbag, finding a felt-tip pen and leather address book. She flipped to a blank page and handed the open book and pen to him.

Jonah noted that Beckwith wore no engagement ring or wedding band. She did not smell of perfume. He started writing out random directions, to nowhere. *Stay on 90 East, to exit 54, Route 9 West . . .* "I take it you're not from around here," he said.

She shook her head. "Washington, D.C."

"Are you a skier?" he asked, still writing.

"No," she said.

"A hiker?"

"I'm just visiting a friend."

"Good for you." He glanced at her. "Boyfriend?" he asked matter-of-factly. He went back to writing.

"College roommate."

No boyfriend, Jonah thought. No wedding band. No perfume. No lipstick. And not the slightest hint of homosexuality in her manner or tone. "Let me guess . . ." he said. "Mount Holyoke."

"Why would you guess a girl's school?" Beckwith asked.

Jonah looked at her. "I saw the Mount Holyoke sticker on your back window when I drove in."

She laughed again—an easy laugh that showed the last of her fear had melted away. "Class of '78."

Jonah did the math. Beckwith was between forty-five and forty-six years old. He could have asked her what she had studied at Holyoke or whether the college was close to her home or far away. But answers to those questions would not give him access to her soul. "Why a girl's school?" he asked instead.

"I really don't know," she said.

"You chose it," he pushed, smiling warmly to take the edge off his words.

"I just felt more comfortable."

I just felt more comfortable. Jonah stood at the threshold of Beckwith's internal, emotional world. He needed to buy enough time to cross it. "Do you know Route 28?" he asked.

"I don't," Beckwith said.

"No problem," Jonah said. "I'll, uh, draw everything out . . . for you." Without thinking to, he drew a line up the page, then another, shorter line intersecting it at something close to a ninety degree angle. He noticed the rudimentary cross on the page and took it as a symbol that God was still with him. Hadn't Jesus, after all, absorbed the pain of others? And wasn't that Jonah's aim? His thirst? His cross to bear? "Why would a coed campus have made you uncomfortable?" he asked Beckwith.

She didn't respond.

He looked at her, saw a new hesitancy in her face. "Sorry to pry. My daughter's thinking of Holyoke," he lied.

"You have a daughter?"

"You seem surprised."

"You don't wear a wedding band."

She had been studying him. She was coming closer. Jonah felt his heart rate and breathing begin to slow. "Her mother and I divorced when Caroline was five," he said. Then he delivered Beckwith this talisman, harvested from Scott Carmady's soul, now a part of his own: "My wife was unfaithful to me. I stayed longer than I should have."

That fabricated self-revelation was all the license Anna Beckwith needed to begin revealing her true self. "I was always shy with boys," she said. "I'm sure that's the reason for Holyoke."

"You've never married," Jonah said.

"You sound so sure," Beckwith said playfully.

Jonah kept writing out his haphazard map, not wanting to interrupt the stream of emotion flowing between them. "Just a guess," he said.

"You guessed right."

"I wasn't exactly marriage material myself," he said.

"I had two brothers," she said. "Both older. Maybe that . . . I don't know."

Jonah heard a whole world within the way Beckwith had said the word *older*. There was resentment and powerlessness in it—and something more. Shame. "They made fun of you," he said. He couldn't resist looking at her again. He watched her face lose its mask of maturity and become open and innocent and beautiful. A little girl's face. He thought to himself that he could never kill a child. And with that thought, the pain in his head fell off to a dull ache.

"They teased me quite a bit," she said.

"How old were you?"

"The worst of it?" She shrugged. "Ten? Eleven?"

"And how old were they?"

"Fourteen and sixteen."

Beckwith suddenly looked anxious, in the same way Jonah's other victims had—as if she didn't understand why she would share such intimacies with a stranger. But Jonah needed to hear more. So he pushed ahead. "What names did they call you?" He closed his eyes, waiting for her emotional wound to ooze the sweet antidote to his violence.

"They called me . . ." She stopped. "I don't want to go there." She let out a long breath. "If you could just give me the directions, I'd really appreciate it."

Jonah looked at her. "The kids at school used to call me 'faggot,' 'wimp,' things like that." Another lie.

She shook her head. "From the looks of it, you've really shown them," she said. "No one would call you a wimp now."

"Nice of you to say." He looked out his window, as if pained by the memory of his childhood traumas.

"They called me . . . 'prissy pussy pants,'" Beckwith said.

Jonah turned back to her. She was blushing.

"I know it doesn't sound like the end of the world or anything," she went on, "but they just kept it up. They wouldn't let me be."

Jonah was with the eleven-year-old Beckwith now, seeing her in a pleated, navy blue wool skirt, proper white blouse, white socks, cordovan penny loafers. It was no accident her brothers had teased her most intensely as she reached womanhood, when they would be, consciously or not, focused on her pants and the soft folds of skin beneath them. And he intuited more toxic goings-on—from the way Beckwith had said that they *wouldn't let her be*. That sounded like code for sexual abuse. He stared at her, hoping she would strip her psyche naked and bathe with him in the warm pool of her suffering. "And besides the name-calling?" he said.

Beckwith stared back at him, the color slowly draining from her cheeks.

"How else were your brothers cruel to you, Anna?"

She shook her head.

"They tried to look at you?"

"I really have to get going," she said.

"They touched you," he said.

Suddenly, the little girl Beckwith disappeared, and the forty-five-year-old Beckwith sat rigidly in her place. "Honestly, it really isn't any of your . . ."

Jonah wanted the little girl. He needed the little girl. "You can tell me," he said. "You can tell me anything."

"No," she said.

Jonah could almost hear a bolt sliding home, locking him out. "Please," he said.

"I need you to leave," Beckwith said.

"You shouldn't feel embarrassed with me," Jonah said. He was straining for air. "I've heard everything there is to hear." He tried to force a smile, but knew his expression had to look more wolfish than reassuring.

Beckwith squinted at him, then swallowed hard, as if she finally saw she was in the company of madness.

Jonah's head had started to throb. "Where was your father?" he asked, hearing the telltale anger seeping into his voice. "Where was your mother?"

"Please," Beckwith said. "Just let me leave." Yet she didn't try to escape.

"Why didn't they help you?" Jonah asked. He felt saliva drip from the corner of his mouth and saw in Beckwith's face that she had seen it.

"If you let me go, I . . ." she started to plead.

The drill bits inside Jonah's skull started grinding again. "What did those little bastards do to you?" Jonah yelled.

"They . . ." She started to cry.

Jonah leaned over her, bringing his mouth to her ear. "What did they do?" he demanded. "Don't be ashamed. It wasn't your fault."

Beckwith's face twisted into the panic and confusion that had seized Scott Carmady—horrified disbelief at what was happening. "Please," she gasped. "Please, God . . ."

Her pleading was simultaneously excruciating and

exciting to Jonah, a terrible and irresistible window on the evil inside him. He pressed his cheek to hers. "Tell me," he whispered in her ear. He felt her tears stream down his face. And he began to cry himself. Because he realized there was only one way to enter her soul.

He reached into his front pocket for the straight edge razor. He opened it mercifully outside her view. Then he placed a thumb under her chin and gently tilted her head back. She offered no resistance. He drew the blade quickly across each of her carotid arteries, severing them cleanly. And he watched as Beckwith wilted like a three-day-old flower.

Blood began to drip down his cheek, mixing with his tears. He could not have said anymore whether it was his blood or Beckwith's, his tears or hers. In this pure and final moment, all boundaries between him and his victim were evaporating. He was free from the bondage of his own identity.

He wrapped his arms around Beckwith, drawing her tightly to him, groaning as he discharged the seed of life between their thighs, marrying them forever. He kept her close as her frenzy faded to exhaustion, until he felt his muscles relax with hers, his heart slow with hers, his mind clear with hers—until he was completely at peace, at one with himself and the universe.

two

Dr. Craig Ellison sat down in the tufted leather chair behind his mahogany desk. He was a kind-looking man, just past sixty, with a ring of white hair and age spots on his scalp. He wore half-glasses, a simple gray suit, a pale yellow shirt, and a blue striped tie. His office bore the trappings of his profession—a deeply hued oriental rug, framed degrees from the University of Pennsylvania and Rochester Medical School, an analyst's couch, dozens of tiny, primitive figures, reminiscent of Freud's. He looked across his desk. "I trust your trip was uneventful."

"Smooth sailing," Jonah said.

"Excellent." Ellison looked over his glasses. "Your resumé said home was Miami. You traveled from there?"

"I worked upstate New York last month. Medina. Near the Erie Canal. St. Augustine's Medical Center."

Ellison smiled. "I'm surprised you'd trade the beach for the mountains."

"I love to hike," Jonah said.

"That explains it. I've been after half a dozen staffing companies to get me a child psychiatrist—every since our Dr. Wyatt retired."

"There just aren't many docs interested in locum tenens work, anymore," Jonah said.

"Why is that?" Ellison asked.

"Fewer psychiatry residents graduating. Staff salaries increasing. You can earn nearly as much staying put as you can traveling."

Ellison smiled wryly. "Twenty thousand a month?"

"Sixteen, seventeen, counting benefits," Jonah said. "Within the last two years, two-thirds of the psychiatrists at Medflex have taken permanent positions at one of the hospitals they were assigned to."

Ellison winked. "That's something we can talk about. I reviewed your letters of recommendation. I've never seen anything like them. Dr. Blake called you 'the finest psychiatrist' he'd ever worked with. I happen to have been a resident with Dan Blake when he was at Harvard. He's not one to hand out false praise."

"Thank you," Jonah said. "But I would get anxious if I didn't move around."

"Maybe we could coax you to stay longer than six weeks."

"I never do," Jonah said. That was his rule. Six weeks max, then move on. Longer than that, and people started wanting to know you. They started circling too close.

"I take it you don't have a family," Ellison said.

"No." Jonah let the word hang in the air, enjoying the crisp sound of it and glad to be able to answer so definitively. Because he had not only forsaken a wife and children. He had completely cut himself off from his family of origin, severed every tie with every relative and childhood friend, cast himself adrift, a man alone on the planet. He nodded toward a silver-framed, black-and-white photograph on Ellison's desk. Two children laughed on a swing set while an attractive woman with windswept hair pushed them. "Yours?" he asked.

Ellison looked at the photograph. "Yes," he said, with

a mixture of pride and melancholy. "They're grown now. Conrad is finishing his surgical residency at UCLA. Jessica is a real estate attorney here in town. Good kids. I'm blessed."

Ellison hadn't mentioned the woman in the picture. Jonah intuited she was the source of the sadness in his voice, sadness Jonah was irresistibly drawn to. "Is that your wife?" he asked.

Ellison looked back at him. "Elizabeth. Yes." A pause. "She passed away."

"I'm sorry," Jonah said. He sensed Ellison's emotional wound was raw. "Quite recently?"

"A little under a year." He pressed his lips together. "It feels recent to me."

"I understand," Jonah said.

"People say that," Ellison said, "but surviving the woman you love . . . it's something you'd almost have to live through yourself to understand. I wouldn't wish that on my worst enemy."

Jonah stayed silent.

"We were married thirty-seven years," Ellison said. "Together, forty-one. I have no complaints."

Jonah nodded, but he knew that Ellison issuing such a denial meant he had plenty of complaints, not the least of which would be with mortality itself, the horrific fact that our lives and those of the people we love are impermanent and exquisitely fragile, that any of us can cease to exist without warning, that loving anyone, anywhere, at any time, leaves you infinitely vulnerable at every single moment.

The thought transported Jonah out of Ellison's office. He was with Anna Beckwith's mother as she answered the phone, a state trooper on the other end, about to deliver bad news. Unthinkable news. A daughter found murdered in the woods near her car, just off the highway. Jonah imagined himself holding Mrs. Beckwith as she sobbed. He stroked her hair. He whispered in her ear, *"Anna isn't really dead. A part of her is alive. Inside me."*

"Dr. Wrens?" Ellison was saying, leaning forward a little in his chair.

"Yes," Jonah said.

Ellison looked over his half glasses again. "Did I lose you there, for a moment?"

"I was just thinking of being with the same woman for forty-one years. You must have loved her very much."

Ellison cleared his throat, settled back in his chair. "You've never married?"

Jonah had asked Anna Beckwith precisely the same question. *You've never married?* He looked askance at Ellison, wondering whether the kindly doctor might be telegraphing that he knew the mayhem Jonah had committed. But that was impossible, and Jonah dismissed his worry as the mental echo of a guilty conscience. For he did feel guilt—more and more with every life he took. "I was married for a short time," he said. "I was young."

"Weren't we all," Ellison said. "You weren't ready for a commitment?"

Jonah shook his head. "I was ready."

"She wasn't," Ellison said.

Jonah gazed down at his lap, tugged nervously at his right pant leg, then looked back at Ellison. "Actually, she died," he said, opting for starker words than Ellison's, *She passed away.*

Ellison's face fell.

"For whatever it's worth," Jonah said, "and I trust

you to keep my confidence, I do know something about what you've been through. I've been through it myself."

"I'm so sorry," Ellison said, his brow furrowing. "What I said must have sounded—"

"Like the truth," Jonah interrupted. "Only someone who's been through what we went through could ever understand."

Ellison nodded.

"Her name was Anna," Jonah said, letting his eyes drift to a corner of Ellison's desk. "We met at a dance at Mount Holyoke College, in Massachusetts." He closed his eyes a moment, then opened them and smiled as if comforted by a pleasant memory. "She'd chosen a girls' school because she was shy—painfully, really. She had two older brothers who had teased her ceaselessly. Really ramped it up when she was about eleven, just in time to inflict the most damage psychosexually. But she came into her own after we were engaged. Blossomed in every way. She seemed to have needed that kind of security." He looked directly at Ellison again. "Security," he said, shaking his head. "She was twenty-three when she died."

"My God," Ellison said. He was quiet a few moments. "Do you mind if I ask what she died of?"

Jonah knew that a woman who died at the age of Ellison's wife Elizabeth was likely a victim of cancer. Heart disease was also possible. A car accident could never be ruled out. "Anna died of cancer," he gambled. He was in the mood to test the limits of his intuition. "Ovarian," he said.

"Breast," Ellison said, of his own loss.

Close enough, Jonah thought. Ovarian. Breast. Neither end was short or painless. Ellison had seen hell, and now he believed Jonah had seen it, too. "People tell you you'll get over it," Jonah said, "given time, given another relationship, given enough Sunday mornings saying enough prayers, but I don't expect I ever will."

Ellison looked at him like a blood brother. "Nor I," he said.

Jonah swallowed hard and said nothing for several seconds, letting the glue of their emotional bond harden. When he did speak, it was with the tone of a man consciously reshelving the memory of a great tragedy. "Well, then . . . okay," he said. "Moving right along . . ."

"Right along," Ellison said.

"Tell me about the ward," Jonah said. "How can I be helpful?"

"You've already been helpful," Ellison said. He smiled at Jonah. "Thank you."

Jonah nodded solemnly.

"But about the ward . . ." Ellison said, refocusing. "As you know, it's twenty beds. We generally run full, with a waiting list. We're the only locked psychiatry unit within two hundred fifty miles. Canaan and the towns around it are blue collar, mostly logging. The parents tend to be high-school educated, if that. Plenty of alcoholism, as you might expect given our locale. Also a fair amount of illicit drug use. Cocaine. Heroin. All of which brings abuse and neglect. And I'd say we have more than our share of depression."

"Tough winters," Jonah said.

"Possibly. Or it may just reflect a population of lower-than-average socioeconomic status." Ellison paused. "What I can tell you is that the kids who come here, probably not unlike other units where you've worked, are severely mentally ill. Major depression, schizophrenia, drug dependence. The insurance companies would deny them admission for anything less. And there isn't a family around here that could foot the bill for an elective stay."

"I like working with very ill patients," Jonah said.

"Then you'll like it here," Ellison said.

"Night call is every third?"

"Right. You'll be working with Michelle Jenkins and Paul Plotnik. I promise they'll be very pleased to see you. They've been splitting Dr. Wyatt's caseload, which is no small burden. He was very popular."

"I hope I measure up."

"I'm certain you will," Ellison said. He looked at a datebook open on his desk. "You'll start the third of the month then, as planned?"

"I can start today," Jonah said, anxious not only to make amends for his destructiveness, but to feed himself the tortuous life stories he needed.

"How about yesterday?" Ellison said, smiling. He stood up. "I'll show you around." He paused. "Come to think of it, we have case conference at noon. Usually Dr. Jenkins or Dr. Plotnik presents the case to me. I interview the patient in front of the staff and see if I can ferret out anything they haven't, pull a rabbit out of the proverbial hat." He winked. "Plotnik is up today. Why don't you sit in for me? That'll be a good way for the staff to get to know your style."

"I'd be honored," Jonah said. "Thank you."

"Thank me after the nurses and social workers get done peppering you with questions," Ellison said. "They love taking pot shots at my clinical assessments. I doubt they'll be any more gentle with you."

"Tell them to shoot away," Jonah said. "I'll take it as a rite of passage."

*

The auditorium of little Canaan Memorial Hospital was an amphitheater that looked newly renovated, with fresh, dark gray carpeting, two hundred or so nicely cushioned, pearl-gray folding seats, and an array of wall sconces that cast pleasant plumes of light against the rose-colored walls, hung here and there with prints of peaceful mountain scenes. Snowy pines. Wafting clouds. An icy brook.

When Jonah arrived with Craig Ellison, men and women were just drifting in. A lectern and honey oak table sat at the front of the room. Behind the table sat two upholstered wingback chairs facing one another.

Jonah had been in dozens of auditoriums just like this one, all of them designed much like he had designed himself—from his clothing to his mannerisms to his choice of words—to hold people and comfort them so they felt safe enough to speak their darkest thoughts. The demons that lurked inside people—those grotesquely disfigured sewer dwellers of the mind, driven underground by the unspeakable emotional holocaust of what we call daily life—were themselves easily spooked, quick to retreat back into the maze of the unconscious, where they might be hopelessly lost and alone and desperate to be touched, but at least safe in their isolation from the kinds of beatings, whether physical or emotional, real or imagined, that they had taken by light of day. Manipulative mothers, violent fathers, lecherous mentors, double-crossing friends, loveless marriages, dead grandparents, dead parents, dead siblings, dead children, death waiting patiently—for them. What they needed was the quiet reassurance of pastels and soft shadows, of endless vistas and clear skies, of a velvet voice like Jonah's, a pale blue gaze like his.

Yet all these things could reach only elbow-deep into the unconscious, leaving the most severe of pathologies untouched. Jonah's reach was far deeper, to the remotest corner of the darkest mind. And the secret ingredient that beyond any other explained the magic he could work with patients was simply this: the palpable presence of his own demons. Those who harbored unthinkable thoughts knew in their hearts they had found a kindred spirit, one who understood the special torture it is to live fractured into pieces, some of them so sharp that to touch them would be to bleed forever.

"There's one of your partners in crime," Ellison said to Jonah, nodding toward an exotic-looking woman with long, straight black hair, in her mid to late thirties, standing in a small group at the far side of the room. "Dr. Jenkins. Let me introduce you."

Jonah followed Ellison over to the woman.

"Excuse me," Ellison said, touching her arm from behind.

Jenkins turned around. She wore a simple but smartly cut black pantsuit, with a lime green, scoop-neck T-shirt. "How are you, Craig?" she said. She acknowledged Jonah with a nod, then looked back at Ellison.

"I'm just fine," Ellison said.

"Paul has a real brain teaser for you today," she said. "A nine-year-old boy. Nearly mute. The poor kid hasn't said more than ten words since he was admitted." She winked at Jonah. "We'll see what the chief can do with him."

Jonah looked into Jenkins's amber eyes, the whites gleaming beside her lustrous hair. The crescent contour of her eyes and the way they sat at a subtle angle above her cheekbones suggested she might be part Asian, as did her tawny skin and long, graceful neck. When she smiled, dimples appeared in her cheeks, making her an accessible, rather than untouchable, beauty. "What were they?" Jonah asked.

"Excuse me?" Jenkins said.

"The words," Jonah said. "What ten words has the boy spoken?"

Jenkins smiled. "I didn't think to ask. I should have."

Ellison chuckled. "Michelle Jenkins, meet Jonah Wrens, the doctor I told you about from Medflex."

"I thought so," Jenkins said, extending her hand. "My savior."

Jonah took her hand. It was soft and delicate, with long, graceful fingers—a hand to rival his own. He noticed she wore a four- or five-carat diamond engagement ring on her middle finger. She probably hadn't had time to have the ring sized since her engagement. Or maybe she wasn't engaged at all, and the ring was an heirloom given her by her adoring grandmother. "Savior may be going a bit far," Jonah said.

"You aren't the one who's been taking call every other night for seven months," she said, tilting her head in a feminine and wonderful way. She let go of his hand. "Every third is going to feel like heaven." She looked at Ellison. "You've worn me out."

"Never know it, looking at you," Ellison said, with a slight bow.

"Time you get your lenses checked," Jenkins said. She glanced over Ellison's shoulder. "Paul's here."

Jonah turned and saw a man in a dark blue blazer and wrinkled khakis heading over.

"Paul Plotnik," Ellison said. "The third musketeer."

Plotnik, a wiry man of about fifty-five, with sparse, unruly hair and narrow, sloped shoulders, joined the group. The sleeves of his blue blazer were a bit short. His khakis were stained above his left knee. "Got a tough one for you today," he said to Ellison, with a slight lisp. His eyes darted to Jonah, then to Jenkins, then back to Ellison. "Ten years old, nearly mute. He hardly moves. Hearing voices, I'd guess. Maybe seeing visions."

"Tell it to Dr. Jonah Wrens, from Medflex," Ellison said, nodding toward Jonah. "I've asked him to sit in for me today."

"Wonderful," Ellison said. He shook Jonah's hand—too hard. "I've heard a lot about you. When did you arrive?"

"Just today," Jonah said. "That's quite a handshake." He noticed that the left side of Plotnik's face drooped slightly. He'd had a minor stroke. That explained his lisp.

"Been told that. Been told that," Plotnik said, finally letting go.

"Dr. Ellison's putting you right to work," Jenkins said to Jonah. "Trial by fire."

"I don't mind," Jonah told her. He held her gaze. Or was she holding his? "Rescue me if you see me going down in flames." He listened to his own words as he spoke them, heard how they married nurturance, sexual passion, and danger. *Rescue me. Going down. Flames.* He hadn't planned to deliver such a potent message.

"I will," Jenkins said, a whisper of seduction in her voice.

Ellison raised an eyebrow.

"Well, then, why don't we get started?" Plotnik said,

smiling a nervous smile. "See what twenty grand a month buys these days."

Jonah laughed.

"Paul, that's inappropriate," Ellison said.

"A joke," Plotnik said, holding both his hands in the air. "A joke. Nothing more."

"No offense taken," Jonah said.

"Dr. Ellison didn't spill the beans," Plotnik said to Jonah. "He's as tight-lipped as they come. I once looked into working for Medflex. I've kept my eye on what they pay."

"You decided to sit tight," Jonah said.

"Craig offered me twenty-two a month," Plotnik said, erupting into laughter.

"When hell freezes over," Jenkins said.

"Why don't we get started," Ellison said.

"Seriously though," Plotnik said to Jonah. "No one's expecting you to crack this case wide open. He's already been on the unit almost three weeks. Get him to string two words together, and you're a hero." He turned on his heels and marched toward the lectern at the front of the room.

three

The auditorium was filled nearly to capacity. Ellison explained to Jonah that Canaan Memorial was one of the few places in Vermont where mental health professionals could earn the continuing education credits they needed to keep their licenses. Social workers, psychologists, and psychiatrists from all over the state attended the weekly case conference.

Jonah listened from a seat in the front row as Paul Plotnik began to present the psychiatric history of nine-year-old Benjamin Herlihey. After the presentation, Herlihey would be brought in to be interviewed.

"Benjamin Herlihey is a nine-year-old white male admitted to the locked psychiatric unit on January third of this year," Plotnik read from prepared notes. "He is the only child born to his father, who works at a local lumber yard, and his mother, who works as a day care provider in the couple's home. According to his parents, Benjamin showed worsening symptoms of major depression for nearly three months prior to admission, including lack of appetite with a seventeen-pound weight loss, decreased sleep with early morning awakening, loss of interest in all activities that once brought him pleasure, decreased energy, and intermittent tearfulness." Plotnik paused, but continued to stare at his notes. He pushed the tip of his pointer finger into his ear and twirled the fingertip, as if removing ear wax.

Ellison leaned toward Jonah. "A nervous habit," he whispered.

Very nervous, Jonah thought to himself.

"Benjamin was treated by an outpatient psychiatrist who prescribed him Zoloft at fifty milligrams, without any improvement in symptoms," Plotnik went on. "The dosage was slowly increased to one hundred milligrams, then to two hundred. No beneficial results were obtained. The patient's symptoms continued to worsen. Desipramine was added at fifty milligrams each morning. But despite the combination of medicines, the patient's energy continued to decline, and his weight continued to fall. He stopped attending school and became more and more reclusive at home. By mid-December, Benjamin had become nearly mute, answering yes or no to questions, but offering nothing more. He began to avoid eye contact. His outpatient psychiatrist then reasoned, wisely by my estimation, that Benjamin, rather than suffering a major depression, was experiencing a first psychotic break, heralding the onset—in childhood—of paranoid schizophrenia."

Whispers in the audience spoke to the poor prognosis of early onset schizophrenia. Major depression, while no cakewalk, was far more treatable.

Plotnik drove his fingertip inside his ear again, twirled it around, then used it to flip to the next page of his presentation. "Since his admission to Seven West on January third, the patient has maintained almost complete silence. He seems, at times, to be distracted, presumably by hallucinations. He looks up toward the ceiling, as if hearing a voice or seeing a vision.

"Benjamin has not maintained a normal diet since falling ill, and his anorexic behavior has only worsened on the unit and now places him in metabolic jeopardy. We are delivering him nutrients by IV, but will need to place a feeding tube within days to ensure his survival. His parents have already consented to the surgery. We plan to initiate electroconvulsive treatment immediately thereafter, in hopes of impacting Benjamin's psychosis.

"Psychodynamically, it seems relevant that Benjamin's father deserted the family with no notice three years ago, almost to the day, that his son's symptoms began. Mr. Herlihey stayed away four months, refusing all contact with his family, then reuniting with them just as suddenly. He did not then—nor has he since—communicated the reason for his abrupt departure or return.

"One would wonder whether Benjamin is replicating his father's silence, starving himself physically as a concrete symbol of the starvation he experienced emotionally." Plotnik looked up from his notes for the first time. "As I feared he would, Benjamin's father dismissed my theory out of hand. He remains unwilling to fill in the gap as to what he was doing—and what his motivations for doing it might have been—during his absence."

Plotnik nodded at Jonah. "We have as our case consultant today the newest member of the psychiatry staff at Canaan Memorial, Dr. Jonah Wrens." Shifting his gaze to a young man standing just inside the door to the auditorium, he said, "Please bring Benjamin in."

Plotnik left the podium and headed for the seat next to Jonah's. Jonah stood. He started toward the wingback chairs behind the oak table, but stopped as the door to the auditorium opened and Benjamin Herlihey, slumped to the left side of a wheelchair, each of his arms hooked up to an IV, was pushed into the room.

Even under a white hospital blanket, Herlihey looked like something out of a World War II concentration camp. His sunken eyes had bluish circles beneath them. His red hair was fine and thinning, his scalp showing through in places. The bones of his legs and arms barely tented the woven white fabric covering them. He seemed ageless to Jonah, nine or ninety, close to birth and close to death.

Jonah walked the rest of the way to the front of the auditorium. He moved one of the armchairs away from the oak table, making room for Benjamin's wheelchair. He took the other armchair. Then the two of them—doctor and patient—sat opposite one another in silence, with Benjamin's head flopped to the side, his vacant eyes peering up at Jonah.

"My name is Dr. Wrens. Jonah Wrens."

Benjamin did not speak or show any emotion.

"Dr. Plotnik asked me to talk with you, to see if I can help."

Benjamin's eyes rolled up and to the left, staring several seconds at the ceiling, then slowly returning to center.

Jonah looked up at the spot where Benjamin's eyes seemed to have traveled. There was nothing there. He looked back at the boy. "Dr. Plotnik told me about the trouble you've been having. I want to understand it."

Benjamin didn't respond.

Jonah was about to ask another question, to prod the boy into uttering a word or two. But he stopped himself, settled back in his chair, and simply sat with him. A minute passed. Then two. Occasionally, Benjamin's eyes would roll up to the ceiling, and when they did, Jonah rolled his own eyes in precisely the same arc.

Two minutes of quiet is more than most people can stand. People in the audience shifted nervously in their seats. Out of the corner of his eye, Jonah could see some leaning to whisper to their colleagues. He could imagine what they were saying. *Who is this guy, anyway? Is he going to do anything? Why doesn't he say something, for Christ's sake?*

Jonah dismissed them all from his mind. Never breaking eye contact with Benjamin, he slowly began moving his own head, neck, chest, arms, hips, thighs, knees, feet into the same positions as the boy's, becoming his mirror image, judging the exact center of Benjamin's equilibrium by the pressure he felt on his skin in some places and not in others, the tenseness in some of his muscles and the lack of it in others.

Another two minutes passed in this state of suspended animation, with the audience getting more and more jittery, and Jonah slumping further in his chair, looking more and more like a clone of the broken boy across from him.

Then, of a sudden, Jonah straightened up in his chair. He stood up. He stepped over to Benjamin, crouched in front of him and looked into his eyes. "I'm going to touch you now," he said, his voice barely audible. "Don't be afraid." He held his hands out where Benjamin could see them.

The room fell completely silent. Psychiatrists do not touch. They maintain rigid boundaries. They heal from across the room.

"What the heck?" Jonah heard Paul Plotnik mutter.

Jonah glanced at Craig Ellison and saw a dubious

look on his face. But he also glimpsed Michelle Jenkins leaning forward in her seat, transfixed.

He focused on Benjamin again. "Don't be afraid," he said. He kept looking into his eyes for several seconds, then turned his attention to the boy's left arm, lying motionless on his thigh. He lifted it about eight inches, let go and watched it fall like a dead weight. Then he lifted his right arm and dropped it. It slowly drifted back down.

Like a man working the extremities of a life-size Gumby, Jonah pushed and pulled Benjamin's arms and legs this way and that. He ran the tip of his thumb along the bottoms of Benjamin's feet, watching the way his toes curled in response to the peculiar pressure. He leaned even closer, bringing his face within a few inches of Benjamin's. He looked left and right, up and down, noting when Benjamin's eyes tracked along with his, as ocular reflexes would dictate, and when they did not.

He sat back on his heels. "Thank you," he said to Benjamin. "I think I see the problem." He stood up and motioned for the man who had wheeled Benjamin into the room. "All set," he said.

He walked to the lectern and waited for Benjamin to be wheeled away. He looked out over the audience and let out a long breath. "This is an unusual case," he said.

"It's an unusual case conference," Paul Plotnik said in a stage whisper.

Nervous laughter filled the room.

Jonah looked at Plotnik, who had broken into a wide grin. "Glioblastoma brain tumors in this age group are exceedingly rare," he said. "In this case," he went on, addressing the whole audience, "the tumor mimics mental illness perfectly, because of its location. Its point of origin lies just lateral to the limbic system, on the right side of the brain, so that the malignant cells invaded the amygdala first, causing mood alterations and changes in muscle function. They then moved into the caudate nucleus, slowing invading upward, into the medial sulcus of the cortex, which is, of course, the primary speech center." He paused and looked at Paul Plotnik again. "Dr. Plotnik," he said. "Did you get a CAT scan?"

"Of course," Plotnik said defensively.

"I knew you would have, because of how thorough your presentation was," Jonah said. He wanted to save Plotnik from looking foolish and save himself from making an enemy. He looked out over the audience again. "The trouble is that eight percent of glioblastoma lesions show up only on MRI. And we don't generally order MRIs on patients whose symptoms seem to be explained by depression—or schizophrenia." He paused. "Benjamin doesn't need electroconvulsive therapy. He needs surgery—and right away. Glioblastomas are aggressive, but treatable if caught early."

"What about the psychosis?" Michelle Jenkins asked. "How do we explain that?"

"I don't think Benjamin is seeing visions," Jonah said. "His eyes drift upward and toward the left because the nerves to the ocular muscles which center the eye are weak. The tumor is destroying them."

A young woman near the back of the room raised her hand.

Jonah nodded toward her.

"How did you figure this out?" she asked.

"By listening to Benjamin," Jonah said.

"He didn't say a word," the young woman said.

"Exactly," Jonah said.

"Exactly, what?" another man in the middle of the audience asked.

"Benjamin's complete silence was my first clue to what was wrong with him," Jonah said. "If he had uttered a single word, I would have been tempted to wonder what it meant psychologically. If he had cried, I may have taken time trying to get him to tell me about his sadness, or what other symptoms of depression he might be experiencing." He paused. "Benjamin helped me to focus. The key was to sit with him in silence and observe what I could without words or feelings getting in the way."

Paul Plotnik cleared his throat as he raised his hand.

Jonah nodded to him.

"Before we call in a neurosurgeon, shouldn't we get that MRI?" he asked. "Can you be certain it won't be normal?"

"I can't be certain," Jonah said, "but I would be shocked if it were."

Plotnik looked away. His shoulders slumped even more.

Jonah wanted to rehabilitate him. "Dr. Plotnik's psychological theory," he said to the audience, "strikes me as very plausible, by the way. Benjamin's illness could indeed have been caused by his father's abrupt departure from the family."

Plotnik looked back at him. "Didn't you just say he has a brain tumor?"

"Glioblastomas incubate as long as six years before spreading," Jonah told him. "That takes us back to the time Mr. Herlihey walked out on his family. Let's not forget: the limbic system is the brain's emotional control center. No one can know for sure that losing one's father couldn't spark a malignancy there. Why should that be less likely than stress damaging the heart?"

Plotnik stared back at Jonah.

"And who's to say," Jonah continued, shifting his gaze back to the entire audience, "if Mr. Herlihey had told the whole truth about the months he went missing whether that could have somehow bolstered Benjamin's immune system, raised his level of antibodies, maybe even made his tumor remit? Truth has the power to heal."

Jonah saw that Craig Ellison was watching him with a kind of reverence. He decided to go the extra mile and bring out the whole truth about why Paul Plotnik had missed the boat with Benjamin. He looked back at him. "What's equally interesting, Paul, from a psychological standpoint, is that you know from your own experience something about what Benjamin has suffered neurologically."

Plotnik looked at Jonah quizzically. "Are you talking about my stroke?"

"Yes," Jonah said. "Would you mind terribly if I use your experience to make a teaching point?"

"Not at all," Plotnik said, no resentment left in his voice.

"Your stroke," Jonah said, "was minor. But judging from the particular facial muscles affected and the over-compensation of muscles on the right side of your body— that strong handshake of yours—the brain injury was probably in an area of motor cortex adjoining those that control mood and language."

"Exactly," Plotnik said, incredulous.

"So that right after your stroke you would have not only felt physically weak, but would have had trouble with word finding—and with depression."

"A bit."

"And both largely resolved as the affected brain tissue healed."

"Resolved completely," Plotnik said.

Jonah didn't feel the need to point out that Plotnik's speech and appearance had not completely returned to normal—and never would. But Plotnik's refusal to accept the continuing impact of the stroke reinforced Jonah's suspicion. "It's possible that your not wanting to think about your brain injury would make it that much harder to recognize Benjamin's. Your first impulse might be to try *not* to think of it."

Plotnik squinted at Jonah.

"I think that's going out on a limb," Craig Ellison said. "As you've said, none of us would have been likely to get an MRI in a case like—"

"No, Craig," Plotnik interrupted. "I think he's right." He turned to Ellison. "Diagnosing Benjamin's pathology would have meant revisiting my own—thinking about my stroke again. That's something I haven't been willing to do."

"So you presented the case here," Jonah said. "You knew there was something about Benjamin you might not be seeing."

Plotnik nodded. "A clinical blind spot."

"And you dealt with it by bringing him before other eyes. Ours. You got him the help he needed."

"If I did," Plotnik said, "it's thanks to you."

Jonah winked at him. "Assuming the MRI doesn't come back normal," he said.

Jonah planned to spend the rest of the day and night on the locked unit, reviewing the medical charts of six patients being transferred to his care from Dr. Jenkins and Dr. Plotnik. Craig Ellison had offered to let Jonah get his feet wet with just a few patients, but Jonah had jumped at the chance to immerse himself in a half-dozen young lives.

He sat in his borrowed office on Seven West, poring through what amounted to chronicles of soul murder. Naomi McMorris, six years old, raped at age three by her mother's live-in boyfriend; Tommy Magellan, eleven years old, born addicted to cocaine and now addicted to both cocaine and heroin; Mike Pansky, fifteen years old, hearing voices telling him to kill himself, fully ten years after his psychotic mother had tried to kill him.

With every page he read, Jonah felt further and further from Route 90 East and Anna Beckwith's frozen corpse. He had another chance to redeem himself, another chance to be a healer, and he was intoxicated enough by the river of psychopathology flowing at his feet to believe he could make that commitment—and keep it. He would do no more harm. Like an addict with a needle in his vein, he could not see past the high. He could not see that drugging himself with other people's demons would never purge him of his own.

He sat back, closed his eyes, and imagined living through parts of a day or night as Naomi McMorris or Tommy Magellan or Mike Pansky. He felt the ceaseless tug-of-war they fought hour by hour between instincts to love and to hate, to trust and to fear, to hope and to despair. He understood—not only with his mind, but with his heart—how an ego stretching to bridge such extremes could collapse, leaving a boy like Mike in a free fall from reality, his inner feelings of worthlessness boomeranging back to him as disembodied voices demanding he kill himself. He imagined waking from a deep sleep as little Naomi might, not simply embarrassed to have wet the bed, but utterly undone by it, shrieking, clawing, inconsolable, her shame and terror at losing control of her bladder rooted in a rape that had robbed her of all control. He shuddered with the unquenchable desperation of Tommy as a newborn, wrenched not only from the peace of the womb, but from a constant infusion of cocaine, every cell in his body already craving a chemical he would always and forever unconsciously connect with comfort and safety.

As Jonah absorbed these children, he felt the raging tides in his own soul ebb, with an easing of his skeletal muscles, a watering of his eyes, the familiar stiffening in his groin. He felt as though he could shed his own skin and slip inside any other life. He felt free.

He opened his eyes and started to reach for a fourth chart, but stopped at a knock on the office door. He took a long, dreamy breath, stood, walked to the door, and opened it.

Michelle Jenkins smiled at him. "Settling in?" she asked.

Jonah turned and looked back at the office. It was a barren space, with a pressed wood desk, a black leather desk chair, a single upholstered chair for a patient, an empty bookcase, and a beige metal filing cabinet. The walls were off-white and freshly painted, decorated with two framed mountain scenes like those in the auditorium. "It needs something," he said.

"Jim Wyatt had every inch of this place stacked with books and journals. The walls were covered with photographs he'd taken and landscapes he'd painted. He'd been here almost twenty years."

"I don't think I'll do it justice in six weeks," Jonah said. He walked to the desk, sat on the edge.

Jenkins stepped into the room. She nodded at Jonah's briefcase sitting beside the desk—an oversized, well-worn brown leather satchel with a combination lock. "You never know," she said. "There's a touch of character already."

"I've had it since residency," Jonah said.

"Where did you train?" she asked.

"New York," he said.

"Don't make me work so hard. Which hospital?"

"Columbia Presbyterian."

"Impressive."

"And you?"

"Mass General, in Boston."

"Very impressive," Jonah said.

"Not really," Jenkins said. "I was all the diversity they needed, in one tidy package. I'm sure I was the only half-Latino, half-Asian woman who applied for a residency there. Being from Colorado couldn't have hurt, either."

"You're a long way from home," Jonah said.

"I followed a ski instructor," Jenkins said. "He turned into my husband. It was all downhill from there."

Jonah laughed. "Still together?"

"Divorced," she said. "Eleven months ago."

"May I ask how long you were married?"

"You can ask me anything," Jenkins said. Her amber eyes held Jonah's as she sat down in the chair opposite his desk. "Five years. Somewhere between twenty-five and thirty mistresses. I lost track. Women still call looking for him."

"I see," Jonah said. Jenkins was a woman scorned.

He glanced at the diamond on her middle finger. Nothing she had said explained it.

"Not from him," Jenkins said, still looking at Jonah as she ran her thumb over the stone. "My mother's. She died when I was a teenager."

Death. Again. The one constant. The funereal melody playing in back of all life's happy-go-lucky scores. "I'm sorry to hear that," Jonah said.

Jenkins shrugged. "We didn't get along," she said. "I went through real growing pains as an adolescent. We were constantly at each other's throats. As it turned out, we didn't have time to work through it."

Jonah tilted his head and studied Jenkins. Even for a psychiatrist, she seemed especially open, ready to divulge a great deal about herself.

"So what's with the pickup line in front of my boss?" she asked. " 'Rescue me if you see me going down in flames.' Not very subtle."

"I didn't mean it as a pickup line," Jonah told her.

"Then you must *really* want to pick me up," Jenkins said, "if that message came directly from your unconscious."

It *had* come directly from Jonah's unconscious. He did feel something for Jenkins. "You're a good psychiatrist," he said.

"Sometimes I think so," she said. "Then I see someone do something like I saw you do today with Benjamin at the case conference. And I realize I have a lot to learn."

"Beginner's luck," Jonah said.

"Sure." Jenkins stood up, caught her lower lip between her teeth. "So here goes. If you don't have plans this weekend, I could give you the grand tour of Canaan."

Jonah said nothing.

"We won't need more than a night," Jenkins said. "There's one decent restaurant and one discount movie theater."

Jonah felt a pang of regret. Jenkins was beautiful and kind and perceptive, and he might have liked listening more to her, even touching her. She had the lithe, dancer's build he preferred in women. Small breasts, slender waist, narrow hips, long legs. But ever since taking his first life he had resolved to keep to himself, until he could keep himself in control. He didn't need anyone getting close enough to see the darkness inside him. To penetrate a woman was to become penetrable to that woman. "Another time," he said. "I look forward to exploring new places myself— at least at first. It's part of what I like about locum tenens work."

"Being alone," Jenkins said, with no ill will.

"Maybe so," Jonah said.

She shrugged, took two steps back toward the door. "You're an interesting case," she said. She started to walk out, but turned back to Jonah. "You might like to know," she said, "Paul did get that MRI on Benjamin."

"Oh?" Jonah said.

"Glioblastoma, like you said—right where you said it would be."

"Early enough?" he asked.

"Maybe," Jenkins said. "Paul has a neurosurgeon and oncologist consulting on the case."

"A neuroradiologist would be best," Jonah said. "Gamma knife radiosurgery is the best route to go with a glioblastoma in that location. It's a fairly vascular part of the brain. They'll need to get Benjamin to an academic medical center. Johns Hopkins would be ideal. Baylor in Houston would be my second choice."

Jenkins nodded. "I'll mention it to Paul." She paused. "What happened at case conference wasn't beginner's luck, Jonah. You're extraordinary. You have a gift." She turned and walked out.

Jonah watched the door close behind Jenkins. He stood up, stepped to the side of his desk, and reached down for his briefcase. Then he carried it to the small closet in the office and gently placed it behind his coat.

four

Frank Clevenger's feet were on his desk, his gaze directed out the window of his Chelsea waterfront office at three Coast Guard cutters as they zipped around a fleet of tugboats pushing and pulling an oil tanker to its docking station on the Mystic River. Chelsea was all about oil and grime, a tiny, fierce port city in the shadow of the Tobin Bridge, its steel skeleton arching into Boston, its giant concrete feet set deep into the Chelsea jumble of triple deckers, greasy spoons, keno joints, and meat factories. Oil floated on the river and seeped into the ground. You could smell it in the air. It literally made the streets flammable, and twice, in 1908 and 1973, dozens of blocks burned.

Clevenger loved the place. It was a city without pretense, two crazily overbuilt hills kissing a chaotic valley where people were struggling simply to live, not obsessing over how to live well.

The tankers used to drift in, be drained of their black blood, and drift away without a show of force, without drawing any more notice than the smokestacks that silently spewed soot onto Chelsea's neighborhoods or the soft-soled sneakers of the drug dealers padding along Broadway. But that was before the world changed on September 11. Now anything that could be blown up

47

seemed as though it might get blown up. The whole country had come down with a bad case of post-traumatic stress disorder. Bad for us. Good for Eli Lilly and Pfizer and Merck. Eventually, they'd put Prozac and Zoloft and Paxil in the drinking water, see whether that kept the anxiety at bay. Because nobody really wanted to figure out anything anymore, not when the knots in the world's psyche had gotten so tight that untying them might mean unraveling a preconception or two. Better to keep the serotonin flowing, bathe our brains in the calm water of denial.

These were some of the thoughts in Clevenger's mind when his phone began to ring. It rang five times before he reached for it. "Frank Clevenger," he said, as if to remind himself.

"Dr. Clevenger, this is Agent Kane Warner," a raspy voice on the line said. He said it as though it were a question, the end of the sentence rising: . . . *this is Agent Kane Warner?*

People from L.A. spoke that way, like they never wanted to commit to anything. Clevenger glanced at the Caller ID screen. 703. Virginia. The FBI was headquartered in Quantico. "What can I do for you?" he asked.

"I'm the director of the Behavioral Sciences Unit at the Bureau. FBI. I'd like to speak with you about helping us with an investigation." Warner finished with that interrogatory flourish of his again: . . . *an investigation?*

"What case?" Clevenger asked.

"I'd prefer we talk in person?"

"I'm in the office most of the day tomorrow," Clevenger said.

"Actually," Warner said. "I was going to suggest my office."

"Afraid to fly?" Clevenger said.

Warner didn't laugh.

"It was a joke," Clevenger said.

"Okay," Warner said stiffly.

"Before I could meet with you," Clevenger said, "I would have to know . . ."

"I really would rather wait until we sit down," Warner said.

Warner didn't sound friendly—especially for someone asking for help. "I'd rather not wait," Clevenger said.

A pause. "The Highway Killer."

Clevenger pulled his feet off the desk, pulled his eyes away from the harbor. He'd been following news coverage of the Highway Killer for years. "Twelve bodies, twelve states," he said.

"Thirteen bodies," Warner said.

"As of?"

"This morning."

"Where?"

"A young couple driving Route 90 East in New York, headed to their ski house, stopped in a rest area. Their dog ran off. They chased him into the woods, and the girl twisted her ankle on something. It turned out to be a frozen arm."

"Male or female?"

"Female," Warner said. "Anna Beckwith. Forty-four years old. Single. From Pennsylvania." He paused.

"So that's eight men, five women," Clevenger said.

"Thirteen victims. Thirteen states."

"That you know of," Clevenger said. He reached for the package of Marlboros on his desk, lighted one, took a long drag.

There was an uncomfortable silence. "That we know of," Warner allowed.

"Why me?" Clevenger said, smoke drifting out with his words. "You've got experts in house."

"There seems to be agreement here that we could use a forensic psychiatrist with a fresh perspective. Someone outside the agency."

There *seemed* to be agreement. Clevenger smiled wryly. How many more bodies would it take for *definite* agreement? "You could use someone outside—or someone a little 'out there?' "

"You have a reputation for working on the edge," Warner said. "You're . . . unorthodox. We understand that. It may be time for us to think outside the box."

It *may* be time. Clevenger turned and looked out his window as a red Porsche Carrera pulled to a stop alongside the docks. North Anderson, a tough, black, forty-three-year-old former cop, got out. "I have a partner," Clevenger said.

"Who you work with is your business," Warner said. "But for our first meeting, we'd like to speak with you privately—until we know whether you're signing on. We're playing this as close to the vest as possible. I'm sure you understand."

"What time did you want to meet tomorrow?"

"Is there a chance for later today?"

"Booked. Parent-teacher conference."

"How's Billy doing?" Warner asked.

"Fine," Clevenger lied, taken aback. He sometimes forgot his adopted son was as well known as he.

"Good," Warner said. "It must have been tough rebounding from a bum rap like he got."

"Yes, it was," Clevenger said. *Still is.*

"I'll leave it to you, then. Anytime tomorrow," Warner said.

"I'll be on the six A.M. US Air shuttle to National," Clevenger said.

"I'll have a car waiting for you," Warner said. "I look forward to meeting."

"Same here."

Warner hung up.

"Skipping town?" North Anderson said from Clevenger's door.

Clevenger clicked the phone off and looked at Anderson. They were close in age, each of them with a nearly shaved head, each of them standing nearly six feet tall, each of them having worked his body until it was lean and muscular. They shared an intensity of gaze, a kind of insistent sincerity that could elicit confessions from con men and romantic concessions from women. If Anderson hadn't been black, the two of them would have looked very much like brothers, instead of just feeling that way. "The Highway Killer," Clevenger said.

"FBI?" Anderson asked.

Clevenger nodded. "They found another victim this morning. A woman in upstate New York. Shallow grave, like the others."

"We've got plenty on our plates right now, if you ask me," Anderson said.

"I don't think they have a single lead," Clevenger said. He dropped his cigarette into a coffee cup, listened to it sizzle.

"Doesn't sound like the kind of team we need to be signing on with," Anderson said.

"He's killed at least thirteen people," Clevenger said.

"Maybe thirteen's his unlucky number."

"The Bureau wouldn't call unless they were at a dead

end," Clevenger said. "My bet—they've got zero. No leads." He tapped another Marlboro out of the package.

Anderson shook his head. "Listen," he said. "The FBI may want to believe they're ready to bring somebody like you in, because they're desperate, but they're not gonna give up control. They'll never let you make the moves you need to make."

Clevenger smiled, lit the cigarette. "Nobody's tried reining us in before?"

"This is different," Anderson said. "This is the FBI. They're experts at it."

"No harm talking to them."

"Maybe not," Anderson said. "Unless all they want to do is talk."

"Meaning?" Clevenger asked.

"Talking to you isn't necessarily the simple thing it used to be, Frank," Anderson said. "Not since Nantucket."

Nantucket meant the Bishop family murder, an infanticide in the home of billionaire investor Darwin Bishop during 2001. By the time that case had ended, Darwin Bishop and his son Garret had been jailed, Bishop's wife Julia had been deemed an unfit parent, and Clevenger had ended up on the cover of *Newsweek*, beneath a headline that read, FORENSIC PSYCHIATRIST FRANK CLEVENGER SOLVES MURDER OF THE DECADE. He'd also ended up adopting Bishop's other son, an emotionally troubled boy named Billy who had been the lead suspect in the killing—until Clevenger proved him innocent. Billy's photograph, inset beside Clevenger's on the *Newsweek* cover, had carried the caption, ". . . And Gives Young Billy Bishop a Fresh Start."

Billy had been only sixteen years old at the time of

the murder and should have been shielded from the media. But the public had had an insatiable appetite for the Bishop case, and the district attorney's office had been only too eager to feed them anything and everything on Billy—so long as it made him look guilty. When he was finally cleared, the media feeding frenzy only intensified. Billy was young, tough, and handsome. His prior history of violence made him every little girl's bad boy fantasy. Leno called. Couric actually visited Billy just before his release from jail. The producers of *Survivor* offered him two hundred grand to be a contestant. Luckily, Clevenger was his legal guardian by then and turned them down.

"You really think the FBI needs the PR?" Clevenger asked.

"They need something," Anderson said. "They're taking major heat for this guy still being on the streets. If they leak a meeting with you to the press, they get instant headlines. They look like they're pulling out all the stops. They get the public off their backs—at least for a while. As long as you're officially on the case, everybody's going to focus on you. And you're the one who'll take the heat when another body turns up."

"So maybe I don't end up looking good," Clevenger said. "Since when did we start worrying about my image? You're my partner. You want to be my agent?"

"Do what you have to do," Anderson said. "Just remember, I warned you."

"I wasn't planning to do it alone."

Anderson ran a finger along the thick, pink scar over his right eye, something he did when he saw trouble on the horizon. "Like I said, we've got plenty on our plates. The Conway case. Bramble. Vega. They may not be national news, but they came through the door first. I'll hold the fort down here."

"We're not *that* backed up," Clevenger said. "You have that bad a feeling about this?"

"I just don't need it," Anderson said, staring at him. "That's all."

"Ah," Clevenger said, leaning back in his chair. "I get it now. You think I do. You think I want the publicity. I *need* it."

Anderson held up his hands. "Forget I said anything."

"No. Please. Tell me what you think."

Anderson shook his head. "You don't want to hear it."

"Unless you're really only worried about me over-feeding my ego—or bruising yours."

"What's that supposed to mean?" Anderson asked.

"Maybe I do like it when I make headlines," Clevenger said, shrugging. "And, deep inside, maybe you don't."

"I'm jealous?" Anderson said, smiling. "You think that's what this is about?" He folded his thick arms. "Okay. Here's what I really think, deep inside: I think you put down the booze and you put down the coke and you stopped betting your future at the track and you're doing a great thing raising Billy and you ought to leave well enough alone. Because you're still a gambler at heart, Frank. You still like the highs and the lows more than you should. Deep inside, you still want to lay it all on the line. But now you're betting more than your future. There's Billy's, too. And mine. Because we are partners. So why not take it slow? I'm not saying forever. Just for now."

"I feel all right," Clevenger said. "I'm not in the same place I was."

"Exactly. That's my point here. I remember what you were like coming off Nantucket."

"You think I forget?"

"Maybe. Maybe you do," Anderson said. "Because if you take this case, you take on a world of trouble. Never mind the travel around the country. Never mind the media breathing down your neck, staking out your apartment, camped out where you get your fucking laundry done. I know you. When another body turns up, then another, no one's gonna have to come pin the blame on you. You'll nail yourself to a cross. Because in your heart, you think you can solve this."

"I am talking to the same person who convinced me to take the Nantucket case in the first place," Clevenger said.

"Same person," Anderson said. "I didn't doubt you then and I don't doubt you now. I'd take any odds you break this thing wide open. But this is a guy who's killed thirteen people over three years across the United States while the FBI has been hunting him like he's bin Laden. And he's not even worried enough to dispose of the bodies properly. He leaves them with their driver's licenses, just in case anybody might get confused who the decomposing remains belong to. If you make a big difference here, Frank, you cut this maniac's run from ten years to five. But that still leaves you in hell for the next two. Not to mention Billy. And he's not exactly coasting right now."

"I didn't say I was taking the case," Clevenger said. "I'm going to a meeting. Then I come back, and we talk things through."

Anderson looked down at the ground, took a deep breath, looked back at Clevenger. "Like I said, you do what you got to do." He turned and walked away.

*

Auden Prep in Lynnfield, Massachusetts, was seven miles north of Chelsea, but a world away. Its two hundred-acre campus had more lawn than existed in the whole of Chelsea's two square miles. Counting interest on trust funds and inflated stipends for summer internships, its 1,500 male students netted substantially more per-capita income. Lynnfield was land-locked and flat. There was no soot and no grit.

Clevenger disliked the place, especially today, waiting for more bad news about Billy. He was sitting in the reception area outside the office of Stouffer Walsh, Auden's Dean for Student Affairs, taking in all the carved mahogany woodwork, the crown moldings, the gleaming chair rail, breathing the stuffy air, wishing he had never agreed to enroll Billy in the first place. The kid probably would have done better at Chelsea High, where his street smarts might have been prized enough by street-smart teachers to mold it into something else—like moral courage or grace under pressure. But Auden Prep had been cited in the Massachusetts Department of Social Services "Action Plan" for Billy, so Clevenger had signed him up.

His grades had lagged from the start, but that was to be expected. Billy had been fresh from losing his baby sister to murder and losing his father and brother to jail sentences. He himself had come close to being framed and sent to prison for life. So a C– in French and even a D+ in geometry weren't the end of the world. Even his first fistfight had been handled by the deans like a bump in the road. Nobody had been badly hurt, nothing more than a bloody nose for the other boy and a fat lip for Billy. It really looked like kid stuff. The other boy was more to blame. On top of that, it was football season.

And Billy could stop just about anyone from taking a step over the line of scrimmage. He was already five-foot-ten, 170 pounds—all of it muscle—with the reflexes of a panther. So the Prep was lenient with him. A quick month of academic probation, volunteering at a local shelter two nights a week. Then the month was over, and all was forgiven.

But six weeks later, Billy was in trouble again. He'd had another fight, this one with two friends of the first boy he'd tangled with. Billy got the better of both of them. One went home with a hairline fracture of his jaw. The other needed six stitches to close a gash in his scalp. Still, it had been two against one, and it was still football season, so Dean Walsh didn't seem terribly concerned. Another month of probation. Another month of community service.

Clevenger himself had been much more worried. Because he knew Billy's past in greater detail than Dean Walsh did. He knew that Billy's having stopped himself at inflicting a bloody nose or a fractured jaw was due as much to luck as self-control. Maybe his opponents had said "uncle" soon enough and loud enough. Maybe they had been smart enough to run away. Or maybe Billy half-liked the three of them despite the fact they were getting in his face. Because there had been other times in Billy's young life—during the years he'd split his time between a Manhattan penthouse and a Nantucket oceanfront estate—when he hadn't been able to control himself at all, not until some bully was lying motionless, with a cracked skull and vacant stare, barely breathing.

Clevenger knew that Billy's violence, taken together with his repeated Youth Services arrests for breaking and entering and destruction of property, had once made him look very much like a garden variety sociopath.

Most ominous of all, Clevenger knew that Billy was a victim of severe and sustained childhood abuse—savage beatings at his billionaire father's hand, beatings that had left scars across his back and deeper ones across his psyche. And that kind of abuse can short-circuit a person's capacity to gauge the suffering of others. Sometimes, forever.

Clevenger and Billy had been living together just over a year, sharing a 1,900-square-foot Chelsea loft in a converted factory. And as tough as the adjustment had been for Billy, it had been tougher for Clevenger.

At least Billy wasn't being beaten anymore, wasn't being viciously ridden by a billionaire intent on remaking him in his own twisted image. At seventeen, he could finally start being himself, a little bit at a time.

Clevenger, on the other hand, had had to rein himself in—at least the parts of himself that seemed incompatible with fathering an adolescent. That meant keeping himself sober, keeping himself away from the track, keeping the door to the loft from reverting into the revolving door for women that it had been as long as Clevenger could remember. It meant freeing himself from all the soothing addictions that had kept his own emotional pain at bay. And that had not been easy. It still wasn't. North Anderson was right about that much.

Of course, nobody had said it would be easy. The Department of Social Services had initially fought Clevenger's bid to adopt Billy, citing their concerns not only about Clevenger being a single parent, not only about the dangers inherent in his line of work, but also about his underlying motivation. Clevenger had lost an adolescent patient named Billy Fisk to suicide several years before, and his contacts at Social Services worried he might be trying to raise the dead, to pay a penance, not simply do a good deed.

What the Department of Social Services didn't understand, what the Dean of Student Affairs couldn't understand, was that Clevenger was indeed performing a resurrection—not of the boy who had suicided, but of the parts of himself and Billy Bishop that had nearly been snuffed out by their brutal fathers. Such was the Herculean task he had undertaken: to heal the boy and heal the boy inside himself at the same time. He needed to get better—and fast—in order to get Billy better.

One of Dean Walsh's secretaries, a middle-aged woman dressed in a navy blue wool suit, wearing a choker of pearls, approached Clevenger in the waiting area. "The dean will see you now," she said, with a smile that really wasn't a smile at all, more of an amiable grimace.

Clevenger followed her past two other secretaries, to the open door of the dean's office.

Walsh glanced up from the papers he was signing, signed a few more sheets, then stood behind his desk and extended his hand. He was an anxious man near sixty, in a blue-and-white pinstriped shirt with three-button cuffs. His hair looked unnaturally full and unnaturally black for his age, enough to make Clevenger wonder whether it might be some sort of newfangled toupee or weave. "I'm glad you could make it on short notice," he said, shaking Clevenger's hand. "And without my having gone into great detail. Please, have a seat."

Clevenger sat in the wooden chair Walsh had

indicated, pressing his back against the gold-leaf emblem of Auden Prep—Atlas hoisting a fountain pen overhead.

"As I alluded to," Walsh said, sitting down, "I'm afraid Billy finds himself in trouble again."

"What sort of trouble?" Clevenger asked.

"Drugs," Walsh said, folding his hands on his desk.

"Drugs?" Since getting Walsh's call at work, Clevenger had been guessing what Billy might have done. Another fight had seemed most likely. Cheating on the geometry test Billy had had that day also seemed possible, as did playing some unwelcome, foolish prank on a teacher or fellow student. But drugs just hadn't crossed Clevenger's mind, maybe because he was always fighting not to think of them. Maintaining his own sobriety was still a battle he needed to win every single day.

"Marijuana," Dean Walsh said.

"Billy was smoking pot?"

"I wish it were that." Walsh opened his right-hand desk drawer and pulled out a Ziploc bag with enough marijuana to roll about fifty joints. He held it aloft between his thumb and forefinger, like a contaminated bird. Then he dropped it back in his drawer. "It was found in his locker."

"How did you come to find it there?" Clevenger asked.

"Another student came forward," Walsh said, joining his hands as if in prayer. "We have a code here at Auden."

"Another student came forward and said . . ."

"And said, 'Billy Bishop is selling pot. He keeps it in his locker.' "

Clevenger let his breath out. Other kids might be able to fool around with drugs and come away unscathed, but Billy was already fragile psychologically. Drugs could be really bad news for him, a surprise actor on the stage of his existence, capable of stealing the show and turning it into a tragedy. "Where's Billy?" Clevenger asked.

"Cleaning out his locker," Walsh said. "He's been expelled."

"I see," Clevenger said. "Did he have a lot of money on him or something? I mean, how did you corroborate the report of the other student?"

"The bag was in his locker. You don't think he was planning to use all that marijuana himself, do you?" Walsh asked. He paused to give his rhetorical question more impact. "Your son is extremely intelligent," he went on. "Truly gifted intellectually. No one would debate that. His character, however, is another matter."

"How did Billy explain himself?" Clevenger asked.

"By denying everything," Walsh said. "He insisted the drugs were placed in his locker by someone else."

"Is that possible?" Clevenger asked.

Walsh smiled. "This isn't a case that would require your good skills, Doctor. There's really no forensic work to be done. What has happened has happened." He shook his head. "We did have hope for Billy. Not just I. The other deans, as well. But I think we've been very fair."

"And football season is over," Clevenger said.

"Excuse me?" Walsh said.

"You were especially fair during football season," Clevenger said.

Walsh stiffened. "If you're referring to Billy's fisticuffs during the fall," he said, "that event did not rise to the level that this offense does. This event is a crime. This time, there is no other boy to share the blame. *This* is a whole different kettle of fish." He paused again, looking a little shocked to have offered up such a tired cliché. "Luckily for Billy," he said, "we have a policy at Auden that possession of an illicit substance does not trigger a call to the authorities. Selling an illicit substance does. But no staff member actually witnessed a transaction. Otherwise, you wouldn't be picking up Billy here, you would be bailing him out of jail."

Clevenger nodded. No sense shooting the messenger, even when the messenger was someone as self-impressed as Stouffer Walsh. "Thank you for that," Clevenger said. "Just so you know, I'm not angry with anyone but Billy. If I've given you another impression, I apologize." He stood up.

Walsh stayed seated. "As for the appeals process . . ."

"I didn't realize there was an appeals process," Clevenger said.

"You could certainly avail yourselves of it," Walsh said, "but I wouldn't recommend that. Given the clear facts in this case, it might be seen as, well . . . contentious. In addition, a transcript of the proceedings becomes part of Billy's academic record. It would be available to other schools, including the public system. Better to let the infraction speak for itself and spare any additional negative commentary that might be forthcoming about Billy. I am certain there would be."

"It doesn't sound like we'll be appealing," Clevenger said. "Thank you." He turned to go.

"There is one last, rather uncomfortable matter," Walsh said, finally standing. He placed his palms flat on his desk.

Could something else have gone wrong? "What's that?" Clevenger asked.

"The matter of Billy's tuition."

"I believe I'm paid up. Is there some sort of quit fee?"

"No, no, no. Nothing like that," Walsh said. "You are

paid in full. I simply needed to remind you there are no partial refunds following a disciplinary action. I know it's awkward even to mention at a time like this, but attempting to resolve all potential financial issues is part of our exit policy."

"Consider them resolved," Clevenger said.

"Very good, then. Billy should be waiting for you in the reception area. I do wish the two of you well, Doctor."

"Right. Thanks, again."

Billy was sitting in the reception area with his head in his hands, his longish, dirty blond hair, all done up in dreadlocks, hanging in front of his eyes. As Clevenger walked up to him, he could see the muscles of his jaw contracting rhythmically. "Ready to go?" Clevenger asked him, working to keep his voice steady. He got no response. He put a hand on Billy's broad shoulder. He could feel the tension in his muscles. "What do you say we talk about this in the car?"

Billy looked up. His ice-blue eyes were full of rage, his upper lip trembling. When he was in the best of moods, his face, though movie-star handsome, still had a menacing quality, something brooding and dark about the combination of his full lips, prominent forehead, and deeply set eyes. The thin gold ring through his left nostril didn't help any. When he was angry, even a little angry, he looked dangerous. Like he did now.

"You've got to be kidding," Clevenger said. "*You're* pissed off? At *yourself*, I hope."

"Fuck this place," Billy said. He stood up and walked out of the reception area.

Clevenger felt half like chasing him and hugging him,

half like chasing him and throwing him to the ground. So he kept himself in check and walked slowly out of the reception area and down the hall toward the exit. He always seemed to be searching for the perfect alchemy to respond to Billy—how many parts reassurance to how many parts discipline. It was hard to know whether the broken parts of his character would heal best if rigidly splinted or gently bathed in warm waters. He wanted to do the right thing by him, to be the right father for him, but it was tough, especially because he'd never been fathered much himself.

Even Billy's appearance raised the question about how firm to be with him. His dreadlocks, for one thing. They had clearly put Billy on the fringe of acceptable style at Auden Prep. But Clevenger knew that Billy's personal development had been stunted for years. So when he had come home with the new look a couple of months before, Clevenger had taken it as a sign, albeit sudden, of Billy's growing sense of self. And he had simply smiled and told him the truth, "I think it looks cool."

On the nose ring, Clevenger had been no less honest. "It's just not my kind of thing," he had said. "But I'm not the one wearing it."

That was the point, wasn't it? Billy was searching for an identity. His. No one else's.

The tattoo Billy had gotten across his back was a little more concerning. It had been inked over the haphazard scars left by his father's strap. A blue-black, four-inch skull and crossbones sat between his shoulder blades. Beneath it, in flowing script, was the title of his favorite Rolling Stones song, "Let It Bleed."

Billy had explained the tattoo was his way of making the scars his own, transforming them into a reminder that he was better off letting his real emotions surface—confronting his pain, instead of burying it.

Who could argue with that?

But maybe, Clevenger thought, he should have argued. Maybe he should have laid down the law a little more often, even if he erred on the side of overreacting. Because Billy's choices for himself were tending more and more toward darkness.

When he got to the Auden Prep parking lot he found Billy leaning against the front fender of his black Ford F-150 truck. He walked past him, headed toward the driver's side door.

"I didn't do what Walsh said I did," Billy said.

Clevenger stopped with his hand on the door handle. He shook his head.

"I didn't do it," Billy said, more emphatically.

Clevenger turned around and saw that Billy was facing him, eyeing him over the hood. The expression on his face had taken a turn from rage toward outrage. He looked sincerely insulted by the accusation lodged against him. But that was part of the problem with Billy. Growing up with a father who was likely to reward a confession with a beating had made Billy a good liar. "Get in the car," Clevenger said. He opened the driver's side door and climbed inside.

Billy's jaw muscles started churning again. He flipped his hair to one side and walked to the passenger door. He got in, then sat silently, staring straight ahead.

"They found a bag of marijuana in your locker," Clevenger said. "Can we at least agree on that much?"

"Yes," Billy said, still staring.

"Not your bag, though," Clevenger said, predicting Billy's defense. "You were just holding it for somebody."

Billy turned to Clevenger. "I wasn't holding it for anyone, either."

"What, then?"

"Did Walsh happen to . . . ?"

"*Dean* Walsh," Clevenger said.

Billy rolled his eyes. "Did *Dean* Walsh happen to mention who tipped him off to look in my locker in the first place?"

"No. He didn't. But it doesn't—"

"You didn't ask him very many questions," Billy interrupted. "You just figured they'd caught me red-handed. Period. Guilty as charged."

Clevenger didn't like the way Billy was trying to turn tables on him and maneuver him into the witness seat. He especially didn't like being accused of not sticking up for him, not after he'd laid everything on the line to save him from growing old in prison. "If you've got a point to make," Clevenger said, "make it. Otherwise, please skip the self-righteous bullshit so we can spend our time figuring out where to get you help for the drugs—if you're using—and where you should finish school, if you intend to."

"Scott Dillard," Billy said smugly.

"Scott Dillard," Clevenger echoed. Dillard was the leader of the trio who had been hounding Billy. "Scott Dillard turned you in."

Billy nodded.

"So what? Has he got the combination to your locker or something? You think he planted the drugs there? Give me a break."

"They don't change the combinations year to year," Billy said. "He must have gotten it from somebody who had it before me."

This whole discussion, Clevenger thought, was vintage Billy Bishop. He was offering up a plausible, if improbable, explanation for the jam he was in. It was the kind of defense that might go over in a courtroom, the punch line about recycled locker combinations delivered Perry Mason-style, which was probably what bothered Clevenger the most about it. Billy always seemed to be banking on the proverbial shadow of a doubt. "I suppose I can't know for sure what happened," he said, "but . . ."

"I just told you what happened," Billy protested.

"What I do know for sure is that Auden Prep doesn't want you back."

"They're suspending me?" Billy asked. "For how long?"

Clevenger looked at him. Had Dean Walsh really not told him? Or hadn't Billy been ready to hear what Walsh had to say? "They're not suspending you, Billy. You're expelled." The words didn't seem to register. "Dismissed. Permanently," he said.

"Expelled," Billy said.

Clevenger watched Billy's eyes get watery. And the part of him that wanted to hold him, rather than hold him to any standard, started to grow. But even with that impulse, he had to wonder whether Billy's tears were genuine or contrived. You couldn't know with this kid. He wasn't just movie-star handsome. He was a very good actor.

"Why don't you at least ask Dean Walsh whether they change the combinations every year?" Billy asked.

"It's not going to make a difference to him," Clevenger said. "Maybe if it hadn't been for the fights, but . . . his mind is made up."

"Fuck it, then. I'm done with this place. I don't care

what Walsh thinks, anyhow. I care what you think. No one else."

That sounded like playing to the crowd. "Sure," Clevenger said. "I can see how you're always looking to make me proud." He shook his head, started the car, and backed out of the space. When he glanced back at Billy, he saw him staring straight ahead, tears streaming silently down his face.

Clevenger shifted the truck into park again. "Hey," he said.

Billy didn't look at him.

"Here's what I think," Clevenger said, in a calm voice. He waited for Billy to turn to him. "I'm in this with you for the long haul. Got that? Nothing you could do would make me walk away. Nothing. Not getting bounced out of Auden Prep, not selling grass. So the only difference between telling me the truth and lying to me is that I can't get you the help you need if I don't have the facts. I can't be a good enough father to you without the facts."

Billy nodded.

"I'm going to ask one more time," Clevenger said, "because it's important we both know the score if we're gonna win the game here—were you selling drugs or not?"

"No," Billy said.

"Using them?" Clevenger asked.

"You can drug-test me right now," Billy said. "And any time you want after that."

Clevenger looked into Billy's eyes, to detect any duplicity there, but Billy's gaze was as impenetrable as the space he had occupied on the Auden Prep defensive line. "Okay," Clevenger said. "I'll make some phone calls tomorrow morning, and we'll see whether Chelsea High School is an option. That is, if you want me to."

"I do," Billy said. "I want to stay in school."

"Good. And I'll take you up on that offer about the drug testing. Once a week."

"Fine," Billy said.

Clevenger put the truck into gear, started out of the parking lot.

"I know you're not proud of me," Billy said.

Those words cut through the last layer of Clevenger's tough love to the soft stuff underneath. He reached out and cupped his fingers around the back of Billy's neck. "It's not that I'm not . . ."

"You will be, though," Billy said. "You'll see. Even though things look bad right now? You will be."

five

Clevenger had put his meeting with the FBI off a day in order to settle Billy down and to visit with his friend Brian Coughlin, the superintendent of schools in Chelsea. Now, headed to Quantico in the Crown Victoria sedan Agent Kane Warner had sent to pick him up at National Airport, he was thinking he should have canceled altogether and just stayed home. Because all of a sudden leaving Billy alone in Chelsea felt risky. And signing on with the FBI would mean leaving him alone a whole lot more.

At least Coughlin had come through for them. Clevenger had met with him the night before at Floramo's, a steak joint near Chelsea High, and hammered out a plan for Billy to continue his education starting the fourth quarter, in April. To keep him off the streets until then, he'd gotten him a job with Peter Fitzgerald, the owner of the shipyard down the street. And to keep him off drugs, he'd scheduled him for drug screens twice a week at the Massachusetts General Hospital satellite clinic in Chelsea.

He glanced at the dashboard clock of the Crown Victoria: 8:26 A.M. Just a few more miles to Quantico. He wondered whether Billy had dragged himself out of bed yet, wondered what the chances were he'd get himself to the first of those drug screens by nine, like they'd agreed.

He thought of calling to make sure Billy was on his way. But he worried that that kind of hand-holding would sap his will.

The sedan slowed as it drove through the gates of the FBI Academy, which shared a sprawling campus with the United States Marine Corp and the Drug Enforcement Agency.

The nerve center of the Academy was an interconnected network of nondescript buildings that looked like an overgrown corporation. Recruits in dark blue sweat suits, with the FBI insignia emblazoned in gold across their chests, jogged along the road leading to it. Marines with high-powered rifles stood at every intersection. Helicopter blades beat the air. A palpable sense of mission, grandeur, and secrecy permeated the place.

Clevenger felt two things, at odds with one another. The first was suspicion. He distrusted institutions, even law enforcement institutions, because their very size and structure could stifle the three things he valued most in the world: courage, creativity, and compassion. Those were three qualities a person needed to find inside him- or herself, sometimes searching his or her soul for decades before finding them—if ever. Being part of an organization made the search harder, not easier. A failure of courage or creativity or compassion could be shared by the group, allowing each member to escape the full measure of guilt that ought to derive from things like cowardice or cruelty.

But the second feeling Quantico inspired in Clevenger was a kind of reluctant pride. The Bishop case had made him a celebrity, but it hadn't won him any stamp of approval from the law enforcement community. If anything, the fact that he'd embarrassed the Nantucket Police Department and Massachusetts State Police by proving Billy innocent had made him more of an outsider, not less. Now the FBI was coming to him for help. The federal government was coming to Frank Clevenger, one half of a two-man operation in oil-soaked Chelsea.

Clevenger was escorted through two sets of security doors, down a long hallway, then through a third set of security doors and into an elevator which descended six floors to the Behavioral Sciences Unit, or BSU. The elevator opened onto a shiny, hardwood hallway, lighted by hanging brass fixtures, with portraits of former FBI notables in gilded frames lining the walls.

A tall man with brown, wavy hair and bright white teeth stepped in front of the open elevator doors. "Dr. Clevenger," he said, in a raspy voice that came across even less friendly than it had over the phone, "I'm Kane Warner. Welcome to the Academy."

Clevenger stepped out, shook Warner's hand.

"Your trip went smoothly?" Warner asked, trying not to show how taken aback he was by Clevenger wearing what he always wore—blue jeans and a black turtleneck.

"No trouble," Clevenger said.

Warner smiled, flashing his gleaming teeth. He was handsome, late thirties, with high cheekbones, an unmistakably healthy hue to his skin, and bright green eyes—a Ken doll decked out in a dark gray pinstriped suit and red silk tie. His shirt was as white as his teeth, pristinely pressed and starched. "Everyone's waiting in the conference room," he said.

Clevenger followed Warner down the hallway. "Quite a campus," he said.

"Three hundred eighty-five acres?" Warner said, delivering his statement as a question, the way he had on the phone. "Self-contained. A city unto itself. Classrooms? Dorms? Dining hall? Library? A thousand-seat auditorium? Eight firing ranges? Four skeet ranges? A one-point-one mile racetrack for defensive and pursuit driving? Hogan's Alley? It's all here."

"Tell me about Hogan's Alley?" Clevenger asked.

"A mock town," Warner said. "For hostage rescue training, that sort of thing?"

"Handy," Clevenger said.

"Very." He stopped in front of a set of double doors. "I hope you decide to join us in this," he said.

Clevenger gave Warner a mirror image of his own wide smile and left it at that.

Inside the conference room, two women and three men sat around a long, polished mahogany table. A back-lighted, computerized map of the United States glowed on the wall, thirteen red dots shining along the highways where victims of the Highway Killer had been found. Warner took a seat at the head of the table and nodded for Clevenger to take the seat next to him. "Let's start with introductions," Warner said. "I think everyone is familiar with Dr. Clevenger's background," he said to the group. He glanced at Clevenger, then nodded in turn at each person around the table. "Dorothy Campbell, who works with our PROFILER computer system; Greg Martino, an analyst with VICAP, the Violent Crime Apprehension Program; Bob White and John Silverstein, from our Criminal Investigative Analysis Program, CIAP; Dr. Whitney McCormick, our chief of forensic psychiatry; and Ken Hiramatsu, our chief pathologist."

Clevenger's eyes were still on Whitney McCormick

when Hiramatsu was introduced. She was no more than thirty-five, slim and very pretty, with long, straight blonde hair, and deep brown eyes. She looked completely at ease, entirely self-confident, yet the way she held her head and the way she looked at him, even the pale rose lipstick she wore, made him sense that she had not surrendered her femininity, that the sensitivities and intuitions that were her birthright had survived medical training and FBI training and all the horrors she had to have seen on the job. That was quite a feat. Even as he forced his eyes over to Hiramatsu, McCormick's image stuck with him. He was that vulnerable to feminine beauty. Almost permeable. His commitment to fathering Billy the past year had done a lot to keep women out of his bedroom, but it hadn't done a thing to get women off his mind. "Nice to meet everyone," Clevenger said, making eye contact with each person around the table, then letting his gaze return to McCormick for a few seconds.

"Why don't we start with an overview, Bob?" Kane Warner asked.

Bob White, serious, somber, about forty, looked up at the lighted map on the wall. "First, the stats, which I trust you already know, Dr. Clevenger: Thirteen bodies. Eight men. Five women. Each found within ten yards of a highway, in a shallow grave or simply dumped on the ground. No attempt to disguise their identities." He stood, opened a folder and took out a short stack of photos. He spread them on the conference table and began listing the towns where the victims had been found. "Carlhoun, Alabama; Patterson, Idaho; Bellevue, Iowa; Brownsville, Kentucky; Northfield, Maine . . ."

Clevenger looked at the display of carnage. Thirteen bodies, limbs poking up through the soil, through leaves, through snow, others simply sprawled on the ground. Thirteen victims. He felt their absolute terror, the awful recognition that their lives were being cut short, that they were dying without any chance to reach out to the people they loved, without the chance to say good-bye, to voice regret or a final thank-you.

"They were all fully clothed, some face up, some face down," White was saying. "No discernible pattern as to age or race or gender. No consistency in terms of where they're from or where they were going. Their throats were all cut, but using different implements. Some of the wounds were inflicted with a short blade, like a carpet knife, others were inflicted with a long blade, like a pocket knife or steak knife." He paused. "The perp doesn't seem methodical. Not a lot of planning here. He kills spontaneously. It doesn't matter who you are. And he isn't on a cross-country journey, because the chronology of the killings puts him north, south, east, west, without any discernible rhyme or reason." He nodded toward the picture furthest to Clevenger's right. "You can be an old woman." He nodded toward the picture furthest to Clevenger's left. "Or a sixteen-year-old boy. You can be black or white, young or . . ."

Clevenger looked from the woman to the boy, letting his eyes stay with the body of the sixteen-year-old, sprawled in bloody snow, wearing a puffy, down-filled jacket, blue jeans, and green suede Nike high-top sneakers. It can end just like that, he thought. Even for someone's beloved sixteen-year-old son. Even for someone like Billy or for any kid decent enough to help a stranger carry a bag of groceries to a van, or kind enough to help jump-start a car stranded in the night, or stupid enough to walk into a darkened park to buy a couple joints or a bag of heroin or a couple pirated CDs. Then you get a call one day from a cop. Very serious tone. Maybe you think your son or daughter has been nabbed for speeding or—worse—driving under the influence. So you brace for bad news. You might even think of a lawyer you know or the punishment you're going to dole out. Then the cop starts with the description, trying to let you down easy, sounding kind, not angry, which makes your heart sink, for some reason. Did your son or daughter leave the house wearing this jacket, that pair of pants? And maybe you still have hope when he mentions that jacket—the blue, down-filled one with the hood—and even those jeans with the frayed bottoms. Because they could belong to anybody. So it could be a mistake. I mean, you're talking a million teenagers a day in America wearing the same get-up to express their individuality. But there is the unmistakable fact of the phone in *your* hand, that *you* have the gotten this call, not one of those other couple of million parents. So there must be more coming, another fact whizzing toward you to shatter your world. And then the cop mentions the green high-tops. The green Nike high-tops. And all your breath leaves you and your head is in your hands and you hear the telephone hit the floor. And you look up at the clock, maybe because you need to see the second hand moving to believe any of this is real. And then you know that it is. And you know you will never forget 4:24 in the afternoon, that you will dread the leading edge of evening the rest of your days, and that nothing, but nothing, will ever be the same. Because death—the devil himself, the scourge of the universe—has come to your door.

"Entirely random," White finished up.

"I see," Clevenger said.

"One consistency," said Ken Hiramatsu, an Asian man who looked to be in his early thirties, "is the lack of signs indicating a struggle. Relatively little bruising. Not much in the way of torn clothing. No ropes. No duct tape. These people got comfortable with the man who killed them. They let him get very close to them."

"Drugged them?" Clevenger asked.

"No signs of that on toxicology," Hiramatsu said.

"Seduced them, more likely," Whitney McCormick said, looking at Clevenger. Her voice was pretty seductive stuff itself, combining a soft, girlish tone with a level of self-assurance that was disarming. "I don't mean romantically, necessarily. Although I'd bet he's good-looking. Appealing, anyhow. A nice face. A pleasant voice. Well coiffed. Maybe obsessively so. He dresses well. But the main thing is that he's smooth. A charmer. Somehow he gets his victims to trust him so much that they can't quite believe he's killing them. They're so shocked at what's happening that they don't struggle a whole lot."

"And he doesn't have sex with them," Clevenger ventured.

"No," White said. He glanced at Hiramatsu.

"No semen was recovered," Hiramatsu said. "He doesn't leave any bodily fluid inside his victims, he takes some of theirs away with him."

"Meaning?" Clevenger asked.

"On every body, we found evidence of phlebotomy," Hiramatsu said. "A small bruise and puncture wound at the antecubital fossa, consistent with a hypodermic needle."

Bob White laid three more photographs on the table. Each was a close-up of the crook of a victim's arm.

"He takes a blood sample?" Clevenger asked.

"Apparently," Hiramatsu said. "Unless he's injecting them with something we can't detect."

"And the venipuncture is competent?" Cleveneger asked.

"He gets most of them on the first stick," Hiramatsu said.

"We're right with you," White said to Clevenger. "He could be a hospital worker. A nurse. A phlebotomist. Even a doctor."

"He doesn't collect anything else, so far as we can tell," Greg Martino, the VICAP analyst said. "Just the blood. He's not snatching purses or wallets. No indication he wants a lock of hair or a piece of jewelry."

"The blood keeps them close to him," Clevenger said.

"He gets close and he stays close," McCormick said. "You start to wonder about abandonment. Is the guy an orphan? Did his father or mother or a childhood friend die on him precipitously?"

Clevenger thought of Billy, again. He'd lost his baby sister to murder, his father to life in prison. How would those losses ultimately play out in his life? He shook his head and shook the question out of his mind. "Or did *he*?" Clevenger said.

"Did he, what?" McCormick said.

"Die," Clevenger said, looking at her. "Did something make him feel dead? Maybe that's what he wants to watch—the reason he needs to get so close to his victims in the first place. Maybe they're substitutes for looking at the dead parts of himself."

"Sexual abuse?" Kane Warner asked, from the head of the table.

"Possibly," Clevenger said. "But the fact that he doesn't violate his victims sexually argues against it."

"The penetration of the needle could be a sexual equivalent," McCormick said.

That was high-end psychological reasoning, and it told Clevenger that McCormick was no lightweight. "Could be," Clevenger said. "No question. But what's clear to me is that he's searching for comfort, not thrills. Intimacy, not excitement. This isn't a power trip for him. It's something he's driven to. He's not enraged. He's not looking to maim or disfigure. He kills with a minimum of violence. A single laceration. He takes the time to bury his victims when he can, not so much to hide the evidence, but because he feels badly for them, and probably feels badly about what he's done. But he's not going to risk anything to be a nice guy. He's cool and collected, even after the kill. When it's too chancy to take the time to bury a body, he leaves it exposed. He doesn't want to be caught."

"They all do," Kane Warner said. "Deep down."

Clevenger disagreed, but said nothing. Plenty of killers would be happy to go on killing forever. They didn't want to get caught. But they did wish to be known. That's what seemed to trip them up every time. Good old ego. A killer content to remain anonymous forever just might be able to.

Warner nodded toward Dorothy Campbell, a bookish woman in her fifties who ran the PROFILER system, a database of millions of facts about serial killers, including the behavioral patterns and geographic locations of known violent criminals. "Obviously, by statistical probabilities, we are dealing with a male offender," she said. "Above average intelligence. Probably college educated. Maybe more. He's extremely socially competent—likeable—but a loner at heart. He's more of a traveler than a vagrant, someone who very much wants to keep moving, given the highway as his hunting ground. And he doesn't kill on the outskirts of Manhattan or L.A. He doesn't like cities. He can't stay anonymous enough. He goes close to the mountains in Vermont or near a state park in rural Kentucky or close to the Iowa plains. He needs his space. He may be an outdoorsman—a hunter or hiker or camper." She looked at the lighted map, then back at Clevenger. "The part that doesn't make sense is that he blurs the boundaries between the organized criminal and the disorganized criminal."

"Forget 'blurs,' " Bob White said. "He *shatters* them."

Clevenger knew the distinction Campbell and White were drawing. An "organized serial killer" would be likely to plan out the murders, to target strangers, to require submission by his victims, to restrain them before killing them, and to kill them in a very gruesome manner. A "disorganized killer," on the other hand, would strike out much more spontaneously, exploding at people he knew, speaking little to them, not using restraints, possibly having sex with his victims' corpses, and generally leaving a weapon at each crime scene.

"This is someone," Campbell said, "who doesn't seem to plan his murders, but somehow comes to know his victims—or behaves toward them as though he has some intimacy with them."

"He's been destroyed," Clevenger said. "He knows what they're going through. He feels their pain." That line made Clevenger think of Jesus Christ. "He probably considers himself religious, or in touch with God, much more than the devil. He may think he's doing God's work."

McCormick nodded.

"He leaves the bodies pretty much where they fall," Campbell said, "as if he's horrified by what he's done. Yet he wants a reminder of them. Another dichotomy."

"The only thing that seems crystal clear," Kane Warner said to Clevenger, "is that the paradigms we've developed in-house don't yield a clear picture of this guy. So what I'm suggesting is that Whitney get you fully up to speed on the case over the next couple of days and that you join the investigation, reporting directly to me. It's probably best you stay right on the base for the time being?"

Talk about being put on the spot. And Warner's tone reminded Clevenger of yet another thing North Anderson had warned him about. The FBI wasn't likely to set him loose on the investigation. Warner wanted Clevenger on a leash, and he wanted to be the one holding it. That's what the whole *reporting to me* clause was about, not to mention the one about sleeping in an FBI dorm. It was as good a time as any to show he didn't train well. "You already made that offer on the phone two days ago," Clevenger said. "Except for the room and board. But I'm still not convinced you're ready to catch this guy."

"Excuse me?" Warner said, never losing his politician's smile.

"I mean you've got the fancy map and everything, and these people have done impressive work on the computer and in the lab. Whitney is probably dead right about some of the killer's psychological characteristics. But you're still going at him from a distance. And this is a guy you might be able to reach—if you've got the stomach for it."

"Be more specific, doctor?" Warner said.

"The killer gets close to his victims before he kills them," Clevenger said, looking at the people around the table. "He makes them feel that he cares about them. And he probably does, or at least he thinks he does. The trouble for him is that he can only take intimacy in small doses. That's why he has to keep moving. No long-term relationships. Which causes him great pain, as it would anyone."

"We always want what we can't have," McCormick said.

Clevenger looked at her. "Always," he said. He looked slowly back at Kane Warner. "The key to making this guy mess up, the way to trip him up psychologically, is to keep his victims in his face. Trot out their relatives. Show pictures on the television news of them as kids. Bring the relatives together for meetings every month somewhere. Let the public know about each reunion. Now our man is excluded. He's an outsider who really feels it. He may have thirteen blood samples, but these people on television have much more. Photographs, memories, real tears. And they have each other. His need for closeness—*his* brand of closeness, whatever it is—will increase. He'll start getting hungrier and he'll start making mistakes. Maybe he'll feel the need to revisit one of the murder scenes. Maybe he'll make a call to a grieving mother or brother. He might even let us catch him, if only to lay eyes on his extended family, to sit in the same courtroom as the families of his victims."

"Interesting," Warner said, without much feeling.

"I think Dr. Clevenger is right," McCormick said to Warner. "It's almost like this guy is so good at keeping people away that he's keeping us away. We have to reach out to him."

Dorothy Campbell nodded.

"I've been saying we should take the fight to this animal for months," said John Silverstein, from the Criminal Investigative Analysis Program. It was the first time he'd spoken during the meeting. "There's no traditional pattern here to figure where he's from or who he is or where he might strike next. We've got to flush him out."

"But that could be dangerous," Bob White said. "What if you increase his need to kill and he *doesn't* get careless? I mean, this guy can wait between feeds. Thirteen bodies in three years. If he picks up the pace a hundred percent, he can still pick and choose his spots."

Warner nodded in agreement.

"You might find that out," Clevenger said to White. "And then you notch up the psychological pressure even higher. You have to be willing to accelerate his violence until he crashes. It won't be pretty. But it's the price you have to pay to stop him."

There was a knock at the door. It opened. A twenty-something woman stood in the doorway. She looked at Kane Warner.

Warner stood and walked to the door. The woman whispered something to him. Warner let out a long breath, shook his head. Then he turned around and closed the door. "Number fourteen," he said. "In a pond twenty yards off Route 7, in Utah. A handicapped man— in his wheelchair."

A weightiness filled the room.

Clevenger looked at Whitney McCormick, who shared the kind of glance with him that he remembered from medical school, when he would be standing with a nurse over the bed of a patient about to die, knowing that being so close to the end of life had suddenly dissolved all the usual boundaries between them. And that single glance from McCormick nearly enticed him to commit to the investigation then and there. In it was an invitation to let his personal and professional lives become one thing, to let his need to live fully and to love fully and to be loved completely express itself in the only forum he had ever really found—the hunt for a killer.

"According to the local pathologist, the body is at least three months old," Warner went on. "The remains are on the way here." He looked at Clevenger, and his politician's mask suddenly dropped. "Just so you know," he said, with no hint of a question in his voice, "I sleep and eat this case. I want this guy more than you can imagine." His mask was back just as suddenly. "Let's take whatever time we have today to give you all the information you'll need to make your decision about joining us."

By the time Kane Warner walked Clevenger to the front door of the Academy and delivered him into another black sedan, Clevenger had the beginnings of a profile of the Highway Killer in mind. He had stayed in the conference room over two hours, gathering more details on each of the crime scenes and pressing each of the players around the table for their gut feelings on the case.

He believed the killer was indeed probably male, not only because statistics said so, but because of the force with which the blades had sliced through the carotid arteries and the fibrous windpipes of his victims. He was probably at least forty, because it was hard to imagine someone younger having the social skills and bearing to make victims feel so comfortable with him. He was good-looking, but not particularly sexual, which made him nonthreatening to women. He had been around hospitals or first aid or blood banks, given his proficiency with a needle. And he was probably an only child, because his need for closeness—"blood relatives"—was so extreme that it was hard to imagine such a need developing in the presence of a sibling. Whitney McCormick's theory that he had been orphaned or abandoned was a decent bet.

No part of the profile was for sure, and it wasn't much to go on in any case, but Clevenger did feel certain about one thing: there would be other bodies to examine and other crime scenes to study. The killer needed to keep killing. He was hooked.

As the sedan made its way back to National Airport, Clevenger thought again of the thirteen photographs Bob White had spread across the Behavioral Sciences Unit conference table. Thirteen lives. And now the body count was up to fourteen, with no way of knowing how many corpses had yet to be found.

Clevenger imagined the killer might be thinking of his victims, too. At that very moment he could be driving a highway, anxious for the sun to go down, thirsting to extinguish another life and extend his family, his bloodline.

He felt a familiar hatred fill him. Antipathy. Because for Clevenger the end of life was the enemy. He despised death, no matter what form the beast took—cancer, old age, or murder. He had simply chosen the cause of death he could short-circuit using what he had learned and the ways he could think. And if people sometimes said he went overboard doing his job, they just didn't get it, as far as he was concerned. An investigation was a war. You were staring death down and you had to be willing to throw everything in the kitty if death upped the ante—even sacrifice yourself, if need be, to end the carnage.

The sedan dropped him outside the US Air terminal. The first two shuttles from D.C. to Boston were canceled due to fog at Logan, and by the time he landed back home it was 5:15 P.M. He drove his truck out of Central Parking and used his mobile phone to dial the lab at Mass General. "This is Dr. Frank Clevenger," he said to the woman who picked up. "I'm looking for the result of a toxic screen on Billy Bishop."

"Date of birth?" she asked.

"December 11, 1987."

"One moment, doctor."

"Please be negative," Clevenger whispered. Not that he thought marijuana was the end of the world. Not that most sixteen-year-olds didn't smoke a joint now and then. But if the stuff was in Billy's blood, then Billy had lied to him, straight out—about using, and probably about selling. And that meant his character was anything but on the mend.

A minute went by. To Clevenger, it felt like ten. "Hello?" he prodded.

"Just one second," the woman said. "My computer . . . Okay . . . No. We have nothing on record."

"He didn't come in?" Clevenger asked.

"Apparently not," she said.

"Could the result be recorded anywhere else?"

"If he'd had a tox screen, it would be in the computer, even if the results were pending."

"Well, thanks for looking," Clevenger said, feeling the odd cocktail of anger and frustration and sadness that only Billy Bishop could provoke in him.

"Not at all." She hung up.

Clevenger dialed his loft, got no answer. He dialed Billy's cell phone and got his terse recorded message, "You know what to do," then the beep. He hung up, dialed the cell phone again, got the message again. "Pain in the ass," he said aloud, clicking off. He tossed the phone onto the passenger seat and headed for home.

six

Billy Bishop sat on the weight bench he'd set up in his room in Clevenger's Chelsea loft, blaring the Doors and staring out the Paladian windows at the Boston skyline shimmering beyond the Fitzgerald Shipyard.

The room was barren except for the weight bench, a simple bureau, his bed, and the stereo components he'd stacked against one wall, a tangle of wires connecting them. Posters of the rock groups Puddle of Mud, Pearl Jam and the Grateful Dead covered the walls.

He had maxed out at six reps of 200 pounds. His body was pumped, and his thoughts were coming fast.

He was feeling pretty good about himself. He'd gone down to the shipyard, talked to Peter Fitzgerald, and landed a job starting the very next day. Sure, the whole thing was a favor to Clevenger, but at least he hadn't blown it. He'd closed the deal. Which had to count for something, right? And it was actually pretty cool stuff. He'd get to learn to fix tugboat engines. He'd get to hang with the guys who captained them. And he'd get ten bucks an hour cash to start, which was chump change, but a whole lot better than volunteering. Dean Walsh and his tight-ass secretary, and Scott Dillard and the rest of Auden Prep could go to hell, bunch of fucking hypocrites.

Dillard and his tough-guy friends just didn't like getting the shit knocked out of them. That was pretty much the whole story, which was pretty funny, considering they'd picked both fights—Dillard talking all kinds of trash about Billy's hair style and nose ring, then his buddies figuring they'd get revenge for the beating he'd taken.

As far as Billy was concerned, you didn't start something you couldn't finish. If you did, you sucked it up and took your punishment.

Not Dillard and company. They'd ratted him out.

He stood up and walked to the mirror over his bureau. He was ripped. His torso looked like a gladiator's armor—perfectly defined pecs, a six-pack abdomen, not an ounce of fat anywhere. He flexed his arms and watched his biceps bulge rock-hard.

That's what they all were: hypocrites. To think that Dillard had turned him in for having marijuana in his locker when Dillard had been one of his best customers. The scumbag had been nursing a habit of an ounce a month until he'd decided to start in on Billy about his dreadlocks—joking at first, but then going overboard and really hassling him. *From Jamaica, mon? Off de island, mon?* So Billy had cut him off. Cold. Not a single joint. Don't bite the hand that feeds you.

That was the real reason Dillard had wanted to fight: he was hungry for his smoke and couldn't get it.

Billy leaned closer to the mirror and inspected his nose ring, making sure the piercing was healing up. Then he stepped back and sat at the end of the weight bench. He laced his fingers behind his head, rotated his shoulders left and right, stretching before his next set.

Walsh throwing him out over a bag of reefer was a real

joke in the first place. Could anybody seriously believe the dean wasn't having himself a couple of martinis every night he went home to his five-foot wife with the thick legs and bright red lipstick? How was that different than having yourself a joint? Or a line? Other than the government taking a cut of the profits on the booze? Also, booze could destroy your liver or make somebody roadkill, whereas pot and an occasional blast wouldn't hurt you at all.

He lay down on the weight bench and gripped the bar overhead. He'd added ten-pound plates to each side, bringing him up to 220 pounds. He took a deep breath and pushed the bar off its pegs. He lowered it to his chest. Then he blew all the air out of his lungs and pressed the bar back up. Solid. He did another rep, struggled through a third. On the fourth, his pecs shook from his effort to slow the bar as it fell. His arms felt as though they might give out. But he reached deep inside himself and imagined that the bar *wanted* to rise, that gravity was working in reverse, that all he had to do was work with it. He shut his eyes, craned his neck and pushed with everything he had, gritting his teeth as he powered the bar back up, extending his arms, holding the weight steady a split second before letting it crash back onto the steel pegs.

"Nice," Clevenger yelled over the music, from just outside the room.

Billy sat up, breathing like a bellows, covered in sweat.

Clevenger nodded at the stereo. "Mind lowering that?"

Billy walked over and dialed down the volume. "You could have spotted me," he said, turning back to Clevenger. "I almost lost it there."

"No, you didn't," Clevenger said. He stepped into the room. "Not even close."

"Two-twenty," Billy said. "Four reps."

"A new record," Clevenger said. "Congratulations." He nodded at Billy's cell phone on the floor beside the weight bench. "I tried you on my way back from the airport."

"I didn't hear it," Billy lied.

Clevenger nodded.

"I talked to Peter Fitzgerald today," Billy said. "I start work tomorrow."

"Good," Clevenger said, in a reserved tone.

"Ten bucks an hour," Billy said, injecting more enthusiasm into his voice than he felt, hoping the energy might propel the discussion past any mention of the drug test. "And these guys who run the tugs turn out to be—"

"Talk to me about the drug test," Clevenger said.

"I couldn't get there," Billy said automatically. He reached for his T-shirt. "I'll go tomorrow," he said, pulling it on. "First thing."

"What do you mean you 'couldn't get there?' "

"By the time I finished at the shipyard it was like four-thirty, and I promised Casey, this new girl I met, that I'd call her, which took till like five-fifteen, five-thirty, then it was dark, so I figured I might as well wait."

"Why didn't you get the test done before going to the shipyard, like we agreed?" Clevenger asked.

"A million things," Billy said.

"A million . . ."

"Honestly? I slept in 'til like noon, then ended up going for a run to kind of clear my head, grabbed lunch and whatever. Then I got worried how jammed the clinic might be, that I might miss Peter. You know? But I can definitely go get it done tomorrow morning."

Clevenger knew enough about drug abusers—himself included—to know they were always stalling to avoid turning over their bodily fluids, buying time for their bodies to detoxify, for their kidneys and livers to obliterate the truth. "How about right now?" he asked. "We can drop by my buddy Brian Strasnick's lab in Lynn. Willow Street Medical Center. He's there half the night."

"I told Casey I'd meet her," Billy said.

"Meet her afterwards," Clevenger said, trying to stay in control.

Billy smiled, shook his head. "She's not gonna like—"

"I don't give a fuck what she likes," Clevenger sputtered. "We had a deal that you'd have a tox screen done at Mass General, then you'd go to your interview at the shipyard. And you let me down. So now you're gonna take the ride to Lynn with me."

"Because you don't trust me," Billy said, trying to sound wounded.

"Because you didn't hold up your part of the bargain," Clevenger said.

Billy shook his head. *Fuck it,* he thought. Maybe this Strasnick's machine was a dud. Maybe he'd get the chance to add some water to his urine and dilute any drug metabolites below their recognizable concentrations. If none of that worked, he'd still get another night out with Casey before the shit hit the fan with Clevenger. "Fine," he said. "Let's go."

"How was Quantico?" Billy asked, as soon as they'd climbed into Clevenger's truck.

"I think it went pretty smoothly," Clevenger said. He hoped Billy would let him leave it at that—for two reasons. First, he was too angry to make small talk. Second, and more important, he wanted to keep Billy at a distance from his forensic work, to avoid feeding him a steady diet of darkness.

"What case do they want you on?"

"A murder case."

"The Highway Killer?" Billy asked excitedly. "How cool would it be working on that?"

"They asked me not to talk about our meeting," Clevenger said tightly. He glanced at Billy, saw him deflate. "Not to anyone."

"Sure," Billy said.

"That's the way they want it."

"But you told them you don't keep anything from North."

Clevenger could feel Billy jockeying for position. There was part of Billy that wanted nothing to do with Clevenger and part of him that wanted to get as close as he possibly could. Closer than anyone else. And maybe if Billy had followed through with the drug test, Clevenger would have told him a little more about his meeting. Nothing too grisly. Nothing truly classified. Just something to let him know Clevenger was taking him into his confidence. But that would be sending the wrong message now. Billy had to learn that trust was something you earned. "North hasn't let me down in a long time," he said.

Billy turned away and stared out the passenger window.

They drove in silence the next few minutes, headed down Route 16 East through Revere, Clevenger wondering what Billy was thinking, figuring he was probably less focused on the drug test than on whether he would be done with the drug test in time to catch the train out of Lynn to meet his girlfriend at the North Shore Shopping Center ten miles away in Peabody, something he'd arranged to do just before leaving the loft. Maybe he was wondering whether Tower Records would have a CD he wanted or whether he had enough cash for a room at the Motel 6 up the street from the mall.

But Billy wasn't thinking any of those things. In those two minutes of silence, staring out his window, he was thinking what it would be like to open his door and leap out of the truck. He imagined a powerful mixture of panic and pleasure just before hitting the road, much of that pleasure deriving from how horrified Clevenger would be. He heard the screeching of brakes as Clevenger skidded to the side of the road, the sound of footsteps as he ran to where Billy lay facedown, bleeding on the pavement. And although Billy could not fully explain the satisfaction he felt turning over and seeing the grief and panic in Clevenger's face, he knew it was connected to the fact that Clevenger was not willing to hurt him nearly so badly as he was willing to hurt himself. That was his end run, his ace in the hole, even if he could not say what game he and Clevenger were playing, even if he missed entirely the fact that Clevenger's self-restraint was something called love and that his own lack of it was something called self-loathing.

Billy Bishop could worship his physique and hair, and the little gold ring through his nose, and the blue-green letters and the skull and crossbones tattooed across his back. He could gloat over being a good fighter, a great football player, and a magnet for pretty girls. But his

vanity was just a defense against what he felt inside—
ugly, rotten to the core, worthy of every beating he had
ever taken and would ever take. Like nearly every
abused child, deep in his soul he had given the benefit of
the doubt to his abuser, to the man with the strap.

But Billy didn't end up on the pavement. As the two
minutes of silence came to a close, he leapt in another
direction. He turned to Clevenger. "We don't need to get
this drug test," he said.

"We're getting it," Clevenger said.

"I can tell you what it's gonna show."

Clevenger glanced at Billy and saw he was serious.
He swerved into the parking lot of a Dunkin' Donuts and
threw the truck into park. "Okay. What will it show?"

"Marijuana," Billy said, resisting the impulse to smile.
"I smoked a couple joints I couldn't sell at school."

Clevenger's heart fell. For a few seconds he felt
utterly powerless, foolish to be trying to father a boy
when he hadn't been fathered himself. Who was he trying to save anyhow? Billy? Himself? Why not just admit
the two of them were hopeless together, the blind leading
the blind? "How much have you been . . ."

"That's not all it would show," Billy said.

Clevenger let out his breath, wondering what else was
coming.

"Marijuana . . ." Billy went on, watching the way the
word seemed to injure Clevenger all over again. "And
cocaine . . . and steroids."

Clevenger could tell from Billy's tone that he had
intended to hurt him, that he was trying to engage him
in the only way he knew how—negatively, through con-
frontation. And that reminded him that rescuing Billy
had never looked like anything but a marathon. The

opposition of the Department of Social Services to his adopting Billy had at least helped him see that much. More than half the kids adopted at Billy's age, with histories like his, ended up homeless, jailed, or dead before the age of twenty. Winning the fight for his soul meant holding his hand while slowly, painstakingly uprooting his demons. It meant fighting for years, losing plenty of battles. "So what do you figure we should do?" he asked.

Billy shrugged, still watching Clevenger's face intently.

"You figure that's my job," Clevenger said, mostly to himself.

Billy turned and stared through the windshield.

Clevenger did the same. "There is the standard response, 'You're grounded,' " he said. "Which won't work here, if you ask me. I think you'd be pretty content up in the loft for a month with your weights and your stereo, sneaking in girls." He paused. "There's another one that goes something like, 'You're out of the house, on your own, unless you get yourself into a thirty-day program.' And there's some merit to that kind of thinking. The 'tough love' thing can work. But it's risky with someone like you. You're so unhappy with yourself you might feel at home on the streets. You may figure that's all you deserve. And I don't want that for you. Truth is, I couldn't stomach it." He glanced at Billy to see whether he would respond to that olive branch. He didn't. "Other parents just call the cops," he went on. "Let the DA get a conviction against their kid for possession and hope a judge will make Narcotics Anonymous and drug-testing part of a deal for probation." He shrugged. "That isn't always a terrible idea. Having a jail sentence hanging over your head can make it tougher to enjoy getting high."

"Or more exciting," Billy said, still staring straight ahead.

Clevenger turned to Billy, saw the smug look on his face. And right about then it would have felt really good to grab him by the neck and drive his head into the windshield, to smash the smirk off his face, to teach him that as tough as he thought he was, there were people a hell of a lot tougher than him. Maybe that's the lesson Billy needed to learn, the one no one had been able to teach him in the school yard at Auden Prep.

But as Clevenger felt the rage gather inside him, felt his heart begin to race, his jaw clench, he realized a beating was exactly what Billy was angling for. He was unconsciously trying to resurrect the relationship he had had with his father, casting Clevenger in the role of his abuser this time. Clevenger shook his head, thinking how hard the past died. He was just one mistake away—a slap, a punch—from becoming his own father, completing the pathologic journey from victim to victimizer. Seductive stuff, this repetition compulsion. The only way out was to speak the dynamic, instead of acting upon it. "Of course," he said, "there are parents who just lose it, knock the living crap out of their kids."

Billy looked at him. "I don't give a shit. Go ahead, if you want."

"It's what *you* want."

Billy rolled his eyes.

"I used to be in the same rut you're in," Clevenger said.

"What rut is that?" Billy asked.

Clevenger looked out through the windshield again.

"Trying to show how strong I was by surviving one beating after another. First from my father. Then, when he wasn't around anymore, I filled in for him pretty well. Nearly killed myself with cocaine and booze."

"You?" Billy said. "Cocaine?"

Clevenger squinted into the night. "It dulled the pain. That's the obvious part. But it did something else. It kept the dream of my father alive for me. The dream that I had a father who cared about me."

"I don't get it," Billy said.

"As long as I was abusing myself," Clevenger said, looking at him, "as long I didn't deserve any better, I could believe he loved me. Me, the fuck-up. Me, the addict. The liar. So what if the old man was a fall-down drunk? So what if he grabbed a belt when he was pissed at me? It wasn't like I didn't deserve it. All I had to do was look in the mirror to see that I did."

Billy was listening more intently.

"There's a lot of grief headed your way when you realize you're a worthwhile person, Billy," Clevenger went on. "I mean, *really* worthwhile—because of your heart, not your hair or your face or your body. Because then you start to feel how much it hurt to have that belief beaten out of you, how much you suffered before you finally let go of it. You start to add up how much it cost to have a father who *didn't* love you. And then you start to bleed for real."

"Or bleed out," Billy said.

That comment took Clevenger by surprise.

"Everybody's always saying how you should face up to stuff," Billy said. "Like that's gonna make you happy. But who's to say it won't make things worse, even make you lose it?"

Clevenger nodded. Billy was right. If you let down your defenses and confronted your demons, there was always the chance they would win. "I won't lie to you," he said. "That happens to some people. Sometimes the pain is too much to bear. But it doesn't happen nearly as often to people who team up—like you and I could. If you were willing to tell me when you feel like using drugs, instead of using them, if you and I could talk the most when you're low instead of high, we'd end up beating this thing."

"You're not my shrink, though," Billy said.

Clevenger wondered for a moment whether Billy was finally asking to see a therapist, something he had been hounding him to do. But then he realized Billy was asking for something more. "No," he said, "I'm not your therapist. I'm trying to be a father to you." He watched as Billy swallowed hard—which either meant he'd been moved by what Clevenger had said or that he was acting that way. "So tell me where to take you, champ. Your decision. I can drop you at the mall, take you back to the loft, or over to Strasnick's lab. Whatever you pick, I'm still with you one hundred and ten percent."

"Why would we need the lab?" Billy asked. "I already told you what the tox screen is gonna show."

"It's too early for me to take your word on that. There are plenty of other drugs you could be using. Without the lab, I still have to worry whether I know what we're up against. And I'd rather not."

Billy looked out the passenger window. He thought how he really owed Clevenger a lot. He thought how what Clevenger had said made sense—the parts of it he could understand, anyhow. But mostly he thought how he'd already spilled his guts about everything he was taking, except for Ecstasy now and then. And he hadn't used that for about a week. So it definitely wouldn't show up on a tox screen. And he'd already told Casey he couldn't get to the mall until later that night. So, long and short of it, he really had nothing to lose by giving up a little blood and urine. He turned to Clevenger. "Let's go to the lab," he said.

seven

It was nearly 1:00 A.M., but Jonah had no desire for sleep. He lay in bed, in jeans and nothing else, spread-eagled on the mattress, smiling up at the ceiling. The perfectly sculpted muscles of his chest, shoulders, arms, and legs rippled with excitement. The apartment was still foreign to him, still freeing to him. The anonymity of the place— its vacant walls, new white sheets and towels, freshly cleaned beige wall-to-wall carpeting, plastic plates and utensils, vinyl couch and wood veneer dining room table—made him feel reborn. No one in the apartment building knew him. No one along the three-mile road to the hospital knew him. During the weeks since arriving in Canaan he had installed no phone, connected no cable, ordered no newspaper. He either grabbed food at the hospital cafeteria, or wolfed takeout from the Chin Chin Chinese restaurant two blocks from his apartment or the Canaan House of Pizza just around the corner.

Michelle Jenkins had asked him out twice more, but he had politely turned her down each time. He didn't need a woman. His caseload had grown to eight patients who transfused him not only with their pain, but with that of their troubled fathers and mothers and siblings who came for family meetings on the locked unit. Eight life stories quickly became sixteen, then thirty-two, then sixty-four. Each workday was a nonstop orgy of suffering.

It satisfied Jonah.

He laced his fingers behind his head, closed his eyes, and thought of six-year-old Naomi McMorris, raped at age three. She had sat silently in his office the first thirty minutes they had spent together, her ankles crossed, her little girl legs swinging back and forth, too frightened to look at him for more than a few seconds. She was beautiful, though skinny, with straight blonde hair and green-blue, soulful eyes that were far more knowing than they ought to have been at her age, eyes that hinted at how much she had seen, too early, of human cruelty. Her mother's rapist boyfriend had come and gone, but he had left adult and foreign knowledge inside her. That was the reason Naomi cut herself habitually, clawing her wrists open when she couldn't get her hands on a knife or fork or broken pencil, staring at the blood as it oozed. Because a six-year-old could not find words to express the terror it had to be to feel herself penetrated—her *self* penetrated—the unspeakable pain, the desperation. Cutting herself open could tell the story without words—the breach in her body's integrity, the warm, red fluid dripping to the carpet. Time and time again she would step out of her room on the locked unit or stand up in the cafeteria and hold out her bleeding wrists for everyone to see, her eyes wide, triumph on her face, as if to say, "Let there be no secret now. I have been torn apart."

Before retiring from Canaan Memorial, Dr. Wyatt had written orders in Naomi's chart designed to keep her safe. He wrote to file down her nails every other day, to restrict her access to sharp objects, and to check on her safety every five minutes. These were sensible measures to keep her from cutting herself. So, too, were the 75 milligrams of Zoloft she was to take each morning to elevate her mood, the 2.5 milligrams of Zyprexa she was to take each afternoon to calm her agitation, and the 25 milligrams of Trazodone she was to take each night to ward off nightmares.

The trouble was that Naomi's bleeding was mostly internal. Preventing her from cutting her skin would never stop the shards of her shattered childhood from quietly shredding her psyche.

Jonah knew that he would never gain access to a girl like Naomi in the usual way. She was not about to open herself up to him simply because he was called "doctor" or promised to do her no harm. He needed to be a victim, like her. He needed to tap her instinct to comfort and protect another person, an instinct that often survived trauma, even grew stronger because of it.

"I don't like it here," Jonah had told her after sitting in silence with her for that first thirty minutes.

Naomi still hadn't spoken, but she had glanced at him for the first time.

"I hate it here," he said.

Another glance from her. A shrug. Then, looking at her feet swinging: "How come?"

How come? Two words, seven letters, but an opening no less miraculous than the Red Sea parting for the Jews en route to the Promised Land. A six-year-old soul, still new to this terrible world, was inviting *him* inside her. Him, dirtied by over four decades on the planet. Him, whose own sins were beyond words. Him, unto her. Unto God. "Promise not to tell anyone?" he asked her.

She nodded.

"Swear?"

"I swear," Naomi said.

"They're mean to me," Jonah said.

Her legs stopped swinging. "Who?"

"The other doctors."

She looked at him, kept looking at him. "Like how? What do they do to you?"

"Call me all sorts of names. Tease me."

"Why?"

"I guess because they don't like me."

"They don't like you?" she asked.

"They don't want me here. They don't want me to be their friend."

"Why not?"

He shrugged. A six-year-old would not be able to fathom why other six-year-olds had it in for him. And for the moment Jonah was six, making a six-year-old friend. He wanted to forge the kind of fierce allegiance children of that age can. *Us* against *them*. Us against the rest of the world. "This is all a secret," he said. "Just between you and me. I wasn't supposed to tell you."

"I won't say anything," she said.

He smiled. "Can you come here tomorrow?"

"Okay."

Okay. Another victory against Naomi's isolation. A rout. Naomi walked back to her room, and Jonah stayed in his office. But now he knew that little by little, day by day, she would come closer. By appearing vulnerable with her, he would give her the permission she needed to be vulnerable with him. And, together, as victims, they would give her demons an audience, let them scream and cry and mourn and rage as loudly and as long as they needed to.

Jonah opened his eyes and stared at his bedroom ceiling again. He could almost smell Naomi's fresh skin. He wished she were with him at that very moment. He wished Tommy Magellan and Mike Pansky and all his other patients were there, too. He wished he never had to leave the locked unit. He wished he could eat, sleep, and bathe there, among the little broken people. Because locking the door behind him every night was like locking away pieces of himself.

That image of the locked door, with him on one side and them on the other, stuck in his mind and in his throat. Suddenly, he felt more alone than free. And loneliness was the danger zone. Loneliness was the thing that made him want to leave the apartment and walk the streets, searching for truth, scavenging intimacies.

He had never given in to the impulse to take a life in the very town in which he worked, but he had come close. Too close. He had spent November and December of 1995 in Frills Corners, Pennsylvania, just outside the Allegheny National Forest, working at the Venango Regional Medical Center. The child psychiatry unit there was not locked and admitted only patients who could "contract for safety," promising not to harm themselves. That meant the kids could go home for visits or out on "passes" with their parents. The place pretty much emptied out from the day before Christmas until the following Monday. For Jonah, that meant five days of solitude. And late that Sunday night it had all started again—the throbbing inside his skull, the burning in his skin, the awful struggle to get air into his lungs. So he had gone for a walk just after midnight. To breathe. To stop the heat.

She had been waiting for him. Like the rest. Ally Bartlett, twenty-eight years old, not short and not tall, perhaps twenty pounds overweight, with medium brown eyes and curly black hair, sitting at a bus stop outside a bar, dressed in tan wool slacks and a blue wool peacoat. She wore a thick, red scarf wrapped twice around her neck. No hat. No gloves. She was staring at him from the moment he turned the corner. She never looked away as he walked toward her. "You must be freezing," she said, smiling as he sat down a respectful distance from her.

Jonah was wearing faded blue jeans and a gray turtleneck sweater. No coat. But he didn't feel cold. "Someone stole my coat," he told her.

"The bus should be here in a few minutes," she said. "Take this," she said, unwrapping her scarf. "At least until it comes."

"I couldn't," Jonah said, knowing that he would.

"Don't be a hero," she said. "It's freezing." She finished taking off the scarf, revealing the gold cross she wore around her neck.

Jonah nodded in silent acknowledgment of this sign, of God's offering to him. He took the scarf and wrapped it around his neck, breathing in Ally's enrapturing scent, a bouquet of her perfume, makeup, sweat, breath. "My name is Phillip," he said. "Phillip Keane. I'm a doctor at Venango Regional."

"Ally Bartlett," she said. She looked down the street. "Any second now, I bet," she said.

His hunger had him off-balance, and he moved awkwardly into questioning her. "How was your holiday?"

"Terrible," she said, with an even wider smile.

"Why?" He thought he sounded desperate. "What was terrible?"

The smile disappeared. "Long story."

So Ally was closing the door already. Baiting him

with kindness, then shutting him out. In the freezing cold. She would give more to a homeless man on a street corner, begging for change. Jonah, she would happily shortchange. Jonah, a man dedicated to healing others, she would ignore. His head felt like it would split in two. He could picture his basilar artery, along the base of his brain, pulsating, the angry nerve cells in its fibrous wall screaming in agony as they stretched with every beat of his heart. He needed relief, if only the relief that would come with hearing Ally's muffled scream, looking into her terrified eyes, knowing her pain. He reached into his pocket, grasping the stiletto knife he was carrying. He glanced at the all but deserted bar room behind them, then scanned the street. They were alone. "Where is that bus?" he said, his voice shaking. He stood up. And he would have started over to her, would have—with no more joy than Abraham raising a dagger over Isaac—taken the life he needed, the life God was giving him. But she spoke.

"This will sound crazy," she said, "but do you want to get a drink or something? I mean, you never know who you're really meeting—or why."

A drink *or something*. Jonah relaxed his grip on the knife. He took a deep breath, let it out.

Ally tilted her head. "I mean, here you are. Here I am. No bus. Freezing cold. And there's a bar about fifteen feet away." She held her palms in the air. "It's kind of like God's trying to tell us something, don't you think?"

"You never know with God," Jonah said. He pretended to hesitate. He let go of the knife. "Why not?" he said, after a few seconds.

The two of them took a table at the back of Sawyer's Grub and Pub, ordered a couple of beers.

"You have an incredible voice," Ally said. "Do people tell you that?"

"Sometimes."

"It's strange, almost."

Jonah raised an eyebrow.

"I didn't mean it that way," she said, with a delightful laugh. "Not strange, weird. Strange in a good way. Kind. But more than kind. Comforting or something."

"So why was your holiday so terrible?" Jonah asked.

She looked down at her beer. "Persistent, aren't you?"

"People do tell me that. All the time."

She looked back at him. "My father"—her voice fell off to a whisper, her eyes started to close—"is dying." Then she began to weep.

Jonah sat silently, transfixed. Maybe, despite what he had become, despite all the terrible things he had done, God had truly sent him an angel.

Ally opened her eyes, looked back at him. She kept wiping away her tears, but more and more streamed out of her eyes. "I'm sorry. I didn't ask you to come in here so I could fall apart like this. I just can't seem to . . ."

"To . . ." He leaned forward.

She let her tears roll down her face. "Deal with this."

Jonah reached across the table and took one of her hands in both of his. She didn't resist his touch at all. "What is your father dying from?" he asked her.

"Some kind of virus infecting his heart," she said. "It's swollen and won't pump right. Endo . . ."

"Viral endocarditis," he said.

She used the sleeve of her sweater to dry her eyes. "You really are a doctor."

"I really am."

"A heart doctor?" she asked.

"In a way, I suppose," he said. "A psychiatrist."

She smiled again. "Ah, no wonder," she said.

"No wonder, what?"

Her smile mellowed to something especially warm, almost loving. "No wonder I feel like I could tell you anything," she said.

Jonah felt the tension leaving his muscles, the heat leaving his skin. He realized his head had stopped aching. "Tell me about him," he said.

And Ally had. Without Jonah having to pry or prod or threaten, she gave him her truth. She told him the things she loved about her father and the things she hated. She told him what growing up in Ithaca, New York, had been like for her. She told him about being raped by a Cornell college sophomore when she was fourteen. She told him that her father had asked her what she had done to make the boy think she wanted sex, and that her father had held her as she cried, stroked her hair, and promised her that everything would be all right. She told him she wished she could do the same for him now. She told him her mother, a religious woman, was remarried and had visited her father in the hospital just twice. She told him her older brother was in a federal penitentiary, sentenced to ten years for transporting cocaine across state lines. She told him how memories of her rape still got in the way of her sexual pleasure.

Ally Bartlett, Jonah concluded, was indeed an angel. And he had taken her home with him and made love with her and slept beside her that night. That night and never again. Because he knew that Ally would ultimately want to know him in the ways she had let him know her. She would not be fooled by the pieces of lives he had harvested from others.

Jonah sat up in bed. The memory of Ally Bartlett, like the memories of his patients on the locked unit at Canaan Memorial, only made him feel more alone. His apartment was beginning to feel more like a prison than a fortress.

It was nearly two o'clock. He hungered to wander the streets. He hungered to find someone. To have someone. He reached for the bottle of Haldol on the bedside table, opened it, and chewed three milligrams of the stuff, the pill fragments scratching his throat as he forced them down. Then he looked out the bedroom door at his old, belted briefcase sitting on the floor of the living room.

He didn't want to do it. It was dirty and disgusting and he didn't even know what had possessed him to think of doing it in the first place. Maybe it was something hardwired in his brain, some genetically programmed aberrant appetite. Maybe it was a vestige of primitive rituals buried somewhere in the tangle of billions of neurons that made up his cortex. People were sometimes born with webbed hands or feet, after all. Maybe his was a behavioral throwback.

Whatever its roots, whatever its strange power, once he had given in to the habit the first time, it became nearly impossible to resist repeating it. Because it did partly satisfy his hunger. When he had lasted through days of solitude, it could sometimes get him through the last terrible hours.

He stood up. He walked into the living room, picked up his briefcase, and sat down on the couch. He unfastened one of its straps and then the other. He aligned the wheels of its combination lock and clicked it open. Then he pulled apart its jaws, reached inside, and took out a small, zippered black leather case, of the kind that might be used to hold a blood pressure cuff or a stash of diamonds.

He sat back on the couch, fondling the case, feeling the glass tube inside. Occasionally just touching the thing, knowing it was there, was enough. But it would not be enough tonight. He was already sweating. He was already salivating. He was already imagining the terror in Anna Beckwith's eyes that night on Route 90 East.

He unzipped the case and took out the thing he needed—a test tube half-filled with blood. He rolled it between his palms, warming it. He ran the smooth glass base along his lips, then past them, into his mouth, almost tasting the precious liquid.

He felt intensely guilty. Shameful. But why? Was an infant to be condemned for suckling? Did churchgoers feel guilt consuming the body of Christ? Were we not all, ultimately, one glorious being? And if Jonah felt this more than others, knew it better than others, was he to be condemned?

He slid off the couch, sinking to his knees. He pulled the light purple rubber stopper from the top of the tube. He poured a few drops of the blood onto his tongue, spread another drop over his lips, then carefully pushed the stopper back in place. The blood was warm and tasted salty, of birth and death and, most important, of others. All the others. A fantastic collage of their lives, without boundaries, swirling together, inside him. A reincarnation of the primordial sea from which all life once sprung. He began to relax almost immediately. Within half a minute he began to feel truly at peace. His heart slowed, and his breathing eased. The pain in his head evaporated, leaving behind a pleasant tingling at his temples, at the nape of his neck. God willing, he would make it through the night. He would make it to the morning, when there would be Naomi and Tommy and Mike and Jessie and Carl and the rest of them. The rest of him.

Morning came drizzly and gray and cold. Jonah rushed to the locked unit, arriving just before 7:00 A.M., as had become his habit. He delighted in being there early because the place had yet to fall into its regular rhythm. No other psychiatrist was there. The nursing staff was in flux—the night nurses leaving, the day nurses arriving. Some of the patients were still sleeping, some shaking off sleep, some drowsy from a night without any sleep at all. Some were fresh from showers, some still wearing pajamas. Most of their beds were unmade. Jonah could smell the sweet musk of their sheets, pillowcases and blankets, their matted and tousled hair, their night sweats. It was the time of day when these five and six and ten-year-old shut-ins felt most homesick, most institutionalized, and it was the time Jonah felt most needed and most at home, most a part of his extended family.

He went immediately to Naomi McMorris's room. Her door was ajar. He looked inside and saw her lying awake in bed, her golden hair fanned over her pillow, her fist clutching the floppy ear of a pale pink bunny. He knocked softly, pushed the door open a bit further and waited for her eyes to find his. When they did, it seemed to him that all the love dammed up inside him began to flow, and he felt the kind of exquisite release he imagined a woman feels as her infant begins to nurse at her engorged breast. "You didn't tell anyone our secret, did you?" he asked.

She sat up in bed, shook her head.

"Good."

"Did *you*?" she asked.

Jonah felt shivers at the back of his neck. Naomi wanted all of him as much as he wanted all of her. "Never," he said.

"Good."

Jonah winked. "See you later?"

She nodded.

He started to leave.

"I dreamt about you," she said.

Jonah froze, afraid to believe he had actually heard what he thought he had—that Naomi and he had been together in the night, even as he lay in bed in his apartment, staring at his ceiling. He stepped into the room and waited.

"Want me to tell you about it?" she said after a few seconds.

"Please," he said.

"We went for a walk next to this really deep lake," she said. "It was sunny and warm and beautiful, and I was . . ." She blushed.

"You were what?"

"Holding your hand."

Jonah nearly gasped. He could feel Naomi's hand in his. "And?"

"And then . . ." She began to giggle.

"Then . . ."

She struggled to stop laughing. "I pushed you away from me, and you fell in and drowned." She shrugged. "I guess you couldn't swim. Sorry."

"And then you woke up," Jonah said.

"Uh-huh."

"You felt really cold."

"Freezing," she said.

"And you were having trouble catching your breath."

"I could hardly breathe at all." She squinted at Jonah. "Hey, how do you know the rest of my dream?"

What Jonah knew about Naomi's dream was that she was projecting her own fears onto him. Her real worry was that *he* would push *her* away—coaxing her close to her deepest feelings, then shoving her over the edge, to sink or swim alone. And in her heart Naomi feared that if Jonah did that, it would kill her. She would not be able to keep herself afloat after another betrayal. That's why when she awakened *she* was the one who felt as though she were drowning. "I know a lot about dreams," Jonah said. He paused. "Want to know the most important thing about yours?"

"Yeah. What?"

He winked at her. "I'm gonna hold your hand really tight if we ever go near a lake."

She rolled her eyes. "I would never push you in for real," she said.

"I would never push you in, either," he said. "You can count on that."

"Okay," she said.

"So I'll see you later?" he asked.

"Later, alligator."

"In a while, crocodile."

eight

Clevenger got into work just after 9:00 A.M., hung his jacket in the hall closet, and poked his head into North Anderson's office. "How goes it?"

"Richie Egbert needs this report ASAP," Anderson said, barely glancing at him. "Turns out some of the witnesses against Sonny Raveno have serious credibility problems." He started typing. "Egbert's cross-examining them tomorrow."

"I guess that's good news."

"For Sonny," Anderson said. The phone rang, but he kept typing.

"Want me to get that?" Clevenger asked.

"It's been ringing off the hook." Anderson grabbed a pile of pink message slips off his desk, swiveled in his chair, and held them out. "I got to get this report out."

Clevenger took the slips, flipped through them. The first was a message to call Cary Shuman at the *Boston Globe*. The second was to call Margie Reedy at New England Cable News. The next three were from Josh Resnek at the *Chelsea Independent*. "What the hell?"

Anderson reached for a newspaper on his desk. "Today's *New York Times*," he said, handing it to Clevenger.

Clevenger scanned the headlines. "Am I missing something?"

"Don't be offended. You're under the fold."

Clevenger flipped the paper over. His eyes locked on the headline at the lower right-hand corner of the front page: FBI TAPS OUTSIDE FORENSIC EXPERT IN HIGHWAY KILLER CASE. "That fucking . . . I decided not to take the case."

"You told them 'no' flat-out?" Anderson asked.

"I said I needed time to think it over. I decided last night."

"I guess the Bureau has its own needs. While you were mulling over yours, they were putting theirs out on the news wire."

Clevenger felt his blood pressure rising as he read the first two paragraphs:

ASSOCIATED PRESS

The Federal Bureau of Investigation, under increasing pressure to solve the string of murders known as the Highway Killings, has enlisted the aid of Frank Clevenger, MD, a Boston-based forensic psychiatrist most well-known for solving the murder of infant Brooke Bishop, daughter of billionaire Darwin Bishop, two years ago on Nantucket.

"This agency will leave no stone unturned," Kane Warner, director of the Bureau's Behavioral Sciences Unit, said. "We're reaching out to the best and brightest and giving him everything he needs to assist us."

"I got in at eight this morning," Anderson said. "We already had eleven calls on voice mail. All of them from reporters. So I went out and grabbed the papers. The *Washington Post*, the *Globe* and the *Herald* are on your desk."

Clevenger walked across the hall to his own office, grabbed the phone, and dialed Kane Warner, spreading the newspapers across his desk as he waited for someone to pick up.

"Director Warner's office," a man's voice answered.

"It's Frank Clevenger."

"One moment, Doctor."

Clevenger flipped through the papers. The *Globe* story wasn't any more extensive than the one in the *Times*, but the *Herald* had run two full pages on the Highway Killer, complete with a rudimentary map of where bodies had been found and a three-column photograph of Clevenger fielding a question at the news conference he'd given on Nantucket at the conclusion of the Bishop case.

"Dr. Clevenger?" Warner finally answered.

Clevenger started to pace. "What are you trying to pull here?"

"I'm sorry?"

"I told you I hadn't decided whether to sign on."

"You're upset about the news coverage?"

"You know what? Go fuck . . ." He started to hang up.

"Hold on. Please. I didn't leak the story."

Out of the corner of his eye Clevenger saw a New England Cable News van pull up beside the office building. "You expect me to—"

"I responded when the AP called. 'No comment' wouldn't have buried the story anyway. But I swear to you I didn't drop a dime on this. I've asked every person who sat in that room with us yesterday; they all deny leaking it. I'm sorry it happened. I don't know how it did."

"Let me save us both a lot of time and trouble," Clevenger said. "I'm not working the case."

"I'd ask you to think about it a little longer. You—"

Another phone line in Clevenger's office started to ring, then a third. "My decision is 'no,' " Clevenger said. "Categorical. Final. Got that? I'll be telling the press I turned you down for personal reasons. You can tell them the same thing. I hope that saves you face. I'm not looking to embarrass anyone."

"Would a discussion about your compensation help?" Warner asked.

"Did you hear a word I just said?"

The phones stopped ringing just as a second television van—this one from Channel 7—pulled up outside.

"I've got clearance to go as high as five hundred an hour. That's a big number for us."

"Listen to me," Clevenger said, watching satellite poles rise out of the vans. "No number will turn the key here. It's not about money." Out of the corner of his eye he saw North Anderson at the door to his office. He motioned him inside.

"How about the number fourteen?" Warner asked.

Anderson sat down in the armchair in front of Clevenger's desk.

"Fourteen . . ." Clevenger said.

"Victims."

Clevenger said nothing.

"Fourteen dead people, Doctor. And I'm going to tell you straight out: we're nowhere on this. You're not window dressing to me. I need you."

Forty-nine-point-nine percent of Clevenger wanted to say "yes," wanted to pit his energy against that of the Highway Killer, to pour all of himself into a worthy and consuming quest that would swallow any doubts he had about his own existence—like whether he was fully alive, whether he was wholly good, whether he could father a son. Add in potential romance with Whitney McCormick, and his feet wouldn't have to touch ground at all. "I can't. Not now," he said. "This isn't something to nickel and dime. Getting into this case means getting in all the way. It means living it and breathing it for as long as it goes on. I'm not in a position to do that."

One of the other phone lines started ringing again.

"Tell me what would change your mind," Warner said.

"I hope you get this guy," Clevenger said. "I'd really like to see you nail him. But you'll have to get him without me." He hung up. He picked up the other line, hung that up, too.

Anderson glanced out the window at a man and woman unloading a television camera, tripod, and sound gear from the back of the New England Cable News van. The other crew was already on its way to the front door. "You want me to tell them?"

"My job," Clevenger said. He squinted out the window and shook his head.

"What's the real reason you're turning them down?" Anderson asked.

Clevenger didn't respond.

"Because if you're holding back because of me," Anderson said, "don't. I was out of line with what I said the other day."

"No. You were right," Clevenger said. He looked at Anderson. "Billy's been using drugs."

Anderson took the news like a kick to his gut. "Jesus, Frank, I'm sorry."

"Selling, too. They expelled him from Auden."

There was a knock at the front door.

"Let them wait," Anderson said. "When did you find this out?"

"Two days ago."

"Marijuana?"

"Among other things."

"Does he need to detox?"

Clevenger shook his head. "I'm not exactly sure what he needs. But I think it all adds up to needing me more than ever. This is no time for me to disappear." He took a deep breath, let it out. "I've never really let anyone rely on me." He saw Anderson about to protest. "On the job, sure. I hope you know by now that I'd back you up no matter what. I think my patients have always known they could count on me. But outside of that, in my personal life, I haven't taken responsibility for anyone but myself—and that's a pretty recent phenomenon. No wife. No kids. Billy's the first one who made me want to step up to the plate, put somebody else first. I've got to follow through with that. I've got to do the right thing by him."

A third television van pulled alongside the building.

"If there's anything I can do, just say the word."

"Keep telling me when I'm about to screw up."

The phone started ringing again.

Anderson broke into a wide grin. "Only if you promise to do the same for me."

"Done."

As Clevenger was walking out of his office to meet the reporters gathered there, Jonah Wrens, 208 miles north in Canaan, Vermont, was opening his office door for Naomi McMorris. She had her hair in pigtails, tied with pink ribbons. She was wearing denim overalls with three mice and a wedge of Swiss cheese embroidered on the chest. The nurses had bought her white leather sneakers decorated with light-up, red plastic hearts that glowed every time she took a step. "Is now okay?" she asked.

"Now is perfect," Jonah said.

Naomi took her seat in front of Jonah's desk. This time Jonah took the one beside hers. He looked at the bandages along her forearms. He had seen the battle-worn skin underneath, some scarred, some raw and freshly sutured. "Why do you cut yourself, Naomi?" he asked.

She turned her arms over so Jonah couldn't look at her bandages.

"Why?" Jonah repeated.

"Just because," she said shyly.

"Because . . ."

"It feels good."

"What part feels good?" Jonah asked. "The cutting? The blood coming out? The way people get scared when you do it? All of it?"

She stared down at her lap.

"You can tell me. It's okay."

She stayed silent.

"How about if I tell you another secret of mine first?"

She looked up him.

"As long as you still promise not to tell the other doctors," he said.

"Never," she said.

Jonah unbuttoned his sleeves, rolled them up, and turned his arms over. He watched Naomi's eyes widen as she stared at the horizontal scars up and down his forearms—the record of his suicidal gestures. "I've done it, too," he said.

"Why?"

Jonah looked at her as if to say, *You know why.*

"To get the yucky stuff out," she said.

Jonah nodded. He stared at his scars, but he saw Naomi's rapist forcing apart her knees, pictured the fear and confusion on her face. Confusion dominated, because there was no way for her to guess at the horror that was about to unfold. What she knew was that her body was being manipulated in a way that it never had before, arms out, legs out, making way for a man, a man whose face was closer than she wanted it to be. And though her confusion would grow as the man forced his way even closer, her fear would skyrocket, eclipsing everything. Then the man would force his way inside her, and her whole world would go black. Thinking of it, feeling it, Jonah's eyes began to fill with tears.

Naomi looked at him in the way a knowing child can, a child new enough to this world that everything around her—including the suffering of others—still burns as warm and bright as the noonday sun. She instinctively wanted to give him more of herself, more of the pain she had kept bottled up inside her. Because he seemed to want it. Or need it. "I felt it go in me," she said. "Yucky, sticky stuff."

"And you don't know if it might still be in there."

Now Naomi's eyes started to get wet.

"Talking about it this way makes you want to cut yourself right now," Jonah said.

A tear started down her cheek. She started rubbing her hands together.

"I know another way to make sure it's all gone. The yucky stuff."

"How?"

Jonah held out his hands to her. "With these." He saw her knees clamp shut. "We trust one another. Right?"

She nodded, but crossed her ankles.

"Close your eyes for me," he said. He held his breath, waiting to see if she could do it, if she—unlike Anna Beckwith and the rest of them—was ready to be healed, able to be cured. Because the ability to trust, which requires trust not so much in the kindness of others but in one's own strength, was what Naomi really needed, more than she needed Zyprexa or Zoloft or Trazodone. She needed to place herself in another person's hands and see that she could emerge unharmed. That was the antidote to everything her rapist had left inside her.

Jonah closed his eyes and prayed silently to the God he loved, the God who loved him, for some of the Lord's strength to fill the part of him that was this beautiful little girl. And when he opened his eyes, she showed that strength. She closed her eyes and held them shut, crow's-feet fanning out from the corners, her whole forehead visibly straining with the effort not to open them right back up again.

His skin turned everywhere to gooseflesh. "You're going to feel my hands on you," he said, his voice more melodious, more reassuring than ever. "Promise me you won't open your eyes," he said.

"Promise," she whispered.

Jonah stood and placed the palms of his hands gently on her head. "I can tell if there's bad stuff inside you," he said. "If there is I can draw it out of you—and into me."

He moved his hands to her temples, then her cheeks, thrilling as he felt the wetness from her tears.

"It won't hurt you?" she asked, pulling back slightly.

Her concern for him nearly took his breath away. "I'm older than you are," he said, "and very strong. I can hold a lot more inside me." He spread his fingers over her ears, brought his hands to her neck, lightly pressed his thumbs into the soft flesh beside her windpipe. "I'll be fine. And you'll be fine."

The crow's-feet beside Naomi's eyes lightened, then disappeared. As Jonah's thumbs massaged her jaw, the tension there melted away, too. She sat still as his hands traveled down her shoulders, down her sides, and over her abdomen. She didn't move at all when he crouched in front of her, his hands on her thighs. Only when his hands settled on her knees did she tense up again. "We're going to be all right," he whispered. "All the bad stuff is going away. I can feel it."

She relaxed enough for him to slip his hands between her knees, then for him to run his palms up the insides of her thighs. Only when the crook of each hand was close enough to frame each side of her groin—without ever touching her there—did he pull his hands away. He massaged her calves, then her ankles, took off her sneakers and worked at the soles of her feet.

Finally he stood again and laid his hands back on her head. "Open your eyes," he said.

Naomi did as he asked.

He knelt in front of her and looked into her glistening, green-blue eyes a long time. "It's gone," he said.

"Are you sure?"

"Yes."

Her brow furrowed as she surveyed the internal landscape of her soul. "I think it is." She nodded. "It is. It's gone."

He sat back in his chair and smiled at her.

"Where did it go?" she asked.

"First, into me," he said. "Then to God."

"Do I need to pray to keep it away from us?"

"I think that's a very good idea."

"Then I will," she said. "Every night."

"I will, too," Jonah said. "That way no matter where you are, no matter where I am, we'll be together."

"Forever," she said.

part two

one

His brain burned white hot. His knuckles had gone white. The BMW's stereo blared white noise. He had started out from Canaan with every good intention, driving 480 miles to hike Pennsylvania's Pine Creek Gorge, bathing in crystal clear water, breathing pristine mountain air, purifying himself. But just three days back on the road and he was in agony again, his head pounding, his neck and jaw stiff, his heart and lungs straining. He had swallowed five milligrams of Haldol, even dipped into the precious ruby fluid in his briefcase, but neither had stemmed the tide of evil rising inside him.

Every cell in his body screamed for those he had left behind: Naomi McMorris, Mike Pansky, Tommy Magellan, fifteen other patients he had taken inside him at Canaan Memorial, hundreds before them. He longed to touch their skin, to feel their pain, to see his reflection in their eyes.

He longed, too, for Michelle Jenkins. She had invited him to dinner his last night in Canaan, and he had accepted.

"Where do you go from here?" she asked him at the restaurant.

"I'll take a few weeks to relax before my next

129

assignment," he said, "and then, who knows? I can pretty much take my pick of states."

"Mysterious to the end," she said, with a smile.

With her silky black hair shining and her white teeth glistening, Jenkins looked as beautiful to Jonah as any woman he had ever been with. He wanted her. "I'm sorry we weren't able to get to know one another better," he said. "I know I keep people at a distance." He paused for effect. "Especially when I feel drawn to someone." He watched her face as she received this confession, this ode to what might have been, and saw in her eyes that it had sparked that potent combination of nurturance and sexuality he could elicit from women.

"Why do you put up so many walls?" she asked softly.

"I don't think I know the complete answer to that question," he said. "Part of it has to do with moving again and again when I was a child. Everything I built— friendships, adolescent romances, achievements on the football field—got torn down every year or two. After a while I realized it didn't make sense to put down roots at all."

"Your father's job?"

Jonah nodded. "Railroad. He was an engineer. We went wherever they were laying track. By the time I was twelve, we'd lived in nine states, all over the country."

She tilted her head, stared into his eyes. "You *had* to move with him as a boy. You don't have to *keep* moving as a man. It just feels that way. You could build something that lasts."

"Sometimes I think so," he said, glancing at Jenkins in a way to make her feel that he associated her with his potential for commitment.

She took a deep breath, reached to the center of the

table, and linked pinkies with him. "So I guess it's no accident you waited until your last night in Canaan to spend time with me," she said.

No accident. Nor was it an accident that Jonah felt free to make love with her that evening, free to be with her completely, because he was leaving her forever. Naked together, he anticipated her every movement, unlocked desires tucked deep in her unconscious, touched her and tasted her in ways she could not bring herself to ask for. He made her come again and again with the slightest pressure from his fingertip or tongue in precisely the right places at precisely the right times. And when he did finally penetrate her it was at the very instant she desperately wanted him to, so that they truly began to move as one person, in the ultimate way men and women fantasize about but never quite achieve, because they are separate, autonomous beings.

Not so with Jonah. He could shed his skin, slip inside a woman's, and do everything to her that she would do to herself, if only she knew herself well enough to do it. Because he had become her.

In the haze of her own pleasure, listening to his contrived groans, Jenkins probably failed to notice that he had not ejaculated. He never did during sex. He wanted women to release their warm, wet erotic energies into him, not the other way around. His pleasure was in absorbing theirs.

Now, driving through the night, he had run dry again. Bone dry. And no one could know the depth of his suffering in that desiccation. No one could fathom the horror of living without personal boundaries, without ego, an existence in which the lives of others—their suffering and hopes and fears and passions—became his own, only to be cleaved from him again and again and again. His existence was an endless miscarriage, burying him under layer upon layer of grief—solitary grief, without the closure of a funeral, the solace of a headstone, the comfort of a shoulder to cry on.

Imagine loving so many, then losing every one.

Each of the past two nights he had dreamed the same dream. He was lying on a bed of spring flowers in a lush valley, the sun warming his face, a gentle breeze sweeping over him. He felt truly at peace, connected to all living things, finally healed and whole. He closed his eyes, stretched his limbs, and breathed deeply of the new morning.

He was nearly asleep when he sensed a shadow falling over him. He opened his eyes and saw a radiantly beautiful woman with golden hair, sparkling emerald eyes, and perfect, ivory skin kneeling beside him. "Who are you?" he asked.

When she spoke, it was in the most gentle voice he had ever heard. "Your heart is not your own."

It seemed to Jonah an elegant metaphor for love. "I would gladly give it to you," he said.

"But it isn't yours to give. It hasn't been for a very long time."

How true. How absolutely right. Jonah felt he had finally found a kindred spirit, one who understood his special place in the world, his special burden. "I carry many souls inside me," he said.

The woman began unbuttoning his shirt, laying the cloth aside, kissing his chest.

He tilted back his head and closed his eyes, waiting for her to move to the button at his waist, to the zipper below, to take *him* inside *her*.

"You're so tired," she whispered, running the tip of her tongue down his abdomen. "You need to let go."

"Yes," he breathed. He arched his back with pleasure, lifting himself toward her. And with that he felt the first searing flash of pain over his sternum. He tried to sit up, but could barely raise his head. He glimpsed the blade of a scalpel, wet with blood. His blood. He was desperate to flee, but his hands and feet were frozen. Then he felt her beginning to feast, her razor-sharp teeth ripping through his skin, through muscle, scraping so furiously at the sternal bone below that it began to splinter. The pain was unspeakable, a hellish torture that woke him from sleep, screaming, shaking with terror, his sheets soaked with sweat.

He could find no refuge from his isolation. Not by day. Not by night. And his next hospital assignment was a full week away.

The road was a blur. He was nearly blind with hunger for another human being. He took the next exit, heading onto Route 17, toward the Ottawa National Forest. If he could make it there, he might outlast his cravings. He had enough food and water to camp out a week. He could hike Mount Arvon, climb closer to God, further from temptation.

But God had another test waiting for him. A mile off the exit a man wearing a backpack turned around and held his thumb out for a ride. In the middle of the night. In the middle of nowhere. A man in precisely the wrong place, at precisely the wrong time. Jonah looked away, gritted his teeth, and drove past him. Then, half against his will, as if drawn there by the part of him that was nine-year-old, wheelchair-bound Benjamin Herlihey, his gaze drifted up and to the right, into the rearview mirror.

He saw the man at the side of the road shake his head and throw down his fist in frustration. And he saw something more. The man was wearing a patch over one eye.

A simple thing, that patch. There could be a dozen explanations. A workplace accident. A birth defect. A lazy eye from multiple sclerosis. A retinal hemorrhage from diabetes. A beating. For anyone other than Jonah it would have remained nothing more than a curiosity. Something seen and then forgotten one or two miles down the road. But for Jonah that curiosity landed inside him like a grappling hook, sinking through his flesh, into his soul. It slowed him down, reeled him in, then pulled him to the curb and held him there.

Jonah watched as the man started toward him. He looked slim and strong. He had a spring in his step, even under the weight of his pack.

He walked up to the passenger window.

Jonah turned to him, saw he was about thirty, handsome in a rugged way, with a few days' growth of beard and shoulder-length, reddish hair under a gray-and-black striped ski cap. He lowered the window.

"Any chance you're headed toward Trout Creek?" the man asked nervously.

"Close enough," Jonah said, rubbing his stiff jaw. He forced a smile. "Throw your pack in the back seat."

The man slipped out of his pack, put it in back and climbed in beside Jonah. He extended his hand. "Doug Holt."

"Jonah Wrens." He shook Holt's icy hand.

"I didn't think I'd catch a ride all night. Nobody stops anymore."

"I used to hitch a fair amount," Jonah said, unable to take his eyes off Holt's patch. "I had to, to visit the girl I was dating during med school. I didn't have the money for a bus." He shook his head, as if remembering the lean years. "I can get you pretty much the whole way to Trout Creek."

"You don't know how huge that is," Holt said. "God knows how long I would have . . ." He paused, suddenly aware he was being studied. He touched his eye patch. "BB gun. A buddy of mine. I was five."

Was this Ally Bartlett again, ready to reveal all to Jonah? Was Doug Holt another angel, in the nick of time? "Did you manage to stay friends?" he asked.

"To this day. Only thing is, Troy moved halfway around the world. He's teaching English over in Japan. Plus he's married, three kids. I talk to him a couple of times a year."

That was more information than Jonah had asked for. He savored every word. The pain in his head began to ease. His vision began to clear. He put the car in drive, pulled back onto the road. Maybe he would make it through the night after all. "How about you, Doug? Are you married?"

"Hoping to be," he said. "I'm headed to my girlfriend's parents' place. She's there waiting for me. I'm going to pop the question tomorrow night. Bended knee. The whole nine yards."

"Tomorrow night." Jonah felt excitement begin to eclipse his desperation. "How wonderful."

"She's a great lady."

"In what way?"

Holt shrugged. "That unconditional love thing, you know? She'd stick by me no matter what."

"How did you two meet?"

"Fate."

"Oh?"

"She's a resident in ophthalmology. I went for a checkup with my usual guy, and she was doing some sort of rotation with him." He shrugged. "Weird how things work out, huh? Troy shooting that BB took something away from me, but it gave me back something—twenty-five years later. I never would have met Naomi otherwise."

Naomi. Could that name be a coincidence? Jonah pictured Naomi McMorris sitting in his office. He felt a warm wave of reassurance wash over him. God was still with him. "The Lord works in mysterious ways," he said, smiling at Holt.

Holt smiled back, winked.

Jonah stared at him a few seconds, then turned and looked down the road. His pulse began to race. A dull ache rose up the back of his neck. Because he knew that Doug Holt—if that was even his name—had been lying to him. A man blind in one eye from the age of five never learns to wink, never chooses to close his one good eye and blind himself. Not even for an instant. "She's pregnant, actually," Holt went on, wistfully. "Four months along. So I've got a lot of new things happening in my life. I've got a lot to look forward to."

Jonah didn't hear much excitement in Holt's voice, probably because his supposed engagement and new baby were lies. "Did you tell Naomi that tall tale you told me—the one about your buddy Troy?" he asked. "About being shot in the eye?"

"Sure," Holt said. He shrugged. "I mean, she was working under my doctor."

"Where did it happen, anyhow?"

"What?"

"The accident. The BB."

"The fields in back of my house," Holt said. "There was a pond where we'd horse around, play cowboys and Indians. Troy didn't even know it was a BB gun. It was his older brother's. He took it from his room."

"I see," Jonah said. "Does your handicap allow you to work?"

"I'm an artist," Holt said.

"What sort of art?"

"Glass sculpture, glass jewelry, stained glass."

"How interesting."

"It can be," Holt said. "When the glass does what I want it to do." He paused. "How about you?"

"Psychiatrist."

"Wow. Now *that* sounds interesting."

"It always is. I love being able to find out the truth about people." Jonah looked over at Holt, kept looking at him until Holt grew visibly tense. Then he stared back down the highway. "This may sound bizarre to you, but I'd like to see it."

"My glasswork?"

"No. Your eye. Or whatever's left of it." He glanced at Holt, who suddenly looked very worried. "Is that asking too much?"

"You're kidding, right?"

"I'm quite serious."

One of Holt's hands moved to his door handle. "I promise it's not pretty. It's covered for a reason."

"People always cover up for a reason," Jonah said. "But I've seen—and heard—very ugly things in my life. You can show me." A few seconds passed in silence. "Go ahead."

"I never show anyone."

Jonah forced a smile. "If there's a reason you're wearing that patch other than the one you gave me, you should just tell me."

"What do you mean?"

Jonah slowed the car, pulled to the side of the road. "All I want is the truth, Doug. If that's your name."

Holt's other hand inched toward the electric lock button on the center console.

Jonah dropped his hand to the hunting knife he kept taped to the bottom of his door. It had an eight-inch blade, sharpened to a razor's edge. He didn't want to use it, knew that using it would be a sin against the God he loved, but he was desperate for the truth, even if the only truth he could get from this man would be his genuine panic at having his throat cut. "I'll give you an example. Let's say that patch was just a clever way to get noticed by the side of the road, increase your chances of being picked up. It wouldn't matter now. What matters now is that you be honest about it."

Holt sat motionless and said nothing.

"Just tell me the truth," Jonah said. "I'm begging you."

Holt turned and looked out his window. "Okay," he said. "Here goes." Then, with no more warning than the tensing of his forearms, he pressed the button to unlock his door, then pulled the door handle. His movements were coordinated, but a little too slow. Because as his door was swinging open, Jonah's arm was swinging, the knife in his hand slicing through Holt's carotid arteries, esophagus, and windpipe.

Holt turned and looked at Jonah with the bewildered gaze of all Jonah's victims. His eyes may have focused long enough to see Jonah reaching for him, weeping. And he was probably still alive to hear two words whispered in his ear, words that would have sounded completely sincere, because they came from the bottom of Jonah's heart.

"I'm sorry."

He dragged Doug Holt four feet into the woods and left him there, with his two good eyes staring up at the black sky, his eye patch tied like a tourniquet around the arm Jonah had drawn blood from. He grabbed his pack out of the backseat, dumped it beside him, and turned to go. But then curiosity got the better of him. He turned back, walked over to the pack, and crouched down to see what Holt had been carrying with him—who he had been, after all.

He found the expected items: changes of clothes, a nylon tent, a climber's pick, a squeeze bottle of water. But then he found the unexpected—chapters of Doug Holt's life story.

The first was a summons, dated eleven days before, for Holt to appear before the Trial Court of Bristol County, Connecticut, on charges of marijuana and cocaine possession with intent to distribute. That explained his rudimentary disguise. He was on the run.

Second were two United Airlines tickets to Brazil—one in Holt's name and one in the name of Naomi Caldwell, MD. They were about to leave the country together.

And then Jonah found what cut him to the core: a photograph of a brunette in her early thirties, her hands cradling her pregnant abdomen; a black velvet box with a modest diamond engagement ring inside; and a larger, white cardboard gift box that held a magnificent conch shell of blown glass, a rainbow swirling inside it.

Inside the gift box was a tiny envelope. Jonah opened it and read the card inside:

For Mr. and Mrs. Caldwell,
Please accept this small token of my undying gratitude
for you having brought Naomi into the world. She has
changed my world forever.

—Doug

Undying. Jonah sank to his knees on the frozen earth. Holt had been telling him the truth, even from behind his disguise. Not about everything. Not about running from the law. But about the important things. The woman he loved. The infant about to be born to him. And Jonah, in his arrogance, in his angry panic that he was being duped, that he was being kept from the life blood he so desperately needed and so justly deserved, had failed to resonate with that truth, had failed to follow its path to Doug Holt's heart.

Of all things, he had failed to listen.

Tears streamed down his face. His mind was flooded with questions for Holt. Did he and Naomi plan the pregnancy? How did he feel about becoming a father? What was his relationship like with his own father? Did he know the child's gender? Had they chosen a name?

Holt would have told him. He would have answered those questions and more. Truthfully. And in so doing, he would have made Jonah part of his growing family.

Instead, Holt was dead, and a baby would be born fatherless, with a gaping wound already cut in his psyche.

God had indeed sent another angel, but Jonah had

failed to receive the gift. Failed miserably. He had killed a man and absorbed almost nothing of that man's soul. He had laid waste to him. Obliterated him.

Forever.

As he sped down the highway, he felt self-loathing greater than any that had visited him before. He felt vile. Grotesque. And he felt this all the more because the pain in his head and jaw and heart and lungs were gone. Holt's murder itself, without any potential for his resurrection inside Jonah, had filled the raw void of his own existence.

Only a monster would be satiated by pure destruction.

He thought again of suicide, but fleetingly. He still thirsted for what Christ had promised on the cross. He wanted to be healed in this life. Forgiven. He wanted redemption. Even if he had to risk everything for it. Because then—only then—could he die in peace.

two

The *New York Times* ran Jonah's letter front page. By the time Clevenger drove up outside his office at 9:00 A.M., an army of reporters was waiting for him, thrusting microphones emblazoned with insignia from CNN, Fox, CBS, and Court TV at his window. He looked toward the office, made eye contact with North Anderson standing outside, looking very uneasy, his massive arms crossed over his chest, a folded-up newspaper in his fist.

The reporters surrounded him as he stepped out of his truck, shouldering and elbowing each other for position, shouting questions: *Are you in contact with the FBI? How do you interpret the letter? What do you make of his 300 lovers? Will you respond to him?*

Clevenger gave them the standard "No comment" as he pushed past them, climbed the stairs to the office and escaped inside, followed by Anderson.

Anderson locked the door behind them.

"What the hell is going on?" Clevenger asked.

Anderson handed him the newspaper. "The *Times* ran a letter front page from the Highway Killer."

Clevenger shook his head. "And everyone showed up to get my angle on it?" He started to unfold the paper.

"The letter is to you."

Clevenger stopped, looked back at Anderson.

"He must have seen the news coverage when you turned down the FBI. I guess he liked what he saw."

Clevenger unfolded the paper the rest of the way. His heart began to pound as he read the headline in the upper right-hand corner of the front page: *HIGHWAY KILLER REACHES OUT FOR HEALING.* He read on:

Special to the Times

On March 26, 2003, this newspaper received a letter from an individual purporting to be the Highway Killer, the serial killer responsible for at least 14 deaths across the country. The letter, addressed to our managing editor, is an appeal to Frank Clevenger, MD, the Boston-based forensic psychiatrist best known for solving the murder of infant Brooke Bishop on the island of Nantucket. Factual information enclosed with the letter convinced us of its authenticity.

After careful editorial consideration and with guidance from the Federal Bureau of Investigation, we are printing the letter in its entirety. We reserve the right to publish or to not publish any future correspondence.

"Kane Warner," Clevenger said, looking up.

"Has to be," Anderson said. "Someone had to give the *Times* the green light to publish."

"And convince them to publish it without notifying me."

"That way you couldn't get a lawyer to stop the presses."

"You think it's for real?" Clevenger asked.

Anderson nodded. "Take a few minutes to read it, and let's talk about what we do next."

Clevenger heard the *we* loud and clear. "Thanks," he said.

"Any time." Anderson turned and left.

Clevenger sat at his desk, riveted from the first sentence:

Dr. Clevenger:

I am soaked and filthy with the blood of others, yet I have goodness in my heart. I have no motive to kill, but I cannot stop myself from killing. My hunger for the lives of others is greater than for food or sex or knowledge. It is irresistible.

I have thought of destroying myself. I have made halfhearted attempts. Halfhearted, because destroying the whole of me would be no triumph. Nor would there be triumph in surrendering to any "authority," to then be judged by small-minded men and caged like an animal.

The glory would be in defeating the darkness in my soul, freeing the eternal light to shine. And the only proper judge of my success or failure in that great quest is our Lord Jesus Christ, King of the Universe.

Is not my struggle, after all, a reflection of man's great struggle? Is my existence any less than a microcosm of humanity's hope for the triumph of good over evil? In facing my destructiveness am I not taking the first step toward redemption?

And if I am redeemed, are we not all redeemed in small measure? If I am resurrected, does not all humanity rise with me?

I hear the words of Jung:

"The sad truth is that man's real life consists of a complex of inexorable opposites—day and night, birth

and death, happiness and misery, good and evil. We are not sure that one will prevail against the other, that good will overcome evil, or joy defeat pain. Life is a battleground. It always has been, and always will be; and if it were not so, existence would come to an end."

Help me fight this battle. My Armageddon. Help me be reborn, good and decent, as I once was. Be my healer.

I am male. I am in the middle of my life. I have never been imprisoned. I have no history of psychiatric treatment. I hear no voices. I see no visions. I use no alcohol nor any illicit drug. I have no medical illness.

My IQ is in the range of genius, yet my intellect is no shield from the base needs that overcome me.

Were I sitting with you now, I would tell you that I feel a crushing loneliness, a gaping, raw hole inside me. The pain is simultaneously physical and psychological. It makes me weep like a child. And it is this excruciating isolation that leads me to take the lives of others. Something in witnessing the purity and truthfulness of death connects me to all living things and brings me peace. I am laid to rest beside each of my victims.

They are luckier than I: my rest is never permanent. My hunger begins anew, sometimes hours, sometimes days, sometimes weeks later.

I cannot feed my soul in the usual ways. I have no friends, no loving family. I keep no pet. I have no home. I wander endlessly.

My mother was kind and gentle, a woman beyond reproach. My father was a monster. Perhaps I embody that dichotomy.

I was the product of a normal pregnancy and delivery. I was psychologically and physically healthy as a *child, save for having experienced paralyzing school phobia.*

I had few interests as a young man, but achieved academically with ease, dated frequently, but never married.

I have had over 300 sexual partners in my life. I am heterosexual.

Since you were, no doubt, briefed on my case by the FBI, you know that I take blood from each of my victims. I carry that bit of them with me. A talisman, perhaps.

But I also carry their souls inside me. And in that way, they are still alive.

To save you the energy of wondering, I will tell you that I learned the skill of venipuncture as a decorated army medic. Honorable discharge. No disciplinary action.

My proposal: You may put any question to me. I will tell you everything I can, without risking my freedom (which is simply the freedom to find God, something I do not believe I could achieve while incarcerated, likely on death row). I would like you to try to be equally open with me, to minimize the chances that you and I remaining strangers would cause me to feel even more alone and more in need of the lifeblood of others.

To trust you, I need you to trust me.

You solve crimes? What crimes have been perpetrated upon you? Of what crimes, great or small, are you guilty?

You adopted a troubled boy. Were you a troubled boy? Are you still that boy?

Are you, like me—and like young Billy Bishop—struggling to be reborn?

psychopath

Hold my hand, look into my heart, let me see into yours. Unearth my demons and help me exorcise them from my soul.

— *A Man of God*
They Call the Highway Killer

There are moments in a person's life that are like chemical titration points, that crystallize everything that has come before them and change the very nature of everything that will come after them. They are life-altering and life-defining. For Clevenger, reading the words of the Highway Killer was such a moment. His skin turned to gooseflesh. Shivers ran up the back of his neck. He walked to North Anderson's door.

"What do you think?" Anderson said, swiveling in his desk chair to face him.

"It's for real. He's reaching out."

"What are you going to do?"

"Part of me would like to keep my distance, just to burn Warner, but I don't see how I can anymore."

"Neither do I. If I were you, I'd get down to Quantico and learn everything there is to know about this guy. Visit the crime scenes. View the bodies. Don't take anyone's word for anything. If it's your case, make it your case top to bottom. I'll help any way you need me to."

Clevenger nodded.

"You look worried."

"I don't like the part about Billy," Clevenger said. "I don't want him dragged into this. He's been doing great. At work every day. Clean drug screens. And he's really starting to open up." He shrugged. "He came into my room last night and talked about how much he still craves the pot—and the coke. And he told me more about this girl Casey he's been hanging around with."

"Great."

"But I can never be sure the next tox screen won't turn up dirty. I can never be sure of anything with him."

"I'm sure of one thing about him," Anderson said.

"What's that?"

"He knows what it is to lose someone to murder. Deep down, he knows why you do what you do."

"Think about how many reporters are outside already. Day one. It's only going to get bigger. I don't want him to feel like he's losing me. Nothing would be worth that."

"I think if you tell him that he'll see he never could."

Clevenger dialed Kane Warner. The secretary put him right through.

"Doctor," Warner said.

"If we're going to work together," Clevenger said, "no more surprises. I get blindsided again, I'm gone."

"Fine," he said stiffly.

"Did the *Times* publish everything the Highway Killer wrote?"

"They held nothing back."

"I expect the same."

"I understand," Warner said. "But it will be important to work closely with the team you met here."

"I'd like to come down tomorrow."

"I'll expect you."

"One more question," Clevenger said.

"Okay."

"Why did you decide to print it?"

"It wasn't my decision," Warner said.

"I'm supposed to believe that?"

"I asked the *Times* not to publish it. I think it's much too dangerous for you to play Freud from a distance. If you happen to hit a psychological hot button in one of your little 'sessions,' we might pay for it in body bags."

"If you weren't the one who gave the green light," Clevenger said, "then . . ."

"The newspaper went over my head," Warner said. "To the director's office."

"Jake Hanley?"

"Jake's a friend of the publisher of the *Times*, Kyle Roland. He's also considering a run for Senate back home in Colorado. A serial killer on the loose doesn't do much for his popularity. He wants this thing to be over— no matter how it ends." Warner paused. "May I ask you a question?"

"Shoot."

"You wouldn't work with me a month ago. You turned me down cold. So what gives? Is there finally enough publicity in it for you?"

Clevenger was too angry to answer with anything other than obscenities. So he stayed silent. And in that silence he had to ask himself the same question Warner had put to him. Had he been seduced? Had his fee in narcissism finally been paid?

"You probably aren't sure of the answer yourself," Warner said. "It doesn't matter. We're on the same team now—just a couple of bodies later."

Clevenger cleared his throat. "I'll be there by 10:00 A.M. tomorrow."

"Whitney McCormick will meet you in the lobby. She can start updating you."

Clevenger hung up. He looked out his window at the crowd of reporters. He stood up, drew his blinds, then sat back down at his desk. He reread the letter from the Highway Killer. Then he turned on his computer and began to plan how he would respond.

His goal was clear. He believed all killers had been emotionally murdered themselves. In taking one life or many lives they were replaying their own deaths, casting themselves as aggressors, rather than victims—as powerful, rather than weak. He wanted to slowly, methodically trace the roots of the Highway Killer's violence back to whatever early life traumas had spawned it. He wanted to make him grieve over his own destruction, instead of reenacting it again and again.

This would indeed be a resurrection, a rebirthing of the tortured child inside the killer.

That child had a conscience, could experience guilt, and might be coaxed either to surrender the killer or trip him up.

The child craved intimacy. To have any hope of stemming the Highway Killer's violence, Clevenger would have to provide that intimacy.

But the child was also consumed by fear. Trying to get too close too fast would make him flee.

Clevenger started to type:

I agree to respond to each of your letters. I understand you will tell me everything you can without risking your freedom. I will tell you everything I can without violating the privacy of others, including my son.

I know you are not a killer at heart. Your goodness has been overtaken again and again by something foreign to you. A parasite inside you causes hunger so unbearable that you feed it the lives of others. I will call that parasite the Highway Killer. How shall I address the rest of you?

How did you become infected? What in your life caused you the worst pain? What do you remember being most frightened of as a child? Did it ever become clear why you experienced "paralyzing school phobia"? At what age was that condition worst? What was happening at home at that time?

What did your anxiety feel like—physically and emotionally?

To say that your mother was beyond reproach and that your father was a monster leaves much unanswered. In what specific ways did she demonstrate her goodness, and in what specific ways did he cause you to suffer? Did they divorce? If not, what kept them together? Are they still alive?

To whom were your 300 lovers attracted—the Highway Killer or you? Did they help satisfy his appetite or yours? Is this an appetite for emotional union, sexual union, or both?

What war did you serve in? If in Vietnam, in which provinces? Did you see combat?

If we succeed in exorcising the killer inside you, what will be left? Who are you, absent the Highway Killer?

When were you first aware of his existence?

How do you feel immediately after the Highway Killer strikes? How many times has he killed? List all the places where bodies lie.

You asked several questions of me. To answer the first, the crimes perpetrated upon me include having been beaten and humiliated by my father. Like you, I know something about monstrous men. To answer the second, the crimes of which I am guilty include trying for years to quell my pain with alcohol and drugs.

What drugs have you used to try to subdue the Highway Killer?

What do you do with the blood you take from victims?

Because you obviously have read the words of great men, I close with Thomas Hardy's: "If a way to the better there be, it lies in taking a full look at the worst."

So we begin, two men against one killer.

—Frank Clevenger, MD

Clevenger returned home that evening to find Billy Bishop sitting at the dining room table, in jeans and no top, his "Let it Bleed" tattoo looking especially stark across his perfectly defined back, a pile of books and dozens of photocopied newspaper articles in front of him. "What's all this?" he asked, walking up behind him. Then his heart fell as he scanned the newspaper headlines, all of them about the Highway Killer. The books were about serial killers. A sense of foreboding gripped him.

Billy swung his dreadlocks out of his face as he looked up at him. His eyes were pure excitement. "I figured I might as well help out in my spare time."

"Help out . . ."

"A bunch of reporters found me at the shipyard," he said, speaking a little too quickly. "I told them I had nothing to say. Then I ran and got the *Times* myself. I know you're taking the case. How could you not?" He winked. "By the way, there are about twenty messages from reporters on the machine."

Clevenger looked at the articles, again. They were from papers across the country.

"I've got all the coverage on this guy," Billy said. "Everything from the *Oregonian* to the *Washington Post*."

One thing Clevenger hadn't expected was that Billy, far from resenting his involvement in the Highway Killer case, would be drawn to the case himself. But it made sense. The biggest event in his life had been the murder of his infant sister. And before that tragedy, his own brutal father had victimized him again and again. The snuffing out of lives would always resonate with him.

Clevenger sat at the head of the table. "I don't think this is a good idea," he said. "You've got to focus on staying healthy and getting yourself ready for school."

"I couldn't exactly stay at the shipyard with television crews surrounding me. Mr. Fitzgerald told me to take the day off."

"I understand that," Clevenger said. "And I can see you're trying to be helpful." He took a deep breath and tried to collect his thoughts so he could share them in a useful way. "But I also know what you've been through in your life. And I think you need to build a stronger foundation before getting involved in something like this."

"I'm not *involved*. I'm just . . ."

"I don't want you becoming preoccupied with it."

Billy stared at Clevenger a few seconds. Then he threw his head back and gazed at the ceiling. "I get it," he said. "You're worried if I get into this stuff at all, I'll get *too* into it."

"I think it could take up a lot of time," Clevenger

said. "I think it could be distracting. And I think it's pretty depressing stuff, when you come right down to it. You don't need that kind of negativity in your life right now."

Billy looked at him in the piercing way he sometimes could, when his emotional intelligence was working like radar. "What you *really* think is that I could become obsessed. Maybe even go the wrong way with it and end up like *him*. A killer."

"That's not what I'm thinking," Clevenger said, reflexively. But wasn't it? Wasn't it possible that by immersing himself in darkness Billy could be pulled fully into his own shadow? "You've done good things in your life and bad things, Billy. We're only a month past the fights at Auden. You're only clean from drugs a few weeks. I think dwelling on violence is a mistake. That's all."

"No problem," he said flatly. He shrugged, closed the books. "Feel free to look at this stuff. It took a while to put it together." His upper lip began to tremble. "Some of it's off the Web, but I had to find the rest on microfiche at the library." He got up and started toward his room.

"Hold on," Clevenger called after him. He wanted to say something more to honor the part of Billy's effort that really was an attempt to be helpful—to reach out. "I really do appreciate what you—"

"Sure thing," Billy said, without turning around. He walked into his room and shut the door behind him.

Clevenger got up, walked toward the room. When he'd gotten within a few feet of the door, it opened.

Billy stood in the doorway, staring at the floor. "Can

we just drop it?" he asked. "Can you at least respect me
enough to back off when I ask you to?"

Clevenger nodded reluctantly.

The door closed again.

three

APRIL 1, 2003
CHELSEA, MASSACHUSETTS

The door was still closed at 6:30 A.M. when Clevenger left to take the 8:00 A.M. shuttle to Washington, D.C. He met Whitney McCormick at her office in the main building of the FBI Academy in Quantico. She was decked out in straight-legged black pants, a black leotard, and a black blazer that was the perfect backdrop for her straight blonde hair. She looked every bit as beautiful as the last time Clevenger had seen her.

"Welcome to the team," she said, extending her hand. "Some invitation—from the killer himself."

To focus on raising Billy, Clevenger had dialed down his sensitivity to feminine beauty, but not to zero. As he shook McCormick's hand he didn't miss her soft skin, her long, graceful fingers, her manicured nails, perhaps even a special tenderness in her grip. "I finished the first draft of my response last night," he said. "I brought it with me."

"Great," she said. "I can approve it that much faster." She walked behind her desk, took a seat. "Make yourself comfortable." She nodded at a leather sofa at the side of the room.

"Approve it?" Clevenger said, sitting down.

"It's the way we've structured things with the *Times*. Before they print anything, they'll run it by me. If I think it's questionable, it goes to Kane Warner for a final decision."

"I didn't plan on being edited."

"Relax," she said, in a truly soothing voice. "No one's going to get heavy-handed."

"Thanks for the reassurance," Clevenger said. "But just so I know, what kind of content might be 'questionable'?"

"That's hard to say before I see it," she said. "From your side, I guess an example would be if you inadvertently disclosed sensitive information about the investigation. From the Highway Killer's side, I might censor something that would be unbearable for a victim's family to read—something beyond the pale."

"Okay."

"I suppose you and the Agency could also have a disagreement about how deep to go with this guy," she said, in a less comforting tone. "How far to push him."

"The *Agency*? A minute ago, *you* were vetting my letters."

She smiled. "Count on me to go to the edge with you. Okay? From what you said at the last meeting, I know where you're coming from with this guy. We've got to take the fight to him, not be sitting around waiting for the next body. That's why I broke ranks with Kane over whether to publish the letters at all."

"But . . ."

"But I agree with Kane that there's a risk. It could backfire. He could get worse rather than better."

"No question."

"Then we're all on the same page."

"It's early," Clevenger said. He noticed McCormick's degrees from Yale Medical School and the Yale psychiatry residency on the wall opposite him. Beside them hung a white board filled with half sentences, arrows connecting one thought to another, some words underscored three or four times, some crossed out. "Brainstorming?" he asked, nodding at it.

"More like brain fog," she said. "On the surface this guy gives us everything: the bodies out in the open; an unmistakable signature including severed throats and venipuncture wounds; plenty of fingerprints—even on the stamps he used to send your letter to the *Times*. But none of it leads anywhere. The prints obviously don't match anything in our database. The bodies can be found days or weeks or months after he dumps them. And the victims have absolutely nothing in common."

"He's random because he's out of control," Clevenger said. "From what he wrote in the *Times*, he's not moved to kill by seeing a person of a particular gender or body type or hair color or age. He's driven to kill by loneliness. He strikes out. He isn't hunting for his next twelve-year-old, brown-eyed blonde girl to abduct."

"Brown-eyed blonde girl?" McCormick asked, tilting her head. "Where did that come from?"

Clevenger realized he'd borrowed McCormick's hair and eye color for his example. "Sorry about that."

She half smiled. "Remind me not to make you angry."

"Why would I have to remind you?"

A full smile this time. "As driven as this guy is, he's methodical," she said. "We don't have a single eyewitness catching a glimpse of him. We haven't heard of any close call—somebody escaping. He doesn't leave anything trackable at the scene. That adds up to real self-discipline, real planning, even though he's got us believing he just loses it."

"Maybe he'd like to believe that himself," Clevenger said. "It absolves him of moral responsibility."

"And legal responsibility. It's nice groundwork for an insanity plea when he's apprehended. He can say, 'Hey, look, I couldn't stop myself. Just read what I wrote in the *Times*.'" She paused. "What I've started to wonder about is how he feeds himself short of killing. Because he does go long stretches without taking a life. He must be interacting with people other than his victims in very intimate ways."

"Plenty of sexual partners, for one thing," Clevenger said.

"Those don't necessarily add up to intimacy," she said.

"Agreed."

"You wonder about a truck driver crisscrossing the United States," she said. "He picks up hitchhikers who go on and on about their lives, maybe hooks up with a needy woman here and there at a bar or a restaurant, and plays therapist, maybe hires prostitutes and gets them to spill their guts—and sometimes that's enough. But other times he can't connect. And that's when he takes lives."

"Or when he can't connect deeply enough . . ." Clevenger said.

"Say more."

"Maybe if he gets close enough to a person, truly gets his emotional fix, he lets that person go. If he can't, he kills in order to share the moment of death, to play next of kin at the bedside."

McCormick nodded. "That would explain why people wouldn't struggle very much to get away from him. He's gone a long way toward winning them over."

"And if that's true," Clevenger said, "then there are people out there who have gotten exceedingly close to him—and lived. The ones who bond with him most deeply walk away. They've paid their dues."

"Finding them wouldn't be easy," McCormick said. "They probably have no idea how close they came to being victims."

"They might, deep down." He looked directly at her. "You know how you sometimes meet someone you feel close to right away?"

"I've seen it happen in movies," she said. "In reality, I think it's pretty rare."

McCormick couldn't be accused of flirting. "It is rare," Clevenger said. "That's why when it happens, you don't forget it." He leaned forward. "If I could somehow make the point in the *Times* that our man inspires that kind of feeling," he went on, "we might get people thinking about it. Maybe somebody would call in."

"It's worth a try."

There was a knock at the door.

"Come in," McCormick said.

Kane Warner opened the door. He was dressed to the nines again—this time in a dark blue pinstriped suit, blood-red tie, and white tab-collar shirt. "Dr. Clevenger," he said, sounding like an entomologist identifying a bug he had picked off a blade of grass.

"Kane," Clevenger said.

"If you two can take a break," he said, glancing at McCormick, "we've received a package addressed to Frank Clevenger, MD, care of Whitney McCormick, MD. It came Federal Express, a little over an hour ago. The airbill was typed. The sender's name is listed as

Anna Beckwith. Bastard used her credit card number, too."

Clevenger and McCormick followed Warner to the basement of the Behavioral Sciences Unit, into an observation room with a six-inch-thick tilted wall of glass overlooking another, smaller room with a concrete floor, cinderblock walls, and a polished iron door that looked like the door to a bank vault. A nondescript cardboard box about eight inches tall and twelve inches long, sat atop an elevated concrete slab in the center of the room.

Warner picked up a phone mounted to the wall, spoke into it. "All set," he said.

"Where was it mailed from?" Clevenger asked.

"Upstate Pennsylvania. A little town called Windham, close to New York. He used a Federal Express drop box outside a strip mall."

"Any weight to it?" McCormick asked.

"A little under two pounds," Warner said.

The door to the room opened and a man wearing a welder's face mask and carrying a long, Plexiglas shield walked to the box. He reached his hands through holes in the shield, into explosive-resistant gloves fastened to it. The gloves were fashioned with a carbon fiber blade affixed to the palm. He started to cut the seams of the box.

"We sent agents up to Windham to poke around, on the off chance we'd get lucky," Warner said. "No one who works around the drop box recalled seeing anyone unusual. The agents are canvassing motels and RV parks now."

The man opening the box had finished cutting the

seams and was peeling the cardboard down toward the concrete block.

"Could be a hoax," McCormick said. "With this much publicity, people are going to try to jump on the bandwagon."

Warner shook his head. "We lifted fingerprints from the plastic tape. They match ones from the crime scenes and from the letter to the *Times*."

Clevenger watched as crumpled sheets of newspaper fell out of the sides of the box. He squinted at what was left behind: a large glass conch shell, with a swirl of colors inside it.

"What the hell?" Warner said.

The man opening the box carefully pushed the glass shell aside. Beneath it was a small, handwritten card and a typed letter. Warner spoke into the phone again. "We'll take a look at those as soon as they're processed."

The man gave Warner a thumbs-up.

Clevenger looked to McCormick for an explanation.

"They'll dust them for prints, make sure nothing toxic is on them—like anthrax."

"Will that take long?" Clevenger asked her.

"Two, three hours," McCormick said.

"Why not have him show it to us through the glass right now?" Clevenger asked.

"Listen to you," Warner said to Clevenger. "Hanging on this bloodsucker's every word. You think he's at the edge of his seat, combing the *Times* for your letter to him? He's playing you."

"At least we're finally in the game," Clevenger said.

"There's no reason to wait two hours, Kane," McCormick intervened.

"I guess you're right," Warner said. He winked.

"Whatever you two want." He spoke into the telephone. "Would you bring that card and sheet of paper to the window?"

The man took off the explosive-resistant gloves, set his shield against the concrete block, and pulled on a pair of rubber gloves. He picked up the card and sheet of paper, carried them to the observation window, and held them up toward the glass.

The card was the one Doug Holt had written to his fiancée Naomi's parents, thanking them for bringing her into the world.

The typewritten letter read:

Dr. Clevenger:
I frown upon you working with the FBI, understandable and predictable as that initial instinct on your part might be. I extend my hand to you as a brother. I believe you have the ability to help me end my violence. Trying to end it through my capture is a waste of our good time and energy. Let small minds busy themselves with such foolishness.

Have you read Dr. McCormick's writings? They are the writings of a hunter, not a healer. A stalker for the government. She fails to see, as Aleksandr Solzhenitsyn did, that "the line dividing good and evil cuts through the heart of every human being."

Even her own heart.

The attempt to cage me, perhaps to execute me, to deprive me of my God-given right to conquer the evil inside me, can only inflame that evil. Could anyone, after all, fault a lion for turning on one sighting him through crosshairs?

Imagine how violated you or Dr. McCormick would

feel if I were intent on cutting short your journey toward healing.

—A Man of God
They Call the Highway Killer

P.S.

Kindly forward this card and glass sculpture to the parents of Dr. Naomi Williams of Trout Creek, Michigan. Their future son-in-law Doug Holt made the shell in honor of their daughter. He would have wanted them to have it. So do I.

Naomi should have her lover's body.* His soul dwells inside me.

---

*Michigan, Route 17 East, one mile off Route 45 North

The Behavioral Sciences team met with Clevenger in the situation room.

"It's a direct threat," Bob White, from the Criminal Investigative Analysis Program, said, looking down the long table at him. "We should reexamine this whole public psychotherapy idea. He's telling us right out of the gate that the risk is too high."

Kane Warner nodded.

Clevenger leaned forward in his seat. "I certainly don't like the idea of him threatening anyone," he said. "But it may actually be a gain, rather than a loss."

"A gain?" Warner asked.

"We've interrupted his pattern without printing one response in the *Times*," Clevenger said. "Until now he's been targeting strangers, killing at random. If he's really starting to circle this close, to attach his rage to me or to Whitney, we may be able to nail him sooner than I thought."

"He's invisible," White said. "Just because he comes

close—even close enough to kill one of you—doesn't mean we get much of a shot at him. He can disappear back onto the highway, more famous than ever."

"Dorothy?" Kane Warner said, looking at Dorothy Campbell, who ran the PROFILER computer system.

"It's certainly the case that maintaining a dialogue with a subject increases the odds of an arrest," she said. "That's been true for everyone from serial killers to hijackers to the Unabomber. It would have been true at Waco. The wrinkle here is that we're dealing with someone extremely intelligent who obviously has insight into the way we work and—at least in Whitney's case—who we are."

"It's not like he had to break code," McCormick said. "The switchboard will give anyone my name. My photograph is on the Bureau's website."

"My only point," Campbell told McCormick kindly, "is that there is a danger he's manipulating us—even you."

"To what end, Dorothy?" Kane Warner asked.

"To drag us in over our heads," she said. "To get the Bureau deeply involved with him when his sole intention—as Bob already alluded to—may well be to grandstand, to make a name for himself. The letter to the *Times* certainly fits that paradigm." She paused. "So would killing one of the people searching for him."

"He can do that without the *New York Times*," Clevenger said.

"But *with* the *Times*," Campbell said, "he brings millions of people along for the ride. He becomes the most famous serial killer ever. It's one thing to taunt the FBI. It's another to target agents—or consultants."

"I think this guy is setting us up," White said.

John Silverstein, White's partner at CIAP, shook his head. "Maybe he is," he said. "But I still think we have to stay the course. We've been looking for a chance to accelerate the investigation. This is it. We can't back off when he pushes the envelope."

"I don't buy the idea he's dragging us in over our heads," McCormick said. "I think he's hoping we back off. He's trying to scare us away."

"How do you figure?" White asked doubtfully.

"He's the one under seige—psychologically," McCormick said. "If Dr. Clevenger succeeds, then our man is going to face demons his unconscious mind is desperate to keep buried. The killer inside him is looking for a way to short-circuit the therapeutic process and get on with the bloodshed."

Clevenger thought about that. It made sense. "And if we do back off," he said, "he can tell himself he reached out, to no avail. Nobody would help him. He can go on killing with a clearer conscience." He paused. "I think I should call his bluff and reassure him I'm going it alone, that my goal is to heal him, not get him arrested."

"Which it has to be, for this to work," McCormick said, looking directly at Clevenger. "If we capture him, it's going to be because of that healing, not in spite of it. If you do your job, and we do ours, we'll get him."

"I think you should reconsider," Warner told her. "You're overestimating how amenable sociopaths are to psychotherapy of any kind, let alone therapy that unfolds in the public eye. And you're underestimating the personal danger involved."

"I don't think we have a better idea," McCormick said. "And I don't think the public trust is well served if

I focus on keeping myself safe, at the expense of the next victim."

Warner took a deep breath, let it out. "I don't see Director Hanley vacating his original position without a unanimous request from the team." He made eye contact with Bob White, who shook his head in dismay.

"Don't pin this one on me," McCormick said. "Jake Hanley's door is never closed. Anyone who feels strongly we should pull the plug on this should go to him."

"*I* don't have that kind of pull," Warner said. He winked at her.

John Silverstein winced.

Dorothy Campbell cleared her throat.

McCormick lost her game face. "What's that supposed to mean?"

"Nothing," Warner said.

"You actually think Jake Hanley follows my lead?" McCormick asked.

"I'm not trying to get under your skin, Whitney," Warner said. "But I'm not going to pretend the playing field is level on this one. The McCormicks are very important to the director right now. If you don't want to believe that, that's your own business." He gave her an arrogant shrug of his shoulders. "I didn't mean any disrespect."

"Of course you didn't," she said.

The room fell silent.

Warner started collecting the papers in front of him. His cell phone rang. He reached inside the breast pocket of his suit jacket, took it out, and clicked it open. "Kane Warner," he said. A pause. "Very good. I'll make sure Dr. Hiramatsu is notified." He snapped the phone shut. "The state troopers in Michigan found Doug Holt's body," he said, "right where our man said it would be. They're bringing it in by helicopter."

The silence in the room grew heavier.

"Does anyone have anything else right now?" Warner asked, looking around the table.

A few people shook their heads.

"Very good, then," Warner said.

"What was that about?" Clevenger asked McCormick as they headed back to her office. "My dad," she said. "Dennis McCormick."

"*The* Dennis . . ." Clevenger said, but stopped himself when he saw that the answer was already on her face. He was suprised at himself for never making the connection. Whitney McCormick's father was a top FBI agent, turned U.S. congressman, turned political fund-raiser. He had helped crack the Night Stalker and Son of Sam cases before leaving to run for office. More recently, he had helped elect conservative Republican candidates across the country.

"Kane thinks my father has the power to influence decisions at the Bureau. He also thinks my father got me my job."

Clevenger said nothing.

McCormick stopped and faced Clevenger. "Go ahead. Ask."

"Okay," Clevenger said, looking into McCormick's eyes. "Can your father influence Bureau decisions?"

"I don't know," she said.

"Sounds like an honest answer."

"You didn't ask the tough part of the question."

Clevenger hesitated.

"You won't hurt my feelings."

"Did your father get you your job?" he asked.

"I don't know," she said. Her shoulders seemed to sag slightly.

"Another honest answer. Now can I ask you the only question that matters?"

McCormick nodded.

"Do you deserve your job? You're, what, thirty-five? Chief forensic psychiatrist for the FBI? You really that good?"

Something new came into McCormick's face—a mixture of amused pride and fierce determination. It answered the question without her having to say a word.

"I think so, too," Clevenger said. "I've worked with the best forensic psychiatrists in the country. You don't take a backseat to any of them."

She smiled. "Does that mean I have carte blanche to edit your letters to the *Times*?"

"Definitely not."

"Didn't think so."

four

On Thursday, April 3, 2003, the *New York Times* ran Clevenger's letter to the Highway Killer word-for-word, including an assurance from Clevenger that he would not work directly with the FBI. On April 5 they received the Highway Killer's response, sent Federal Express from a drop box outside an office building in Rogers City, Michigan, on Lake Huron, near the Mackinaw State Forest:

Dr. Clevenger:

My earliest memory (changed only slightly to avoid jogging the memories of others) is of a birthday party given me by my mother when I turned four. It was held at a little park near my home. A sunny day in May. Green grass. Flowers. A gentle breeze. A swingset and slide. A jungle gym.

My mother had rented a carousel with brightly painted, carved wooden horses for me and a dozen friends to ride. She laid out a banquet of peppermint-stick ice cream, cotton candy, and cookies. Party favors.

These were rare extravagances. We had very little.

I loved that day. I remember feeling overwhelming pride. This was my *birthday. These were* my *friends.*

psychopath

They doted on me, brought me Hot Wheels cars, stuffed animals, books, paints.

But even more than my birthday and my friends, there was my mother—pretty, vibrant, above all else kind and gentle. Riding my carousel horse, I would catch glimpses of her smiling, laughing, blowing me a kiss. Snapshots of an angel. She gave me a special gift that day which I keep with me even now, a trinket that reminds me I was once pure and vulnerable—a loving child who had not hurt a soul.

My friends and I played for hours. I walked my mother home, feeling like a conquering hero, carrying my booty, my head spinning with what wonders might await a boy as old as four. I was on the cusp of learning to read, of tying my own shoes, of riding a two-wheel bicycle.

The door to our house was open. My mood fell. My father was at home. He came at us the moment we walked inside, backhanded my mother to the floor, ranting that he'd told her there was no money for the "little bastard's fucking party." I stepped between the two of them, and he backhanded me. My vision blurred. I fell to the floor. I tasted blood in my mouth. My front tooth wiggled in its socket as my tongue moved against it. I saw ripped pages from my books, torn pieces of my stuffed animals, my Hot Wheels cars rain down around me. Then I watched as he crushed his heel into each and every one of the cars.

My mother cowered in the corner, weeping. I wished I were older, bigger, stronger, able to defend her. She held a single finger to her beautiful lips, warning me to stay quiet, then blew me another kiss. And even with the taste of blood in my mouth, I felt safe and secure, even victorious over the monster who called himself my father.

I was victorious, with blood in my mouth. *At four years old. Does that account for the calm I feel tasting the blood of others?*

Or is the better clue the helplessness I felt that day, the absolute impotence to help someone I loved. Because in killing, as in sex, there is an undeniable potency, an overtaking, a terrible and final triumph.

There is also union. Did my mother and I die a spiritual death together in that little house of horrors? In embracing a dying man or woman am I returning to her arms, as I sometimes long to do?

Without addressing your direct questions about my immediate family (which might contribute to identifying me), suffice it to say that my father is dead in my life. My mother will always be alive for me.

To answer another of your questions, I believe my anxiety attached itself to school only because I was separated from the person I adored. Perhaps I worried about her safety at home. I cannot recall.

I do remember how the anxiety felt. I was dissolving. There was no physical pain, rather a sense of utter disorder. Entropy. Panic that my reality, my self was adrift and might drift away. Forever.

I feel that same anxiety when my impulse to take a life is greatest. But now physical pain is a major component of my suffering. Terrible headaches. Jaw pain. Palpitations. Shortness of breath.

After killing, all these symptoms abate. I experience profound peace. Perfect unity with the universe.

I have tried alcohol and marijuana to quiet the Highway Killer, to no avail.

psychopath

What to call the frightened boy inside me? How ought my healer address the part of me that swallowed blood on the floor of my parents' home or wept for my mother in the school yard? That good child? Call him Gabriel, a messenger of God, an echo of my innocence.

To give you the final resting place of every body would be premature. Our relationship has only begun. But I do understand the importance families place on bodily remains. All will be returned in time. To begin, search the first fifty yards off Exit 42, Route 70, near Moab, Utah.

Have you ever wanted to kill, Frank? Did you use alcohol and drugs to blunt that impulse? Do you work to understand murderers in order to understand yourself?

How did your father humiliate you? Be specific. If you wish me to continue being forthcoming with you, be so with me.

You cannot hope to reach the core of my psychopathology from a distance.

—A Man of God
They Call the Highway Killer

Within a few hours Clevenger was flying out of Boston to meet Whitney McCormick at the site the Highway Killer had identified in Utah. He had arranged for North Anderson to look in on Billy while he was away.

He started to work on his response during the flight. He wanted to empower Gabriel, the part of the killer that remained innocent and decent.

He believed the main reason Gabriel could not stop the murders was that he was weak—too pure, too good, entirely split off from the dark side of his nature, the "shadow" side that included aggression.

Gabriel was all compassion, a reflection of his mother. The Highway Killer was all rage, a reflection of his father.

To take control, Gabriel would have to tap into the dark side. Like a surgeon cutting out a tumor, he would have to take a scalpel to his own soul and wield it decisively.

The Highway Killer was right to insist Clevenger tell him the humiliations he had suffered as a child. He was right to ask whether Clevenger's work searching for murderers reflected a fascination with destructiveness. Because he needed to learn by example how to transmute his own rage into the desire to protect others.

You cannot hope to reach the core of my psychopathology from a distance.

Clevenger would have to lead with his own scars, his bonafides as a man who remembered what it was to suffer as a boy.

The thought frightened him, partly because he didn't relish the idea of revisiting his traumas, partly because millions of people would read things about him that were intensely personal—and embarrassing.

That included North Anderson. And Kane Warner. And Whitney McCormick. And Billy.

What was the real risk, though? Abandonment? Isolation? Did he not believe in his heart of hearts what he would have told a patient: that revealing oneself—especially the parts that beg to be kept under wraps—is the path to genuine love and self-esteem?

If he couldn't bear to tell his truth in the *New York Times,* how could he ask Gabriel to?

You cannot hope to reach the core of my psychopathology from a distance.

He picked up his pen and started to write:

Gabriel:

My father, now deceased, humiliated me in usual and unusual ways. When he was drunk he used a belt on me. I learned not to hide from him because it made the beatings worse once he found me. I remember wondering how someone struggling just to stand up could ferret me out of the most remote corner of the house—deep inside a closet, curled under a bed, huddled behind an old coat hanging in the basement.

Clevenger let his head fall back against his head rest, remembering. He could almost smell his father's alcoholic breath, see his bloodshot eyes, eyes that stayed frighteningly steady even when he was lashing out. He took a deep breath, then leaned forward to write more.

He would come home ready for a fight. Unlike your mother, mine lacked the courage to absorb his rage. She often greeted him with an overblown complaint about some wrong I had done her during the day. An untidy room. A half-eaten meal. Real or imagined "backtalk."

It got to the point that I would meet him at the door with her, to get it all over with.

Another memory flashed across his mind, then begged to stay off the page. He forced himself to write it out:

I would wear nothing under my jeans because my father yanking down my underwear felt too humiliating and too frightening. More than once, I thought he especially enjoyed that part. And I didn't know if his enjoyment was pure sadism or partly sexual. I suppose I didn't want to know, probably still don't.

Sober, he was even more creative, opting for psychological over physical torture. One of his favorites was to set me up by telling my mother and me that we would be going to an amusement park or to the beach or to buy the dog I desperately wanted. We might get down the street or even to the parking lot of a carnival. And then he would shake his head and laugh. Only the punch line varied:

"You think you're going to play games and go on rides with a room that looks like yours? Give me a break."

"You think I'm going to give you responsibility for a dog when you can't take responsibility for yourself? Give me a break."

"You think you're gonna lay around on the beach when you've got homework to do? Give me a break."

Looking back, the strangest part of the whole tired routine was how many times I fell for it, how much I wanted to believe in his capacity for kindness, how much hope I had that my world might turn bright—even for a day.

I hated him. At some level I still do, even knowing he was a broken man who was suffering greatly himself.

As a child I thought of killing him more than once. Is that killer still inside me?

Clevenger put his pen down and laid his head back again.

The thud of the plane landing at Canyonlands Field Airport awakened him. He met Whitney McCormick at the Wayne County state police barracks. They headed down Route 70 in a state police van with two troopers and Dr. Kent Oster, the county coroner.

A morning of freezing rain had yielded to late afternoon bright sun. As they approached Moab, Route 70 offered up shimmering vistas as it coursed through the San Rafael desert, skirted the majestic Book Cliffs and Arches National Park, then curved north toward the Colorado Canyons.

They pulled over at Exit 42. After just fifteen minutes of searching, Trooper Gary Novick yelled for the others.

When Clevenger reached him McCormick was already there.

"It's bad," she said, staring down a path of matted weeds.

Clevenger looked off in the direction of McCormick's gaze and saw a decaying female body, fully clothed in a simple, floral pattern dress and mint green cardigan sweater. He started toward it, stopped after three steps. The head had been severed from the body. He scanned the ground and saw it several feet away in a pile of leaves, eyes open, staring back at him, wisps of gray hair catching the wind. "My God," he muttered.

Dr. Oster knelt beside the corpse, craned his neck to study the wound. "He's a powerful man," he said. "The spinal column is cut cleanly." He leaned even closer. "She's been here several months, at least," he said. He pulled on surgical gloves, peeked under the neck of the woman's dress, glanced over at the leathery, disembodied face. "Seventy. Maybe seventy-five." He stood up, walked over to the head, and crouched down beside it. "Obvious traumatic facial injuries. We're talking multiple fractures—jaw, zygomatic arch. The frontal sinuses are crushed."

"This isn't the kinder, gentler Highway Killer," said Jackie McCune, the other trooper. "He got a little carried away this time."

"Overkill," McCormick said. "This one got to him."

The troopers started to comb the area for clues.

Clevenger walked to the body. He stared down at the woman's exposed arms. "I don't see any sign he took blood from her," he said.

Oster joined him. He gently raised each arm to inspect the antecubital fossa. "No venipuncture site," he said. "There could be one elsewhere. I'll certainly flag that issue for the pathology team at the Bureau."

Novick came out of the woods carrying a handbag. "Ten yards in," he said. He held up a driver's license. "Paulette Bramberg. Seventy-three years old. Lived out on Old Pointe Road." He looked at Clevenger and McCormick. "That's about ten miles from here. I'll send someone by."

five

It had started to sleet. Both Clevenger's and McCormick's flights were delayed a couple of hours, so they grabbed dinner at the airport.

"This one breaks the mold," she said.

"In more ways than one. I know we've been saying there's no demographic pattern linking the victims," Clevenger said, "but this is the first elderly female victim we know of."

She shook her head. "Why didn't we see that before?"

"It's hard to see a hole in a pattern as diffuse as the one the Highway Killer has created," Clevenger said. "I think Paulette Bramberg is the very center of that pattern. The hot spot. I think she triggered something explosive in him."

"If we're right about his age, she was old enough to be his mother. But he worships his mother. Or says he does." She sipped her sparkling water.

"Idealizes her," Clevenger said. "No one is all good. But with his father abusing him every day, he needed to believe someone loved him perfectly. My guess: she ultimately let him down big-time, and he's never dealt with it."

"Well, let's steer clear of that issue for now. We don't need him connecting with whatever reservoir of rage shifted him from cutting throats to severing a head."

"I don't think there's any way to put the genie back in the bottle," Clevenger said.

The waiter appeared at the table. "Everything all right for now?"

Clevenger glanced at McCormick, who nodded. "Fine," he said.

McCormick picked up where they had left off. "Just don't mention it."

"He sent us to find one body out of who knows how many. Consciously or unconsciously he wants to talk about what we found. And the biggest thing we found is the overkill."

McCormick shook her head. "If you had a patient in psychotherapy who made a stray comment that made you think he might have been abused as a child, you wouldn't necessarily dwell on it. You might just file it in the back of your mind, bring it up much later—and very cautiously."

"You might, you might not."

"My point is you wouldn't want to cause a meltdown by going too far too fast."

"He didn't make a stray comment. He decapitated somebody. He's not being subtle."

She smiled. "Write your letter, and we'll argue it out then."

"Why not now?"

She sidestepped the comment. "Have you started it? The letter?"

Clevenger nodded.

"Want to give me an early look?"

He felt a familiar hesitancy and pegged it as resistance, the trepidation he had felt with his own psychoanalyst before laying himself bare.

"I have to read it eventually," she said.

He reached inside his back pocket, unfolded the letter, and handed it to her.

She read it, glancing up at him a few times with a combination of worry and warmth in her eyes. She placed the sheet of paper on the table. "I didn't know you'd been through anything like that."

"It's not something I would normally publicize," he said.

"You sure you want to?"

"No," he said. "But he told me up front that this is quid pro quo. What I give, I get. And I believe him."

"What if he asks for more than you can deliver? Isn't anything off-limits?"

"I have to go the extra mile. Because, ultimately, I'm going to ask even more of him. I'm going to ask him to surrender his freedom."

"What's the one thing you wouldn't want to tell him?"

Clevenger smiled. "You, first."

McCormick balked. "Here's my point: whatever that thing is, it's your ultimate bargaining chip. Don't put it on the table too soon."

"Good advice."

"Occasionally I come through." A few seconds passed. She put her fork down and looked at him, tilting her head. "Okay, I'll go first."

He figured she was about to offer up a joke. "You sure you want to put it on the table so soon?"

"Why not?" She blushed in the lovely way she had a week before in her Quantico office. "My father's been such a powerful force in my life that every other man has paled by comparison."

Clevenger was taken aback by the revelation.

"I mean, it's definitely not a sexual thing," she hurried to add. "But he's such a talented man. He's interesting on so many levels. And he's always taken very good care of me. When I'm troubled by something he listens to me. *Really* listens."

"And you haven't been able to find that in anyone else."

"I thought I had a few times, but it didn't last very long. It seems like once you go to bed with a guy, he shuts down emotionally, instead of opening up. I don't know if that's about me, or them. And I don't know if it's all men or just the ones I pick."

"Who have you picked?" Clevenger asked.

"Surgeons, ever since medical school," she said. "A neurosurgeon. Plastic surgeon. Ophthalmologist. Even a podiatrist."

"Not exactly listening arts."

She took a deep breath. "Maybe if I hadn't had my father's complete attention I'd be willing to settle for less."

"Or maybe if you didn't settle for less you'd feel like you were trading him in, betraying him."

That registered with her. "Possible . . ."

"Bottom line—you don't need to settle at all," Clevenger said, surprising himself with the obvious affection in his voice.

Her eyes showed she liked hearing it. "Your turn," she said. "What's the one thing you wouldn't want to publish in the *New York Times*?"

The answer came pretty quickly. "I think being

beaten by my father . . ." He stopped himself, squinted to see through to the real truth at the back of his mind. "I think he made me question whether I was worth anything—as a person. As a man. I think my whole life has been about proving that I am."

"Just you?" she asked. "Or are you out to prove everyone is worthwhile at some level? Even killers. Even the Highway Killer."

Now Clevenger was the one taking a deep breath, letting it out. He found himself thinking not only of his life, but of Billy Bishop's. "When your own father doesn't see you as a person, you have to work hard to see yourself as one, to see the part of yourself that's real and substantial—the part that really is worthy of love. Maybe it got to be a habit with me. I probably want to do for everyone what he couldn't—or wouldn't—do for me." His throat felt tight, maybe because he had said enough, maybe because he had said too much. "You know?" he managed.

McCormick answered by sliding her hand across the table, into his.

He ran his thumb along hers, then down the ball of her hand, along the inside of her palm.

"I see you," she said.

The sleet had turned to sheets of rain. The only thing clear about the night was that nothing would be flying out of Canyonlands Field. Clevenger and McCormick headed to the airport Marriott in a taxi.

Clevenger called Billy on the way.

"Hey," he answered. He sounded tired.

"How are you?"

"Fine," he said dismissively.

"I'm rained in here for the night. Why don't we sit down and talk when I get back tomorrow."

"Sure."

"I should be home by three or so."

"Whenever. I'll be here."

"Listen," Clevenger started, "I really miss..." But Billy had already hung up. The sting showed on Clevenger's face as he clicked off his phone.

"He's sharing you with the Bureau," McCormick said. "And the Highway Killer."

Clevenger nodded.

"Maybe you should bring him to Quantico with you next time. We could give him the VIP tour."

"I want to keep him away from what I do," Clevenger said. "He's seen enough violence."

McCormick nodded halfheartedly.

"What are you thinking?" Clevenger asked her.

"It's really not my business," she said.

"Pretend it is."

She nodded. "He ended up living with you because of what you do. You *were* a forensic psychiatrist, after all, when you popped into his life and saved him from going to jail forever."

"And?"

"And you're still a forensic psychiatrist. Why should you pretend otherwise?"

"He's had trouble with violence and drugs lately," Clevenger said.

"And you worry that if he gets too close to your work he could lose it. You think he could become much more violent."

Billy had taken the same message from Clevenger's concern. "Maybe," Clevenger said.

"Interesting," she said.

"What do you mean, *interesting*?"

"You sure you're not projecting? According to the letter you just showed me you're worried there might be a killer deep inside *you*. That doesn't mean there's one inside him."

"I see what you're saying."

"That's what people usually say when they disagree with what they've heard."

Clevenger smiled at her. Maybe it would be better to invite Billy into his professional life, even its darkest corners. Maybe Billy was less fragile than Clevenger thought. But it still seemed risky.

"So . . ." McCormick said. "I should be up front— we're booking two rooms."

"We can book three, if you want," Clevenger said. He took her hand. "I'm in no rush, Whitney." Speaking her name made him feel warm. "Just so you know, though, I won't stop listening to you after we start making love."

"If we ever make love."

"If," Clevenger allowed.

McCormick moved her hand to his knee.

Clevenger stayed up past midnight, finishing off his letter to Gabriel, aka the Highway Killer:

As a child I thought of killing him more than once. Is that killer still inside me?

No doubt. Though embryonic. And the more I can touch that unborn part of me, the more I can feel the gut-level helplessness and rage my father's violence spawned, the less likely it is to ever be born.

I accept my pain. You refuse yours. You describe feeling victorious "with blood in your mouth" because you knew you had your mother's love. But your sense of triumph was only a defense against deeper feelings of terror and weakness. As a four-year-old you never truly faced the horrible truth that it was your blood leaking from your mouth, that you were powerless to protect yourself, and that no one else would or could protect you.

Now you seek the ultimate power over others—whether they live or die—as if that could erase your humiliation and helplessness.

You speak of experiencing great physical pain—migraines, jaw pain. You feel terrible anxiety—palpitations, shortness of breath. But I doubt you feel gut-level sadness or rage. Because the worst of what you went through as a child remains locked in your unconscious.

What trauma have you failed to look at, Gabriel? What buried fury exploded when you were with Paulette Bramberg? What was it about an elderly female (a woman the age of your mother?) that caused you to completely lose control, so that it was no longer enough to be with someone dying, but necessary to kill so brutally. Monstrously. And why did you take no blood from her? Would it be poison to have Paulette Bramberg inside you?

Or was Paulette Bramberg's sin simply that she remained aloof from the Highway Killer, keeping her distance, never coming to feel the extraordinary and instant intimacy I believe you can inspire in others, so that they open up their hearts in a way they never have before; open up to a stranger in a way they would remember all their lives were their lives not cut short?

I asked you for the remains of all the Highway

Killer's victims. You gave me a body different than the rest. Why?

I believe finding the answer will be the beginning of the end of the Highway Killer.

There was a knock at the door to his room. He looked at his watch. 12:50 A.M. "Who is it?" he called out.

"Whitney."

He walked to the door, opened it. She was standing outside, barefoot, in faded blue jeans and a worn, gray FBI sweatshirt. Dressed down, she looked even more stunning.

"Couldn't sleep?" he asked.

"I'm glad we booked two rooms," she said.

"Okay . . ."

"But I don't think we should use both."

Clevenger took her hand, pulled her into the room and into his arms, then gently pushed her against the door as it closed. They kissed deeply, yielding to each other's lips and tongues, feeding one another's hunger. Then, without warning, McCormick pushed him away, almost angrily. She grinned at his surprise, pulled her sweatshirt over her head and dropped it to the ground. She was naked from the waist up. He stepped closer, reached out and brushed his fingers lightly over her breasts, watched her nipples rise at his touch. Then he sank to his knees, unbuttoned and unzipped her jeans, and kissed the lowest part of her abdomen. "I wanted you the first time I saw you," he whispered.

"That could be a bad sign," she said, her words trailing off as Clevenger pressed his hand between her legs.

"Could be," he said. He stood, picked her up in his arms, and carried her to the bed.

They made love tenderly at first, then furiously, two people living on the edge, falling into one another, releasing their passions and frustrations and hopes and needs until they were spent and lay quietly looking into each other's eyes.

"You've been with a lot of women," she said.

"Excuse me?" he deadpanned. "I wasn't listening to you."

She laughed. "Fuck you," she said.

Then they made love again.

APRIL 6, 2003

LEAVING UTAH

Clevenger showed McCormick his finished letter just before they boarded their flights, hers scheduled for 12:25 P.M., his for 12:50 P.M.

She shook her head. "Look," she said. "I promised to back you up, and I will. But you're going for the jugular right away, and I want you to think it over. As he bleeds out psychologically, he could spill a lot of other people's blood."

"Sooner or later, he's going to have to come face-to-face with his demons," Clevenger said. "It might as well be sooner."

An overhead speaker announced final boarding for McCormick's flight.

"If he responds negatively in his next letter, we reassess," she said.

"Deal."

She turned for her gate.

"I'll miss you," Clevenger said, surprised again by his

own words. It had been a long time since he'd allowed himself to care about a woman. It made him feel anxious.

She turned around, self-consciously checking to make sure Clevenger hadn't been overheard by anyone, like one of the state troopers, a cagey reporter, or an undercover FBI agent working the case. Seeing no one, she placed her palm over her heart, then held it out to him.

Jonah Wrens had heard—and seen—everything. He was sitting at the gate in a light gray, pinstriped wool suit, light blue tab-collar shirt, and blue-on-blue striped tie, his briefcase at his feet, pretending to read the Salt Lake *Sentinel and Telegraph*. His heart was pounding. His eyes ached. He had reached out. He had trusted. And he had been betrayed. Clevenger had never intended to join him in his struggle for redemption. He wanted to cage him. He had promised not to work with the FBI, but had gone right along working with them—with Whitney McCormick, the huntress.

Through binoculars, from his perch on a steep hill half a mile away, Jonah had watched the Utah State Police van pull to the side of the road off Exit 42, had waited for each person to step out, praying that Clevenger would not be among them. But then he had seen him, seen him fully for the fraud that he was. And he had felt the all too familiar loneliness begin to gnaw at his soul, hollowing him out, leaving him empty and in agony.

The pain was even worse now. He needed to fill himself up, to fortify his marrow with the lifeblood of another. And who better to feed him than the man who had promised to relieve his suffering.

He stood up from his seat at the gate, reached through a hole in the front pocket of his pants and gripped the handle of the hunting knife taped to his leg. He twisted it free. Then he started toward Clevenger, picturing how he would smile at him as though they were old friends, surprise him with an embrace, then drive the blade up under his sternum, piercing the left ventricle of his heart, at the same time whispering in his ear how much his own heart ached, how desperate he had been for healing, how Clevenger had been his last chance, his only hope. Then he would simply walk away, leaving Clevenger's body behind, escaping with what he could of the man's spirit, the pure truth in his dying eyes.

Maybe that, after all, was the only genuine part of Clevenger to be had.

He closed to ten feet . . . nine . . . eight . . . and then Clevenger suddenly shifted his gaze and made eye contact with him. For an instant or two, no more. The window was there and then it was gone. But through that window Jonah thought he saw straight into Clevenger's soul, saw something of rare intelligence, powerful and even fierce, but also something injured and in need, something empty and alone. He saw parts of himself. And that reflection weakened his grip on the hunting knife and sapped his rage and made everything perfectly clear to him.

He remembered the Dean of Johns Hopkins Medical School, Jonah's mentor when he was a student there, telling him that life would hold such moments— moments of epiphany—but he had never experienced one before. Now he saw the greater plan the Lord had in mind for him: to be healed, but also to heal.

What a glorious and complete circle: he and

Clevenger redeeming one another. Two psychiatrists joining hearts and minds, becoming one.

Who was to say, after all, whether he had reached out for help to Clevenger or Clevenger had reached out to him? Wasn't it plain that the hand of God had directed them to one another? Wasn't it true that he never would have known of Clevenger but for a news broadcast linking the two of them? And hadn't it been obvious—even to the FBI—that Clevenger's whole professional life had led him to this moment?

As Jonah walked past Clevenger he heard, as if for the first time, Clevenger's words of farewell to Whitney McCormick. *I'll miss you.* And he remembered seeing in Clevenger's expression that those words came directly from his heart. Clevenger was falling in love with a woman who could not love, a woman devoid of empathy, a woman who would drag him into a black hole of despair.

Jonah could save him. Jonah could fix what was broken inside Clevenger, whatever fractured pieces of his psyche were getting caught in McCormick's sticky web. And in the process, in God's mysterious way and in God's good time, Jonah had complete faith that he would be saved as well.

six

Back in Chelsea, Billy Bishop was finally waking up. It was 1:10 P.M. He propped himself on an elbow and looked at sixteen-year-old Casey Simms still asleep on the mattress beside him, lying on her side, her long, auburn curls draped over her shoulder, her navel pierced with a diamond, a bar code like the ones scanned in a checkout line tattooed across the small of her back.

They'd been up past 3:00 A.M., having sex again and again, and talking about everything and about nothing in that ceaseless flow of verbiage that good weed can fuel. Casey's weed. They had talked about Billy losing his baby sister and about Billy living with Clevenger and about how cool it was to have his name in the *New York Times*, how everyone at Auden Prep and its sister school Governor Welch Academy, where Casey went, was talking about it, how Billy was more famous than ever. And they had talked about Casey's parents not understanding where she was coming from, how all her father cared about was business and tennis, and all her mother cared about was business and shopping and tennis, and about how Casey wasn't long for her hometown of Newburyport, an hour north of Boston, where the streets looked like a movie set of 1890, with overly quaint storefronts beneath overly quaint wooden, gold-leafed signs, along perfectly bricked sidewalks lighted by pristine gas lanterns that were nothing but lies because they were contrived. Fake. Casey wanted to be real, spontaneous, alive, in the here and now. She wanted to move to L.A., become an actress.

She turned onto her back, showing her real, sixteen-year-old breasts, each nipple pierced by a genuine 14-karat gold bolt. The pair had cost her a week's allowance.

"I got to get out of here before he gets home," Billy said.

He felt a little guilty for smoking the pot, but he hadn't smoked nearly as much as Casey, and he put eighty percent of the blame for his slip on her and Auden Prep and Clevenger and Mr. Fitzgerald at the shipyard. Billy wasn't the one, after all, who had bought the joints in the first place. He wasn't the one who had decided to leave school. He wasn't the one who had picked the fights that ultimately got him thrown out. He wasn't the one who had brought the reporters back into his life. He wasn't the one who'd taken two tugboats into the ship-yard to scrape and paint hour after hour, day after day, when what they really needed was to be sunk in Boston Harbor. And he wasn't the one who had decided he should stay alone in Chelsea while Clevenger flew cross-country with the hot, blonde FBI shrink who Billy had seen on television.

"You going to do it?" Casey asked. "Take off?"

"Just for a while," Billy said. "Two, three days. I have to clear my head."

"Use our cottage in Vermont. I have the key. It's on Lake Champlain, outside Burlington. It's kind of cool. Bare bones. Woodstove, that kind of thing. It was my grandparents'. Nobody's ever up there during the winter."

Billy could not have put into words exactly why he wanted to leave. And he would have denied the truth—that his leaving was a play for Clevenger's attention. He only knew that he felt lousy—a combination of lonely and anxious and angry—and needed to get away from that feeling. "You couldn't tell anyone," he said.

"Like I ever would?" She ran her hand down Billy's smooth, muscled abdomen. "Don't go yet."

He had sex with Casey the way he pumped iron, to prove he was strong, that he was a real man, that he was invulnerable. He wanted to touch her everywhere in order to prove he was untouchable. So that when she tensed her legs, arched her back, and cried out, he felt a great weight being lifted off his shoulders and sighed in a way that young Casey wrongly took to mean that he had come with her. The truth was that he was long gone.

Casey left the loft first. Billy cleaned up the remnants of their joints, wrote out a note saying he'd be away "a couple of days," then left through an exit in the basement to avoid the reporters massed on the sidewalk outside the building. He took the commuter rail from Chelsea to Boston's South Station and caught the 2:50 P.M. departure of the Amtrak "Vermonter" to Burlington, via Springfield, Massachusetts, all in all a nine-and-a-half-hour trip.

He slept all the way to Springfield. The layover there was two hours, so he grabbed a cheeseburger and fries and poked around the shops in the station. He bought a pair of mirrored sunglasses and a bandana. At a magazine concession he spotted the *New York Times*, scanned the front page, and saw they had run another of the Highway Killer's letters, the one Clevenger had read a day earlier, before leaving for Utah to find Paulette Bramberg's body. He tried to make himself walk right past it, tried to prove to himself how little he cared what Clevenger was up to, how he'd gotten the message loud and clear to stay out of his business and out of his way. But he couldn't quite pull it off. Because he did care. He bought a copy and tucked it under his arm, telling himself he'd read it on the train—when and if he felt like it.

With the time change and an hour's delay into Logan, Clevenger didn't get back to the loft until nearly 9 P.M. A dozen television and print reporters were still waiting there and mobbed him, calling out questions about whether he had truly broken ranks with the FBI, whether the Highway Killer was more in control of their public psychotherapy than he was, whether he thought the Highway Killer was old or young, black or white, possibly even female. Clevenger answered with a single "No comment" as he pushed his way through them, fueling a round of much more personal questions to which Clevenger didn't respond at all: Was his drug use truly under control? Had he ever used intravenous drugs? Had he disclosed his use of drugs to the Department of Social Services before adopting Billy Bishop? Would he disclose that information now?

He was almost to his door when Josh Resnek, publisher of the local *Chelsea Independent*, called out a question that made him stop and turn slowly around.

"What happens if you cure this guy but never find him?" Resnek asked. "You okay with that, Doc?"

The other reporters fell silent.

Resnek was a tall, broad man about fifty, half-shaven, with weathered skin and a full head of wild, salt-and-pepper hair. He looked like the drummer in the *Spirit of '76* painting, only about twenty years younger. Back when Clevenger's days had ended with three scotches at the Alpine Lounge up the street from his loft, Resnek—part reporter, part philosopher, part genius, part lunatic—had been about the best company he could hope for at the long bar. The man could talk Chelsea sports, politics, history going back decades. And when the two of them were on their third round, they could sometimes really talk—about the trouble with family, and the difference between the law and justice, and the miracle of feminine beauty, and the fear of death.

"If I cure him but never find him?" Clevenger echoed, stalling.

"That's what he wants, right?" Resnek pushed. "To be healed, without being caught. And you're very good at getting into people's heads. That's why he picked you in the first place."

Clevenger thought about the scenario Resnek was painting. And the answer that came to him was not only the one in his heart, but the one the Highway Killer himself would have wanted to hear, which was a good thing because the reporters—including the ones from national television networks—were listening very closely to what Clevenger was about to say. "I care that he gets well and stops killing people," he said. "The rest is up to the FBI."

He turned and reached for the door, pulled it open.

"Are you saying you won't help them catch him?" a reporter from Fox yelled.

He stepped inside.

"How long will you keep treating him if he keeps killing?" another from CBS called after him.

He pushed the door closed behind him and stood a few seconds with his back to it, then started up the five flights to his loft.

Inside the loft, the smell of marijuana was still thick in the air. He called Billy's name, got no response, checked his room, found it empty. He followed the odor to where it seemed strongest, pulled the wastepaper basket out from under the kitchen sink, and saw the butts and ashes Billy had dumped there. His pulse shot up, and his jaw tightened. The kid was going into detox that day, period. No more cat and mouse games. Detox, or out of the house for good. The choice was his. Then he spotted the note Billy had scrawled on a torn piece of notebook paper taped to the kitchen counter. He read it. "You've got to be joking," he said, his teeth clenched. "Pain in the ass!" But his anger crashed into waves of guilt and worry. Guilt, because he caught himself resenting Billy for taking his attention away from the Highway Killer—as if the investigation, not fathering, were his first priority. Worry, because Billy had stumbled into plenty of trouble right under Clevenger's nose and could end up in a hell of a lot more on the streets.

He tried Billy's mobile phone, but heard it ringing in his bedroom. He called North Anderson at home.

Anderson picked up.

"It's Frank," Clevenger said.

"Welcome back. You got stranded, huh? With McCormick. Some guys have all the—"

"Listen, I could really use your help."

"I got your message about the body," Anderson said. "Decapitated. Your man's throwing curves now."

"Not only with the investigation," Clevenger said. "With Billy. He took off."

"Took off? I saw him yesterday before dinner. He had a date with that Casey girl."

"He left a note saying he'd be gone 'a couple of days.' He also left a bunch of marijuana around. He's back on drugs. And he obviously doesn't care that I know it."

"Jesus," Anderson said. "Any idea where he went?"

"None. I don't know if Casey has anything to do with it. From the amount of ash in the garbage, there was certainly enough marijuana around to have gotten them both high." He shook his head at the realization that he had never met Casey and didn't remember her last name.

"Where is she from?" Anderson asked.

"Newburyport, I think. At least Billy headed up there once or twice to meet her. I know she also met him for lunch a couple of times at the shipyard. Maybe she knows him through someone there. Or she might go to one of the schools Auden Prep has their 'get-togethers' with." He let out his breath. "For all I know, she could be his dealer."

"I'll start with the shipyard, then drive to the Prep," Anderson said. "We'll find her. Hopefully she can tell us where he went."

"I know a few cops up in Newburyport," Clevenger said. "I'll call them."

"I can handle this, Frank. I've done more than a few missing persons cases, remember? A couple of hundred more. You've got your hands full right now."

That stung, even though nothing in Anderson's tone

suggested he meant it to. "That could be the problem," Clevenger said.

"Hey, give yourself—"

Clevenger wasn't about to give himself a break or a little credit or whatever else Anderson was about to suggest. "Call me on my cell the minute you find out anything?"

"Sure thing."

Billy was most of the way to Burlington, Vermont, when he flipped on the light, pulled the *New York Times* out of the seat-back pocket in front of him, and started to read the Highway Killer's letter. He read about the killer's idyllic fourth birthday party at the park, then read and reread the horror story of his arrival back home:

The door to our house was open. My mood fell. My father was at home. He came at us the moment we walked inside, backhanded my mother to the floor, ranting that he'd told her there was no money for the "little bastard's fucking party." I stepped between the two of them, and he backhanded me. My vision blurred. I fell to the floor. I tasted blood in my mouth. My front tooth wiggled in its socket as my tongue moved against it. I saw ripped pages from my books, torn pieces of my stuffed animals, my Hot Wheels cars rain down around me. Then I watched as he crushed his heel into each and every one of the cars.

   My mother cowered in the corner, weeping. I wished I were older, bigger, stronger, able to defend her. She held a single finger to her beautiful lips, warning me to stay quiet, then blew me another kiss. And even with the taste of blood in my mouth, I felt safe and secure, even victorious over the monster who called himself my father.

"Bullshit, you wanted to defend her," he said aloud.

A fat man sleeping across the aisle stirred, grunted, fell back asleep.

Billy squinted at the page, shook his head. "And she blew you a kiss?" he whispered. "Give me a fucking break."

He didn't have to work very hard to remember the feelings his own beatings had sparked in him when he was four years old. His mother had been at home. But he was too scared to think about protecting her. He was busy trying not to cry, because tears didn't extinguish his father's violence, they inflamed it. And his mother wasn't blowing him any kisses while his father's strap broke skin. She was locking herself in the bathroom so she wouldn't get whipped herself and wouldn't see what was happening to him.

Did he hate her? No. She was irrelevant, powerless, a prisoner like he was. But she certainly didn't make him feel safe and secure. That part of the Highway Killer's letter was just more bullshit.

The Highway Killer was fantasizing, maybe even deluded. A psychopath. Maybe the guy actually *believed* this woman was alive in his house, his guardian angel making goo-goo eyes at him while he got the crap beat out of him.

Billy laid his head back, closed his eyes. And after a minute or two he remembered something key. He remembered his own fantasy while his father was taking that strap to him. It wasn't for a waif of a mother who would cower in the corner and whisper sweet nothings. It was for a father who would love him. A man who would take care of him.

What he fantasized about was the very opposite of the father he had, and he was willing to bet the Highway Killer was fantasizing about the very opposite of his mother. *She* was the one who had backhanded him to the floor, crushed his toys, called him "little bastard."

He felt eager to tell Clevenger what he thought of the letter, which made him feel foolish. "Like he cares what you think," he scolded himself.

He would have completely dismissed the impulse to reach out were it not for another revelation that visited him as his train sped north. He realized that Clevenger was the kind of person he had fantasized about all those times his father had stood over him, ranting and swinging. Someone who would stand by him. Fight *for* him, not with him. Maybe that was what made it so hard to live with him. Maybe that's what all the drugs were about. Maybe he was having trouble believing in something he had dreamed of—a real father, a man who really loved him.

"You are one sad case, Bishop," Billy muttered. "The guy doesn't give a shit about you." But the words didn't stick because they were made out of fear and nothing else. The fear that he was unlovable. The fear that he could lose what he had found, that Clevenger might fail him, turn out to be an illusion. And that would be sad as hell, and embarrassing, too. Because the truth was that Billy was starting to love Clevenger right back.

That's what had him getting high. That's what had him riding the rails.

He pulled into Burlington at 12:55 A.M. He would

have taken a train right back to Boston's South Station, but there wasn't one until 7 A.M. So he stepped out of the station, into the icy edge of a Vermont morning, and started walking along Route 7, headed toward Casey's parents' cabin.

Clevenger didn't sleep at all that night. Neither of the Newburyport cops he contacted knew any "Casey." Peter Fitzgerald at the shipyard had seen her around, but couldn't offer anything more. Then at 3:37 A.M. the phone rang. North Anderson's home number showed on the Caller I.D. Clevenger reached for the receiver, but his hand froze with worry that he was about to get bad news, that this was that call the unluckiest parents in the world got, that their kid had overdosed or been hit by a car or murdered. 3:37 A.M. Would he remember that time the rest of his life, wake with a start more nights than not, staring at those blood-red digits splayed across his alarm clock? He made himself pick up. "Find out anything?" he asked.

"He headed to Vermont," Anderson said.

"Vermont?"

"I found his girlfriend about an hour ago. She's a sophomore at Governor Welch Academy up in George-town. Goes by Casey, but her real name is Katherine Paulson Simms. One of Newburyport's first families. She was tight-lipped, a real stand-up girl—until I bluffed and told her the cops might want to talk to her about the pot she left behind in your apartment."

"Why's he headed to Vermont?"

"He told Casey he needed time to think, a little space, that kind of thing. The Simms have a cabin on Lake

Champlain. She gave him the key. I called Greyhound and Amtrak. He took the train, used an American Express—yours—to pay for his trip. He got in just before one A.M."

"Thanks," Clevenger said. "I'm going up there now."

"Listen, Frank," Anderson said. "Tell me if I'm stepping out of line, but maybe he was being straight with her. He might need a little time to think something through, get his head screwed on straight."

"He needs detox," Clevenger said.

"This could be his way of getting clean. Who knows? Maybe the couple of days will do him good."

"So, what am I supposed to do? Just wait?"

"Sometimes that's all you can do. At least it's all I can do with my Kristie. She's still too young to hop on a train, but she's been way out of reach a few times. That can happen when she's right down the hall. It won't be any different with Tyler."

"He's, what, five months old? You don't need to start worrying."

"I started the day he was born."

Clevenger took a deep breath. "Is there a phone up there?"

"None in the cabin. No heat, either. But there's a woodstove and a half cord stacked on the porch."

"Why not send a cruiser by, see that he got there?"

"I'll take care of it."

"Let me know if . . ." Clevenger started.

"If there isn't a light burning or smoke coming out of the chimney, I'll call you," Anderson interrupted. "Otherwise, get some sleep."

"Will do. Thanks."

*

He slept about an hour altogether, dozing off for five or ten minutes at a time, then waking and listening to the silence in the loft, hoping to hear a door slamming or the shower running or Billy's footsteps falling across the floor. But he heard nothing.

He awakened for good at 6:20 A.M., remembered he'd arranged for delivery of the *New York Times*, and grabbed it outside his door. He sat down on the couch and reread his front-page response to the Highway Killer's last letter. He imagined the killer reading it at the same moment—at a truck stop or a rest area or having a nice, hot breakfast at some diner that might be just a quarter mile from where he had left another body. And he felt sick to his stomach. Because he imagined that body as Billy's. And he wondered whether losing him would change the answer he had given Josh Resnek from the *Chelsea Independent*—that healing the Highway Killer was what mattered to him, that catching him was up to the FBI. He wondered how well his empathy would weather a murdered son.

But it wasn't really supposed to hold up, was it? That's why juries and judges and the whole rule of law existed in the first place—to buffer the understandable desire for vengeance in the bereaved. Because if justice were left to victims, gallows would outnumber jails a hundred to one.

Together, as a society, we can aspire to act like Christ or Ghandi. Left alone, most of us would act more like the Terminator.

The phone rang. North Anderson again. Clevenger picked up.

"I think he may be heading back your way," Anderson said.

Clevenger looked at the ceiling, closed his eyes, and thanked God. "How do you know?" he asked.

"After the Burlington police told me there was activity at the cottage, I drove up here," Anderson said. "Just to make sure he stayed safe."

"You drove to Vermont? In the middle of the night? You told me to sit tight."

"*You* can't be tailing him. You're his father." He chuckled. "Anyhow, he's up and dressed and out the door, walking toward the train station. Maybe roughing it doesn't suit him. He'll probably use your charge card again. I'll track it. Just in case he decides to take a detour."

"Maybe you should just stop him and bring him home."

"If that's what you want," Anderson said. "It's your call."

Clevenger thought about that—how much better he would feel about Billy for the moment, and how much the same he might feel in a day or a week. "I guess we better let him decide where he's going," he said.

"Tough, isn't it?" Anderson asked.

"What?"

"Loving a kid like you love him."

Clevenger's throat tightened. "Does it get easier?"

"Harder and harder."

"Great," Clevenger said.

"Yes, it is," Anderson said.

Clevenger smiled. "Thanks, again, North."

"Talk to you soon."

seven

Jonah Wrens began reading Clevenger's letter for the fifth time just before a family meeting with the parents of his newest patient, nine-year-old Sam Garber. That morning he had begun two weeks of coverage for a vacationing psychiatrist on the inpatient unit of the Rock Springs Medical Center at the foot of the Aspen Mountains. But he could barely focus on his work. The letter had infuriated him. The parts about Clevenger's own life were interesting enough. His revelation that he fantasized about killing his father seemed honest. But then the letter veered into self-righteousness and outright manipulation.

I accept my pain. You refuse yours. You describe feeling victorious even "with blood in your mouth" because you knew you had your mother's love. But your sense of triumph was only a defense against deeper feelings of terror and weakness. As a four-year-old you never truly faced the horrible truth that it was your blood leaking from your mouth, that you were powerless to protect yourself, and that no one else would or could protect you.

Now you seek the ultimate power over others—whether they live or die—as if that could erase your humiliation and helplessness.

psychopath

You speak of experiencing great physical pain—migraines, jaw pain. You feel terrible anxiety—palpitations, shortness of breath. But I doubt you feel gut-level sadness or rage. Because the worst of what you went through as a child remains locked in your unconscious.

What trauma have you failed to look at, Gabriel? What buried fury exploded when you were with Paulette Bramberg? What was it about an elderly female (a woman the age of your mother?) that caused you to completely lose control, so that it was no longer enough to be with someone dying, but necessary to kill so brutally. Monstrously. And why did you take no blood from her? Would it be poison to have Paulette Bramberg inside you?

Why would Clevenger lie? Jonah wondered. What possible reason could he have for misrepresenting the body Jonah had left by Route 80 in Utah—the body of a man at least seventy, a man the age of his father? A man named Paul. A man who had died quietly in his arms, no more horribly than any of the Highway Killer's other victims. What sort of mental trap was Clevenger trying to lay, challenging Jonah's memory of his mother, a mother he still longed for, every day on the road? Why descend to the ugly trickery of besmirching their relationship, implying Jonah had some unconscious store of rage toward the only person who had ever truly loved him, the only person he had ever truly loved?

The last of the letter made Jonah's pulse race even faster. His teeth began to grind. Because he saw the hook Clevenger had set for readers of the *Times*, his not-so-subtle attempt to catch him by jogging the memories of the good and giving people he had set free, to turn them, too, into hunters:

> Or was Paulette Bramberg's sin simply that she remained aloof from the Highway Killer, keeping her distance, never coming to feel the extraordinary and instant intimacy I believe you can inspire in others, so that they open up their hearts in a way they never have before, open up to a stranger in a way they would remember all their lives were their lives not cut short?
>
> I asked you for the remains of all the Highway Killer's victims. You gave me a body different than the rest. Why?
>
> I believe finding the answer will be the beginning of the end of the Highway Killer.
>
> —Frank Clevenger, MD

Jonah closed his eyes and imagined himself back at the airport in Utah, plunging his knife into Clevenger's heart. At that moment he wished he had done it, wished he had put Clevenger out of his misery, rather than trying to heal him or be healed by him. Because Clevenger was obviously infected to the bone with Whitney McCormick, lost inside his lust for her.

He reached into his pocket and took out the trinket his mother had given him at his birthday party at the park, a tiny, enameled carousel horse. He ran his thumb back and forth over its mane, the black coating worn away from so many years of touching, and made himself consider how God might be testing him, what was now required of him.

A knock at the door brought him back to the moment. He shook his head clear, opened his eyes. "Come in," he called out.

The door opened and Sam Garber's parents, Hank and Heaven, walked in, looking like a couple of items off humanity's closeout rack—the husband maybe sixty, short, nervous, and wiry with bloodshot eyes; the wife much taller, no older than thirty-five, at least three hundred pounds, looking irritated.

"Please, sit down," Jonah said. He opened Sam's chart to a line drawing from the emergency room that showed the locations of his physical injuries. The nine-year-old had been admitted to Rock Springs Medical Center after his gym teacher found fresh bruises and healed burn marks on his abdomen, back, arms and legs, leading the Wyoming Department of Social Services to temporarily remove him from the Garber household. "You do understand why Sam has been admitted to this unit?" he began, looking from Hank to Heaven, then back again.

"On account of that Mr. Daravekias getting the wrong idea," Hank said.

"About the bruises," Jonah said. "And the burns."

"Already explained all that to the social worker," Hank said.

Jonah looked directly at Heaven, who stared right back at him, still chewing her gum. "From what I've read," he said, "you told the social worker Sam fell down a flight of stairs recently and fell off his bike a while back. And there was something about him falling into the fireplace?"

"All of which is what Sam says himself," Hank said.

"How did he fall down the stairs?" Jonah asked Heaven.

"Tripped, I guess," Hank said. "Kid's always losin' balance. Love him to death, but he's got the coordination of a frickin' mule."

Love him to death? Not if Jonah could help it. "Did you see him fall?" he asked Heaven.

She stared back at Jonah for several seconds. "I don't suppose I can be watching him every minute," she finally answered, chewing over some of the words.

Jonah kept looking at her. For an instant he saw his own mother's face, much thinner than Heaven's, far paler, her eyes lighter and brighter. Through an act of will he forced her out of his mind, silently chastising himself for letting her image mingle with a beast's. "There was one other worrisome finding," he went on, staring into eyes that had gone back to being Heaven's—dirt-brown and lifeless.

"You might be worrying over it," Hank said. "We ain't."

"Worrisome to me," Jonah allowed, glancing at him. "Worrisome to the social worker, too."

"Well, you, the social worker, and anybody else can relax yourselves," Hank said. "We're raisin' our boy right. Accidents do happen."

Jonah looked down at his hands, folded on the desk in front of him. And for a split second he pictured them around Heaven Garber's thick neck. He closed his eyes, tried to diffuse the rage building inside him. "We got a full series of X rays on your son," he said. "We found two fractures. One on his left forearm, all healed up. The other mostly healed, but newer, near his right biceps." He opened his eyes, looked at Heaven.

"Like I already made mention," Hank said, "Sam is always falling over himself."

"The X rays showed what we call spiral fractures," Jonah told him. "The way a stick would break if you twisted it like you were wringing water from a dishrag."

He held his fists in the air, rotated one toward the Garbers, one back toward himself. And again he saw his hands wringing Heaven's neck. "You get an S-shaped crack in the bone as it gives way," he said, his voice shaking.

"That could of happened the couple times he fell off his bike. Probably caught his arms the exact wrong way," Hank said.

"It happens when someone becomes angry with a child," Jonah said. "Say someone were to grab hold of Sam and decide to teach him a lesson." He looked directly at Heaven Garber again.

"I know everybody's bad-mouthing Heaven and me," Hank said. "But hear one thing—Sam would never tell a lie about us. And I'm here to tell you we ain't never—"

Jonah shook his head. He nodded at the door. "The door is locked," he said, just above a whisper. "This office is soundproof."

Hank glanced slowly over his shoulder, looked back at Jonah warily.

"I know about children," Jonah said. "Sometimes they get out of control."

"Not Sam," Hank said.

"Tell me the truth," Jonah said, shifting his gaze to Heaven, his hands clenched.

"Like I said, ain't nothing to—" Hank started.

"Shut your mouth," Jonah shot back, still staring at Heaven, who stopped chewing her gum.

Maybe Hank heard the killer inside Jonah. Or maybe he just saw the muscles rippling in his forearms. What-ever the reason, he didn't say another word.

"The spiral fractures in Sam's arms run counterclockwise," Jonah said to Heaven. "That, together with the pattern of bruising over the newer fracture, proves that whoever caused them is left-handed. Like you."

Heaven turned to Hank. "I ain't gonna listen to this. Let's . . ."

Jonah saw his mother's lips moving as Heaven spoke. Her words ran together into an indecipherable drone. And his hatred for Clevenger and Whitney McCormick and this woman became one storm inside him, the thunder and lightning obscuring the memories trying to surface from his unconscious—memories of his mother's unspeakable cruelty.

He tried to stand, but his legs would not budge, a paralysis that had besieged him before while meeting with parents who had abused their children. It was as if his mind was turning his muscles off, lest he do to Heaven Garber everything he wanted to do to her. "Listen to me," Jonah said, interrupting Heaven's rant. "I don't believe you're evil."

Heaven looked blankly back at him.

"Something happened to you to turn you into a person who would attack a little boy. Probably something horrible, probably when you were very young. Maybe when you were exactly nine, like Sam." Jonah thought he saw a flicker of recognition in Heaven's face. Then it was gone. "I can help you remember. I can help you heal. And maybe then you'd get your son back some day."

Heaven stood up. "A lawyer's all the help we need."

Hank stood, but slowly, as though Jonah's last words—about the loss of his son—had knocked some of the fight out of him.

Jonah tried to raise his hands, but they were dead

weights. "I'll be working here two weeks," he said to Heaven. "Come see me. I'm willing to meet with you every day."

Heaven's lip curled, baring teeth that gapped in the center, exactly like Jonah's mother's. Or did Jonah only see them that way? "You doctors think you know every-thing," she seethed. "Well, I got—"

Hank grabbed hold of her meaty arm and began pulling her toward the door.

"Please," Jonah said. "Wait."

Heaven pulled her arm away from her husband, turned back to Jonah with a fragile indulgence on her face, as though expecting an apology.

"You've grown large in size because of how small you feel inside," Jonah said. "But you can't swallow or drink or smoke all your suffering. Surely, you have ulcers already. Have they started to bleed yet?"

Heaven was breathing hard, but seemed to be half listening.

"Your pain is choking your heart, too. You feel it every time you walk up that flight of stairs—the one you say that Sam fell down."

Heaven shook her head. "You don't know nothin' about me," she protested, but weakly, a hint of fear in her voice—fear of the Truth, which is no different than the fear of God.

"You know that I do," Jonah said. He squinted at Heaven's lips as they turned deep red—the color of his mother's lipstick. Oh, how he missed her. What he would give to be held by her. To smell her hair, nuzzle against her warm neck. He closed his eyes, saw her again hud-dled in that corner, blowing him a kiss. And when he finally opened his eyes, the Garbers were gone.

*

At 6:10 P.M., Clevenger heard a flurry of activity on the street below, looked out the window, and saw Billy make his way through the mob of reporters and disappear through the front door. He felt a profound sense of relief. But as Billy began climbing the five flights to the loft, Clevenger's anxiety level started climbing, too. He was worried for him. He was back on drugs and troubled enough to have run off without saying where he was going.

Clevenger was also worried over the exact right thing to do. And he didn't want his anger to get in the way of him doing it. "Don't jump down his throat about the pot," he reminded himself. "Or the credit card."

The door opened. Billy walked in. He had a couple of *New York Times* newspapers tucked under his arm, which made Clevenger concerned he was dwelling on the Highway Killer case. He closed the door behind him, nodded to himself as if working up the courage to say something important.

"What?" Clevenger gently prompted him.

"I can't stay here right now," he said.

Clevenger felt like he had been kicked in the gut. "You've got to tell me what's going on with you, Billy. You can't expect—"

"I've got to get into detox," he said. "I need it. That, and AA or NA or whatever. I can't stay away from the drugs. You've been good with me, but I need more help."

Sometimes, if all too rarely, the world gives you what you want. Clevenger felt like this was one of those times. "Fair enough," he said.

"Maybe you could take me over to North Shore Medical Center? A couple of guys from school went there when they had problems."

"Of course," Clevenger said. "You don't have to do this by yourself." And then he did the one thing that seemed the most natural to him and the most uncomfortable at the same time, maybe because his father had never done it to him. Not once. He walked over to Billy, put his arms around him, drew him close and held him tight. And after a few moments, he felt Billy do the same to him. And then he journeyed further still, turning and kissing his adoptive son's cheek. And he knew that with everything that had happened to each of them and between them, with everything that they still had to face, that it would all be easier for that embrace and that kiss and the ones that could follow. Because they could face it all together.

Billy's eyes were full when Clevenger let go of him. But there was something different about his tears this time. This time he was trying to hold them back. This time they were undeniably real. They made him tremble. He had to clear his throat to speak. "I'll trade you one favor for another," he said. He pulled the newspapers out from under his arm. "You give me that lift to the hospital, I give you a hint about the Highway Killer."

Clevenger hesistated. He really didn't want Billy involved in the case. But for the first time he realized he might not be able to stop him. Billy was standing right there with the *Times* in his hand, five days from having been named in the Highway Killer's first letter, two minutes from having been hounded by reporters for his comments.

Even more important, Billy clearly *wanted* to help.

He wanted to help catch a killer. And maybe letting him feed that urge would help him do with his potential violence what Clevenger had done with his own—transmute it into a desire to heal, a commitment to protect. He thought of a few lines from the Highway Killer's latest letter:

> *Have you ever wanted to kill, Frank? Did you use alcohol and drugs to blunt that impulse? Do you work to understand murderers in order to understand yourself?*

Yes, Clevenger thought. "Yes" was the answer to each of those three questions. And maybe Billy was no different than he was. Maybe he wanted to help Clevenger with the investigation in order to help himself. Maybe he was ready to harness his pain in service to relieving pain in others. "It's a deal," he told him.

Billy sat down on the couch, spread the newspapers in front of him. "This guy supposedly gets attacked by his father, right?"

Clevenger nodded.

"And he's thinking about his mom?" He shrugged. "I never did. Not when I was being beaten." He shrugged. "Did you?"

Clevenger thought about it. He thought about all the nights he had absorbed his father's violence, how it had taken every ounce of strength he had just to control his fear. "No," he said.

" 'Course not," Billy said. "You were praying for it to stop. And if you were like me, you found yourself wishing you had a normal father. I actually fantasized I had one somewhere, that he'd blow through the door one day and carry me out of there."

"Same here," Clevenger said.

"So the way I see it this guy is making up the woman in the corner of the room," Billy said. "He wants to believe he's got a good mother, a guardian angel. But he doesn't. He's got the worst. She's the one attacking him." He leaned forward, started to speak faster. "There wasn't any birthday party in the park. There weren't any gifts. There were just the beatings. He invented all that happy horseshit. He didn't live with a devil and an angel. Just a devil. A she-devil. The guy's schizo."

That last word, *schizo*, helped Clevenger crystallize the idea that had begun to form in his mind as he listened to Billy. "Unless she was both," he said.

"What do you mean?" Billy asked.

"It's easier to survive something predictable. Something that's always bad news. Like when my dad would come home. I at least knew what to expect. I knew what he was."

"So you could psych yourself up to get through it."

"And I could hate him."

Billy looked at him quizically. "That's good?"

"It keeps the hate from going underground, building steam," Clevenger said. He paused. "If the Highway Killer had a mother who was kind and loving some of the time and sadistic at other times, he would never have been able to discharge his rage. It would all get dammed up in his unconscious. Because what he loved in the world—that ideal mother he writes about—is also the one torturing him. So there's nowhere for the hate to go. Attack the 'she-devil,' and you attack the 'angel,' too. Kill one, they both die."

"Which is why he kills other people, they're just stand-ins for her."

"Could be." That idea certainly explained why the

Highway Killer would get so close to his victims, mimicking the idealized maternal bond, then cutting it off—literally. Paulette Bramberg was just too close a facsimile. Probably a woman the age of his mother. Possibly a woman who even looked like his mother.

"So maybe she did give him that party," Billy went on, "and he did get all those gifts, and then they get home, and she's a completely different person. Beats on him, out of the blue. Starts screaming about not having enough money. Busts up his toys."

Not bad, Clevenger thought. The kid was following right along. "And when that happens," Clevenger said, "he splits off the image of the angel, keeps it alive in the corner of the room, and takes his beating. He can't bear to think his mother is attacking him. So he invents an abusive father." He nodded to himself. "My guess? He didn't have a father at home at all. Or he had a very, very weak one."

"So what do we do now?" Billy asked, excitedly.

Clevenger winked at him. "We get you to detox." As the words left his mouth, he knew they sounded abrupt. Dismissive. He watched Billy slowly wilt before his eyes. "And when you're out," he quickly added, "I want you to come down to Quantico with me and learn more about the case."

The energy came right back into his eyes. "Are you serious?" he asked. "You'd take me with you?"

"You're good at this," Clevenger said. "I could use your help."

eight

Jonah left his room at the Rock Springs Ambassador Motel at 12:20 A.M. He was having one of those "really dark nights of the soul" his beloved F. Scott Fitzgerald had written of. His spartan suite felt like a coffin.

He could not sleep more than fifteen minutes without being awakened by his usual nightmare, but with a horrifying twist. The woman with flowing blonde curls who carressed him, then gnawed through his flesh and bone, hungry to devour his heart, now looked at him through his mother's eyes. Light brown. Luminous. And in his sleep he felt himself thirsting for her love even as he struggled to escape her, and stayed asleep longer than he should have, long enough to tell her that he loved her, but long enough, too, for the beast to scrape past his sternum. So that when he did awaken, it was with a shriek, clutching his chest to keep his ravaged heart from tumbling out of his body.

Was this what Clevenger and McCormick were plotting? To deprive him of the only true comfort he had ever had? To take the memory of his mother? Defile her? Drive him over the edge of loneliness, into insanity?

His temples pounding and jaw aching, he got into his X5, turned on Mahler's *Tenth Symphony* and headed for Route 80 East. He took it about sixty miles to the exit for

Bitter Creek, far enough away from the hospital to avoid being seen out alone, past midnight. He was a visitor at the hospital, and, hence, a natural focus of curiosity. He didn't need to inspire more.

He pulled into the empty parking lot of an all-night diner, went inside with his copy of the *Times*, and ordered a large, black coffee from the plump, sixty-something woman tending the place. Then he sat in a booth sipping the coffee and pretending to read Clevenger's letter while stealing glances at her, just to reassure himself she was moving and breathing, to reassure himself he was actually awake, actually alive. Like her.

With a trembling hand he took a folded sheet of paper and a pen from his coat pocket, unfolded the paper, and reread the beginning of his response to Clevenger:

Dr. Clevenger:
How does it feel to fall in love? Is it the pure bliss they say it is to feel one's ego boundaries melt away, to join another human being erotically?
Or is it simply another intoxicant? Are you addicted to Dr. McCormick the way you were addicted to alcohol and drugs? As an escape from your pain? Is it really any better to lose yourself in her than in a bottle?

He took a long drink of his coffee, not noticing how it scalded his lips, mouth, and throat. The woman behind the counter looked over at him. "Everything all right?" He smiled back. "Perfect." He picked up his pen and started writing:

The killer inside you shall not remain embryonic, but will walk the earth as the Highway Killer. Every day I remain ill I will represent your unwillingness to love your fellow man, the limits on your empathy, your failure as a healer. I shall cast not only my Shadow, but yours.

It remains more important to you to serve man's law than God's law, more important to catch me than to cure me. Where is the Lord in that plan? Do you really believe evil can be locked away behind bars? Do you not understand that I am already inside you, that the struggle for my soul has now become a struggle for your own?

His vision had gone blurry, and he could feel his pulse bounding behind his eyes, but he pressed on:

You think you can avoid that struggle by submerging your heart and mind in the sex act. You choose the huntress to avoid choosing a true self, to avoid the question that haunts you. Are you—at core, in the darkest moment of your night—a healer or a hunter, my physician or my executioner?

I will help you answer that question. Because I am—unlike you—a man of my word.

One by one, I would have returned each and every body to you, to be reunited with its family, but you have proven yourself unworthy, arriving in Utah with the FBI (after promising to disavow them), then lying about my offering in order to make me question my love for my mother, my defender, my angel.

To what end? To leave me even more isolated? To make death my only angel? Did no one love you purely, Frank Clevenger? Have you loved no one deeply? Is it so impossible for you to fathom that emotion that you must denigrate it?

Your father lied to you, and you have become a liar.

Your father tortured you by raising your hopes, then dashing them. You would do the same to me—were I to permit it.

I shall not. I shall not let you destroy me, nor shall I abide your self-destruction. We were destined to save one another. Staying true to that great journey is my path to redemption.

And I am yours.

—A Man of God
They Call the Highway Killer

Jonah set the pen down, gulped more of his coffee. He believed he had indeed embarked on a great journey, but knew it was also a daunting one, no less so than the journey of Christ finding God inside him, then helping others find Him inside them.

The difference was that Jonah was determined to avoid the cross, determined to finish in this life the work that lay before him—even if that meant coming face-to-face with the devil.

He did not get to bed until 4:50 A.M., having driven another hour east to deposit his letter in a Federal Express drop box in Creston, Wyoming, then two hours back to the Ambassador Motel in Rock Springs. He set his bedside alarm for 7:00 A.M., wanting a few hours' rest and feeling oddly at peace, no terrible hunger to see his patients, the pain gone from his head, clear vision restored to his eyes. He had said exactly what he had needed to say. He would do what he needed to do. He felt better than he had in a long, long time and fell easily off to sleep.

Having suffered for weeks with shattered sleep, he

savored deep slumber, untainted by nightmares, and actually awakened refreshed. Maybe he had turned a corner, he thought to himself. Maybe God could see the effort he was willing to put forth. Maybe he was finally on the right path.

He walked into the bathroom, turned on the light, and looked into the mirror. And what he saw made him lose his breath: his face and neck were splattered with blood.

He ground the heels of his hands into his eyes to clear away the illusion, but it kept staring back at him. He shook his head in disbelief. The man in the mirror did the same. He reached out, tried to wipe him away. But the man in the mirror reached out, too. And as their fingertips touched, memories of what Jonah had done hours before began to surface.

He saw himself walk to the counter of the coffee shop, smile, and ask the woman whether he might use the rest room. He saw her guide him through the kitchen, point to an open door. And then he saw himself straddling her waist, his hands around her neck, her gray-blue hair fanned out over the pink ceramic tile floor.

He yanked his hand away from the mirror as if it were on fire. "No," he begged.

But his reflection only mimicked him, and the images kept flashing through his mind. He saw himself grab the woman's hair and pull her head back, saw the blade of his knife power through her windpipe and pharyngeal muscles, felt the warm spray from her severed carotid arteries cover his face.

"It couldn't be," he pleaded. "Please, God." He turned away from the mirror.

Panic gripped him. Anyone could have witnessed

what had happened in the diner. Anyone could have spotted him driving away. Someone in the motel could have seen him returning with blood on his face or noticed blood on his car.

Epinephrine poured from his adrenal glands, fueling him for the task at hand, but also driving up his blood pressure, painfully dilating the arteries feeding his heart and brain.

He grabbed his bloodied clothes off the floor, stripped the sheet off his bed, stuffed everything into a trash bag. Then he showered, pulled on a clean pair of pants and a shirt, grabbed a wet towel and stepped out to the parking lot, expecting his X5 to be a mess and feeling relieved to find only a few red smears on the steering wheel. He wiped them away.

He returned to the room trembling. He began to pace. "Calm down," he told himself again and again. "No one is knocking at the door. There was no police cruiser outside."

He turned on the television, flipped channels, and found what he was looking for. A young, pretty television reporter stood in front of the Bitter Creek Diner, interviewing a man about fifty, with a pot belly and balding head, two days' growth of beard on his ashen face.

"Sally worked here fifteen years," he said. "I just . . ." He cleared his throat. "Nothing like this . . . It's a nightmare. I don't know what to say."

"No one had threatened Ms. Pierce, to your knowledge?" the reporter asked. "There hadn't been anyone suspicious at the restaurant? A traveler? A new employee?"

"Not so far as I know."

The reporter turned to camera. "That's it from here,

J.T. A brutal slaying in the quiet town of Bitter Creek. A woman decapitated as she worked the overnight shift at the local diner. No witness. No known motive. And police are refusing to speculate whether this is or is not the work of the Highway Killer."

Jonah clicked off the television. He sat down at the edge of the bed, hugging himself, rocking back and forth, his mind pulling in too many directions: guilt over what he had done; fear of being caught; sheer panic at having lost touch with reality, of losing control so completely that he had taken a life without even being conscious of it. Then there was the terrible truth that killing had calmed him again, that he had slept like a baby after spilling a woman's blood.

He had slept like a baby after spilling a woman's blood. He heard his own thought through his ears, as though someone else were speaking it. Was it God? Was the good Lord promising him rebirth, even at this dark moment? Or was he losing his mind?

He wanted to leave Wyoming that very moment, to climb back into the mountains to try to regain control, but he knew a sudden departure would raise suspicion. The FBI would be searching the area, asking questions. They might even show up at the hospital. He had to stay focused, go to work as if nothing at all had happened.

He picked up his bottle of Haldol and swallowed a milligram. He decided to take the medication three times a day, every day, to try to keep himself harnessed to reality.

As Jonah was watching coverage of the killing, Clevenger was driving Billy to the detox unit at North

Shore Medical Center in Salem, about forty minutes north of Chelsea. He'd gotten calls from Kane Warner and Whitney McCormick detailing the crime scene in Wyoming and asking him to attend a meeting at FBI Headquarters at 3:00 P.M. Warner had sounded even more hostile than usual. McCormick had sounded worried. He'd booked a noon flight.

An intake worker named Dan Solomon, about fifty-five, his skin weathered and worn, a diamond stud in one ear, his eyes sapphire blue, interviewed Billy about his drug use and psychiatric history. "Just marijuana and cocaine, then?" he asked.

"That's it," Billy said. He glanced at Clevenger.

"Is there more?" Solomon asked.

Billy shrugged. "Ecstasy, occasionally."

"Would it be easier if I left the room?" Clevenger asked Billy.

"No. Stay."

"Listen to me," Solomon said, his eyes glowing brighter. "It doesn't make any sense to hold back. I know you think it does. I used to lie to counselors myself. It's like you figure you're here, you're gonna get the full ten-day treatment anyhow, so what do you get for coming clean? But remember this: *coming clean is half the battle.* Because what this really comes down to is becoming a truthful person—owning your pain, not trying to drug it away or lie your way through it. Telling me everything you've swallowed or smoked or snorted or mainlined is a big step in that direction."

Billy glanced at Clevenger again, looked back at Solomon. "Oxycontin, a couple of times. And I, uh . . . I injected the cocaine twice."

Solomon stared at him.

"Three times," Billy said.

He kept the stare going.

"Smoked it once," Billy said.

"You used crack," Solomon said, jotting notes.

"Once," Billy said.

Clevenger's heart felt like it was in a vice, but he tried not to show it. "Is that absolutely everything?" he asked Billy.

"That's it," Billy said definitively.

"I'll take you at your word," Solomon said, "until you give me reason not to. Fair enough?"

Billy nodded.

"Any history of depression?" Solomon went on.

"I don't know if I have a history of anything else," Billy said.

"Ever hospitalized on a psychiatric unit or treated with medicine?"

"They put me in a hospital once," Billy said. "After my sister was murdered."

Solomon didn't break stride. Like everyone else, he'd heard of Billy Bishop and the murder on Nantucket. "Ever had thoughts of suicide?"

Clevenger hoped Billy's answer would be "no," mostly because Billy's prognosis would be better, partly because he couldn't help feeling that Billy's mental health—or lack of it—would be some sort of verdict on his parenting. He had only been in Billy's life a few years, but he wanted to believe those years had made a dent in Billy's psychopathology.

"A couple of times," Billy said.

The vice tightened on Clevenger's heart, but he kept his game face.

"When?" Solomon asked.

"I don't know," Billy said. "Maybe when I got kicked out of school. A couple of times around then."

"And you thought of doing . . . what?" Solomon asked.

Billy shrugged. "Overdose. Inject a shitload of coke or something."

The image of finding Billy stroked out in the loft made Clevenger close his eyes.

"Sorry," Billy said.

Clevenger opened his eyes, saw Billy looking at him. "You have nothing to be sorry for on that one, champ," he said. "I'm sorry I didn't ask you the question myself when you were that down."

"I wouldn't have told you," Billy said.

"Thinking of hurting yourself now?" Solomon asked.

"No way," Billy said. He remembered the thoughts he had had as Clevenger drove him to Brian Strasnick's outpatient laboratory in Lynn to be drug-tested, the desire he had felt to make Clevenger suffer by watching him leap out of the car, hit the pavement. He looked over at him. "I don't want to hurt myself or my dad, anymore," he said. And he meant it.

Jonah Wrens showed up for work on time, at 8 A.M. He was wearing a starched lavender button-down dress shirt, perfectly knotted deep blue and lavender tie, trademark gray flannel slacks, kidskin loafers. He walked into the nurses' station, nodded good mornings to the unit secretary and the head nurse, and sat down to flip through the charts of the patients assigned to him for the next two weeks.

"Hear about the murder?" the head nurse, Liz Donahue, asked.

Jonah looked over at her. She was a forty-something, twice divorced, childless woman who could have been beautiful, were she not bulimic. "The murder?" he asked.

All the affability in Donahue's face evaporated, leaving behind sullen eyes, hollowed-out cheeks, cat-thin lips. "At the Bitter Creek Diner?"

Was he imagining the suspicion he heard in her voice? He shook his head.

"A woman was decapitated," she said.

"It's so disgusting," the unit secretary said, swivelling in her seat to face Jonah and Donahue. She was in her early thirties, plump, with a blonde braid that hung to the small of her back. "People are so sick. Whoever did it, I hope they find him and cut *his* goddamn head off. Tie him to a chair, take little breaks along the way. Let him watch it happen in a mirror."

A mirror? Jonah's eyes narrowed. Could the two of them know what he had done? Was he wearing the face of a killer? He touched his cheek, glanced at his fingertips to make sure they did not come away stained with blood. "They don't know who did it?" was all he could think to say.

"It's got to be the Highway Killer," Donahue said, her face suddenly alive with excitement. "I guess we'll all be reading about it in the *Times*. I know I will."

She likes the letters, Jonah thought. She likes them the way people like *People* magazine and TV movies. Is that what he and his suffering had become? A sideshow?

The unit secretary was all smiles, too. "He probably did the same sicko thing to that Paulette Bramberg woman Clevenger wrote about in his last letter. In Utah?

He said she was brutalized—probably cut her head clean off just like this one."

As the secretary spoke, Jonah saw Paulette Bramberg's eyes staring up blankly at him from the bed of leaves off Route 80 in Utah. The image lasted only a moment, but long enough to convince him Clevenger hadn't lied to him in his last letter. He had killed a woman with brutal force before. But only once before?

"Hates women," Donahue said. "Ask me, that's Sam Garber in twenty, thirty years."

Jonah knew he should say something, knew it was his turn to speak. "Sam Garber?" was all he could manage.

"He's been admitted five times in the last eighteen months," the unit clerk said.

Donahue shook her head. "He's got the whole pedigree of a budding sociopath: lights fires, hurts animals, wets the bed."

"We have to keep his mother away from him," Jonah said.

"Good luck," Donahue said. "Social Services hasn't lifted a finger to protect him."

"Why not?" Jonah asked.

"He goes with the party line. Parrots back the stories his parents feed him about how he got hurt. No one's been able to prove otherwise."

"No one *wants* to prove otherwise," the ward clerk chimed in. "It's not like every group home in the state would be lining up to take him. He's a pain in the ass. Assaulted the staff a bunch of times. Tried to set fire to the hospital twice."

"He needs to set fire to his mother," Jonah said automatically, horrified to hear his own words as they came out of his mouth. But were they his words? What was happening to him? He laughed to take the edge off what he had said, but his laughter sounded hollow, mechanical.

The ward clerk and Donahue glanced at one another.

"I suppose that's one way to look at it," Donahue said. She cleared her throat. "Get up on the wrong side of the bed this morning, Dr. Wrens?"

He summoned every bit of positive energy he could. "A little joke," he said with a wink.

Dr. Corrine Wallace, the hospital's chief of psychiatry, appeared at the door to the nurses' station. She was an attractive woman about forty, with shoulder-length brown hair and a rare and infectious optimism that her staff and patients relied upon. But now her face and her voice were somber. "May I see you a minute?" she asked Wrens.

"Of course," he said, tentatively.

"It's about what happened at the diner."

Jonah froze as his paranoia soared.

"We were just talking about it," the ward clerk said, "hoping they fry that bastard."

Maybe he had been spotted at the crime scene, after all, Jonah thought. Maybe the police were waiting for him this very minute, outside the door to the locked unit.

"Shall we?" Wallace asked him.

The two of them walked silently down the hall, into Jonah's office.

"Care to sit down?" Jonah asked.

She shook her head. "We work very closely with police departments in the area," she started. Jonah slipped his hand inside the front pocket of his pants, gripped his folding knife.

"A Sergeant John "Buck" Goodwin called this

morning," she went on. "He's the detective assigned to the murder in Bitter Creek. I told him I would help him."

Were they using Wallace as the "good cop"? Jonah wondered. Did they actually think he might roll over and let them search his hotel room without a warrant? "In what way?" he asked her.

"The owner of the diner and the employees were just absolutely wrecked by this thing," Wallace said. "The victim—Pierce, her name was—was very well liked. Her daughter happens to waitress there, too. The whole staff is like a big, extended family." She paused. "Normally, I would never ask a locum to do this, but I have to be out of town for a seminar later today. And Dr. Finnestri really isn't comfortable with trauma victims."

Jonah could hardly believe what he was hearing. Was Wallace really about to ask him to counsel Pierce's coworkers? Her daughter? Was this God's way of punishing him, making him see firsthand the suffering he had wrought? It terrified him and touched him.

"I don't think it would take more than two or three hours of your time," Wallace said. "But if there's any way you could talk with these people by phone. The daughter, especially."

"I'd like to help," Jonah said, speaking not only to Wallace, but to God. "In fact, I'll invite each of them to visit with me right here at the hospital."

"This is clearly not in your job description. We can pay you something extra."

"I wouldn't think of it. It's the least I can do," Jonah said.

*

Jonah met with Sam Garber half an hour later. It felt good to lose himself in the boy, to forget what had happened the night before.

Sam was stocky and much taller than most nine-year-olds and spoke in a monotone that made him sound older, too. Only his soft skin and the bangs cut straight across his forehead gave him away. He sat bolt upright in the chair opposite Jonah's desk, his brow furrowed, a slight frown on his face as he told Jonah how clumsy he was, how he'd fallen down and hurt himself again and again, how all he wanted was to go home to his mother and father.

"That's not going to happen this time," Jonah said.

The furrows in Sam's brow deepened. "I know you can't keep me here," he said tentatively.

Jonah heard a plea in Sam's words. *You* won't *keep me here. You can't rescue me.* He knew he had to demonstrate his resolve, to prove Sam could place himself in his hands. "I can and I will," he said. "There is no possibility you will go home from here. You'll go somewhere safe. Because I know *exactly* what your mother is doing to you."

"She's not doing anything."

"Have you ever seen me at this hospital before?" Jonah asked.

"No."

"Do you know why they call me in?"

Sam shrugged.

"I can read minds," Jonah said.

"Tell me about it," Sam scoffed. "What are you, some sort of superhero? Got X-ray vision, too?"

"I'll show you."

Sam hesitated, which told Jonah he wasn't so certain

mind-reading was impossible. "Go ahead," he said. "I don't care."

Jonah stood and walked over to him. "Can I touch your head?" he asked.

"This is dumb," Sam said. But he dropped his head slightly.

"Close your eyes," Jonah told him.

Sam did as he was told. He might look twelve or thirteen, might have suffered through much more than his age would predict, but he was nine, still suggestible, still willing to believe and able to hope that there were rare people in the world with special powers—maybe even enough power to save him.

Jonah laid his hands on the boy's head, closed his eyes, and took a deep breath. He pictured the S-shaped spiral fractures of Sam's radius and humerus. "When your mother hits you," he said, "she holds you by the arm, and you twist and turn to get away."

Sam stayed silent.

Jonah remembered Heaven Garber's tall tales about Sam falling down the stairs, falling off his bicycle, backing into the fireplace. Having listened to countless victims and countless perpetrators, he knew that her stories probably contained elements of truth. Combining fact and fiction creates the most powerful deception. "One time," Jonah ventured, "you tried to get away from her while she was holding you that way, hitting you, screaming at you, and she let go all of a sudden, and you fell down the stairs."

Sam shut his eyes more tightly, as though fighting off the memory.

"Did she laugh at you?" Jonah asked. "Call you clumsy?" He felt Sam's head nod once under his hands.

"Did the same thing happen with the fireplace? She let go?"

"Uh-huh," Sam said.

"You fell back into the screen."

Sam nodded again.

Jonah pictured Heaven Garber taunting Sam as he cried. He could almost hear her cackling. He moved his palms to the sides of the boy's face, felt his tears begin to flow, then felt himself fill with sadness. How wonderful to be swept away by that tide of grief, carried far from his own worries of what he had become, what he was capable of doing. "Where was your father?" he asked, as quietly as though he were praying.

"I don't know."

"Did you ever tell him what really happened?"

"She said he'd never believe me," Sam said. "She said she'd make him send me away to a reform school for lying—and the other stuff, like with those animals. Hurting them. She said I'd never see him again."

"And you thought he would choose her over you?"

Sam shrugged.

Jonah let all his breath out, kneeled in front of Sam. He looked into the boy's eyes. "It's out in the open now," he said. "No changing your story, no matter what. Deal?"

"But what's she gonna do to me?"

"She can't do a thing."

"Why not?" Sam asked.

Jonah thought of the way Hank Garber had been taken aback when he had mentioned losing Sam forever. "Because your dad will choose you," he said. He smiled at him. "You're kind of a superhero yourself."

"Me?" He shook his head. But he was hooked. "What do you mean?"

"You had all the power all along. Not your mother. You just didn't know it."

"You sure about that? I don't feel very powerful."

"Sure as sure can be," Jonah said. He looked deeply in Sam's frightened eyes. "What do you say? We have a deal? Your story doesn't change?"

Furrows fanned across Sam's brow again. He caught his lower lip between his teeth, chewed it a few seconds. "Deal," he said.

nine

An agent named Phil Steiner escorted Clevenger from the lobby of the FBI Academy to the pathology laboratory. Kane Warner and Whitney McCormick were already gloved and gowned, standing beside another woman who was inspecting a female body laid out on a stainless steel dissecting table. Clevenger pulled on the necessary garb and joined them.

"We figured we might as well start our meeting here," McCormick explained as Clevenger reached the table.

Kane Warner acknowledged Clevenger with the briefest of nods.

"The body from Wyoming came in about an hour ago," McCormick went on. "Sally Pierce, sixty-two."

Clevenger looked at Pierce and lost his breath. She had been beaten beyond recognition, her eyelids puffed out like a toad's, her cheekbones dented, her lower lip dangling from ruby shreds of tissue, her broken teeth coated with dried blood. Clumps of her hair were missing, her scalp below pounded so thin in places that bone showed through. Her ears were the color of eggplant. A jagged laceration and black and blue contusions encircled her neck.

Clevenger looked up at McCormick. The contrast between the corpse and her natural beauty made her look otherworldly. He felt the urge to hold her, to kiss her, to be alive with her.

"I'm Elaine Ketterling," the woman at the head of the table said, holding out a gloved hand. "Assistant Chief of Pathology."

Clevenger shook her hand.

Ketterling motioned toward Sally Pierce's head. "As I was pointing out, we obviously have severe contusions to the face, ears, and scalp, consistent with a sustained and extreme beating. We're certain to find facial fractures and brain hemmorhaging once we demask and get an MRI." She curled her fingers under Pierce's chin, gently tilted back her head. "The closed head trauma would have been enough to kill her," she said, "but she also sustained a fourteen-centimeter-deep laceration to her neck, six centimeters above the clavicles." As Ketterling exerted more pressure, the jagged laceration around Pierce's neck opened to a red-purple cleft, then gaped to a canyon that exposed Pierce's transected windpipe, jugulars, and carotids like a schematic out of *Gray's Anatomy*. "The wound extends partway through the spinal column," Ketterling said, "bowing toward the end, consistent with the bent blade of the knife found at the scene. It couldn't quite do the job."

"Did he use a knife that was already in the diner?" Clevenger asked McCormick.

McCormick nodded. "The owner IDed it. No weapon to trace."

Ketterling moved alongside the dissection table, running her hands along Pierce's shoulders, down her arms, over her forearms, wrists, and hands. "The bruising on the upper extremities is much less severe," she said. "Much more diffuse. There's no sign her arms or wrists were bound. More likely the perpetrator knelt right here to keep her from moving." She pointed out two large, elliptical bruises along Pierce's biceps. Then her hands continued to travel—down Pierce's legs and ankles, to her feet. "No obvious lacerations anywhere other than her neck," she said. "I suspect her fractures will be confined to her facial bones and skull. I'll have more definitive data after we get a full-body CT."

"No venipuncture site?" McCormick asked.

"I went over her skin very carefully," Ketterling said. "No sign of phlebotomy. Of course, he could have taken blood from one of the vessels he severed. Carotids. Jugulars. There had to be massive hemorrhaging." She moved to the end of table, nodded toward Pierce's groin. "I did note the large volume of dried blood at the vulva and upper thighs," she said. "I'll do a full pelvic exam later to look for any injury and test for semen."

"No semen," Clevenger said, mostly to himself.

"Excuse me," Ketterling said.

"His rage is pure now," he said, still looking down at the body. "He can't contain it. He was hungry to destroy this woman—and Paulette Bramberg—not get close to them."

"Well, that's pretty obvious," Warner said. He looked at Clevenger. "We had an emotionally conflicted killer, now we have one with a clear mind. I guess I'm having a little trouble seeing how that brings us closer to catching him."

"He has anything but a clear mind now," Clevenger said. "He's losing it."

"Excellent," Warner said. "I'll put out a press release about how the slaughter in Wyoming is actually a *good* sign."

McCormick looked at Warner. "Can we please save it for later?"

"No problem," Warner said. "See you in fifteen." He walked away.

"It's working," Clevenger said, seated on the couch in Whitney McCormick's office. He turned from McCormick to Kane Warner. "For the first time he's killed in a risky location. He could have been caught in the act or seen fleeing. He acted precipitously. Less planning. It's what we want."

Warner chuckled imperiously. "It's what *you* want, Doctor," he said from his armchair in front of McCormick's desk. "I want to stick with the data. He *wasn't* caught. He wasn't spotted. He didn't use a weapon we could trace. We've had a couple of dozen agents poking around the area today with no leads. If he's so out of control, why didn't he make a mistake? Why didn't he use his own knife and drop it at the scene? Why didn't he kill in broad daylight, in front of eye witnesses?"

"If we keep up the pressure, he will," Clevenger said. "Then we've got him—a lot sooner than we would have."

"Says you," Warner said, leaning forward in his chair. "Maybe he really starts to 'bleed' and decapitates a couple of people in some variety store along any one of fifty thousand back roads across this great nation. Maybe he doesn't get sloppy until the whole country is petrified, and we're on the cover of *Newsweek*, trying to explain why Clevenger-style therapy for serial killers just doesn't look like the right prescription for this particular maniac." He smirked. "Of course, you'd still have that cover . . ."

"Is that what you're afraid of Kane?" Clevenger asked. "The bad press?"

"I'm not afraid of any—"

"You like a slower, steadier killer, somebody who generates fewer headlines, further apart. Let him drop bodies here and there, time to time, string things out long enough for you to get your next promotion, or maybe a really big payday running security at Reagan National or Caesar's Palace."

Warner's neck was turning red. "I don't think I'll match the five hundred dollars an hour we pay you anytime soon."

"You get what you—"

"This isn't getting us anywhere," McCormick broke in. She looked at Warner. "Just tell him," she said.

Clevenger looked at her askance. She wouldn't meet his gaze.

Warner sat back in his seat, straightened his tie. "We met with Director Hanley this morning," he said, sounding triumphant. "You're to confine future correspondence with the Highway Killer to recommendations of how he can contain his violence, with a clear slant toward turning himself in. We don't want you getting the pot boiling, so to speak."

"Sounds like selling abstinence to seventeen-year-olds on the pill," Clevenger said. He looked at Whitney McCormick for support.

She stayed silent.

"You agree with him?" Clevenger asked.

"I'm not sure that I do," she said tentatively. "But I'm not certain I don't."

Clevenger squinted at her. "Paulette Bramberg's corpse was in those woods for months. He decapitated her a long time before he and I started trading letters."

"But you dredged her right up," Warner said. "Whatever you sparked inside this guy, he coughed up a corpse that symbolizes his explosiveness. And now he's killed with even more brutality. I don't like the pattern. Neither does the director."

"Who just happens to be thinking about running for Senate," Clevenger said.

The phone rang. McCormick picked up. "Yes?" Her face fell as she listened. "I see. Thank you. I'll let everyone know." She hung up.

Warner and Clevenger looked at her.

"That was pathology. They found a knife inside the victim—Ms. Pierce."

"Inside . . . where?" Warner asked.

McCormick looked at Clevenger like the news she was about to deliver would be the last nail in his coffin. "The handle emerged from the cervix," she said. "The blade bisected the uterus. No semen detected."

As grotesque as the data was, as much as it horrified Clevenger, it only confirmed what he believed was happening inside the Highway Killer's mind—the shredding of his psychological defense mechanisms. But he could see that he was alone in that belief.

Warner looked at him as though he was personally responsible for Pierce's demise. "You get it now?" he asked. "You need to shift him to a lower gear, get him back in some kind of control. Buy us more time."

"It's the wrong strategy," Clevenger said. "Time was on his side. He liked setting the pace."

"So you refuse," Warner said.

Clevenger saw the satisfaction in Warner's face and

realized he wanted him to quit, was itching to race upstairs to the corner office and tell Jake Hanley that the letters would stop altogether. "Give me one day to think it over," he said.

Warner stood up. "Take as long as you like," he said. "In the meantime, should we receive another letter from . . . your patient, we'll glean what we can from it and let it go at that—unanswered."

"You may let it go," Clevenger said. "He might not. You think he's out of control now? Watch him when he feels abandoned, like no one's listening anymore."

Warner smiled his best glad-hander's smile. "He can always book an appointment right here in this office," he said. "I'll clear you to visit him twice a week at Levenworth." He gave McCormick a little bow. "Take care."

"What the hell is going on with you?" Clevenger asked McCormick once Warner was gone. "You left me all alone there."

"They're worried," McCormick said.

"I asked about you."

"I have concerns."

"What, that he might not crumble instantly, that this might actually take a while? Why would you expect anything else? He's been at this game a long time. Too long."

McCormick stiffened a little. "Not just that," she said, her voice dropping a few octaves.

"Okay . . ."

She leaned forward. "I think you should give a little thought to how your own issues could be alive in this thing."

"My own issues?"

"Your *strategy* is clear. You want to bring his rage to such a fever pitch that he overheats. But I don't think you've even considered whether you have any unconscious motivation to watch the meltdown."

"To watch . . ." Clevenger said, baffled. He shook his head, looked back at McCormick. Then it dawned on him what she was driving at. "You think I'd manipulate him into becoming more vicious—for *me*? To express *my* rage?"

"Never intentionally."

Clevenger laughed. "You're kidding, right?"

McCormick didn't respond.

"You don't think I've seen enough violence?"

"We're seeing more than ever in this case. That's all I know. And you have no second thoughts about it, which worries me. If it were solely up to you, you'd just push harder and harder."

"Until he breaks."

"Without taking feedback from anyone else on the team."

Clevenger looked up at the ceiling, took a deep breath, then focused on McCormick again. "Your father would be proud," he said.

"What the fuck is that supposed to mean?" she shot back.

"His daughter turned out to be a politician, just like him."

"I'm not trying to be a politician, Frank. I . . ."

"Maybe it's in the genes." He focused on her more intently. "You know we're on the right track. Other than the fact that it happens to take place in the *New York Times*, this is no different than any other therapy. You don't get to the other side of any serious psychopathology without going through a little bit of hell. The question is always whether you have the backbone for the trip. Maybe you just don't."

"That's not fair."

"You can't stand up for what you know," Clevenger pressed.

"I can, too," she said, sounding very much like a little girl and looking very bothered her words had come out that way.

He shook his head. "Deep down, you don't believe you have permission to say what you think and defend it. You aren't sure whether this is really your office or your father's. So you're playing it the way he would—safe."

"This *is* my office. And I want you to leave. Now."

"There," Clevenger said. "Now that's backbone. You just have to show it when there's something bigger at stake than your ego—like people's lives." He stood up and walked out.

Clevenger didn't get back to the airport until after 7:00 P.M. He reserved a seat on the 8:20 to Boston, checked his messages at home. There was one from Billy, telling him he was comfortable enough on the detox unit at North Shore Medical Center and thanking him for taking him there. He sounded pretty good, which made Clevenger feel a little bit better than he had leaving Quantico. But the message following Billy's sank his mood.

"Dr. Clevenger," a woman's voice said, "this is Linda Diario at the Massachusetts Department of Social Services. I'm calling to see when we could meet to talk about a discussion I had with one of Billy's clinicians at the detox unit earlier this afternoon. If you could contact me at your earliest convenience, I'd appreciate it."

The Department of Social Services would never call with good news. Clevenger dialed North Shore Medical Center, got connected to Billy's room. "How you feeling, champ?" he asked.

"Like a truck hit me," Billy said. "They're going pretty light with the detox meds."

"It's never easy, but it's worth it. Stick it out."

"I will," Billy said. "How are you?"

"Headed back." He paused. "I heard you got interviewed by a social worker today."

"Some woman came by."

"Did she ask you about our relationship?"

"Sure. I told her we were tight. Tighter than ever. Even working together a little."

Clevenger felt his chest tighten. "Did you mention the Highway Killer investigation?"

"She asked about it. I just told her I was reading up on him, trying to help out." A couple of seconds passed in silence. "Was I not supposed to tell her?"

Clevenger didn't want to saddle Billy with another worry. "It's fine. I think DSS may have a few questions for me, but nothing I can't handle."

"I shouldn't have said anything."

"It's not a problem," Clevenger said. "Honestly." He paused. "What are the rules on visitors there?"

"None for the first three days," Billy said.

"Then I'll call you in the morning."

"Thanks."

"Love you, buddy."

"Love you, too."

Clevenger hung up.

The flight had started to board. Clevenger got in line. He was almost to the door when he heard Whitney McCormick call out his name. He turned around, saw her headed his way.

She walked up to him. "I don't think we should let it end like this," she said.

"Us, or our work on the case?" Clevenger asked.

"Us," she said. "Stay over tonight. We don't have to talk about the investigation."

Clevenger looked into her eyes. They were bright and beautiful and brimming with a certain hunger that he recognized for the first time as the look he had seen in the eyes of addicts, the look in his own eyes when he was chasing drugs. McCormick needed him like a person needs a fix, maybe exactly the way she needed her father's approval, thirsted for his love, when what she really needed was to love herself. "I've got Billy in detox back home," he said. "I need to be around for him."

She nodded, managed a half-smile. "My offer to show him around the Academy still stands."

"We may take you up on that." When she leaned and hugged him, he hugged her back. But when she looked up at him in a way that invited him to kiss her, he looked away.

She let go. "Take care of yourself," she said.

"You, too."

Clevenger checked his messages again when he got back to the loft in Chelsea. North Anderson had called twice while he was in flight. He turned on his mobile, saw that Anderson had tried him on that phone twice. He called the office, got no answer, and dialed Anderson at home.

"Hello?" Anderson answered.

"It's Frank."

"I've got something you need to know."

"Shoot."

"Stephanie Schorow from the *Herald* called me in the office today. She was asking questions about you and Billy."

"What questions?"

"She knew Billy was in detox. She seemed to be saying that your custody of him was being called into question by DSS. She'd already interviewed a couple of sources there. They gave her the 'can't confirm or deny' routine, which got her more interested."

Clevenger dropped his chin to his chest. For the first time he felt like the Highway Killer investigation and his personal life had collided head-on. "Anyone on staff at the medical center could have gotten the bright idea to call the press."

"The press might have stumbled on this one themselves. I'm sure you're being followed most of the time."

"I got a message from DSS," Clevenger said, scrolling through his Caller ID list. "They want to meet." He came to numbers slugged *HERALD NEWS*, then another slugged *NY TIMES*. "The *Herald* tried me, too. And the *New York Times*."

"Whatever they're running, they've put it to bed," Anderson said. "Nothing you can do tonight."

"That won't make me sleep any easier."

"I guess not. How's Billy?"

"So far so good," Clevenger said.

"Glad to hear it," Anderson said. "Anything you need, call me. Understand?"

"Thanks."

Clevenger dialed his voice mail as soon as he had hung up from Anderson. As he expected, the message from the *Herald* was from Stephanie Schorow, wanting an interview about Clevenger's relationship with Billy. But the message from the *New York Times* was from Kyle Roland, the legendary publisher, not some reporter looking for a sidebar to the Highway Killer story. And Roland had left his office number, his mobile number, and his home phone.

It was past 11:00 P.M. Clevenger dialed the mobile.

Roland answered on the first ring. "Kyle Roland," he said, in the throaty yet musical voice that was his trademark. Clevenger pictured the still brawny seventy-year-old in the Manhattan penthouse apartment Clevenger had seen featured in the *Times*'s Style section, every wall a recessed floor-to-ceiling bookcase stocked with classics, great biographies, and the novels Roland loved most: detective stories. He owned first editions of every work by Conan Doyle, Chandler, Hammet. And he had signed volumes from the new greats. Evanovich. Kellerman. LeHane. Coben. Parker.

"Frank Clevenger getting back to you."

"I appreciate the call," Roland said. "I had a difficult decision to make earlier today. I made it, wanted you to know about it, and want to know how you're likely to respond."

"That's a lot of 'want' in one sentence," Clevenger said.

Roland laughed, but got right to the point. "We received another letter from the Highway Killer this morning, Fedex. He makes reference to you and Dr. McCormick being romantically involved. He saw the two of you together in Utah."

Clevenger could hardly believe what he was hearing. "He was watching us?"

"That's what he claims. Which seems possible. He told you where to find Paulette Bramberg's body. He could have driven right by while you were at the scene. He could have been anywhere in those woods. He could have been waiting at your gate when you flew in." He skipped a beat. "Or at your hotel."

"He was that close," Clevenger said, his voice just above a whisper.

"I'm calling because the FBI asked me not to publish the letter," Roland said.

"Kane Warner?"

"Warner and Jake Hanley, both."

"And?"

Roland cleared his throat. "There are legitimate reasons not to publish material—even material as compelling as this letter. I think when something jeopardizes a police matter as important as the Highway Killer investigation, that test is met."

"You couldn't edit out the part that refers to McCormick and me?"

"Edit it out? No way. I think that reference is integral to what the killer is saying. Part of what he's focused on is your alliance with Dr. McCormick. I'm no psychiatrist, but I think that's meaningful, especially given the likelihood that we're dealing with a man with very few, if any, real attachments."

Clevenger let out his breath. It all seemed to add up to politics as usual, even coming out of Kyle Roland's charmed mouth. "If you're not going to run it, why bother talking about it?"

"I did run it," Roland said. "Front page, above the fold, tomorrow morning."

Clevenger felt a wave of energy flow into him. "Then what was all that about it jeopardizing the investigation?" he asked.

"I think it's important for you to know where I'm coming from. I would have pulled the letter *if* I believed it represented a real hurdle to arresting the killer. I don't. I think Kane and Jake are trying to keep their noses clean and keep the public off their backs. And that's not a good enough reason to censor anything— even for a friend."

"Good for you."

"So here's my question: will you respond to the letter without the FBI being involved? Same ground rules would apply. We don't print anything that would make it easier for this guy to get away."

Clevenger felt like another major fork in the road had snuck up on him. If he chose to continue his public psychotherapy with the Highway Killer, he'd not only be playing his own game, he'd be playing without any backup at all. He'd also be working the case while fending off the Department of Social Services and a new storm of media attention certain to begin swirling around him and Billy as soon as the *Boston Herald* hit the stands. Not to mention all the fun the tabloids would have with his apparently DOA romance with McCormick. But with all those reasons to say no, he heard himself say yes, and he felt good about saying it. Settled. And he realized—not for the first time, but perhaps more clearly than ever—that he and his work in this world were inseparable. One thing. Elemental. Billy Bishop's father was married to forensic psychiatry. Call it a profession or an obsession or an addiction. The label didn't matter. The motivation to understand how violent criminals were made and how their minds worked rose above all labels, above all value judgements, above reason. In this life, Frank Clevenger was tied, permanently and inextricably, to understanding destructiveness wherever he saw it. There could be no divorce. Not ever.

"Excellent," Roland said. "If you can get us your response by, say, one P.M. tomorrow, we'll run it Thursday."

"You'll have it," Clevenger said.

"Then let's talk tomorrow," Roland said.

ten

Clevenger didn't sleep at all. His mind kept visiting Utah, replaying his every move, trying to register a face to go with the Highway Killer's words. But he couldn't bring one into focus. Like Roland had said, the killer could have been anywhere—driving by the crime scene as Clevenger and McCormick were getting out of the state police van, at the restaurant where they had had dinner, at their hotel, at the airport. And there was another reason he might not be registering in Clevenger's mind. He blended in. No rough edges, nothing to turn heads. A pleasant-looking man who caused no alarm. A blank slate of a man you could pour out your heart to.

He went to get the *New York Times* the moment he heard it hit the floor in front of his loft. He sat down and read the Highway Killer's letter, rereading part of it three times:

> *You think you can avoid that struggle by submerging your heart and mind in the sex act. You choose the huntress to avoid choosing a true self, to avoid the question that haunts you. Are you—at core, in the darkest moment of your night—a healer or a hunter, my physician or my executioner?*

253

I will help you answer that question. Because I—unlike you—am a man of my word.

One by one, I would have returned each and every body to you, to be reunited with its family, but you have proven yourself unworthy, arriving in Utah with the FBI (whom you promised to disavow), then lying about my offering in order to make me question my love for my mother, my defender, my angel.

Could it be, he wondered, that the Highway Killer didn't remember what he had done to Paulette Bramberg?

The phone rang. He glanced at the Caller ID. Federal Bureau. He picked up. "Frank Clevenger."

"It's me," Whitney McCormick said. "The *Times* got another letter from the Highway Killer."

"I know," Clevenger said. "I talked to Kyle Roland last night."

"You talked to Kyle Roland?"

Clevenger didn't think he should tell McCormick about his agreement with Roland to keep the Highway Killer's therapy going. Kane Warner or Jake Hanley might take another shot at trying to end it. "He wanted to explain why he hadn't withheld the part about you and me from the FBI," he told her. "He felt they should know how focused the Highway Killer is on our relationship."

"Kane grilled me on whether it was true," she said.

"What did you tell him?"

"The truth—that I care about you."

Clevenger was surprised how much he liked hearing that. "Same here," he said. "For whatever it's worth."

"It's worth a lot," she said. "Maybe when this is all

over I can prove how much." She paused. "He wanted to know whether we had slept together."

"He can't ask you that. You work for him."

"He can if he has reason to believe it could affect my work."

"So what happened?"

"I answered his question, and he took me off the case. He said he can't trust me to be objective. Hanley backed him up."

"You sided with them yesterday, not me. How can they say you're not objective?"

"It doesn't matter anymore," she said. "I quit."

"You *quit*?" Clevenger pictured the smug look on Kane Warner's face when Warner had almost gotten him to quit the case. "Why give them the satisfaction?"

"It's not about them," she said. "I thought about what you said in my office. You were right. I've never known whether I really deserved this job."

Maybe McCormick was more vulnerable than Clevenger had imagined. Maybe he'd really shaken her to her roots. "What are you going to do now?" he asked her.

"Earn it."

Clevenger heard a mixture of defiance and intrigue in her voice that told him she wasn't even close to finished with the Highway Killer investigation. "Earn it, how?" he asked her.

"Our man definitely killed Sally Pierce. The letter was stained with her blood. It was mailed from a Fedex box about fifty miles away from Bitter Creek. In Creston. If he's unraveling the way you say he is, maybe he really didn't plan this one at all. Maybe he wasn't just passing through. Maybe he's even still around."

"Do not go after this guy, Whitney."

She didn't respond.

"You're a psychiatrist, not a cop. It's not your place to try to capture him. Certainly not now, without Agency support. And certainly not when he's already focused on you as a 'huntress.' "

"Maybe that's what he's afraid of."

"What?"

"That I'm the one who could actually find him. That I really am my father's daughter."

"Or maybe he's setting you up," Clevenger said. "Maybe he wants you to come after him."

"I can take care of myself."

"There are other ways to prove it without putting yourself in danger."

"That's interesting advice, coming from you. You've never exactly played it safe."

"And it's cost me."

"I'll touch base in the next couple of days," McCormick said.

"Whitney!"

She hung up.

Clevenger dialed North Anderson at home right away.

"What's up?" he asked.

"The psychiatrist I was working with at the FBI, Whitney McCormick, quit her job."

"And?"

"She and I had gotten involved. That's what triggered her resignation. The Highway Killer must have seen us together in Utah. He wrote about it in a letter to the *Times*. It was published this morning."

"Old habits die hard, chief," Anderson said. "Hope she was worth it."

"I think she's got it in her head to try to find the Highway Killer herself, get her job back—whatever. She might just get herself killed."

"You want me to keep an eye on her?"

"I think she's headed to Wyoming," Clevenger said. "I know it's asking a lot, but I can't check up on her without her knowing. And I've got a storm brewing here with DSS."

"I'll get someone to check airline reservations," Anderson said. "If she booked a flight, I'll be on the same one."

"I owe you."

"We're past balancing accounts with each other, partner."

Clevenger spent the next three hours drafting his response to the Highway Killer's letter. He believed the killer was projecting when he asked whether anyone had shown Clevenger pure love: no one had loved the *killer* purely, certainly not the mother he called his "angel." With two mutilated corpses of women in their sixties as data, Clevenger decided to go with the theory he and Billy had come up with: the killer was raised by a woman who could be gentle at one moment, brutal at another. He was mimicking that dynamic—getting close to his victims, then cutting their throats.

It was time to ratchet up the psychological pressure. If the killer truly believed Paulette Bramberg's body was no more horribly disfigured than the rest, then he had the capacity for a real break with reality. Psychosis. And if Clevenger could trigger that break, then the killer's ability to reason, strategize, and avoid being caught would be obliterated.

The finished letter was designed to pull apart the Highway Killer's fragile defense mechanisms, to unmask the insanity smoldering beneath:

Gabriel:

You ask if I have experienced true love, but the question is better put to you. The bodies found in Utah and Wyoming make it plain your anger is directed toward the woman you claim you adore—your mother. Why else would you lose control so completely with women her age? Why else would the most chilling injury you inflicted—to the woman you killed in Wyoming—be to her reproductive organs?

Do you even remember killing Paulette Bramberg? Or has your mind blinded you so completely to the abuse you suffered at your mother's hand that you cannot bear to look upon the destruction you visit upon others in her place?

When you returned home from your birthday party in the park, it was not your father who attacked you. It was your mother, the woman you idealize as your long-suffering defender, the beauty you fantasize cowering in the corner, blowing you a kiss. What a pretty illusion.

Your mother gave you that birthday party, then turned on you and punished you for having it, split your lip, destroyed your gifts. How could your young mind make sense of that dichotomy: kindness and cruelty from the same person? How could you do anything but split her into two—the perfect mother who loved you completely, the demonic other who tortured you?

She was one and the same. She loved you and hated you, nursed you and cursed you, carressed you and beat you.

In what other ways did she terrorize you, Gabriel? What else did she do to completely sever your sensitivity and intelligence from your aggression, so that the aggression floated free, unrestrained by reason, untempered by empathy, and became embodied in the Highway Killer?

I do not believe you search for victims. I believe you search for comfort, for love, for the kind of complete union you fantasize you had with her. But it was a mirage then, and it is a mirage now. Being reminded of that fact reignites the primitive rage you felt as a boy, the infant's pure fury when the breast is pulled from his hungry lips.

Clevenger decided to cast another line for someone who might remember a rare, intimate interaction with a perfect stranger:

Only when someone fulfills your titanic need for closeness can you let that person go. Only when someone connects immediately and intensely—in a way he or she would never be likely to forget—do you feel sufficiently well-fed to forego a blood meal.

You took no blood sample from Paulette Bramberg or Sally Pierce. For them, your violence was pure and unrestrained, possibly entirely unconscious, since it erupted from that dark well you refuse even to acknowledge: your hatred for the woman who brought you into the world.

The pain in your head and in your jaw, the aching in your gut, are your body's reactions to you suppressing the truth: you had no one to defend you as a child. You were entirely vulnerable to the mood swings of the woman upon whom you depended for love. When she provided it, you felt alive. When she withheld it, you felt dead. And as you drive the highways, you are fleeing from the truth that she was two things: your angel and your devil.

The reason you focus on my connection with Whitney McCormick is that male-female relationships always appear toxic to you, full of peril. Because in your mind a woman is never as she seems to be. Behind every kind word, every tender touch, each passionate moment, lurks the unpredictable demon you feared as a child— the demon you wrongly remember as your father.

Did you ever meet your father, Gabriel? Can you bring his face to mind? His voice? Do you have a single possession that was his? Haven't you ever wondered why not? Where has he gone? Disappeared into thin air?

Why did your mother call you a 'little bastard'— literally a fatherless child?

He wanted to make the Highway Killer confront the truth by inducing him to paint a mental image of it:

Put this letter down a moment, close your eyes, and picture the scene you described in your house again. Put your mother's face on the person striking you, berating you, destroying your toys. Can you even bear to do it? And once you put that face on your assailant, can you remove it? Or is it permanently affixed there by reality, by the truth the Highway Killer could never bear to see—that your mother was, like you, both darkness and light, good and evil, heaven and hell.

psychopath

The words of Jung you quoted should speak to you now:

> *The sad truth is that man's real life consists of a complex of inexorable opposites—day and night, birth and death, happiness and misery, good and evil. We are not sure that one will prevail against the other, that good will overcome evil, or joy defeat pain. Life is a battleground. It always has been, and always will be; and if it were not so, existence would come to an end.*

Let go of your illusions. Let yourself be the boy injured by a violent, schizophrenic mother, rather than the living embodiment of her illness. Embrace the parts of you that died as a child and you will no longer hunger to watch others die. Look long and hard at what was murdered inside you, and the Highway Killer will die a vampire's death under the bright light of the truth.

Every day you remain ill does indeed reflect my limitations as a healer, but it also represents your limitations as a human being and as a Christian. Should we fail to stop the Highway Killer, my skill as a physician will be in question. But your stake is infinitely greater: the final verdict on your soul.

You are the one lost in your blind love for a woman, Gabriel, not me. See her for what she was and set yourself free.

He read the letter a few times before signing it. He was going on his gut, which he had learned was the only way to take a giant leap forward—in an investigation or in psychotherapy. The real breakthroughs came when you pushed your intuition to the limit. But there was no turning back when you took that gamble. You either got through to the patient and changed his life or you lost him—sometimes for that session, sometimes forever. And Clevenger had no illusions: losing Gabriel meant other people would lose their lives.

eleven

Jonah took his seat behind his desk as soon as Hank Garber had taken one of the chairs in front of it. Sam was sitting beside his father, nervously drumming his fingers on his thigh. The *New York Times* lay on Jonah's desk, his letter splayed across the front page.

Hank motioned toward the paper. "Another one of them letters out of New York City?" He shook his head. "Bet you'd like to get under the hood of that crackpot."

"Yes," Jonah said, with a smile, "I would." He paused. "I'm glad you were willing to meet. And I think it's just as well your wife wasn't able to. It gives the three of us a little time."

"Heaven's got her own health problems," Hank said, looking over at Sam. "Back went out on her again. She's in a world of pain."

Sam looked down.

Jonah didn't want the boy to lose his nerve. "Trust me on this—your son is suffering far more than your wife," he said to Hank. "That's why I asked you here. Sam wants you to hear firsthand what he's going to tell the Department of Social Services tomorrow. He needs you to back him up, to admit that he's telling the truth."

Hank looked at Sam. "Ain't told nothin' but the truth from the beginning."

Sam shrugged weakly.

"A couple, three accidents," Hank said, his unblinking eyes bearing down on the boy.

"Telling DSS what really happened will help you keep custody of your son," Jonah persisted. "You could take him home with you—provided, of course, your wife isn't living with you anymore."

Hank blinked once, but never stopped staring at Sam. "We had a run of bad luck. But I'm gonna be around a hell of a lot more. Keep track of things. Keep you safe."

Sam looked up at his father.

Jonah could see hope clouding the boy's eyes. The poor kid was thinking things really might be different this time, that maybe he should keep his secret. "Go ahead, Sam," Jonah said. "Tell him."

Sam looked down again.

"You have all the power," Jonah said. He waited for Sam to look at him. "But you have to use it."

Sam gazed into Jonah's eyes several seconds, as if recharging a weak battery running his soul. He turned to his father. "You know how she is to me," he said.

You know how she is to me. Jonah's scalp tingled. Sam had spoken just those seven words, but the words were no less moving to Jonah than the Declaration of Independence or the Emancipation Proclamation or Jesus' words from the cross. Because with them, beaten and abused Sam Garber, shackled to a life that was no life, had suddenly and irrevocably declared himself free, declared himself alive.

Hank held up his hand. "Things are gonna be all right if you just—"

"Won't, though," Sam said, choked up. "You know it."

Hank closed his eyes.

Jonah waited a few seconds before speaking. When he did, his voice was pure compassion. All his rage was blissfully submerged in the tortured lives before him. "Why are you so afraid of losing her, Hank?" he asked. "Why risk losing Sam?"

Hank took a deep breath, shook his head.

"Who left *you* as a child?" Jonah asked.

"Nobody by their own choosing. I can tell you that."

"You lost someone you loved."

Hank suddenly looked angry. "Since you want to know so bad, my parents got killed," Hank said.

"I do want to know," Jonah said, his voice a gentle wave rolling to shore. "How old were you?"

"Six," Hank said.

"A car crash," Jonah said, half to himself. Jonah's breathing slowed. The muscles in his arms went slack. "You were in the car."

Hank nodded.

The last of the background noise in Jonah's brain evaporated. "Who raised you?"

"I got put with an aunt."

Put with. Not *raised by.* Not *taken care of by.* "She was cruel," Jonah said.

"I was a tough little bastard," Hank said. He winked at Sam.

"You couldn't leave your aunt when you were a child," Jonah said. "You had already lost the two people who truly loved you."

Hank stayed silent.

"You would be all alone. A little boy with nowhere to go."

Hank shrugged in the same weak way Sam had moments before. "It's just how she was," he said, then squinted and shook his head, seeming to realize how similar his words were to the ones he had heard from Sam.

"Here's the saddest part," Jonah said. "You *never* really left. Because Heaven is just like your aunt. She probably even looks like your aunt, now that you think of it. A big woman. A blonde woman. Brown eyes."

The look of disbelief on Hank's face proved what Jonah had said was true.

"All you've done is transfer your suffering to your son."

Hank swallowed hard. "Sam's like me," he said, his voice cracking. "Tough."

"He is tough," Jonah said. "But maybe not as tough as you. And Heaven may be more violent than your aunt. That's the big danger when you re-create the past—you can never get it exactly right." He paused. "You survived. That doesn't mean Sam will."

Hank's eyes filled up.

"He's going to tell the truth tomorrow," Jonah said. "That gives you one last chance to be true to him. Don't waste that chance, Hank. Help DSS do the right thing. Back Sam up."

Several seconds passed in silence.

"Dad?" Sam said.

Hank wouldn't look at him.

"Dad?"

Hank wrapped his arms around himself and hung his head.

"It'll be okay," Sam said.

Jonah nearly gasped, watching this victim, this young and tortured soul, become a healer before his eyes.

Hank's chin was quivering. "All right," he said, still looking down. "All right. We'll do this together."

Sam smiled the first real smile Jonah had seen on his face, a full, ear-to-ear grin. He stood up, bounded over to Hank, but stopped short when Hank didn't raise his head.

Jonah literally held his breath as the seconds crawled by, seconds slowed by the weighty question of whether Hank—nothing but a beaten, frightened boy himself— could grow suddenly into a real man, into a real father willing to do for his son what he could not do for himself. Ten, eleven seconds passed in that purgatory. And just as Jonah was about to lose hope, just as he was about to acknowledge that God cannot be everywhere for everyone at every moment, he watched in amazement as Hank opened his arms, grabbed his son, and held him to his heart. And then Jonah felt God's love shining down upon all of them, despite Anna Beckwith and Scott Carmady and Paulette Bramberg and Sally Pierce and all the others. Despite Heaven Garber. Despite his own monster of a father. Despite every evil in the world. Despite his own evil. And he knew in his heart that he would be saved.

Though we often miss it, the world has symmetry, a true pattern. We are connected one to another in mystical, immeasurable ways we know little about. As Hank Garber was embracing his son in Jonah's office on the fifth floor of the Rock Springs Medical Center in Wyoming, Clevenger was being escorted to Linda Diario's office on the fifth floor of the Department of Social Services, 3,354 miles away in Boston.

He was already a couple of rounds into a day that felt like a heavyweight bout. Kane Warner had called around 6:00 A.M., railing against the *Times*'s decision to print the

Highway Killer's letter and warning Clevenger not to respond. "You'd be interfering with an ongoing investigation," Warner had said.

"I happen to have been part of that investigation until you shut me out," Clevenger told him. "Now I have to go my own way."

"You don't care about anyone but yourself, do you?"

"If this is where I'm supposed to start feeling bad for you, book an appointment."

"You've got this guy focused on a sexual relationship between you and Whitney," Warner said. "He was *watching* the two of you in Utah. And the way I read his letter, he's got the twisted idea in his head he can save you from her. You can't know whether the guy is around the corner from her condo right now. And you don't give a shit."

That was the last thing Warner had said before hanging up, and it was still stuck in Clevenger's mind as Linda Diario, the DSS Commissioner, came out from behind her desk to greet him.

"So glad you could meet on short notice," Diario said. She was a grossly overweight woman who might have been forty or fifty underneath all her padding, wearing a tight, navy blue skirt, a belt of shiny gold links, and an ivory-colored silk blouse open too low, exposing more of her generous cleavage than anyone was likely to want to see. She held out her hand.

Clevenger shook it.

"I've asked Richard O'Connor to join us. He should be right along."

"O'Connor? The prosecutor?" Clevenger asked.

"He left the district attorney's office two months ago and signed on with us," Diario said.

Clevenger had testified for the defense in a murder

trial prosecuted by O'Connor. A psychotic woman with postpartum depression had killed her three-year-old daughter. The testimony had helped win a verdict of not guilty by reason of insanity. "I suppose that's alright," he said. "I didn't think to bring an attorney of my own."

"It's a matter of policy for us any time we discuss a child's welfare."

Clevenger nodded. He figured if things got dicey he could put in a quick call to Sarah Ricciardelli, the Quincy, Massachusetts, lawyer who had so expertly shepherded him through Billy's adoption in the first place. Her office was only fifteen minutes away. "Why don't we start and see how things go?" he told Diario.

"Why don't we?" Diario said, looking toward the door. "Richard. I think you know Dr. Clevenger."

O'Connor walked in. He was a wiry fellow about five-eight, late thirties, with a prominent forehead and deeply set ice blue eyes. "Been hearing a lot about you lately," O'Connor said. "Hard not to."

"Occupational hazard," Clevenger said. He noticed O'Connor didn't extend his hand.

The three of them took seats around a conference table that occupied the short arm of the L-shaped office.

Diario let out a long breath, opened a folder in front of her.

Clevenger saw the pages on top were the ones he had filled out when he had first applied to adopt Billy.

"Let me give you a clear sense of our concerns," Diario said.

"Please do," Clevenger said, glancing at O'Connor, who came up with a half-smile for him.

"We're in receipt of a report from one of our

clinicians in the field identifying Billy Bishop as a 'child in need of services,' " Diario said.

That was code for a child at risk. It triggered an official DSS investigation. "What sort of services do you mean, in this case?" Clevenger asked.

Diario sidestepped the question. "We're concerned about Billy's safety," she said. "He's obviously been using drugs."

"Like a lot of kids his age," Clevenger said. "Including plenty who've been through a lot less than him."

"Using them at home," O'Connor said flatly, like the prosecutor he still was at heart.

Clevenger stayed silent. He was starting to think he might want Sarah Ricciardelli in the room, after all.

Diario touched the adoption form. Clevenger noticed that her fingernails had been chewed to the nail beds, a sign of pent-up aggression. "We're concerned whether you were completely candid when you adopted Billy." She flipped several pages, stopped on a grid where Clevenger had recorded his medical and psychiatric history. "When you filled out this form, you entered one word—*no*—where it asked about drug dependency."

"I wasn't dependent on any substance at that time, nor am I now," Clevenger said.

"I think it's clear the question means to address your entire medical history—past and present," Diario said, handing O'Connor the form.

"I don't think that's clear at all," Clevenger said.

O'Connor shook his head. "The spirit of the question is obvious," he said. "A comprehensive answer is clearly called for."

"Look," Clevenger said, "I would have been happy to tell you I'd gotten sober. I'm proud of it." He figured he'd cut to the chase. "I published my drug history in the *New York Times*, for God's sake."

"Well, exactly," Diario said. "That's where I was headed. We had no knowledge you had a . . . problem with alcohol, let alone cocaine. If we had, we would have integrated those facts into our decision on whether you were an appropriate custodian for Billy Bishop."

"And decided I wasn't?" Clevenger said.

"That's not the point," Diario said. "I'm speaking to whether you were truthful with us. We ventured forward with you despite our concerns about you being a single parent and our misgivings about you having met Billy while investigating his sister's murder. We gave you the benefit of the doubt on more than one count, Doctor."

Clevenger could feel Diario laying the groundwork for a formal review of his custody of Billy. "I didn't know I'd been charged with anything," he said, glancing at O'Connor.

"But now it turns out you had a serious drug problem," Diario said. "Would that be fair to say?"

"I certainly didn't take it lightly," Clevenger said.

"Nor can we," Diario said. "Not when Billy is having a serious problem while you are . . . otherwise distracted."

"You mean by the Highway Killer investigation," Clevenger said.

"By that," Diario said. "And, apparently, by a new relationship—at least according to the *Times*."

"You believe everything you read?"

"I suppose the better question is whether Billy believes it," Diario said. "And how he feels about it."

"He did tell a clinician he's working with you on the investigation," O'Connor said. "I'm no psychiatrist, but maybe he feels he needs to, in order to compete for your time."

"He's not involved in the investigation," Clevenger said.

"He's followed the case closely, given you advice from time to time," O'Connor said.

"He ran away from home," Diario added. "He's been using drugs."

"You don't see any connection?" O'Connor asked.

Clevenger knew he should call Sarah Ricciardelli, knew he was shooting from the hip, but he couldn't stop himself. "I think Billy's a very complicated young man," he said. "I think he wants to be closer to me, which is something I want, too. And I also think he has some dark parts of his psyche that he's inclined to harness and channel toward helping people—people who are victims, like him. That's something else we have in common. And I don't see anything wrong with it."

"You see yourself in him," Diario said.

Clevenger knew that question was actually an indictment. Diario was implying he was projecting his identity on the boy, raising him in his image, including his trouble with drugs and his deep psychological connection with violent crime. "I think we have things in common and things that separate us," Clevenger said. "But I won't dodge your question. The answer is yes. I do see parts of myself in Billy."

Diario nodded to herself, took a deep breath, and let it out. The odor of last night's tuna dinner wafted out of her. "Will you submit to random drug testing?" she asked Clevenger.

"Will I *what*?"

O'Connor leaned forward. "Are you willing," he

asked, "to submit to random drug screens to make sure you are not currently abusing any substance?"

Clevenger didn't miss the irony that DSS was asking him for the same tests he had required of Billy. "Would that satisfy you?" he asked. "Clean drug screens, and that's the end of it?"

Diario and O'Connor exchanged glances.

"As soon as the Highway Killer investigation is over," Diario said. "Until then, we'd like to get back to home plate—a clean slate, so to speak."

Clevenger sat back, tilted his head to get a little perspective on the two people across the table from him. "You would try to suspend my parental rights until after the Highway Killer is apprehended? That might not be this month or next. It might not be this year."

"Not 'suspend,'" O'Connor said. "It would be an open-ended probationary period that would, quite frankly, allow for the indefinite suspension of your rights should Billy's condition worsen due to any involvement on his part in the Highway Killer case."

Clevenger knew that translated to DSS living, eating, and breathing Billy and him. They'd have the right to check on them day and night, drag Billy in for endless meetings with social workers and psychologists. "No chance," he said.

"We think it's a reasonable solution to a complex problem," Diario said.

"I don't," Clevenger said. "If you want permission to run our lives, try to get it from a judge."

"We may have to," Diario said.

"We have a proper role in ensuring the safety of minors in this state," O'Connor said, "no matter how famous their parents might be."

O'Connor had shown his cards, and they had come up envy and payback. "You do have that role," Clevenger said. "I have one, too. I'm Billy Bishop's father." He stood up. "See you in court." He walked out of the office.

His anger helped him keep his game face as he walked to his car on the fifth floor of the Government Center parking garage. He opened the door, slid into the driver's seat, shut the door. And then his face fell, and he hung his head and fought back the tears that wanted to come.

He knew Diario and O'Connor had no good reason to pry into his life with Billy. He knew he was doing the best job he could to raise him under circumstances that were anything but ideal. He knew he would take a bullet for him without a second thought. But he also knew DSS was capricious—and powerful. He knew Juvenile Court was highly political: he could draw a judge who liked him a whole lot or one who disliked him a whole lot. He knew there was a chance—not a great chance, but a real chance—that he could lose his son.

twelve

Whitney McCormick landed at the Rock Springs—Sweetwater County Airport at 4:20 P.M., Central Time. She picked up the pistol she had checked through at Reagan National, rented a car, and drove the thirty-eight miles to the Bitter Creek Diner. Her resignation still hadn't been officially accepted by Jake Hanley, and she still had her badge, which seemed like plenty of ID for the Wyoming state cop guarding the crime scene.

She sat in the booth just behind the one Jonah happened to have sat in, looking toward the counter as he had. She imagined him sipping coffee, glancing out the window at the empty parking lot. Maybe he had dropped a quarter in the silver jukebox mounted on the wall beside the table, listened to a little Sinatra or Bennett as he watched Sally Pierce restocking the glass cabinets with donuts and muffins for the morning crowd. Maybe Pierce reminded him of home, of his mother. And maybe that had started his adrenaline flowing, his fists clenching, his mouth salivating for blood.

McCormick could almost feel him beside her right now, a painful hunger mingling with his excitement. She felt a rush of adrenaline course through her system, a transfusion from the killer that made her heart race and her breathing deepen and the delicate blonde hairs on her arms stand straight up.

Crazy as it might be, she had a gut feeling she was going to nail this guy, see him get the death penalty he so justly deserved, show Kane Warner and Jake Hanley and the Highway Killer and her father and—much more important—*herself* that she had what it took, that she didn't need any favors from anyone to open the door to her own office at the FBI.

It was easy for Clevenger to say she didn't need to prove anything. People might disagree with his tactics, might resent his getting rich when they were getting by, might shun him because the press couldn't get enough of him, but nobody thought he was irrelevant, nobody was saying he wasn't one of the best at what he did.

If she got the Highway Killer, nobody would ever say that about her either.

She looked straight ahead at the entrance, then turned and looked behind her at the emergency exit, noting that the Highway Killer wouldn't have had to strain to get a view of the whole length of the place, to make certain he was the only customer being served. But even craning her neck and rising a bit out of her seat, she couldn't quite see into the kitchen, set off from the dining room by a swinging door with a diamond-shaped window.

She stood up, walked to the counter, and stared through that window, but still got only a limited view of the space beyond it. One whole side of the kitchen was blocked. She glanced to her left and noticed how most of the parking lot was now obscured by the far wall. She had to step back four feet to get a decent angle on it.

There was no way the Highway Killer could have had

any confidence there would be no eyewitness to Pierce's murder, whether someone pulling into the lot or walking into the dining area from the kitchen.

McCormick stepped behind the counter, pushed the swinging door open, and saw a three-foot-wide pool of dried blood about seven feet away on the linoleum floor. She walked over and knelt beside it. She pictured the killer crouched atop Pierce, struggling to keep her down, butchering her without troubling himself to watch his back.

So maybe Clevenger was right; the killer might be falling apart, striking out without planning to, maybe without even being fully conscious of what he was doing. But maybe Kane Warner was right, too: at some level the killer *wanted* to be caught. And if he did, then Sally Pierce's body might be more than evidence of his explosiveness, his deepening insanity. It might be a final cry for help, a plea for someone to stop him right here, right now. His travels state-to-state might be over. He might even have come home.

It was remotely possible he might even have known Sally Pierce.

She walked back out through the swinging door, pulled a map of Wyoming from her jacket pocket, and unfolded it on the counter. She found Bitter Creek, then traced her finger east along Route 80 to Creston, where the Highway Killer had left his last letter in the Federal Express drop box. She reasoned that if she were the killer, the momentum of fleeing the scene of the crime would have driven her further from home, not closer. So she traced Route 80 West, past the towns of Table Rock and Point of Rocks, to the larger town of Rock Springs, then beyond it to Quealy. Between Rock Springs and

Quealy sat the Three Patches Recreational Area, near Pine Mountain and the Salt Wells Creek. That struck a cord; she and Clevenger had wondered whether the Highway Killer might be an isolationist, drawn to solitary pursuits like camping, hiking, and mountain climbing. She kept moving her finger west, came to the town of Green River near the Flaming Gorge National Park.

She eyeballed the length of Route 80 she had traced. All told—Creston to Green River—it measured about 250 miles. That felt like as much of a span as she could possibly explore in the next several days.

Part of her felt foolish trying. There were a dozen agents poking around the area, and they hadn't come up with a single lead. There hadn't been any real progress in the investigation during the past three years. But something was different now. Palpably different. The killer had changed. He had killed brazenly. He had left a calling card at the Bitter Creek Diner. And McCormick felt that calling card was meant especially for her.

She took a deep breath. She was going to have to focus her search by making tough decisions from the start. She was going to have to trust her intuition.

That intuition told her to start by ruling out the long-shot possibility the killer had known Pierce. That meant interviewing her family and coworkers. She'd also need to visit as many health care facilities as she could within the 250 miles she had identified as her hunting ground. She knew one thing for sure: the Highway Killer drew blood like a pro. That might simply mean he had been an army medic like he claimed, but it might mean more. He could be a nurse now or a phlebotomist or even a doctor. And if this was his home, he had to have a pretty spotty attendance record while he crisscrossed the country.

Unexplained absences. Out sick for weeks at a time. Maybe fired for absenteeism by one hospital, hired by another, fired from that one, hired by a third, and so on.

She had to face facts. There was no guarantee he wasn't already in Texas. Or California. Or on his way to New Hampshire. There was no guarantee he hadn't been trained to draw blood twenty or thirty years ago by the Red Cross in Florida or Tennessee or New Jersey, never setting foot in a hospital. But here she was in Wyoming, and the only thing to do, the only thing she *could* do, was simply start. Finding one man along a stretch of highway 250 miles long was a shot in the dark, but it was her shot to take.

She stood up. A little of that adrenaline high came surging back. Her skin turned to gooseflesh. It felt good to be on the road, on the hunt—just like the Highway Killer.

She drove back to Rock Springs, grabbed a couple of slices of pizza at Papa Gino's near the Days Inn, and checked in just before 7:00 P.M. She had unpacked, opened her file on the Highway Killer, and started to review the descriptions of the prior crime scenes when her cell phone rang. Unknown Caller. She answered it.

"Hey, Whitney," her father said. His voice was smooth and low, mellowed by time like a rare scotch, flavored with a hint of his childhood deep in the Georgia swamps.

"Hey," she said, standing up. She felt partly comforted hearing from him, partly embarrassed, even a little afraid—like a kid running away from home. She sat on the edge of the bed. "What's up?"

"I just got off the phone with Jake Hanley."

"It's not his place to tell you," she said.

"*You* didn't."

She could see him sitting behind the seven-foot mahogany desk in the study of his farm in Potomac, Virginia, broad-shouldered and silver-haired, wearing a boldly striped Brooks Brothers button-down, pleated khakis, feet up, gazing out the towering, arched window that looked onto the dimly lighted brick patio where he had taught her to waltz before her ninth-grade formal, the same brick patio where he had held her as she cried at age nine after her mother's death. Sometimes she could still smell the cigar slowly burning between the fingers of his trembling hand that unseasonably cool evening, a hand that had seemed impossibly large to her, impossibly powerful. "So what did he say?" she asked.

"He said you'd had a disagreement with the Agency on the Highway Killer investigation and decided to move on. He said it was an honest difference of opinion."

Or else what? she thought to herself. Or else you go to war for me, call in another favor, get some senator to lean on Hanley? She half wanted to tell him she'd gotten taken off the Highway Killer case for having sex with Frank Clevenger, as if the shock of that revelation might finally make him see her as an adult. "That's right," she said. "Honest disagreement."

"But worth leaving for," he said.

"Time will tell," she said. There was a long pause. It worried her. "Dad? You there?"

"You didn't look at the *New York Times* today."

"No. Why?"

"They printed another letter from the Highway Killer. It caught Hanley and Kane Warner completely off guard. They thought Kyle Roland would bury it." He cleared his throat. "There's a good deal in there about you and Frank Clevenger."

McCormick could feel her neck and face flushing. It was bad enough the FBI had learned of her relationship with Clevenger. Now it was public knowledge. Now her father knew. She felt like a little girl caught necking, and that made her angry. "They pulled me off the Highway Killer case because of it, because of . . . Clevenger, which is bullshit. So I quit."

"That was the 'honest difference of opinion?' " her father asked.

"Pretty much." She braced herself for a harangue about letting him down, about not mixing business with pleasure, about the importance of the McCormick family reputation, about the fact that being a McCormick meant you could never think only of yourself. You had to set an example. She'd heard it plenty of times before.

But she would not be hearing it this time.

"You're okay, then?" her father said tentatively, his voice shedding its authority, warming up in the indescribably comforting way it could when he sensed his daughter really needed him.

She sat down on the edge of the bed. "I'm okay."

"We could get a glass of wine at Mario's place, talk in person."

"I'm not home," was all she could think to say.

"Oh."

She knew that sounded like she was at Clevenger's place. She didn't want to leave him thinking that. "I still have to empty out the office and tie up some loose ends on the investigation. I want to download everything I can to Kane in the morning. It's going to be a long night."

"If there's anything I can do, you know I will."

She knew. She knew he would happily tie every loose end in her life and make everything seem all right. But it wouldn't be. Because even if her father got Jake Hanley to reject her resignation, even if he got her reinstated on the Highway Killer investigation, she'd be left with the same question that had followed her as she'd followed in his footsteps from Andover Academy to Dartmouth (college for him, college and medical school for her) to the FBI: was she a substantial person in her own right, or was she substantially the daughter of Dennis McCormick? "I'll be fine," she said.

"Good night, then."

"Good night."

"I love you," he said quickly. "Nothing could ever change that."

"I love you, too." She clicked off the phone. She sat there for half a minute thinking about what her father must be thinking, wanting to call him back, tell him where she was, tell him she was flying back home, back to him. But then she remembered what he had said about reading the Highway Killer's latest letter in the *New York Times*. And she felt her energy start to build again, every hint of worry and fatigue in her body and mind vanishing behind a new wave of determination, powered by unconscious, surging tides of shame. She felt hungrier than ever to find the Highway Killer. Because now she had been publicly humiliated. Now she had something to prove far beyond the gates of the FBI Academy. She had something to prove to the millions of people who had woken up to the *Times* that morning.

Clevenger's day had gone the distance, fifteen bruising rounds that included a sobering phone call with his attorney Sarah Ricciardelli, during which she advised him to gear up for a long and expensive custody battle, a visit with Billy that had started out badly, two run-ins with crowds of reporters manic with excitement over his reported romance with Whitney McCormick and his brawl with DSS, and a call from North Anderson telling him the last thing he wanted to hear: that Anderson had found McCormick's reservation to Wyoming, hopped a flight to D.C., spent two grand to fly eight rows behind her to Rock Springs, Wyoming, then booked a room down the hall from hers at the Marriott Courtyard near the airport.

His head didn't hit the pillow until after midnight, and thoughts of Billy didn't let him sleep until after 1:00 A.M. Billy was already feeling better, requiring less and less in the way of detox meds, which was good news and bad news. *Good*, because the cocaine and booze and Ecstasy was quickly leaving his system. His kidneys and liver were working well. *Bad*, because some of his resolve seemed to be leaving him, too.

"They want me in Day Treatment for six weeks after I detox," he'd complained, pacing the room like a caged animal. "That's like half the spring."

"And you're thinking that's not long enough," Clevenger had said sarcastically.

Billy stopped pacing, looked at him with disbelief. "It's eight hours a day."

"Which leaves sixteen for you to worry about," Clevenger said, struggling to keep his voice down. "Getting the drugs out of your body is easy. Getting them out of your mind is a war. You win that one in six weeks, you're way ahead of the curve."

"Fine," Billy said bitterly. "But I'm not telling anyone anything about me. Everything I say goes in the medical record, which you know is gonna get turned over to DSS."

That was true, and part of Clevenger agreed the less Billy said the better, but he wasn't willing to jeopardize Billy's treatment, even if it meant a tougher case for Sarah Ricciardelli. "No secrets anymore," he said. "Tell them everything. You have nothing to hide."

"I should leave this place right now," Billy said. "We should just go home."

"What?"

"I can sit around at home just like I do here. It's not like they have therapy groups or anything."

Clevenger had heard the same rationalization from countless patients about to bolt from detox so they could drink or drug again. But he didn't think Billy's addiction was the only force driving him out the door. He thought he could hear a fear of abandonment playing in the background of his words. "We'll have plenty of time to be at home together once you're discharged," he said. "Leave now, and you leave us wide open to DSS claiming you're not serious about getting well. And if I let you stay at home with me, they'll say I'm not serious about it, either."

Billy looked down and shook his head in the way he did when he was working up a head of steam to tell Clevenger and the rest of the world they could go fuck themselves, that he could take care of himself. But this time he didn't. This time, he looked up and said, "We're in a bit of a jam here, huh?" Then he smiled. "Don't worry. I'll sit tight. We'll get through it."

Clevenger had smiled then, and he was smiling now, realizing how far Billy and he had come, how much closer together they had gotten. And as he finally drifted off to sleep, he was thinking how strange life was, how it could serve you up the very best things and the very worst things right out of the blue, with no hint at all what was coming.

part three

one

APRIL 10, 2003

Just as Kyle Roland had promised, Clevenger's response to the Highway Killer appeared on the front page of the *Times*.

Jonah picked up the paper first thing at the hospital gift shop and began reading through it the moment he sat down at his desk.

He had five minutes before his scheduled 8:00 A.M. meeting with Hank, Sam, Heaven, and a woman named Sue Collins from the Wyoming Department of Social Services. And in those minutes Clevenger's words passed through the lenses of his eyes, were converted into electrical patterns on his retinas, sparked impulses that traveled the optic tracts of neurons leading to the occipital cortex of his brain, spread synapse-to-synapse to his limbic system and front lobes, and then were conveyed by means still completely unknown into his mind and, deeper still, into his soul.

In that cauldron a strange alchemy defended Jonah from the onslaught of truth in what Clevenger had written, and converted what should have been his grief, his shame, his primitive rage at his mother into fury at Clevenger for soiling an angel's name. And his hatred of Clevenger and Whitney McCormick and the rest of the hunters at the FBI crystallized hard as a diamond and pure as the waters of the mountains that were his refuge.

Clevenger had baited his hook again, casting about for someone who would remember meeting Jonah, remember connecting with him "immediately and intensely—in a way he or she would never be likely to forget." He had shed any pretense of trying to heal him. He wanted only to catch him and cage him.

Even worse was the "prescription" toward the end of the letter, Clevenger's arrogant rejection of the root injury in Jonah's life, his ignorant assertion that the sadistic father who had tortured him had never even existed:

> *Put this letter down a moment, close your eyes and picture the scene you described in your house, again. Put your mother's face on the person striking you, berating you, destroying your toys. Can you even bear to do it? And once you put that face on your assailant, can you remove it? Or is it permanently affixed there by reality, by the truth the Highway Killer could never bear to see—that your mother was, like you, both darkness and light, good and evil, heaven and hell.*

Jonah crumpled the page in his hand, squeezing it the way he would have liked to wring Clevenger's neck. And when he let go, both his hands curled into white, bloodless fists as he pictured Clevenger with Whitney McCormick, tucked away in some office at the FBI Academy in Quantico, ogling one another, pawing one another, stinking of sex, concocting toxic messages to him, trying to undo him, to drive him insane.

Contrast their small-minded attempts to cage him

with his own strivings to free himself from evil. He had taken Dr. Corrine Wallace's invitation. He had sat with Sally Pierce's coworkers and with her daughter, Marie, absorbing their pain. One after the other. For over five hours. He had held Marie Pierce as she sobbed over how much she missed her mother. And he had felt her loss as though it were his own—so much so that he found himself sobbing with her. Like Christ, he had given her grief a home inside him.

He was struggling with every cell in his body to be worthy of heaven, while Clevenger and McCormick worked day and night to consign him to hell.

A knock at the door. He took a few deep breaths, willed open his fists, and stuffed the crumpled front page of the *New York Times* into his briefcase. He tried to stand, but his legs would not budge. His rage had paralyzed him again. He tried a second time. Nothing. "Come in," he called out, unable to screen out the anger in his voice.

The door opened. Sue Collins from DSS, a wisp of a woman about forty years old, under five feet, who could not have weighed more than ninety pounds, stood outside with Hank, Heaven, and Sam Garber. "Too early?" she asked meekly.

"Not at all. Please, come right in." He realized how odd it must seem that he wasn't moving from his chair. He tried to cover up by smiling broadly and extending his hand energetically. "It's a pleasure to meet you," he said to Collins.

Collins's face registered the fact that Jonah remained seated, but she mirrored his smile and shook his hand. Then she took the seat furthest to his right, leaving three others for Heaven, Hank, and Sam.

Heaven groaned and grabbed her lower back as she poured her 300 pounds into her chair.

Hank sat beside her, laying a hand on her meaty arm. "Are you alright?" he asked her tenderly.

"Don't know how I make it through the day," she said.

Sam took the seat furthest to the left, beside his father.

Jonah made eye contact with him and held it, half to reassure the boy, half to anchor himself amidst the tides of rage still surging inside him. It worked. Sam gave him a slight, go-for-it nod of his head, and Jonah could feel the sails of his mind catch wind and begin carrying him toward calmer waters. Nine-year-old Sam Garber, with his concussions, his fractured bones, his psychological contusions, with the certain knowledge that he was risking everything, was nonetheless ready to take his stand, to take on the Goliath of a woman who had very nearly destroyed him. Jonah could almost feel himself shedding his own skin, slipping inside this Boy Wonder superhero, this incarnation of God's grace and power. He felt pins and needles in his thighs and calves as his flesh came back to life. He was reborn in Sam. He turned to Sue Collins. "I appreciate you taking time from your busy schedule."

Collins glanced at Sam. "No thanks necessary."

"What's this all about, anyhow?" Heaven asked Jonah. "Why is *she* here?"

Collins straightened in her chair and brushed lint off her pleated black skirt.

Jonah looked into Heaven's lifeless eyes. "You are all here because Sam is going to tell Ms. Collins what has been happening to him at home."

Heaven crossed her arms, puffed out her chest.

"Unless," Jonah said, "you would rather tell us."

Hank shifted nervously in his seat.

Heaven's lip curled. "We already told you." She turned on Collins. "Hennessey out of your office did his investigation, gave us a clean report. Accidents happen. Said so himself."

Something very much like determination came into Collins's face and bearing. And all of a sudden her appearance changed from wispy to lean and tough—a certain flattening of her upper lip, a squaring of the shoulders, both her feet now flat on the floor. Maybe she'd been pushed around one too many times herself as a girl, maybe that was what had brought her to her work in the first place.

"Sam has something to say," she said sharply. "I intend to hear it and to take appropriate action."

Heaven turned on Hank next. "You gonna sit here for this? Let's get the hell out of here, get us a lawyer." She started to stand.

Hank put his hand back on her arm. "We don't need to get lawyered up just to listen," he said.

Heaven shook her head. "You gotta be joking. These people ain't nothin'." But she reluctantly settled back into her seat.

Hank looked over at Jonah.

"Sam?" Jonah prompted the boy.

Sam shrugged, chewed at his lower lip.

Heaven smelled his fear. "Don't be going telling no tall tales," she said.

"What is it, Sam?" Collins asked gently. "I'm listening."

Sam's skin turned ashen.

Jonah began a silent prayer for him.

"Warning you," Heaven said, leaning forward in her seat to stare at him.

Sam dropped his head so that his bangs covered his eyes.

"You can tell us anything that's on your mind," Collins said.

Sam shook his head ever so slightly.

Heaven chuckled. "Good boy," she nearly sang. "We about done here?" She looked from Jonah to Collins, then back again. "Finished trying to put thoughts in my little angel's head?"

"You can do this," Jonah told Sam. But he wasn't sure anymore that Sam could. His bones and brain tissue had healed. But his soul might still be fractured in too many places to bear the weight of what needed to be done. Jonah's teeth clenched with that realization, and his hatred of Heaven Garber surged. He looked at her, saw with horror that she was wearing his mother's eyes again.

A tear had started down Sam's cheek.

Heaven was feeling bold. "You people just don't understand discipline. You figure kids ought be allowed to run wild."

Jonah wanted nothing more than to rip those eyes away from her. But his arms had gone tingly, and he could hardly move them.

"Sam's gonna be better off for having his limits set," Heaven was ranting. "He's gonna be a good boy, not some hoodlum. Gonna learn respect." She looked at Hank. "These people are paid to sit around. We ain't, last time I checked. Let's get going."

Hank didn't move. He was chewing his lower lip now, like Sam. His spindly fingers were tugging at his pant legs.

"C'mon," she said. She pried herself out of her seat, stood up.

Hank gazed up at the massive figure towering over him. "Go on home, Heaven," he said.

The room fell utterly silent.

"Excuse me?" Heaven said, planting her hands on her hips.

"Bringing you along was the wrong idea. Wasn't what the doctor wanted, but I thought I knew better. Thought it would be best for you to listen in. But it's pretty clear Sam can't do what he needs to get done here with you hoverin' over him. And it's pretty clear I can't neither."

Jonah felt a crown of shivers ring his scalp.

Sam looked over at his father.

"What are you talking about?" Heaven asked, looking truly confused, as though she did not recognize her husband at all.

"I'm sorry," Hank said, choking back tears. "I love you. Least I think I do. But there's right and wrong in this life. And I got to do the right thing here this once or I won't be good for anyone or anything. So you just go on home, get whatever things you need, and stay with your sister for now. I'm taking Sam home with me today."

"We're going home together, all of us, right now," Heaven said, her voice straining. She reached down for Hank's arm, but a flash in his eyes told her that grabbing him would do no good. She was dealing with a different man. A free man. She had lost control over him.

Jonah watched as Heaven shrunk before his eyes, her face falling, her shoulders slumping, her chest no longer puffed out, her hands no longer on her hips, but now on the small of her back as she bent forward in what looked like real pain. "They gone and brainwashed you," she said. "You're not thinking worth anything."

"All I been doin' is thinking," Hank said.

Heaven turned on Jonah, her eyes wild with rage, but now hers again, and now filling with tears. "You did this!" she seethed.

"I've told you that I understand you," Jonah said. "I don't think of you as a bad person. My door is still open. We can meet anytime you like."

"What do you think you are, God, handing out forgiveness? You that much better than the rest of us?"

"I'm no better than you," Jonah said.

She took a step back, almost stumbling, most of the fight gone from her face, a dictator deposed, on the run, with only her mixed-up pride to insulate her from whatever fires of hell had burned the child inside her, leaving her psyche so monstrously disfigured. "I would rather die than come to you," she said.

"I understand that, too," Jonah said.

By 3:10 P.M. Whitney McCormick had used her badge and her charm to gain access to the employment files of seven area health care facilities, including Rock Springs' two largest outpatient clinics, three largest primary care group practices, and two hospitals: Rock Springs Memorial and the Rock Springs Medical Center. She had come up dry. Her selection criteria—someone skilled in blood drawing with many absences from work or with multiple terminations for such absences—had netted her a few older women battling arthritis; a doctor now incarcerated for his seventh driving under the influence arrest; and a young, very troubled male nurse about six-feet-four and 350 pounds with gender identity issues, now living in Paris as Patrice, rather than Patrick, who had sent very pretty photographs of herself/himself back to the hospital nearly every month at various stages of sexual reassignment surgery. Not exactly the kind of person you'd let into your car and pour your heart out to.

Now, waiting for Marie Pierce at Rock 'n' Roll, a coffee shop in Rock Springs, she was anxious to get back on the road to make a 4:45 P.M. meeting with the human resources director at the Red Cross offices in Quealy. She was thinking of Pierce as the longest of longshots to help her catch the killer.

She recognized her the moment she walked in. The loss she had suffered showed on her face. Telltale dark circles. Bloodshot eyes. Flushed cheeks. Yet she was still pretty, in a rough way. She was in her early forties, but her body was as trim as a teenager's. Her hair was bleached blonde, tied in a ponytail. She wore an oversized Harley-Davidson sweatshirt, a metal link belt, tight jeans, and black, ankle-high boots.

McCormick knew Pierce had not slept, had not stopped crying. If the nightmares hadn't started, they would soon. Then, the second-guessing: *If I had just worked my mother's shift that night. If I had just gone by to check in on her.*

She raised a hand to call her over.

Pierce spotted her, walked to the table. "Dr. McCormick," she said.

McCormick stood. "I'm so sorry about your mother."

"Thank you. She was a wonderful person." They sat down.

"I know this must be hard for you," McCormick started. "I appreciate you coming here."

"The police already interviewed me. And the FBI."

"I'm a forensic psychiatrist. My role in the case is a little different."

Pierce nodded.

"I read a short article about you, your mother, and your two daughters all living together in the same household. Three generations. Obviously, you were very close."

"We were best friends. I'll do anything to find the person who did this."

The waitress came by and took their coffee orders.

"My questions are pretty straightforward," McCormick said. "I need to know whether your mother had any conflicts with anyone, whether she had been threatened, even by a relative. And I'd like to know whether she had been seeing anyone. Dating."

Pierce answered simply and directly. No one would want to harm her mother. No one had been romantic with her mother since the death of her father three years before. There was no vagabond, homeless, mentally ill son coming and going. Nothing. "I'm really going to miss her," Pierce said. She took a deep breath, bit her lip.

McCormick readied herself for the part of the interview she dreaded—sitting with Pierce's raw grief. She wasn't especially good at that, never had been, maybe because she had never really grieved her own mother's death.

"In a way, though," Pierce said, "it's like she isn't even dead."

"That's normal," McCormick said, knowing her words sounded much more clinical than compassionate. "Denial is a stage of grief."

Pierce smiled indulgently. "I know that," she said. "I took Death and Dying at Quealy Community College.

Got my associate's in psychology. I'm not saying I don't believe she was *murdered.* What I mean is there were parts of her that couldn't be killed. Like the fact that I miss her and always will, the fact that she's inside me and inside my girls Heidi and Sage." She paused. "Mom's gone, physically. I can't hold her, can't hug her. But her spirit is still around. I feel it. I think I always will. I think I'll always be able to talk to her."

Half of McCormick thought Pierce was deluding herself. Her mother really was dead, after all. Every bit of her. McCormick had seen her lying on a stainless steel table with her face macerated and her throat cut. But the other half of her wished she could have the same conviction about her own mother, the same sense that her mother was still alive inside her. "You're dealing with this remarkably well," she said. "Where do you find the strength?"

"I wasn't dealing at all, believe me," Pierce said. "All I could think about was how much I wanted to die. I wanted to join her. I didn't get out of bed for a day and a half. Then I met with this doctor at the hospital, and I started seeing things differently."

"You've already started counseling?"

"The hospital offered it up. For me, and everyone who works at the diner. I couldn't stop crying, wouldn't eat. So when they called the house, my older daughter— that's Heidi—she pretty much forced me to go to see this Dr. Wrens at the medical center in Rock Springs."

"A psychiatrist?"

Their coffee arrived.

"I think that's what he is," Pierce said, sipping the brew. "He's some kind of therapist, anyhow." She shrugged. "What he really is is a miracle worker."

"Pretty high marks."

"I wouldn't have believed anybody could make any difference at a time like this. But it was like he *knew* me, without ever meeting me. Better than I know myself. I ended up telling him things I've never told anyone." She leaned a little closer and spoke more softly. "He actually cried with me."

McCormick intentionally downplayed the feeling in her gut, the suspicion that she was hearing the story about Wrens for a reason. She sipped her coffee. "He cried with you?" she asked, placing her cup on the table.

"It sounds freaky, I know," Pierce said. "But it wasn't. Not if you were there. He cares that much about people. He felt my pain. It hurt him just like it hurt me. And, somehow, that made me hurt less."

"In one hour."

"The meeting was scheduled for an hour, but he spent almost three with me. He had me tell him everything I could remember about my mother. What I love about her. What I hate about her. The fights we had. My favorite gift from her. Her favorite song. Perfume. Food. Holiday. Movie. Everything. And that's when everything came into focus."

"What changed?"

"I realized that those memories made me happy, not sad. That she was still with me, like I've been saying. That she always will be." She smiled wistfully. "It didn't hurt that he was good-looking. And he has this incredible voice. It kind of puts you in kind of a trance."

"Oh?"

"He's not gorgeous—no George Clooney or Bruce Willis. Just real *nice-looking*. A gentleman. Something about him that's very . . . tender." Her cheeks and neck started to redden. "Almost like a woman—not that I'm saying that's what I'm into, 'cause I'm not, at all. But . . ." She collected herself. "I must sound really crazy."

"He obviously helped you a great deal. Did you make another appointment?"

"I wish I could," she said, shaking her head. "He's leaving in a week."

"Leaving? Why?"

"He's a 'rent-a-doc.' " She smiled. "That's what he called it, anyway. I didn't even know there was such a thing. The hospital hired him to help out for a little while. Then he goes someplace else. Could be two hours away. Could be two thousand miles away."

"A locum tenens," McCormick said, mostly to herself. And with those words, the feeling in her gut intensified.

"A *what*?"

"Locum tenens," McCormick said. "They travel all over the country."

two

As Whitney McCormick and Marie Pierce sat at the Rock 'n' Roll, Frank Clevenger was sitting in Sarah Ricciardelli's office in Charlestown, Massachusetts, planning strategy to keep custody of Billy.

"They can just waltz in and change the rules of the game after an adoption goes through?" Clevenger asked her.

Ricciardelli was a thirty-three-year-old woman with a remarkably kind face, acorn brown eyes, long curls, and a lion's heart. "Only if they can prove you intended to deceive them," she said, lightly tapping a very sharp pencil on her blotter.

"Which I didn't," Clevenger said.

Ricciardelli looked down at her copy of the adoption form. "The courts aren't in the mood to give leeway. Not since O.J. Not since Enron."

"They gave Bush Florida," Clevenger said.

Ricciardelli laughed.

"I didn't lie on that form," Clevenger said. "I sat right here and filled it out."

Ricciardelli leaned forward. "I haven't forgotten that, Frank. We answered every question to the letter of the law. And we'll defend our responses in a court of law." She sat back in her chair. "I just wish you hadn't said anything in front of that asshole O'Connor. Or in the *Times*, for that matter."

Hearing that disclaimer worried Clevenger. "You aren't sure we can win."

Ricciardelli shook her head. "All I'm saying is we may have to get creative if things don't seem to be going our way."

"Creative . . ."

"You adopted Billy at age sixteen. Now he's seventeen."

"Ten and a half months shy of being an adult. I know. But the last thing he needs is to get thrown in some foster home until then. It could ruin him."

Ricciardelli held up a hand. "Who's to say he's seventeen?"

"What?"

"He was supposedly adopted by the Bishops at age six, right?"

Clevenger looked at her askance, pretty sure where she was headed.

"Supposedly," she repeated.

"You're saying he could have been seven, that he could be eighteen right now."

"For all we know—or DSS, or the courts—he might have been eight," she said. "The Bishops adopted him from an orphanage in Russia. You know as well as I do, foreign agencies lie about the ages of their kids. The younger they are, the more marketable they are. So let's get Billy over to Mass General and get an orthopedist to estimate his age using biometrics."

Clevenger nodded halfheartedly. "But if we successfully argue he's eighteen, he can blow out of detox or blow off outpatient treatment. I lose my leverage with him."

"You lose *legal* leverage," she said. "I'm not sure that's the authority you want to rely on as his father."

"Don't kid yourself," Clevenger said. "I'll take any kind of authority I can get." His phone rang. With North Anderson out of the office tracking McCormick, all calls were being forwarded. The Caller ID read *Blocked*. He wanted to let the service pick up, but thought better of it. "Excuse me a moment," he told Ricciardelli.

"Frank Clevenger," he said, answering the phone on his way into the corridor.

"Oh," Ally Bartlett said, taken aback. "I didn't think I would reach you directly."

"Is there something I can help you with?"

"I kind of called to help *you*," she said, "even though I don't know if I can. I mean, I don't know if what I have to say is important. I just . . ."

"Try me."

"I know you're probably getting millions of these calls. But I've been reading your letters in the *Times*. And they made me think of someone—especially your last letter. I called the FBI and asked for you, but I got transferred to about fifteen different people. So I just called and got your number from directory assistance in Boston. You're listed, like a regular person."

The *New York Times* and FBI had both been deluged with tips. They couldn't keep up. And none of the thousand or so leads they had managed to check out had led anywhere. Clevenger didn't have much hope this one would, either. He glanced at Ricciardelli behind her desk. He was anxious to get back to their meeting. "Trust me, I'm pretty regular," he said. "May I ask where you're calling from?"

"Frills Corners, Pennsylvania."

"Could I get your name and number and call you right back?"

A pause. "I need to tell you something that happened to me. But I can't give you my name or my number. I don't want to be involved."

Something in the woman's voice got Clevenger's attention. A dramatic edge and a bit of awe, mixed with very real fear. It was the same tone he had heard in the voices of people he had met who had brushed up against killers. Neighbors of Jeffrey Dahmer. Friends of Richard Ramirez. Two former girlfriends of Ted Bundy. "Okay," he said, "Take your time. I'm listening."

She let out her breath, cleared her throat. "It's like what you wrote about in your letter—someone I've never forgotten," she said. "I only met him once, like six, seven years ago, totally by accident. But I still think about him—every day."

"How did you meet him?"

"At a bus stop. Out of the blue. I was pretty upset that day. My dad was sick, in the hospital. Dying."

"I'm sorry to hear that."

"Anyhow, this man just showed up and somehow got me to talk about my whole life with him. I felt like I could tell him absolutely anything. And I did. I mean, I invited him out for a drink—which I would never, ever do—and I opened up about my dad, my mom, even . . . sex. He had this incredible voice. Not sexy, really, just . . . I don't know. *Inviting.* Totally comforting. I've never met anyone like him."

"Did he tell you his name?"

"Yes and no. He told me his name was Phillip Keane. He said he was a doctor—a psychiatrist—at Venango Regional Medical Center."

"A psychiatrist . . ."

"I believed him," Bartlett went on. "I mean, he was incredibly insightful. It really *felt* like I was talking to a therapist. And not just a regular one. I've had a couple and, honestly, they were no big deal. He was the kind you'd dream about. A perfect listener."

"You have any idea where he is?"

"I couldn't even find him back then. I called the hospital the next day, but the operator said there was no Dr. Phillip Keane working there. So I had her transfer me to the psychiatry unit. And then things got really strange."

"How so?" Clevenger asked.

"I gave the secretary his name, and she pretty much seemed to think I wanted to speak with a patient. It's a unit for disturbed children. She asked me whether I was Phillip's mother. So I just hung up. I figured if the guy hadn't even given me his real name, he wasn't interested in seeing me again."

Clevenger had started thinking of all the psychological reasoning in the Highway Killer's letters, the quote from Jung, the way he layed out his personal history, the arrogant assertion that he could heal Clevenger. Could it be? he wondered. Could the Highway Killer be a psychiatrist, like him? "What did he look like?" he asked.

Another pause. "Handsome in a middle-aged way, I guess," Bartlett said. "But that wasn't why I talked to him. It wasn't about him being, like, hot or anything." A couple of seconds went by. "He just looked like the nicest guy in the world. And he really seemed to care about me. I know it sounds crazy, but I think he really did."

*

Clevenger had to work hard to focus during the twenty minutes it took to finish up with Sarah Ricciardelli. His mind kept wandering to lines from the Highway Killer's letters:

You adopted a troubled boy? Are you that boy?

Do you work to understand murderers in order to understand yourself?

How does it feel to fall in love? Is it the pure bliss they say it is to feel one's ego boundaries melt away?

They were probing questions, potentially healing questions. Deeply psychological questions. The killer being a psychiatrist not only explained them, it explained everything. He would be an expert at getting people to reveal themselves, getting very close, very fast. He would seem trustworthy, with a real bedside manner. And he would remember how to draw blood from his years as a medical student and intern.

He called North Anderson from the street the instant he left Ricciardelli's office, got him on his mobile.

"What's up?" Anderson asked.

"He could be a shrink," Clevenger said, bracing against an icy gust.

"Who? What are you talking about?"

"The killer. He might be a psychiatrist."

"A psychiatrist?"

Clevenger leaned into the wind as he walked toward his car. "I got a call from a woman in Pennsylvania. She met a guy years ago who fits the profile of our man to a tee. He told her he was a psychiatrist, that he worked at the local hospital. He *seemed* like a psychiatrist to her. And he used an alias that turned out to be the name of a kid being treated on the locked unit there."

"This guy's left bodies all over the country," Anderson

said. "He overnighted letters from three states in the last six months. What sort of psychiatrist crisscrosses the country?"

"A locum," Clevenger said automatically, pulling himself into the driver's seat of his car. He sat back and stared straight ahead, amazed the word had come so quickly, after so long, and that it seemed so right.

"A *locum*. Great. What the hell is that?"

"Locum tenens. A traveling psychiatrist. A rent-a-doc from an agency. They fill in for a month or two at hospitals with a shortage of staff psychiatrists, usually in rural areas or isolated locales, places that can't recruit docs. Wide-open places our man would like."

"It fits," Anderson agreed. "But the chances of this woman meeting him, reading the *Times* years later, remembering him, deciding to call you . . ."

"I know," Clevenger said. He had to be realistic. The odds of the hook he had set in the *Times* catching exactly where he needed it to were vanishingly slim. But they weren't zero. Otherwise, he would never have set the hook in the first place. "Maybe she didn't meet the killer. But she got me to think of him as a psychiatrist—a locum tenens psychiatrist. And that turns out to make sense, whether she ever laid eyes on him or not."

"What can I do to help?" -

"I'm guessing there are only a couple of dozen locum tenens agencies with enough reach to place psychiatrists across the country. We've got to get to all of them."

"What about the FBI?"

"Warner probably won't listen to what I have to say, but I'll call him."

"I'm betting Murph—you remember Joe Murphy, Murphy and Associates in Marblehead—can get me a list of the bigger outfits within a couple of hours," Anderson said. "I'll start calling as soon as I get my hands on it. It's pretty clear what we need to know: whether they assigned any one of their docs to all the sites where bodies have been found."

"With the most recent assignment being Wyoming," Clevenger said.

"Got it."

Clevenger thought of McCormick. "What's Whitney up to?"

"Making the rounds of hospitals and clinics," Anderson said. "I'm two cars behind her right now, on 80 West. I tailed her out of the parking lot of a coffee shop in Rock Springs a few minutes ago. She met up with a woman about thirty, thirty-five. Hugged her when they said good-bye. Maybe an old friend, maybe a relative of the victim."

"Thanks for keeping an eye on her. Our man may still be in the neighborhood."

"It's none of my business, but it doesn't sound to me like you're anywhere near over her," Anderson said.

"I've got other things on my mind right now," Clevenger said.

"I guess that's a no, but I won't press you."

"Good."

"You want me to call the hospital where this guy said he worked at in Pennsylvania?" Anderson asked. "See if anyone there can figure out who he was?"

"I'm on it right after we hang up."

"Fair enough. Hey, how's Billy, by the way?"

For some reason Clevenger didn't want to tell him he had another custody battle on his hands. Maybe he just didn't want to get into the details right then. Or maybe he was embarrassed, worried Anderson would give him the *I told you so* routine, which he pretty much deserved, trying to track down a serial killer and create a stable home for a troubled teenager at the same time. He wasn't exactly scoring a perfect ten on either performance. "He's good today," he said. "Tomorrow, who knows?"

"One day at a time."

Clevenger hung up. Then he dialed directory assistance and got the number for Venango Regional Medical Center, suddenly feeling how fragile a lead he was following, how little he really had to go on, and how much he had already put at risk.

three

Jonah sat behind his desk at the Rock Springs Medical Center, a blank sheet of paper and a pen in front of him. He stretched his arms above his head, spread his fingers wide and took the deepest breath he could. He felt more alive than he had in a very long time. His vision and hearing and sense of smell were at their heights again. He could feel the underside of his skin stretching over his bulging muscles. When he sat perfectly still, he thought he could actually sense the opening and closing of his aortic and pulmonary valves as the ventricles of his heart squeezed down powerfully, pumping not only his blood, but the blood of all the others who had died to be reborn inside him.

He had triumphed over his own destructiveness by healing Marie Pierce. He could still feel her warm embrace, her overflowing gratitude.

He had triumphed over Heaven Garber and set little Sam free. He could still see the boy grinning ear-to-ear as he left the locked unit with his father Hank earlier that morning.

He let out his breath, lowered his hands, and picked up the pen to start his next letter to Clevenger. He planned to mail it once he had finished his stint in Wyoming and could head for a week in the mountains before his next assignment in Pidcoke, Texas, near the Fort Hood Military Reservation.

He looked at the clock. 4:27 P.M. He started writing:

Dr. Clevenger:

I have indeed experienced true love—the greatest being my love for God Almighty, King of the Universe. By loving Him I can love others, no matter how seemingly demonic or reprehensible. And through Him I pray that I will, one day soon, come to love myself.

You arrogantly claim that my father did not torture me. You challenge me to put my mother's face on my assailant. But I shall not engage in mental charades that defile her. I will not be brainwashed. For even if she were the actor in the dark memories that plague me, even if she were the devil in my life and not my angel, I would have compassion for her and struggle to forgive her.

You and your lovely Whitney would hide your destructiveness behind mine. You would pretend that extinguishing glorious memories of my mother, in order to weaken me, catch me, and ultimately extinguish me is defensible because you are upholding man's laws. But there are greater laws.

We are all sinners, Frank. We are all sick with violence. The difference between us is my ceaseless struggle to follow the light.

My vision is clear now. Yours is still clouded by your need for vengeance.

That need inside you exists only because you have missed a critical truth, perhaps the most critical of all. And it is simply this: self-hatred is the only hatred in the world. It merely finds convenient decoys.

I am one of yours. I am only the most recent tool you

*have used to escape looking at the killer inside you—
that beaten, humiliated boy who once used alcohol and
cocaine to avoid feeling his pain. Love that boy, and you
will find it in your heart to love me, as I have come to
love you.*

*Isn't it clear you would be a better guide for the trou-
bled boy in your home if you embraced the troubled boy
in your heart?*

*I see so clearly now that the men and women I met
along the highways did not give their lives in vain. They
were stepping-stones to heaven. And not for me alone.
For them, as well. And for you, too, should you choose
the path. For all of us are journeying forward together to
a more perfect place. It matters so little in the grand
scheme which collection of flesh and bones takes the
final leap.*

I hold dear the words of Antonio Machado:

> *I dreamt last night,*
> *oh marvelous error,*
> *that there were honeybees in my heart,*
> *making honey out of my old failures.*

There was a knock at his office door. He slipped the
sheet of paper inside his desk drawer. "Come in," he
called out.

Dr. Corrine Wallace, the medical director, walked in,
looking even more somber than she had that morning.
She shut the door behind her. "We need to talk."

Jonah could see in her eyes that something was very
wrong. He motioned for her to take the chair in front of
it.

She sat down. "I don't know how to tell you this,
Jonah, so I'm just going to say it."

Jonah looked at her and knew. "Sam?" he asked, praying he was wrong.

"I got a call from the police."

He didn't want to ask, sat there several seconds, with only the buzz of the fluorescent lights breaking the silence. "How bad?" he asked, finally.

"She killed him," Wallace said. "Hank let her back in the house." Her eyes filled up.

"He's dead? Sam is dead?" He instinctively looked at the clock. 4:52 P.M.

"She told the arresting officer that all she'd wanted from him was an apology. She said he refused, that he 'pushed her over the edge.' "

"What about Hank? Was he there?"

"Yes. He did nothing to stop her. They're both charged with first-degree murder."

Jonah pictured Heaven Garber, three hundred pounds, a mammoth towering over Sam, screaming at him, "Tell me you're sorry! Tell me you're sorry!" But the brave boy refused. And his silence only enraged the beast more.

Then, in the most horrible transformation imaginable, Jonah watched as his mental image of Heaven's face melted into the face of his own mother, her angelic eyes bloodshot, her beautiful lips twisted with rage.

When he looked again for Sam, he saw himself on the floor, weeping, begging not to be struck again.

Was this some invasion of his mind by Clevenger? Had he succeeded in brainwashing him?

"Are you all right?" Wallace asked, leaning forward in her chair.

Jonah looked at her in front of his desk, saw her for who she was. But an instant later her features, too, fused with Heaven's. He rubbed his fists into his eyes. "I need a little time," he said. "I'm sorry."

"Of course." She stood up and started to leave, but turned back to him. "You did nothing wrong. I want you to know that. There was no way to see this was going to happen."

Jonah didn't respond.

She headed for the door.

As soon as Jonah heard the door click shut behind her, he fell to his knees and let his head fall into his hands.

Clevenger called Kane Warner at the FBI and got a cool response to his suggestion the Agency consider whether the Highway Killer might be a locum tenens psychiatrist.

He didn't waste time worrying about that. By the end of the day he had spoken with the director and assistant director of the Venango Regional Medical Center human resources department, the head nurse for the locked unit, and the hospital CEO. They all insisted he'd need a court order for them to release any personnel files or other information pertaining to whether the hospital retained locum tenens psychiatrists—at that time or in the past. He managed to get connected to the locked unit, but the nurse who answered the phone there had only been on staff eight months, and the description Clevenger gave didn't remind her of any psychiatrist she knew.

At 6:40 P.M. EST he decided to give it one more shot, MD to MD. He had the medical director paged. The operator told him to hold for Dr. Kurt LeShan.

LeShan answered five minutes later.

Clevenger introduced himself. "I'm sorry to bother you after hours."

"Not all. I feel like I know you," LeShan said. "I've been following your work in the *Times*. Fascinating. To what do I owe the call?"

"I'm following up on a tip—someone you may have had on staff."

"Who is that?"

"I'm not sure of his name."

"Some tip."

"I think he worked at your hospital during 1995. Around Christmas. He may have been a locum."

"We usually have at least one locum around here. Recruiting staff docs is impossible."

"Tall. Longish gray hair. Blue—"

"Jonah!" LeShan broke in. "Jonah Wrens."

"Can you tell me anything about him?" Clevenger asked.

"I can tell you this—he was the best psychiatrist I've ever hired, the best I've ever worked with, locum tenens and staff docs included. Absolutely top-notch."

"Any chance he treated a boy named Phillip Keane?"

"Possible. Keane's a frequent flier here. Quite psychotic. Why do you ask?"

"Dr. Wrens apparently introduced himself as Phillip Keane, on at least one occasion—to a woman he met."

"Maybe he didn't want her to know who he was. Keane's name probably popped into his head, so he borrowed it. It isn't gentlemanly, I suppose. Certainly not professional. But it hardly merits the attention of a forensic psychiatrist."

"Do you remember what agency Wrens was from?"

"I do. But tell me something first—why are you looking for him?"

Clevenger didn't want to imply Wrens was a suspect

in the case, which he wasn't. Not officially. Not even rationally. He was what had turned up on a hook cast blindly into the sea of millions of *New York Times* readers. "We received an anonymous call stating that a doctor with Wrens' description may know something important about the Highway Killer."

"You think he might have crossed paths with him, treated him?"

"Possible."

"Well, if anyone could help that lunatic, it would be Jonah," LeShan said. He chuckled. "No offense to you."

"None taken," Clevenger said. "What makes Wrens so extraordinary?"

"You know how it is. Either you have it or you don't. He has it, in spades. The gift. The third ear. He could get patients to open up who wouldn't talk to anyone else on staff. And if we were dealing with a violent person, everyone knew to call Jonah right away. When he walked up to a guy who was out of control, that guy settled down. Period. End of discussion. Something about his presence. He put out a vibe. Very calming. Very strong."

"You liked him—as a person, I mean, his professional abilities aside."

"Everyone did. Nothing *not* to like about Jonah. You'll see. If he can help you out, he will. He's that kind of guy."

"And he was from which agency?"

"Communicare," LeShan said. "We use them almost exclusively. They're out of Denver. Hold a minute, and I'll get you their number."

*

Whitney McCormick had moved her meeting at the Red Cross to the following day so she could stop back at the Rock Springs Medical Center. It was 5:45 when she pressed the buzzer beside the iron door to the locked psychiatry unit.

"Yes?" a female voice said through a speaker.

"My name is Dr. Whitney McCormick. I was hoping to see Dr. Wrens."

"Certainly. He's expecting you."

Hearing that did nothing to put McCormick at ease. Pierce had obviously called to let Wrens know she would be stopping by.

A nurse came to let her in, then escorted her to the door to Wrens's office. She knocked, got no response, knocked harder. Still, nothing. She was ready to try the door when it opened.

"Dr. McCormick," Jonah said. "How might I help you?"

McCormick noted how flushed he looked, as though he had been screaming or crying. Even so, he was everything Marie Pierce had described. A man with a voice and a face and a bearing that promised understanding. "I'm sorry to bother you," she said. She noted his wavy, silver hair, blue eyes, perfect skin, the soft hues of his pleated gray wool trousers, brown suede shoes, and deep blue mock turtleneck. "Would you mind if I ask you a few questions?"

"Not at all." Jonah turned around, walked back into the office.

McCormick followed him, intentionally leaving the office door ajar. "I'm looking into the murder that occurred at the Bitter Creek Diner," she said.

"A senseless killing," Jonah said, standing with his

back to her as he filled a box on his desk with books and folders.

"You helped Marie a great deal. She's feeling much better."

Jonah kept packing.

"I wondered whether you'd found out anything that might be of value to the investigation," McCormick said.

"It was very much a therapeutic intervention," Jonah said. "I wasn't conducting an interrogation."

McCormick didn't miss the edge in his voice. She wanted to push him a little bit. "I can handle that part," she said. "It's my specialty. Is trauma work yours?"

Wrens didn't respond. He finished filling the box, closed the top. Then he finally turned to face her. "I'm afraid your timing is poor," he said. "A patient of mine was murdered by his mother today. I'm not in the mood to swap resumés."

McCormick was taken aback. "I had no idea you lost a patient. I'm . . ." Her cell phone started to ring. She fumbled around in her jacket pocket to turn it off.

"Did you want to get that?" Wrens asked, sarcastically.

McCormick shook her head. "How old?"

"Nine," Wrens said. He cleared his throat. "I discharged him back home. I thought he would be safe. That was a very big mistake. An unforgivable mistake." He placed his hands flat on his desk and spread out his fingers, as if to steady himself.

McCormick suddenly realized the office was completely barren. Wrens had tossed everything into the box on his desk. "Are you leaving the hospital today?" she asked him. "I thought Marie said you would be here another week."

"I'm not feeling terribly confident about my skills right now. I wouldn't be much help to anyone."

McCormick wanted to know more about Wrens, but she wasn't sure how to engage him. "I do have a few more questions," she said.

"About?"

"Your impressions of Ms. Pierce," was all she could think to say.

"Do you suspect her in the murder of her mother?"

McCormick shook her head. "Of course not. I'm just trying to be thorough."

"You want to be thorough," Jonah said. He stared into her eyes. "My patient died today, Dr. McCormick. He was murdered. You may be immune to hearing that sort of thing, but I'm not. I feel very deeply for my patients." He walked past her, pulled open the door. "I need for you to leave now."

Clevenger got through to Communicare just as the office was closing. It took a little convincing, but the owner recognized his name from the *Times* and looked up Jonah Wrens in her files. She read off each of his placements for the last thirty-six months.

He hadn't worked near any of the locations where bodies had been found.

"Where is he working now?" Clevenger asked.

"He's not—at least not for us," the woman said.

"He works for other agencies?"

"Like just about everybody, these days. I wish we had an exclusive on him. He's the most well-regarded psychiatrist we've ever had. Every hospital that hires him begs to have him back. But he doesn't do repeats. He wants to see new places, fresh faces."

"I guess that's not so unusual," Clevenger said, feeling deflated. "Why else would you work as a locum?"

"Honestly? These people would never last in an organization."

"They last in yours."

"With lots of hand-holding, believe me. Lots of troubleshooting. Don't get me wrong, some of them are very talented. Even gifted. But they're gypsies at heart. They don't like routine. And they don't want people getting too close to them."

"Do they choose where they're placed?" Clevenger asked.

"It's a discussion," the woman said. "When we get a referral, we call whoever's next on the list. If that person turns it down, we move on. No hard feelings. We've got lots of doctors. But every agency is different. Some of them will cut a doc loose if he refuses two or three placements in a row."

"I see."

"Why exactly are you looking for Dr. Wrens?" she asked.

"Just following up on a lead." He realized that that statement didn't clear Wrens the way he deserved to be cleared. He borrowed an idea from Dr. LeShan at Venango Regional. "I thought he might have treated the man we're looking for. But it doesn't look like they crossed paths, after all."

"You mean, the Highway Killer?" the woman said.

"Yes, right."

"Do me a favor. When you catch that animal, you slice his throat before he has a chance to spout any more of that nonsense he writes in the *Times*. All that crap about empathy when he's going around killing people. I'm a grandmother, for Christ's sake, but I'd be happy to cut his fucking head off myself. See how much psychobabble comes out of his mouth then."

"A lot of people would be in line for that job," Clevenger said. Enough people, he thought, to keep the death penalty alive in most states.

"You take care yourself, doc. And good luck. God bless."

"Yes, well, right." He hung up. His heart sank. He was at a dead end.

He dialed Anderson's cell phone and got him in his car outside the Rock Springs Medical Center, waiting for McCormick to come out. "I'm batting zero here," he said. "Anything on your end?"

"I got the list from Murph," Anderson said. "I've called five agencies. No go. Two refused to talk to me. None of the other three assigned a doc to the towns this guy has killed in." He paused. "I don't know. Maybe he doesn't mix business with pleasure."

That cliché made something click in Clevenger's mind: matching the killer's work assignments to the places where bodies had been found was all wrong. It flew in the face of the profile Clevenger had developed with the FBI—that of a man who needed to get very close to others, who killed when he couldn't feed himself intimacy in any other way.

"You still there?" Anderson asked.

"You're absolutely right," Clevenger said.

"Of course I am. About what?"

"He doesn't kill on the job. He doesn't need to," Clevenger said. "Getting close to patients satisfies his thirst for intense human connections. People bare their souls to him. He kills between assignments. That's when he feels most isolated, most alone. That's when he has nothing to distract him from his own pain. Every childhood trauma he's tried to bury threatens to break through into consciousness."

"But your letters might have made him break stride. Maybe this time, in Wyoming, the patients weren't enough."

Clevenger was right with him. The most likely location where the killer would have struck "on the job" was Bitter Creek. Unravelling, unable to soothe himself even through his work, he could have spun out of control. And if that was true, he couldn't flee. He couldn't risk raising suspicion. He had to stay focused, finish his month or two as though nothing had happened. Whitney McCormick's instincts in that regard had been right on. "It's possible," Clevenger said. "It's still a huge reach, but he could be close by."

"I'll start calling every hospital around here and lean on them to tell me whether they have a locum tenens psychiatrist working there."

"The operators might even know. If not, ask for the locked psychiatry unit directly."

Just then, Anderson saw McCormick leave the hospital and walk quickly to her rental car. "Whitney just finished her rounds," he told Clevenger. "Safe and sound. She doubled back here—Rock Springs Medical Center—but she didn't stay long."

"I doubt she was looking for a locum," Clevenger said.

"I'll double-check each place she visited."

"Call me with anything you find."

"You know I will."

Clevenger hung up and dialed Whitney McCormick's cell phone. It rang just once before her recorded message came on. She had the thing turned off. "Call me right away," Clevenger said. "It's important."

four

McCormick watched the hospital exit from inside her car. She wasn't sure what to make of Dr. Jonah Wrens. On the one hand, he fit the profile of the Highway Killer—a middle-aged white man with appealing looks who could get very close to people very fast. He traveled the country. His voice did indeed have the hypnotic effect Marie Pierce had spoken of. On the other hand, he was clearly suffering over the loss of his young patient. He didn't lack empathy. He felt guilt. There was nothing that seemed calculating about him; he hadn't tried to implicate Marie Pierce—or anyone else—in Sally Pierce's death.

It also strained her imagination to think there was any chance she would find the Highway Killer so serendipitously, one step from the murder victim's daughter. Yet she knew that didn't mean she *hadn't* found him. The Psychosniper case had turned on one tip called to the FBI. Other killers had been apprehended after running a red light, wearing a victim's shirt on one occasion ten years after the murder, or making mention of a killing to one acquaintance in a drug rehab center, twenty years later.

Wouldn't the Highway Killer have relished the chance to talk to Marie Pierce? Would he not warm to the bloodline of his victim?

She thought of calling Kane Warner for backup, but realized how amateurish she would look if Jonah Wrens turned out to be innocent—a good doctor trying to do his job. She was on a quest to redeem herself; expending Agency resources on a decent man wracked with grief over losing his nine-year-old patient wouldn't win her any points.

Bottom line, she couldn't tell Warner she was still working the case until she was pretty sure she had solved it.

She needed to know more about Wrens. And she had no choice when to start digging. If Wrens was the killer, he knew she was closing in. He could leave town at any moment, escape into the mountains for months—or forever.

She waited in the hospital parking lot twenty-five minutes before Wrens walked out the sliding glass doors, carrying his briefcase and the box he had packed. He climbed into his BMW, started it up, and drove off.

She started her car and followed him.

Jonah glanced at McCormick's headlights in his rearview mirror. He was trying to divine God's plan for him, to understand why He would send him a woman teeming with evil on the very same day as he had taken away a boy as innocent as Sam.

Ultimately the only message he could take from such symmetry was that good and evil were in constant flux, that Armageddon was not a single battle but a constant campaign, that the death of an angel might be balanced for all eternity by the death of a devil.

Was it possible that McCormick's demise had been

Jonah's task from the outset? Had he reached out to Clevenger knowing he would ultimately reach McCormick? Was his resurrection as an innocent possible only upon the destruction of the huntress? Was she the one who had truly incurred God's wrath?

The poetry was plain: he would be forgiven once he removed from the planet one like her, utterly unable to forgive.

He felt a wave of calm blanket him, as if his long and tortuous journey might be nearing an end. The final mile of his road to redemption could well be the mile he was traveling that very moment.

McCormick followed Wrens to the Ambassador Motor Inn, saw him park in front of Room 105. She took a space twenty yards away. He got out of the X5, disappeared into the room.

She reached down to her calf, adjusted her gun in its holster. Then she got out of the car. As she did, she saw North Anderson pull in five spaces away, look at her, then look quickly away. That confirmed what she had suspected on the highway: she was being followed.

Only Clevenger knew she was in Wyoming. She had never met his partner, but she knew he was a black man. She glanced at his license plate, saw the car was a rental.

She walked over to him, knocked on his window.

He rolled it down. "Can I help you with something?" he asked, as offhandedly as he could.

"You would be North Anderson," she said.

Anderson didn't see any use in protesting.

"Tell Frank I'm a big girl. He doesn't need to watch my back."

"I think he figured you might be right about the killer still being around here. If you are, you might *like* the backup."

She thought fleetingly of filling Anderson in on Jonah Wrens, but she just wasn't willing to look foolish in front of him, or Clevenger. She wanted to be left alone to do her job. "I mean, if he really wants me to," she said, "I'll call him and give him a blow-by-blow of what happens in that motel room." She smiled. "But I'm not here on business. So how about you get lost? It kind of ruins the moment, thinking of you out here."

Anderson nodded, taken aback by McCormick's directness.

She walked to Room 105, knocked on the door.

Wrens opened the door just a few seconds later. He was barefooted, his hair tousled, his shoulders slumped. His shirt was unbuttoned, showing his washboard abdomen. His sleeves were rolled up. His socks and his belt were in his hand. He looked like he was on empty, anything but dangerous. "I really need to sleep," he said. "Surely, this can wait until the morning."

"I understand," McCormick said. "I won't take more than a few minutes. I promise."

He seemed reticent.

"It's important."

Wrens closed his eyes and took a deep breath as an image appeared before his eyes—his knife at McCormick's neck, her hair in his fist. He opened his eyes and looked at her standing there. The devil at his door. "I apologize for being curt with you at the hospital. Please, come in."

Now McCormick was the one hesitating. Because she

saw something that bothered her—a series of faded, horizontal scars on Wrens' forearms.

She knew there could be innocent explanations for those scars. The barbs at the top of a fence could have caused them when Wrens was a boy. A hot grill. And even if Wrens had intentionally cut himself in childhood or adolescence, he certainly wouldn't be the first psychiatrist with a history of psychological trauma.

Still, if the scars were from cutting, it meant Wrens had suffered severe emotional trauma. And the only way he had achieved a sense of control over his pain was by inflicting his own wounds. Then he could calmly watch himself bleed, detached completely from his own suffering—and from his underlying rage at others.

Wasn't that the profile of the Highway Killer?

"Dr. McCormick," Wrens said, "you seem tired yourself. Why don't we meet tomorrow? Perhaps somewhere for breakfast?"

"No," she said. She flexed her calf to feel the gun strapped there. "I'm fine." She walked inside.

Wrens closed the door as she stepped past him. And with her back toward him, wasting not an instant, he looped his belt around her neck and dragged her to the ground.

She reached for her gun, but Wrens kicked her hand away from her leg, then pulled the belt tighter, choking her, making her instinctively claw at the leather ringing her neck. He straddled her lower back. She felt his hand at her ankle, then moving up her pant leg and taking the gun. He flipped her over, faceup, and jammed the barrel into her mouth.

He leaned close to her ear.

"What was your first question?" he asked. He pulled the strap even tighter.

As North Anderson waited in his car outside the Ambassador Motor Inn, he imagined a very different scene unfolding in Room 105. He had tailed McCormick as she followed a man—a very good-looking doctor, with a very expensive car—back to his motel. She had knocked on his door, been greeted by him half-dressed, then disappeared inside his room.

It looked to Anderson like McCormick had maybe bumped into someone she went to college or medical school with and decided to try to recapture the past.

In any case, she was right: it was none of his business. And he certainly wasn't about to mention it to Clevenger.

He wasn't about to get lost, either. He'd have to be more careful tailing her, but he could pull that off.

He figured he had some time before McCormick hit the road again. He looked over at the motel coffee shop near the exit. He was starving, and it did feel pretty strange lurking out in front of that room.

Whitney McCormick awakened atop Jonah's mattress, in four-point leather restraints, with Jonah staring at her from a chair beside the bed. She struggled against her tethers, to no avail. She twisted her wrist to look at her watch, saw she had been unconscious less than ten minutes.

"The FBI knows I was headed here," she said. "You can't get away—let me go."

Jonah smiled. "Would you have let me go, had you captured me?"

She said nothing.

"You would have told me to go to hell." He paused. "Am I right?"

McCormick watched, wide-eyed, as Jonah opened his folding knife, held the blade over her face.

"Is there anything you want me to tell your father in my next letter to the *Times*, Whitney?" he asked her. "I know I should consider him a coconspirator of sorts. Certainly some flaw in his rearing of you contributed to you growing into a woman devoid of empathy. Still, I'd like to do what I can to lessen his pain. Losing his wife, then his daughter . . ." He took a deep breath. "How does a man recover from that?"

McCormick saw that Jonah was going to kill her. Pleading would only embolden him, reinforce her status as a victim, his status as all-powerful. She needed to take control, even while bound. "This isn't even about me," she said. "That's the pathetic part."

Jonah placed the edge of the knife at her throat. "Now *that* sounds like denial. Trust me, when you feel your blood start to flow, you'll know this is happening to you, no one else."

"This is about your mother, Jonah. Frank tried to help you see it. You're just too much of a coward to open your eyes. She was the one devoid of empathy—for you. She tortured you."

He pressed on the knife, denting, but not quite cutting her skin. " 'The Lord is my shepherd. I shall not want. He maketh me to . . . ' "

Fear, rage and the will to live had the wheels of McCormick's mind spinning like runaway cylinders inside a combination lock. She felt as though her brain might overheat.

" 'He restoreth my soul. Yea, though I . . . ' "

Something clicked. The boy who was murdered that day, killed by his mother. It had truly rocked Jonah. "Think about your patient who was killed today," she said. "Don't you see why it was so devastating for you? You sent him home to die, Jonah. *You* murdered him."

Jonah stopped his praying, shook his head. "Sam died so I could see that you need to die. He served God's will. He's in heaven now."

"You knew what his mother was," McCormick persisted. "Deep inside, you knew exactly what was going to happen. She had beaten him before. She had never stopped. It was only going to get worse."

Jonah pressed hard enough on the knife for the blade to break her skin.

McCormick felt lightheaded, but she knew she couldn't let up. "You failed that boy because thinking of what was about to happen to him would have put you back in touch with what happened to you. The beatings. You made yourself believe he was safe. You probably convinced him he was safe, too. You sent him into hell, in your place."

"Good-bye, Whitney." He drew the blade an inch along her throat. Blood began to trickle from the wound.

She felt like crying out, but knew that if she did, he would kill her immediately. "I'm going to die tonight, Jonah. Why would I lie?" She gathered her courage. "You killed that boy."

He blinked nervously.

"Your mother is the force behind every killing," she went on. "She's the one you really want to murder. And that's why you'll never be redeemed. Because you would rather kill strangers than face the truth—she destroyed you, but you take revenge on others, because you're still frightened of her. You're a coward."

Jonah moved the blade another half-inch along McCormick's skin. Her blood ran thicker.

"You destroyed that boy today."

"No," Jonah said, his voice shaky. His eyes filled up as he thought of all the false promises he had made Sam: *I can read minds. You're a superhero. You have all the power.*

McCormick decided to take a final risk, to go on her gut again and try to crush Jonah with the truth, to force him into a psychotic state. She remembered his first letter to Clevenger. And she began acting out the part of his mother. "Your little fucking day at the park!" she said in a grating voice full of anger. "Did you have a nice birthday party with your goddamn friends?"

He looked even more pained.

She kept the pressure on. "Where exactly do you think we're supposed to find the money to pay for it, you little bastard?"

With that last word, Jonah's face took a turn toward agony.

"And now that the damage is done you're all apologies," she said. "Well, I'm going to teach you a lesson. Then you'll really feel sorry."

He literally tasted the blood that had filled his mouth the day his mother slapped him to the ground, crushed his Hot Wheels cars. He moved his tongue against his tooth, thought he felt it wiggle.

He looked at McCormick and saw his mother.

"You bastard!" she said.

He closed his eyes. And he saw his mother holding open her arms, calling for him to come to her. He remembered the feeling of warmth that radiated through his entire body at the sound of her voice when she was calm, the special blanket of contentment that only a mother's love can spread over a child. He remembered walking toward her, wrapping his arms around her, her arms embracing him.

But then another memory intruded, a memory of something he had felt—his mother's body stiffening, her softness retreating, her arms extending, pushing him away. And when he did look at her, he saw all the love had left her face, leaving pure hatred behind. He saw her hand swinging, in slow motion, toward his head.

Then he saw something else, out of the corner of his eye—a man observing the scene. A man not old and not young. Perhaps fifty. A man close to his own age. A man who shared his broad forehead and pale blue eyes. A man just watching, neither celebrating Jonah's plight nor protecting him.

He turned and glanced at his mother's hand closing in on him, then looked back at her face, wanting to know why—why she would embrace him and then beat him, why she would love him, then rant that she hated him. "Why?" he asked aloud. "Why did you do it to me?"

McCormick looked up at Jonah. She could see he had lost touch with reality. "Because I'm sick, Jonah," she answered him softly. "Don't you see that? I can't help it."

A tear ran down his cheek. Was it that simple? he asked himself. Had Clevenger been right all along? A schizophrenic mother. A schizophrenic son. Good and evil, darkness and light, healer and killer in one body?

Were his irresistible impulses to destroy and his extraordinary impulses to love no more than peaks and troughs in the dopamine and norepinephrine levels in his brain?

"I did the best I could," McCormick said.

Now Jonah was weeping. Because he saw that he really had sent Sam back to his house to die. He had pretended that Hank would choose his son over his sadistic wife. But that was a fantasy.

It hadn't happened that way for Jonah. Ultimately, his own father had walked out, leaving him alone with the beast. He remembered it now the way he knew he had hands and feet, eyes and ears. It was an undeniable part of him, a part long suppressed but now back in force.

Jonah hadn't been rescued, and neither had Sam.

He had killed the boy trying to replay his own life story, trying to make it come out right.

He looked down at McCormick, saw his mother lying there. And not just her face. Her broad shoulders, her powerful arms. "I can't forgive you," he said. "You should have gotten help. You couldn't expect me to cure you. I was a child."

"I didn't want to hurt you," McCormick said. "I loved you."

"I wanted to love you, too," he whimpered, closing his eyes. "But . . ."

"Please, forgive me."

He shook his head. "Only God can forgive you. You have to go to God." He opened his eyes and looked back at McCormick. And the mask of his mother slipped away. He saw McCormick for who she was. The huntress. He grabbed her hair and yanked her head back, hovered over her. "Do you forgive me, Whitney?" he asked.

She looked at the knife in Jonah's hand, then looked into his eyes and saw her own reflection. She didn't say a word.

"Tell me you forgive me."

She thought of her father, of the crushing, unspeakable grief he would feel losing her, and she felt a tidal wave of rage swell inside her. Rage as great as Jonah's. "See you in hell, you fucking bastard," she said.

He smiled, then laughed a horrible, demonic laugh that ended with him crying again. "You're not exactly cured," he said. He shook his head, put the knife down on the mattress. "Everything in time. God is patient." He stood up, walked to his briefcase and took out two vials and a syringe, carried them over to the bed.

McCormick saw the labels on the vials—liquid Thorazine and Versed, each a potent sedative. In high dosages, they could be lethal. "Don't," she said. "Please."

Jonah drew each of the liquids into the syringe. He brought the needle to McCormick's thigh, buried it deep in her muscle and discharged the contents. "Good-bye, Whitney," he said. "I hope you find a way to heaven. And I hope I see you there."

Was he planning to kill himself? she wondered. A murder-suicide?

Her head felt heavy. Breathing was becoming difficult. She tried to think who would be the one to call her father to tell him what had happened to her. And she hoped it would be Clevenger.

"It's time for me to go home," she heard Jonah say. "It's time I stop running from the truth. Thank you for helping me see that."

*

Clevenger had just hung up with another locum tenens agency, without a breakthrough, when his phone rang. He picked up. "Clevenger," he said.

"Kane Warner." He didn't give him time to respond. "I started to follow up on the locum thing," he said.

"And?"

"Something turned up. I'm not sure whether to bet the farm on it, but it feels right."

All of a sudden Clevenger was a member of the team again. "Shoot."

"I had agents canvass eleven placement services on the east coast. None of them sent a psychiatrist to all the locations where we found bodies. Only one of them sent a psychiatrist to any of them. One match. And that psychiatrist happens to be a fifty-seven-year-old female."

Clevenger's hopes sank. Was Warner actually pitching the idea that the Highway Killer was a woman? "That's what you found?" he asked.

"Give me a break. You think I'd call you with nothing?"

"I'm tired."

"Stay with me. Here's what we found. One of the three agencies I called personally has a director who's run the show twenty-odd years. Staffpro, down in Orlando, Florida. Wes Cohen. He really got into the matching game, spent a couple of hours going through his computer files. When he called back, he said he had an answer for me—but not to the question I had asked him."

"Meaning?"

"He didn't place a psychiatrist in any town near a murder scene. But he was intrigued, so he ran a different search on his database. He keeps track of when his docs *refuse* placements. Five refusals, and you're off his roster.

That's his rule. And he came up with one psychiatrist who turned down four of the towns where we found bodies."

"Four out of fourteen. Almost thirty percent."

"What are the odds? Maybe this guy wants nothing to do with the places where he claims his victims. Maybe he thinks of them as scorched earth."

"Possible," Clevenger said. It did feel right, but it also felt thin. He got that sinking feeling again that he was way out on a limb. "What's this psychiatrist's name?"

"Wrens. Jonah Wrens."

Clevenger's heart began to pound.

"Brilliant guy, but odd, according to Cohen," Warner went on. "And get this—he spends almost all of his time between assignments mountain climbing. Has all his mail delivered to his mother's place in Montana."

Clevenger had started to pace. "Is he assigned to a hospital now?"

"That's the part that really got my attention. He's on assignment to Rock Springs Medical Center in Wyoming. Fifty-one miles from Bitter Creek."

"He's our man," Clevenger said. "I'm sure of it. I've got even more on him."

"I've got agents headed there."

"Whitney's already poking around," Clevenger confessed. "She got there yesterday. She wanted to close the case herself, to prove something—I guess to you, or maybe to me. I don't know. I tried to argue her out of it."

"You've got to be kidding me. Where is she?"

"She's staying at the Marriott Courtyard in Bitter Creek. My partner North Anderson flew out to keep track of her."

"Good move," Warner said. "If you want, get yourself

to Logan, and I'll have a plane meet you at the Cape Air terminal and fly you out. You ought to be there when we nail this guy. You deserve to be there."

That was an olive branch Clevenger had no problem taking. "I'm on my way." He grabbed his coat and ran.

On his way to the airport, he called North Anderson to fill him in.

Anderson answered from his seat at the coffee shop counter. "Got a description?" he asked, after getting filled in on Wrens.

"About six feet tall. Shoulder-length graying hair. Blue eyes."

"Christ!" Anderson said, bolting for the motel room. He noticed that Jonah's car was gone. He kicked down the door, saw McCormick on the bed. His eyes scanned the rest of the room to make sure Wrens was really gone. He checked the bathroom. Empty. He raced over to her. He couldn't rouse her. He felt her wrist, got a decent pulse. Then he unbuckled her restraints, gently tilted her head back to open her airway and listened for breath sounds. She was breathing.

He noticed the two empty vials on the bedside table, took out his cell, and dialed 911.

"Bitter Creek Police," a woman answered. "This call is being recorded."

"I need an ambulance. The Ambassador Motor Inn. I have a woman unconscious after being drugged."

McCormick heard the last sentence of Anderson's 911 call. She opened her eyes.

"Room 105," Anderson told the operator.

"Jonah Wrens," McCormick whispered, working to get the words out.

Anderson turned to her, saw her looking back at him.

He let out a sigh of relief. "We know," he told her. "There'll be a hundred agents searching the whole . . ."

"He's going home," she said, as if remembering something from a dream.

"Home?"

Suddenly she knew with dead solid conviction where Wrens was headed. "Find out where his mother lives. He's on his way there to kill her."

five

Jonah Wrens sat on the green crushed velvet sofa in the living room where he had spent his childhood, looking across a simple wooden coffee table at the woman who had raised him from birth. The wall behind her was covered with crucifixes she had collected over the years, gifts from family and friends and parents of the fourth-graders she had taught for forty years at the local elementary school.

He picked up the cup of tea she had made him, turned and glanced out the window as he took a sip. He could barely make out the shadow of a police cruiser waiting in the blackness outside the ranch-style house—waiting, no doubt, for more hunters. They had him cornered. Or so they thought.

"I'm so glad you woke me up. I missed you," his mother said, in a melodious voice much younger than her seventy-nine years. "You stayed away so long this time. Six months. They must have really needed you."

"I missed you, too," Jonah said.

He meant it. Yet it was also a lie. And he knew that was because he was talking to two very different women.

It was strange how she had lived more than one life. Here was his mother, at seventy-nine, gray and sickly and kind beyond measure, a religious woman making peace with the world she would leave in a year or a decade, or perhaps two. A mother to pine for. A mother to come home to. And yet he knew now that somewhere inside her was the mother who had tortured him, the psychopath who had oscillated between loving him and hating him, comforting him and terrorizing him, until whatever runaway circuits in her brain or mind or soul simply burnt themselves out.

Maybe time had healed her. Or maybe her conversion was real. Maybe she was reborn.

The irrational thing was the rage he felt now for *this* woman, the woman who had brought him his tea. It made his heart pound and his head throb, made him hungry in precisely the way he had hungered for intimacy on the highways. And though he knew now the source of that hunger, that knowledge did not take the hunger away.

Something was fundamentally misshapen in his psyche. His need for intimacy was a voracious and insatiable beast that screamed always to be loved, always to be held, lest it drown in the terrible anxiety it had been to wonder which mother would be at home any particular day, any particular hour, any particular minute—the angel or the devil.

"Did you have many interesting cases?" his mother asked.

"A few," Jonah said. He smiled through his pain. "A boy named Sam Garber. He was the most interesting. A very brave boy with very big problems."

"And you helped him." She gazed lovingly at him. "I'm sure his parents were grateful."

"No," Jonah said. "I couldn't help him."

"Come now. You're always so hard on yourself."

He shook his head. His eyes had filled up.

"Jonah? What happened?"

He heard the sound of more cars coming up the road. He stood and went to the door, saw two black trucks— SWAT trucks—park alongside the cruiser. And he watched as black-suited men with rifles spilled out of them. He turned back to his mother. "Would you pour me another cup of tea?" he asked her. "Then I'll tell you everything."

She stood up slowly, grimacing at the pain in her joints, pushing herself onto diabetic, ulcerated feet, because her son, who she loved, wanted a second cup of tea. And this was her pleasure after a long and tortured life. This was what she waited for when he was on the road. The chance to boil a cup of water, float a tea bag, add a little sugar, a little honey, the way he liked it. Wash his sheets. Press his clothes. Simple things, but meaningful things. Loving things. Little, infinite apologies for what she had been, the monstrous ways she had failed him.

She felt hot and dizzy standing over the stove and backed up. She wiped her brow. Maybe her sugar was low, she thought. Maybe a little of the honey would help. She took a teaspoon from the kitchen drawer, dipped it in the jar, and then slipped the sweet, sticky stuff between her lips. It tasted good and it made her feel better.

When she turned around, Jonah was there, holding his open knife in his hand.

"Jonah?" she said. "What are you doing?" But she knew.

He stepped closer to her and wrapped his arms around her.

She felt even more lightheaded. Was that why she

didn't try to run? she wondered. Or was it that her son's arms felt so good around her. Because she really was tired and she really had missed him and she really did love him.

Suddenly, beams of light streamed through the windows. And Jonah found himself shielding his mother's eyes from the glare. He wondered if that instinct to protect her was a reflex hardwired in him. A child's instinctive impulse to protect its bloodline. Or perhaps it was only another of the devil's tricks, designed to distract, to make him lose his nerve.

A few moments later Clevenger's voice came to Jonah, as if in a dream. "Jonah, this is Frank Clevenger. Come out, and no one will harm you."

Maybe, Jonah thought to himself, his whole life had been a dream. Maybe morning was right around the corner. He carried his mother out to the living room, sat her down on the couch. She didn't struggle, didn't plead with him.

"Jonah," Clevenger bellowed. "There's no other way out."

Jonah reached to his calf and grabbed McCormick's pistol. He aimed at one of the windows toward the front of the house, pulled the trigger, and the window shattered. "I didn't know you made house calls, Frank," he shouted. "I'm honored."

"It doesn't have to end this way."

"Of course it does. You know it does."

Ten, fifteen seconds passed in silence. "If you won't come out," Clevenger said finally, "let me come in."

Jonah took a deep breath. There was something exquisitely beautiful about the idea of Clevenger watching how his "therapy" would end. He smiled at God's wondrous poetry. "The door is open," he called out. "I promise you won't be harmed. You have my word. As God is my witness."

Clevenger slowly walked through the door to the house and saw Jonah sitting on the couch beside his mother, holding her close to him, a knife to her throat. The gun lay on the cushion beside him. "Close the door," Jonah said.

Clevenger shut the door behind him.

"We finally meet."

"Finally," Clevenger said, taking a few steps closer.

"That's far enough," Jonah said. His hand drifted toward the pistol.

Clevenger stopped. "Our work isn't done. Let's talk."

Jonah shook his head. "Let's face it, Frank. We're exhausted. You and me, both. It's been a long road."

"What is it that you want?"

"I suppose, what I've always wanted." He smiled and held up his knife.

Clevenger looked on in horror as Jonah ran the blade of his knife across the palm of his hand, opening a deep gash. He took his mother's hand and cut her palm the same way.

She winced, but somehow kept herself from screaming.

Then, placing the knife back at her throat, Jonah took his mother's lacerated hand in his own. He closed his eyes an instant, took a deep, dreamy breath, then opened them again.

"Give me the knife, Jonah. Let's walk out of here together. You see the truth now. Let that be enough."

"As it often is," Jonah said. "But not always." He pressed the blade of the knife harder against his mother's throat.

"Don't do it," Clevenger said. "All the other killings happened because you were blind to your rage. Out of control. Not this one. God won't forgive this one."

Jonah looked at Clevenger with sympathy. "You did a good job, Frank. A great job. But some people can't be healed by men, not even a man like you. Or me. Some people can only be healed by God." He kissed his mother's cheek tenderly.

"It's all right, Jonah," she said, real love in her voice. "You do what you need to do."

Jonah's eyes filled up. "What did you say?"

"I forgive you."

He started to weep.

"It's my fault, Jonah," she said.

"Let her go," Clevenger said.

"I came here to kill her," Jonah said, smiling through his tears. "I did. But the woman I was looking for, the evil one? She doesn't even live here anymore. Do you know why?"

Clevenger didn't answer.

"Of course you do. It's because she's inside me."

Clevenger saw Jonah's hand drift toward the pistol. He saw him smile a peaceful, almost innocent smile.

Clevenger took a step toward him.

He picked up the pistol, pointed it at Clevenger.

Clevenger stopped moving.

"It's all right," Jonah said. "I know exactly where I'm going. And you should go home. Love that son of yours the way he deserves to be loved."

Clevenger rushed him.

"I want to be free." He pushed his mother into Clevenger's path, put the barrel of the gun into his mouth, and fired a single shot into his brain.

"No!" Clevenger yelled.

Jonah's mother screamed. She scrambled back toward her son, threw her arms around him. "Oh, God, no," she cried. "Oh, God." She tried to stop the blood from spilling out of him, but it just poured over her hands. She sat down, cradled his head and shoulders in her arms, and began to rock him.

The pain inside Jonah's head was unspeakable. He could not catch his breath. His heart fluttered like a wounded bird in his chest. But in the haze between life and death, or between this life and the next, he suddenly felt the sun begin to shine brightly on his face. He felt the air turn clean and crisp and cool. The pain began to drift away. And he found he did not need to breathe at all.

He looked up and saw that his fingers were deep inside fissures in the face of the most beautiful mountain he had ever climbed. He saw with astonishment that the scars on his arms were gone.

The muscles of his arms and thighs and calves powered him higher. His feet found solid shelves of rock everywhere.

He knew he had been climbing a long time, but he was not tired. He felt stronger, in fact, with every step. Both stronger and younger. He flexed his right arm and moved still higher, latching on with his left hand. His mind grew clearer. He tried to search himself for feelings of fear or anger, but could find none.

With every step he took, he shed a year off his life, so

that he felt childish as he neared the summit, and a little timid about finishing the trip. What would become of him if he climbed all the way to infancy? What would he then be, devoid of his life history?

How would he know himself?

And then he understood. He had to let go of that self, with all its rage and all its fear and all its superior knowledge. He had to find the pure light beyond it.

Suddenly, he felt completely at peace. At one with himself and the universe. Because he knew then that his wish was being granted. He had the chance to be reborn. He had the chance to be redeemed. He had gotten where he needed to go.

Finally, his healing was in sight.

six

Judge Robert Barton, one of the toughest and wisest judges in the Commonwealth of Massachusetts, looked down at the stacks of paper arranged before him, took off his half glasses, and stared out at the court. He was a boulder of a man, broad-shouldered, barrel-chested, with a booming voice and piercing eyes. He made eye contact with Clevenger and Billy at the defense table, then looked back down at his stacks of paper.

Barton had listened to Richard O'Connor present the Department of Social Services' position that Clevenger should be placed on indefinite probation as Billy Bishop's guardian, pending a three-month "cooling off" period during which Billy would be placed in foster care and psychologically evaluated in greater detail. And Barton had listened to Sarah Ricciardelli present evidence suggesting Billy was actually eighteen and outside the control of both DSS and the court.

The courtroom was utterly silent. It was time for Barton's judgment.

"Dr. Clevenger," Barton said. "I want to be perfectly clear with you. I think this adoption form you filled out is, formally speaking, accurate. But I think it's obvious you answered the questions to comply with the letter of the law and not its spirit."

Clevenger's heart fell.

"You have battled addiction, is that correct?"

Clevenger glanced at Sarah Ricciardelli.

"You don't need to ask her what to say," Barton said. "Just tell me."

"Your honor, I . . ." Ricciardelli began to object.

"Yes, I have," Clevenger broke in.

"And, of late, so has Billy Bishop," Barton said.

"He has."

Barton nodded.

Richard O'Connor glowed.

"And what is your position here? That love will conquer all?"

Clevenger thought about outlining the detox program Billy had just completed, noting again that he had himself stopped using drugs the moment he decided to adopt Billy, that he had never picked up again. But all that had been put into evidence by Ricciardelli. "I think it goes a long way," he said. "I . . ."

Ricciardelli put a hand on his elbow to stop him.

He stepped away from her, toward Billy. "The fact is I do love him," he told Barton. "Maybe that love has roots in what I went through as a child myself. It probably does. But that doesn't change the fact that I'd go to the ends of the earth to help him. I think he's also ready to help himself. And I think if we're holding those cards, we beat almost anything."

"You a gambler, too?" Barton asked.

O'Connor chuckled.

Ricciardelli leaned forward. "I object to that line of questioning, Your Honor."

"Noted," Barton said.

"I am a gambler," Clevenger said. "It used to be dogs

and ponies, but I'm gambling right now, telling you what I really think. Telling you the truth. But I think it would be a bigger risk having Billy not know how I feel about him. About us. That, I'm not willing to gamble."

Barton smiled. "Indulge me, Doctor. What do you figure the odds are of you two making it together? Ten to one, against?"

Clevenger thought about it. "I wouldn't bet against us."

Barton looked at Billy, then looked over at O'Connor. O'Connor gave him a conspiratorial wink.

"Do you have children, Counselor?" Barton asked.

"Two nephews," O'Connor said.

"I didn't think so," Barton said. "You should have a child. It changes you completely." He looked back at Billy. "I don't buy for a minute that you're eighteen, my friend. But for my money, I think your best shot at getting there is the guy standing next to you."

Whitney McCormick was waiting near the exit to the courthouse when Clevenger walked out with Billy. A couple of dozen reporters were massed outside.

"Give me one second," he told Billy. He walked over to her.

"Congratulations," she said.

"Thanks."

"You think we could get dinner next week?" she asked. "I mean, after I settle back in at the Bureau, and you get back in stride with Billy?"

"I don't know, Whitney. I don't know if it's a good idea."

"Right," she said, trying to look unphased. "Well, then good—"

"I mean, it's not a good idea this week, or next," Clevenger said. "Let's give it until the beginning of the month, check in, and see where we are."

"I'd like that."

"Try to stay safe, will you?"

"Sure. You, too."

Clevenger walked back over to Billy. Then the two of them walked down the steps of the courthouse, headed for Clevenger's truck and the short drive home.